The Place of a Skull

The Place of a Skull

Skull

KEITH FRANCIS

iUniverse, Inc.
Bloomington

The Place of a Skull

This is a work of fiction. All of the characters, names, incidents, organizations, and dialogue in this novel are either the products of the author's imagination or are used fictitiously.

iUniverse books may be ordered through booksellers or by contacting:

iUniverse
1663 Liberty Drive
Bloomington, IN 47403
www.iuniverse.com
1-800-Authors (1-800-288-4677)

ISBN: 978-1-4759-7201-6 (sc)
ISBN: 978-1-4759-7202-3 (ebk)

Library of Congress Control Number: 2013900875

Printed in the United States of America

iUniverse rev. date: 01/30/2013

Table of Contents

Author's Note

Although *The Place of a Skull* is a sequel to my *Death at the Nave* (Writers' club Press, 2002), it can be enjoyed perfectly well on its own—no previous knowledge is required. The earlier novel was set in the fictitious city of Chelcester, but readers familiar with the West of England will have had no difficulty in recognizing Chelcester as a thinly disguised form of Gloucester, and the Nave School as a conflation of the Crypt School and Sir Thomas Rich's School. As far as American readers are concerned, none of this matters in the slightest.

Preludes

(i)

London, England: October 19th, 1940

In the living room of an old house a few miles south of Big Ben, Dick Smith sat next to a gramophone. He was wearing his Saturday garb of a white open-neck shirt and baggy gray-flannel trousers, and there was a look of intense concentration on his face. Being used to listening to music four minutes at a time, and knowing to the second the moment when the music would stop, he was ready to pounce on the machine, lift the needle out of the groove, turn the record over and gently replace the needle. The Luftwaffe's systematic destruction of London had began in late August, and had continued for more than fifty consecutive days and nights, but Dick and his family still found hope and comfort in the sound of a great orchestra, playing music that seemed to them to express the triumph of the human spirit over the forces of evil.

Jessica, Dick's fifteen-year-old only child, lay on her back on the sofa. Her eyes traced the crack in the ceiling that had appeared one night when a house on the other side of the street had been demolished by one of Hitler's bombs, but this didn't prevent her from being deeply involved in the music. When it stopped abruptly at the end of the first side, it struck her that if she ever heard Beethoven's Fifth Symphony in a concert she would expect it to stop at this precise place, and would be overwhelmed with pleasure when it didn't. Dick had mastered the art of the quick flip, so the music started again in less than ten seconds.

As the V-for-victory rhythm became ever more intense, Jessica pulled her long black hair over her eyes and felt the defiant, heroic measures surging through her. Like many British people at this time, she reveled in the spirit of the work and didn't care tuppence for the fact that it had been written by a German. "Well, he was more than half Dutch", Dick used to say, although this was less than half true.

The music stopped again. During the longer pause, while Dick replaced the first record with the second, the other two occupants of the living room continued a conversation that had been going on before the music started. One of them was Jessica's mother, Jean, and the other was Jean's younger sister, Jenny. They were talking about Jenny's divorced husband.

"I do hope James will get here soon", Jenny said impatiently. "I'm sure it's not his fault and it's just the trains, but it's rather annoying, considering the effort it took for me to get here tonight."

Jean Smith looked thoughtfully at her sister but didn't say anything. Jenny seemed to get the message.

"All right, I know I'm being unreasonable. I suppose the fact is that I can't help worrying. I still love him, you know."

"Yes, dear, I do know. It's funny how things turn out, isn't it."

"Yes, it is. You're lucky, you know. You love Dick *and* you can tolerate being married to him."

The music started again and the conversation stopped, but for once Jessica was not immediately absorbed. Instead she was puzzling over Aunt Jenny's last remark. Uncle James was kind, patient and wealthy, and seemed to have the rare virtue of always being in a good mood. Having been bowled over by him in his rakish undergraduate days, Aunt Jenny had been very disappointed to find that once past the first flush of youth he lost interest in everything except finance and politics. Concluding that her supposedly artistic temperament and genuinely mischievous sense of humor were being wasted, she had persuaded James to oblige her with an arranged divorce, and had gone off to live it up with an actor. That had been early in the spring of 1938, when Jessica was twelve, and the girl still remembered her aunt's return, a few months later.

"Well, you know", Jenny had said quite cheerfully, "I thought I was in love with him, but I suppose it was just the excitement . . . But it was wonderful while it lasted."

So Aunt Jenny loved Uncle James but couldn't bear to live with him, and she didn't love the actor but had a wonderful time with him. It was all very odd and made Jessica feel lucky that her parents seemed to be having the best of both worlds. They were teachers at the local grammar school, which seemed prosaic enough, but they loved music, dancing and good-humored disputation, and they took Jessica to the theatre whenever they could afford it. Sometimes people dropped in for hilarious impromptu parties that went on into the small hours, and Jessica would get just as merry on her ginger beer as the grown-ups did on their cheap wine. Then, as now, she would lie on the sofa, listening to conversation about everything under the sun.

"I think Jessica's asleep", someone would say.

"No, I'm awake—I just like to listen."

"Then we want to know what you think about . . ."

Often she didn't have anything to say, but people listened when she did. All that seemed long ago, however. Since the war began there had been very few parties and not much wine, but Jessica had gone on thinking, and her thoughts were so all-encompassing, and at the same time delicately personal, that she felt she would never be able to communicate them to anyone. Sometimes, looking at her parents, it struck her how strange it was that these people, who had brought her into the world and whom she loved desperately, should have so little knowledge, or even possibility of knowledge, of what went on in her mind. She had asked her mother about love.

"Mummy, what's the difference between loving someone and being in love with someone?"

Jean had looked at her child with pity in her eyes and said, "You'll know soon enough when it happens."

"Is it wonderful—I mean like being in heaven?"

"It's like that for some people, but not usually for very long."

"Are you in love with Daddy?"

Jean hesitated and answered obliquely.

"It's not really like that. It changes, you see. And it's not really like being in heaven—it's too uncomfortable."

Jessica was thirteen when that conversation took place. Now, at the age of fifteen, although she still had no first-hand knowledge of being in love, the thought of it filled her mind and body with indescribably mysterious feelings for which no language existed except music. So in

3

her deepest thoughts she communed with Chopin instead of her parents and friends, and let the nocturnes carry her into realms of unfulfilled longing, where love and the loftiest idealism were indistinguishable from each other. And she thought that perhaps her mother was right, but not in every case.

Soon after the divorce, Uncle James had joined the army and taken a commission. He was seriously wounded during the evacuation of Dunkirk, but after three months of convalescence and rehabilitation he could walk quite well and was expecting to be sent overseas again soon. Jessica, who didn't take Aunt Jenny's protestations about love very seriously, thought that the real purpose of Uncle James's visit was to see his former in-laws, including Jessica's grandparents, with whom he was still a great favorite.

Jessica's grandparents on her father's side had died when she was a baby, but her mother's parents had continued to live in their old house, and had been delighted whenever Jessica, with or without her parents, appeared on the doorstep. One day in 1936 Granny Bess had said to Jean, "You know, this house is much too big for us. We're having the basement turned into a nice flat and we want you to come and live here. You can have the whole of the rest of the house and do whatever you like with it. Just think of the money you'll save in rent." Dick was not very happy about the idea of living with his in-laws, but his objections were based more on principle than on the actual situation. He liked the old people very much and, in any case, he was outvoted by his womenfolk.

Jessica thought that she could understand why Aunt Jenny needed to get away from Uncle James, but on the whole her sympathies were with her uncle, who never said an unkind word about anyone, not even his hare-brained wife. One of the good things about him was that although he was very wealthy, he didn't flaunt it, performing his acts of generosity as unobtrusively as possible. After deciding to join the army, he had presented his cat, Montmorency, and his grand piano to the Smiths, with the remark that he had never been very musical and wanted the piano to go somewhere where it would be appreciated. Then he had told Dick and Jean that since Jessica no longer had to tinkle on a ramshackle old upright she might as well have some proper lessons, and he had persuaded them to let him pay for them. What Jessica didn't know, although she had her suspicions, was that Uncle James was also paying for her to go to Greville's School. This was a cut above the grammar school and her teachers felt lucky to have her. His last gift, which was as much a matter of pulling strings as providing money, had been to have an air raid shelter built in the back garden—a long deep trench, walled and roofed with corrugated iron, covered with the soil and sod that had been dug out, and now topped with a profusion of grass and weeds. The tubular, submarine-like interior was big enough to accommodate people from several neighboring houses, who sat facing one another across a narrow central gangway. The atmosphere of the place was oddly convivial, being a concentrated essence of the feeling of the whole country, compounded of fear, defiance and wry humor.

Jessica was so lost in thought that she missed most of Beethoven's slow movement and the whole of the grim *scherzo*, and was brought back to consciousness of her surroundings by the triumphant *finale*, which started in the middle of side 6 and was interrupted two minutes later while Dick made the final change of record. It was in that moment of silence that the air raid sirens sounded, sending the family into a routine that had become firmly established. Jessica picked up Montmorency and went straight to the shelter. It was pitch dark outside, but she had made the trip so many times that she could almost do it in her sleep. Her grandparents stayed in the basement, which they considered just as safe as the shelter, and her parents scurried around the house retrieving a few precious belongings before following Jessica to the shelter. Aunt Jenny was looking for her handbag and couldn't remember where she had left it. As Jessica was entering the shelter, she heard the beat of approaching engines and the outbreak of anti-aircraft fire.

"I do wish they'd hurry", she thought, but Dick and Jean had Aunt Jenny to deal with. So when the bomb fell they were still looking for the errant handbag.

As the earth heaved and shook, the lights in the shelter went out and people were thrown in all directions, some unconscious, some bleeding and some moaning and crying. Some were active enough to try to get out, but the door was hopelessly jammed. By the time Uncle James arrived twenty minutes later, the raid seemed to be over, and a rescue party was on the scene. There was little that they could do, however; the bomb had made a direct hit and penetrated to the basement. What remained of the Smiths' house was engulfed in flames.

James grabbed the arm of one of the rescuers, ignored the warning shouts of the others, and made his way between the flaming ruins of the Smiths' house and the neighboring building. The shelter seemed to be intact, but the door was blocked by debris that had fallen from the roof, and it took them several minutes to get it open. The first to emerge was Montmorency, who disappeared into the night with a frenzied yowl. He was followed by a slow stream of dazed humanity, too numb to think and unable to take in the sight that confronted them. Finally came Jessica, walking unsteadily, and apparently unaware of the devastation all around her.

"Hello Uncle James", she said, as if apologizing for keeping him waiting, "There were people on top of me and I couldn't get out and I've lost Montmorency."

James recognized shell-shock when he saw it, but he had an urgent question.

"Jessica, where are your parents?"

Jessica looked at the burning house and her knees gave way. James caught her in his arms and carried her out to the street, murmuring, "My poor darling child, what am I going to do with you?"

(ii)

Gloucester, England: April, 1965

As the slow, heart-rending music died away, Wilhelmina Marjoribanks glanced at the middle-aged man sitting next to her, felt as much as saw the pain he was enduring, and canceled the whispered comment she had been about to make. So while the four instrumentalists tinkered delicately with their instruments, she sat silently in the little church in the shadow of the cathedral, and thought about her husband, who had died on the night of Queen Elizabeth's Coronation, twelve years previously. In some ways Greg had resembled John Hume, her present companion. As City Chief Librarian he had possessed an encyclopedic knowledge of literature, and he had found an enthusiastic student in his wife. He had also been a great music-lover with a voracious appetite for both the old and the new—"Everything from Anon to Zarzuela", he used to say. He had been a quiet, studious man when not holding forth about music or literature, and the only other things he had been passionate about were his wife and his two sons. After his death, Wilhelmina, whose name had been shortened first to "Billie" and finally to "Bill", had worked as a secretary at the library, but for more than a year now she had been the headmaster's private secretary at the Nave School, where John Hume taught chemistry.

John certainly knew about music and literature, but the passion never bubbled out as it had done with Greg. Bill smiled as she recalled the description given by one of John's colleagues:

"Hume is an immemorial bachelor. He occupies a large flat, reads prodigiously, gets enormous pleasure from his grand piano, which he plays very badly, and is adored by his landlady. He appears to have no social life whatsoever, except when there's a concert he wants to go to."

Bill, who loved music in an ignorant sort of way, found herself in complete agreement. John was courteous and punctual, and knew more about music than anyone she'd ever met except Greg, but he never made her feel ignorant, and struck her as being completely asexual. He was always very apologetic about asking her, explaining that he needed her for protection, because going to a concert on his own was apt to induce a fit of melancholia.

Satisfied with their tinkering, the quartet started up again. Now the music was strong and rhythmical, but still with an undercurrent of unresolved emotion. John remained slumped forward in his seat, with his chin in his hands and his eyes cast down.

"Well", Bill thought, "as far as protecting him is concerned I seem to be a complete failure. If I'm going to enjoy the rest of this concert I'll just have to ignore him."

"I'm sorry for being such bad company", John said afterwards, as he saw Bill to her car. "Schubert always has that effect on me."

"Then why do you go to hear him?"

"I don't know—it's too hard to explain. I mean, why do people go to see *Hamlet* or *Death of a Salesman*, or read *Jude the Obscure*?"

7

"Well, in the last case it's probably the bit about the pig's penis. But I suppose I see what you mean."

It struck Bill, however, that it wasn't really the same thing, and that it was the kind of question that she could discuss with her new boss, Colin Woodcock, with whom she was already on very friendly terms.

1940: Thursday, November 14

London, Paddington Station

Jessica looked at the big sign: "IS YOUR JOURNEY REALLY NECESSARY?" it asked. She wasn't quite sure. London, she had been told, was no place for a fifteen- year-old girl who had lost her entire family in the blitz, and whose only remaining relative, who wasn't really a relative at all, was a wounded soldier who would be required to return to the front in a few days. London was where her friends were, friends who had given her food and clothing, and would have been glad to take her in if she hadn't still been too numb with grief to do anything but accept the advice of her uncle and most of her teachers. With her green school blazer, her pale face and her soft black hair wound so tightly into a bun that very little of it showed below her round regulation hat, she looked every inch an English schoolgirl; but Uncle James, spotting her as he limped into the station, said to himself, "My dear young lady, you're going to be turning a few heads in a year or two."

"Hello, Jessica. Sorry I'm late. I have to sail for foreign parts the day after tomorrow and there's a lot to do before I leave. Have you got everything you need?"

"Yes, Uncle James. Miss Edwards brought me here, made sure I had my ticket, and gave me some sandwiches. She actually kissed me when she left."

"She likes you very much, you know. Why didn't she wait and see you off?"

"She said that she thought you would prefer to have a few minutes alone with me."

Miss Edwards was the gym teacher with whom Jessica had stayed while arrangements for her evacuation were completed. Uncle James, who had met her, thought that it might have been Miss Edwards who wanted to say her goodbyes while she was alone with Jessica, but he kept the idea to himself.

"Do you think she wanted you to stay?"

"She didn't actually say so—she only said she would miss me."

"What about you? Would you have liked to stay?"

"I'm not sure. I thought it would be very awkward staying with a teacher, but she was really marvelous. Most people either gushed over me or stood about looking sheepish because they didn't know what to say. At first I couldn't talk at all and she just left me alone and didn't tell me I would starve to death if I didn't eat, and that sort of thing. Later on I realized that she could talk about ordinary things just like a normal person."

"Well, you know, most teachers *are* normal people."

"I suppose so", Jessica acknowledged dubiously.

"And I don't know how much longer you could have stayed. She told me she was thinking of joining the Wrens."

Jessica seemed taken aback.

"She didn't tell me that."

"Maybe if you had stayed with her she wouldn't have. Anyway, I think she'll look good in a navy uniform, and you'll be much better off in Gloucester. Much safer, at any rate, and Mr. and Mrs. Simpson seem to be very decent people."

"Yes, Uncle James."

They made their way to the train, which, like Paddington Station on that raw November morning, was big, grimy and relatively empty. Doubts about her forthcoming journey almost surfaced, but all she did was to ask her uncle to tell her more about the Simpsons.

"Mrs. Simpson is a nurse at Gloucester Royal Infirmary", he explained, "and I settled on her at the suggestion of some old friends who know her quite well."

The station clock moved ponderously to 10.50.

"Five minutes" said Uncle James, as he put Jessica's suitcase and overcoat on the luggage rack. "It looks as if you might have the compartment to yourself."

Jessica missed her parents terribly, and passing through some of the uglier parts of London did nothing to cheer her up. She felt that she was going to dislike Gloucester, the Simpsons and her new school, Blenheim Hall. She didn't believe that Miss Edwards had any intention of joining the Wrens, and wished she had tried harder to stay in London. Miss Edwards had been more than kind—she had even given up some of her precious clothing coupons so that she could buy Jessica an extra blouse and a nice cotton nightgown—and Jessica had discovered that it was possible to take a few mild liberties without reproof and even with some encouragement. It was when she pictured herself still living with her gym teacher that she realized that in the last few days there had been something slightly uncomfortable in the atmosphere. Was it that Miss Edwards had seemed a little too anxious to please and to defer to Jessica's wishes? It was faintly embarrassing when a teacher behaved like that. And it was odd that although Jessica usually liked a hug and a kiss, there had been something slightly awkward and unsatisfactory about Miss Edwards's final embrace at the station. She had seemed reluctant to let go, and when she did she had held on to Jessica's hand before finally turning away. Like everything else it seemed strange and inexplicable. As she thought more about what it would have been like to stay in London, with no parents and no real home, it seemed to her that there might after all be something to be said for going to Gloucester and getting away from all the things that painfully reminded her of her old life.

The first sight of open countryside cheered her up a little and she began to feel that she was someone starting on an adventure, not just an obedient child being packed off to the country. This made her think of food, so she got out her packet of sandwiches and discovered that Miss Edwards had made another special effort on her behalf. There was real butter on the bread, and how her teacher had managed to get hold of the slices of roast beef Jessica couldn't imagine. The nourishment fortified her sense of adventure so, following an impulse that she barely understood, she took off her blazer and hat and removed the nest of pins that held her bun in place. The proportions of her face echoed the tall, slender elegance of her body, but the hint of asceticism in the high cheek-bones and slightly pointed chin was softened by the fine black hair that cascaded over her shoulders and conspired with her dark eyes to produce a startlingly un-schoolgirl-like sense of mystery, of which she was quite unaware. She felt freer and more comfortable without the bun, but one of the effects of its removal was to draw her attention to the rest of her attire—the plain white blouse, green school skirt the regulation four inches below the knee, and lisle stockings. Thank heaven, at any rate, that her parents didn't make her wear the kind of elasticized knickers that most girls of her age had to endure.

She looked at the stockings. Lisle was always ugly even when it wasn't wrinkled, but bare legs were unheard of and might in any case look funny with sensible school shoes. Well, she had a pair of gym shoes in her suitcase, the train was practically empty and a quick check reassured her that there was no one in the corridor. The change took only a few minutes and left her with an odd sense of tingling anticipation. She looked at the hat on the seat beside her, which obviously hadn't been designed to be worn over a head of long flowing hair. Presumably she would have to get a new one at Blenheim Hall, so she lowered the window and tried to send it skimming out into a cow pasture. Unfortunately at that moment the train entered a tunnel and the wind snatched the hat out of her grasp and into the darkness, while the noise became deafening. Raising the window was much more difficult than lowering it had been, but eventually she managed it and returned to her seat panting a little. The train began to slow down. Perhaps the Simpsons would be shocked. Was there time to change back? No, the train was stopping.

As it turned out, this was Swindon and it would be over an hour before they reached Gloucester. Three young soldiers got into her compartment. One sat next her and two opposite. They looked at her with great interest, nodding as they caught each other's eyes.

Sergeant Willis, passing along the corridor ten minutes later, saw the broad back of a soldier blocking the window of a compartment door.

Being old and experienced he scented mischief and slid the door open so violently that the soldier fell backwards into the corridor. Another soldier was kneeling over a young girl who was stretched out on the floor with her blouse open and her skirt rolled up to her waist, while a third held her wrists over her head.

The soldiers looked up as they heard Willis enter.

"Just having a little fun, sergeant", one of them said brazenly.

"Get out", growled the sergeant. "I'll deal with you later."

Sergeant Willis, who was a married man with two grown-up daughters, saw Jessica as a child in acute distress and made no bones about helping her with her blouse and skirt. He was amazed at her stoicism and couldn't understand why she hadn't screamed for help. He was also confused by the way she was dressed—the blouse and skirt were obviously part of a school uniform, but they didn't seem to go very well with the gym shoes, bare legs and streaming hair. If the soldiers had removed her stockings, they would hardly have replaced her shoes. He asked Jessica if she was hurt—it sounded like a stupid question, but he couldn't think of any other way to phrase it.

"Not really. They had only just . . . started. I think it must have been my fault."

"How could that be?"

"Because I wasn't properly dressed. I wanted it to be an adventure and I didn't want to look like a schoolgirl."

Jessica's eyes strayed to her suitcase, and at last she began to cry.

Willis looked at the suitcase, saw Jessica's name, and figured out what had happened to her stockings and her school blazer.

"Listen, Jessica", he said, "You might have been safer in your full school uniform and with your hair in a bun, but that doesn't mean it was your fault. My girls always hated their school uniforms and they would probably have done the same thing. Where are you going?"

"Gloucester."

"Is someone meeting you?"

"Yes."

"Well then, you come along with me and I'll put you into a compartment with two captains and a major, and we may be able to raise a cup of tea out of a thermos. We'll soon have you as right as ninepence. And if it's any consolation, there will be some nasty consequences for the men who did this. It just shows how much sense there is in putting half-trained eighteen-year-olds into uniform and calling them soldiers."

Soon Jessica was sipping tepid tea in the company of several professional soldiers who were all extremely polite and attentive. Sergeant Willis was wrong about one thing, however; it took Jessica a long time to feel better, but when she did it was more like a million pounds than ninepence.

The last few miles of track into the Great Western Station at Gloucester ran through a wilderness of marshalling yards which the train negotiated very slowly. Sergeant Willis wanted to make sure that Jessica had no more misadventures, so he stood with her in the corridor until the train stopped and they saw a naval officer and a very trim-looking young woman in a long black overcoat standing in the middle of the otherwise deserted platform.

"I didn't know he was in the navy", said Jessica dubiously.

"Well, I'll just come along and make sure they're the right people."

"All right, but don't tell them about . . . that."

But there didn't seem to be any doubt since, by this time, the couple were waving and walking towards Jessica.

"Goodbye. Thank you for taking care of me. I'll be all right now."

When Sergeant Willis got back into the train he was still bearing the impress of a fervent hug and wondering if the kid hugged everyone like that.

"Jessica?" the young woman asked with a smile. "I hope you've had a tolerable journey—one could hardly expect it to be pleasant. You seem to have made a friend, at any rate."

Jessica, acutely self-conscious in the absence of her hat and her stockings, and feeling the unseemliness of bare legs, gym shoes and hair blowing in the wind, blushed furiously. She was afraid that somehow this woman had guessed what had happened. She decided to put her best foot forward.

"Yes, Mrs. Simpson. Sergeant Willis was afraid I would get lost."

"Actually I'm not Mrs. Simpson. Her husband is ill and we're going to take you in until he's better. Our name is Berkeley—my husband is on leave from his ship for a few days."

Captain Berkeley was in his early thirties, tall, loose-limbed, soft-spoken and a few years older than his wife.

"Hello Jessica—is that all your luggage."

"Yes, it's all I have. Our house was . . ."

She trailed off, unable to finish the sentence.

Berkeley looked at her sympathetically.

"I'm sorry—silly of me. Let's go and find a bus."

They walked to King's Square, where after a considerable wait they got on a bus that lumbered out to the house on the Cheltenham Road, a mile or so north of the city center. Sitting between the Berkeleys, Jessica felt safer than she had at any time since the bomb fell.

CHAPTER II

1965: Friday, October 29

The Nave School in the City of Gloucester

The miscellaneous collection of buildings known as the Nave School was situated in St. Mary's Square, which was also the home of St. Mary's Church. The square was connected to the busy thoroughfare of Eastgate Street by a lane known rather confusingly as Knave Street, the name being a relic of *Sankt Marie des Knaben,* the obscure German saint after whom the Church, the square and the school were named. Almost in the middle of the square stood the science building, and at three o'clock on a chilly afternoon in late October, Colin Woodcock was watching it go up in flames. Woodcock, in his second year as headmaster of the Nave, had never liked the science building, which had been put up in a rush immediately after the Second World War. The place always smelt of gas and the janitor had to buy fuses by the dozen, so Woodcock had already set the wheels in motion to have it replaced. He would have been glad to see it go if it hadn't chosen to disappear in such a spectacular fashion, and if he hadn't been so anxious about the safety of the hundred or so boys and teachers who were inside when the fire started.

"Well, that's going to move things along a bit." The voice in Woodcock's ear belonged to Charles Ferrier, the Director of Education for the Gloucester district. "We won't have to persuade anyone of the need for a new building."

The headmaster found himself disliking Ferrier even more than usual.

"Perhaps", he replied. "The question is, what kind? My guess is that we'll be looking at another temporary piece of jerrybuilding that will stay here until it falls to bits."

Woodcock had a habit of being right; he was soon informed that removal of the old foundations was planned for the last weekend before Christmas, and the installation of a new prefabricated building was supposed to be complete by the time school re-opened in January.

On the morning of December 17th, the last Friday before the Christmas holidays, most of the boys and teachers at the Nave School were thinking the same thing—if the idiots who decided the calendar had shown even a little bit of common sense, school would be closing at noon and everyone would soon be on their way home for the vacation. But with the prospect of another three days of school next week, lessons would continue as usual until four o'clock, homework would be set, teachers would spend the weekend with piles of exercise books, and another Monday morning would arrive with depressing speed. So the routine went on and the boys of A. G. "Aggie" Bagwell's history class—healthy, curious fourteen-year-olds—found it quite easy to draw their teacher into the kind of long digression that makes it unnecessary to take notes or even to stay awake. They might have found the Tory Reformers of the 1870's quite interesting if Aggie's main purpose hadn't been just to make sure that they could memorize the list of Acts that they passed. There was no way of knowing that a casual reference to Shakespeare would have very surprising consequences.

"Factory Act, Artisans' Dwelling Act, Trade Unions Act, Public Health Act, Education Act . . . You can easily remember all these Acts because their initial letters spell the name Fat Phebe."

"Who the hell was Fat Phebe?" Terry Carter muttered to himself as he wrote it down. He raised his hand.

"Sir, who was Fat Phebe?"

17

"Fat Phebe is a character in *As You like It*."

"Is that Shakespeare, Sir", asked Dai Davies, knowing perfectly well that it was.

"Yes", replied Aggie, who was almost as bored as the boys. "Phebe was an ill-favored shepherdess."

Derek Hunt was puzzled.

"What does 'ill-favored' mean, Sir?"

"It means that she was not comely—her face was not her fortune."

Carter decided to push things a little.

"Is it true that Shakespeare once slept in St. Mary's church?"

Aggie, a keen local historian and amateur archaeologist, took the bait gladly.

"There was certainly a strong rumor to that effect. He is known to have had some correspondence with the Duke of Gloucester, who had written several very bad plays and was trying to get someone to perform them. He visited the Duke in 1601 and is supposed to have had an affair with the Duke's daughter Margaret. The story is that when the Duke found out what was going on he tried to have Shakespeare arrested, but he escaped on a horse provided by Margaret. It was late at night and he dodged his pursuers by riding his horse up the steps and into the church. Early the next morning he rode down the steps and set off for Stratford, which is only about fifty miles from here."

"What happened to Margaret, Sir?"

"The story doesn't tell us, but we know that the Duke actually did have a daughter called Margaret and that she died in 1602. She was, in fact, buried in the graveyard of St. Mary's Church."

"But Sir, the church hasn't got a graveyard."

"It had in those days, but there has been so much building and rebuilding that nobody is quite sure where it was. The general opinion is that it was south of the church, but my researches have led me to believe that it was somewhere near the middle of the square."

Carter looked out of the window at the ruins of the old science building just in time to see the arrival of a large mechanical digger and a crew with pneumatic drills.

"Might it be under the old labs, Sir?"

"Part of it might well be", replied Aggie, a fanatical look coming into his eye. "I have always wanted to excavate this square. St. Mary's

Church is one of the oldest buildings in the city and parts of it go back to the twelfth century. Who knows what might be found?"

"Why don't you, Sir?"

"I'm not a professional archaeologist and I've never been able to get the authorities to take any interest in the project. It would be very expensive, for one thing, since most of the free area is paved."

"But they could do the bit under the old labs."

"Yes, it's a priceless opportunity, but now they say there isn't time—the builders have to get everything finished by the time we come back to school in January."

"Perhaps Margaret is under there."

"Perhaps she is, but we shall never know. With that mechanical contraption they might remove a whole graveyard without noticing it. Something ought to be done about it, but no one seems interested." He looked at his watch. Happily only ten minutes of his lesson remained, but he probably ought to try to finish Fat Phebe.

"How old was she when she died, Sir?"

"She was eighteen."

"Wasn't she a bit young for Shakespeare?" Hunt asked. "He must have been about thirty-seven."

"Perhaps, but such things do happen. They were just about the same ages as Abelard and Heloïse."

"Who was Abelard, Sir?"

"That's the one who had his genitals amputated", Davies remarked in a penetrating stage whisper.

Halfway along Knave Street was Nave House, home of the school administration, a trim little redbrick building with white windows and three steps leading up to a bright green door. A visitor would first encounter the receptionist, a charming young woman by the name of Dorothy ("Dotty") Ayers, and, if important enough, might then be ushered into the front office, which belonged to the headmaster. Those of lesser rank usually had to be content with admittance to the rear office, occupied by the headmaster's secretary.

When the demolition experts arrived in St. Mary's Square, Mrs. "Bill" Marjoribanks (pronounced "Marchbanks") was sitting in the headmaster's office. Bill was officially a resident of Hartpury, a small village a few miles north of Gloucester, but a few weeks previously she had gone out to dinner with Woodcock and ended up in bed with him, and her neighbors had seen very little of her since then. She was tall, fair-skinned, red-headed and angular, so she made a good contrast with Woodcock, who was short, round, pink and balding. It was just a week before Christmas Eve and the city was dressed for the season; but no carols pierced the din that had just broken out in St. Mary's Square.

"I thought they weren't supposed to start until after four o'clock", said Bill.

"So did I", replied Woodcock. "Perhaps they've finally realized that they'd better hurry."

"Possibly", Bill admitted, "but they'll never get it done in time."

"I know. If they'd started when I wanted them to we might have been able to move in in January. I still don't understand why we had to have six weeks of bickering about planning, estimates, contractors and whatnot. It seemed very straightforward to me."

"Nothing is straightforward to our city fathers. Most of them have an axe of some sort to grind."

"It" was the removal of the concrete slab which had served as the foundation of the old science building, most of the above-ground remains having been deemed dangerous and removed soon after the fire. Woodcock started to say something about vested interests, but the noise of deconstruction grew louder and his remarks were lost in the uproar.

"Let's go out and see what they're doing", yelled Bill.

The bell for morning break was ringing when they stepped out into Knave Street. Boys and masters were emerging from doors all over the square, most of them with just one thing in mind—the inexplicable joy of watching a group of workers dig a hole in the ground. By the time Bill and the headmaster arrived at the roped-off area, the crowd was four or five deep. Spotting Jim Selwyn, the physical education master, and a couple of other teachers, Woodcock called a quick conference.

"We must get the boys away from here before someone gets hurt", he said, making a considerable effort to be heard above the noise of the drills. "It's nearly the end of break, so the best thing to do will be to send them to their classrooms immediately."

Selwyn blew a few piercing blasts on his whistle, penetrating enough to catch the attention of the drillers and produce a momentary lull. He and the other masters scurried around, shepherding the boys to the area of the square where they lined up before returning to class. Woodcock noticed that two boys were still gazing at the operation.

"Carter, Davies", he called, and pointed to the other side of the square where the boys were assembling.

"Sorry Sir", they said in unison, and ran off to join their classmates.

The headmaster decided to have a few words with the foreman, whom he identified as the one worker who appeared to have nothing to do.

"The square is going to be full of boys again at half past twelve and we're going to need something stronger than this rope to keep them at a safe distance."

"I don't know, Sir", the man said dubiously, "I don't think we've got anything else."

"Oh come now, all we need is one of those green canvas fences, six feet high so that they won't be able to see what's happening. If they can't see they'll be less likely to hang about."

"Well, Sir, we might be able to borrow something from Public Works, but I don't know . . ."

"I'll find out", said the headmaster firmly. "Who are you, by the way?"

"Charlie King, Sir."

"And you are in charge of the proceedings?"

"Yes Sir, but Mr. Sandman should be here soon."

"When he appears would you tell him that I'd be glad of a few words with him?"

Herbert Sandman was the proprietor of Sandman and Co., the builders who had finally landed the contract. Woodcock's first telephone call was to their office, but Sandman was already on his way. The Department of Public Works produced a tepid response and thought that something might possibly be done by the middle of next week. Charles Ferrier, at the Education Office, pointed out that it was already a quarter past eleven and that Public Works could hardly be expected to accomplish in an hour what would normally take at least a week. So the headmaster produced his trump card in the person of Inspector Jack Phelps, with whom he had cooperated in the investigation of the fire in St. Mary's Square, and who fortunately happened to be in his office at Gloucester Central Police Station.

"No more arson or dead bodies, I hope", said the inspector. "If it's just a matter of fencing off a dangerous area I'll get Public Works on it straight away."

"They didn't think they could manage it today."

"Don't worry—they will when I get on their tails."

So by lunchtime the six foot green canvas fence had appeared, and the boys streaming out from their classrooms were disappointed to find that there was no longer anything exciting to see. The only ones who approved of the transformation were Carter and Davies, since the fence would be helpful in a little scheme that they had been cooking up. Meanwhile Sandman, having conferred with Charlie King, assured the headmaster that his men would do their best to keep disturbance to a minimum. By the end of the afternoon all that remained of the original foundations would be gone and the excavation for the basement would begin early the next morning.

By four o'clock, when school ended for the day, the sun had set behind layers of thick cloud and there was a hint of snow in the air. The drills were silent and a large dump truck was being loaded with chunks of concrete by a mechanical giraffe with huge mandibles. After the traffic in St. Mary's Square had thinned out, Carter and Davies held a conference with their friend Ted Berry. Carter, who was the tallest, slimmest and most intelligent of the three, was standing on Davies's shoulders, looking over the fence and doing the talking.

"All the concrete is gone and it's just bare earth now."

"Look out, here comes the Humerus", muttered Berry.

John Hume, with a briefcase in one hand and a shopping bag full of exercise books in the other, was on his way to his car, but now he seemed to be just as curious as the boys about what was going on behind the green fence.

"What are they doing?" he asked Carter as the boy slid abruptly down to earth.

"Just taking away the old concrete, Sir."

Hume paused irresolutely before walking over to the fence and peering over it for a few moments.

"Well, don't get into mischief!"

"No, Sir", the boys chorused.

After Hume had driven off in his old Ford Prefect, Carter put his plan forward.

"I don't know about mischief, but I'd like to find out what's under there before they start building on it again. If we each brought a spade and a flashlight we could do a proper investigation. With this fence no one would be any the wiser. You never know—we might find Margaret. And just think how happy old Aggie would be."

Berry, a melancholic who was rumored to have been behind the door when brains were given out, was dubious.

"What if it's snowing?"

Davies, short, round and mercurial, turned the objection aside.

"We'll do it anyway. It'll be more fun."

That evening the three boys got their parents' permission to go to a movie together. The spades were a difficulty and only Carter managed to provide one, but each had a flashlight and Berry had purloined a trowel which he said would be useful when they got close to something. It hadn't occurred to the authorities that the building site was of any particular interest, so there was no difficulty in getting in through the canvas flap that served as a door. By half past seven they were busy dividing the area into small squares and doing some very cautious digging around the center of each one. This, they thought, would give them the best chance of finding something, if there was anything to find. By half past eight Berry's doubts surfaced again.

"I don't believe there's anything here. We'd have had a lot more fun at the pictures."

"Come on, we still have an hour", urged Carter. "We might as well keep trying."

By nine o'clock it was snowing lightly and a chilly wind was swirling around the Square. Berry announced that he was cold and fed up with crawling about in the dirt, and if the other two wanted to keep looking they could, but he was going home.

This annoyed Carter, and he banged the spade down into a small hole that he had made in the middle of one of the squares. He was about to speak when he realized that the spade had penetrated a further six inches with hardly any resistance.

"Come here quick", he called, trying to control his excitement.

They knelt around the point where the spade had entered and started carefully removing the soil with trowel and fingers. A few inches down they found the rotting remains of a wooden board. A minute later they were looking into the eye-sockets of a human skull.

CHAPTER III

1940: Thursday, November 14

Cheltenham Road was lined with modern two-storey houses, each one standing in its own plot of well-tended garden and shrubbery. The Berkeleys' had a green front door with two steps leading up to it. Above the door was a little stained glass window with intertwined red and green leaves, and to the right was a large bay window. All the houses had names rather than numbers, this one being called "That'll Do", a whim, as Mrs. Berkeley embarrassedly explained, of the previous occupants.

"We'd change it if we expected to be here very long, but a week from now my husband may be on any one of the Seven Seas and I never know where I'm going to be for more than a month or two at a time, so there really isn't any point. I expect you'd like some tea after that long journey, and I'll do the best I can, but unlike most of our neighbors we don't know any of the right people, so we actually have to make do with our rations. By the way, I don't suppose . . ."

"Yes", said Jessica, realizing that Mrs. Berkeley was delicately touching on the question of a ration book. "Miss Edwards—she's—she was—my gym mistress—managed to get a new one for me."

"I think perhaps . . ." began Captain Berkeley.

"Yes, John", said his wife with a sigh, "You're quite right. We should save it for the Simpsons. You can leave your hat and coat in the hall closet, Jessica, and I'll show you your room. Then we'll have some weak tea and bread and margarine."

Mrs. Berkeley left her hat and coat next to Jessica's, and the girl saw that she was wearing a nurse's uniform and that her hair was confined in a bun just as tightly as Jessica's own had been at the beginning of the day.

Jessica's room was small and contained only a bed, a chair and a chest of drawers, but it was charmingly situated in the front of the house just under the eaves, looking over the lawn and out on to the road. It was now four o'clock and getting dark, but there were no streetlights, in fact no lights of any kind.

"Have you had any air raids?" Jessica asked.

"There was one a few months ago. We weren't here then but the locals say that one of the German pilots got lost and thought he'd better drop his bombs before going home. I'll leave you to settle in. John's lighting a fire, so when you're ready you can come down and we'll sit round it and have a nice chat."

Jessica put her few belongings into the chest and sat down on the bed. Now that the journey was over she felt paralyzed. In the presence of the officers on the train, and later, while she had been with the Berkeleys, she had been able to suppress the horror of the attempted rape, but now, when there was no one to comfort her, it overwhelmed her. Possibly Mrs. Berkeley could have helped if she had known, but the idea of talking about it was intolerable. The sense of adventure that she had felt earlier in the day had been destroyed by her attackers. Now she experienced the move to Gloucester as an exile, a banishment from everyone and everything she knew and loved, hated or was indifferent to. Above all, crowding out even the hateful images from earlier in the day, there was the huge aching space left by the loss of her parents. She might well have burst into tears, but at that moment she heard footsteps on the stairs. She didn't want to be found weeping, so she stood up, wiped her eyes and opened her door.

"Hello", said Captain Berkeley. "I was just coming to see if you were all right."

"I'm all right", said Jessica. "I was just coming down."

Jessica went to the kitchen to help with the tea, but was soon sitting on a stool and listening while Mrs. Berkeley talked and bustled at the same time. She told Jessica that she was nominally attached to Gloucester Royal Infirmary, which was how she had come to know Mrs. Simpson, but most of her time was spent training nurses for army hospitals, which involved traveling all over the country. Jessica saw that her resemblance to Miss Edwards was not as strong as she had thought. Her former gym teacher's short and compact figure had inclined a little to stockiness, whereas Mrs. Berkeley seemed to Jessica to be perfectly proportioned. Her hair, which was now hanging about her shoulders, was more golden than red, and her freckles were less obvious. There was something about the eyes and the ready smile that suggested a sense of fun, even of mischief, a quality notably lacking in Miss Edwards. The effect on Jessica was to make her feel just a little more calm and relaxed.

"Mrs. Berkeley", she said impulsively, "you have the most beautiful hair I've ever seen."

"Well", her hostess replied, "It's funny you should say that. I was just thinking the same thing about you."

They took the tea things into the living room and sat in armchairs in front of a cheerful blaze.

"Coal is rationed like everything else that makes life worth living", Captain Berkeley remarked, "but fortunately a tree fell down in the back garden. I'm sure there's some regulation about the proper disposal of firewood, but I borrowed an axe and made sure that our neighbors wouldn't give us away by giving them some of the wood."

Conversation was difficult. Jessica might have found it possible and even helpful to talk about her parents, her school and the air raids, but the Berkeleys were too tactful to ask. John Berkeley admitted that he was in the navy and that his ship was a destroyer called the *Masai*, but he could tell Jessica nothing about his past and future activities.

"'Careless talk costs lives'", he quoted wryly. "I don't think there's anything I could tell you that would be the slightest use to the Germans, but we have strict instructions."

Talking about the difficulties of wartime travel, Mrs. Berkeley gave a humorous description of her last trip to London. Jessica felt that she was expected to talk about her journey from London, but it was something she couldn't possibly do. Sensing that there was something behind this reticence, Mrs. Berkeley let the matter drop, and her husband quickly changed the subject.

"Have you ever thought of going into nursing?" he asked Jessica. "If you have, you can pick Susan's brains. She's an expert on the subject."

This had never occurred to Jessica, but she expressed a polite interest and soon discovered that although Susan took her profession very seriously, she could see the funny side of things. The conversation brought Jessica up sharply against the idea of the future, something which she had never thought much about, possibly because the present had been so absorbing. She had enjoyed being a child and, until her house and her family had been destroyed, she had enjoyed being an adolescent. She liked her schoolwork and felt no pull in any particular direction. Her path had been laid out for her for the next several years—school certificate, higher school certificate and then perhaps university, perhaps teaching or secretarial work, perhaps marriage. The last part had been remote and vague. School and her friends and family had been enough to be going on with, but now she seemed to be colliding with the future. How long would she be in Gloucester? She was there because of the war, but how long would the war go on, and where would she go then? She couldn't expect to stay with the Simpsons indefinitely. She had no idea what they were like and wished she were going to stay with the Berkeleys. Uncle James might know some of the answers, but he would soon be a thousand miles away.

Jessica was too tired to wrestle with these problems. The fire was warm and her armchair was deep and comfortable. She realized with a start that Susan Berkeley was talking to her and that she had changed from her nurse's uniform into a long green dress.

"I'm sorry, Mrs. Berkeley. I think I must be getting sleepy."

"Actually you've just taken a two hour nap. Don't apologize, you've had a tiring day, but I don't want you to go to bed with just a slice or two of bread inside you. I had a piece of luck today—one of my nurses is a farmer's daughter and she brought me a dozen eggs. So we'll scramble some of them, make some toast and pretend that Adolf Hitler doesn't exist. And, by the way, since John and I are not that old and not relations, we think you should call us by our Christian names."

It takes an English cook at least twenty minutes to scramble eggs properly, so Jessica sat in front of the fire with John Berkeley while Susan patiently stirred eggs over the lowest possible flame. In the fireplace the flames leaping above mysterious little red caverns died down and Jessica drifted again towards blessed oblivion. As quietly as possible John lifted a log from the neatly stacked pile at the side of the grate, but Jessica stirred and opened her eyes.

"Time to add another precious log or two. Would you like to snooze a little longer or shall I tell you how your Uncle James and I became acquainted? It's a funny story."

"I didn't know that you were acquainted. He only said that some old friends had told him about Mr. and Mrs. Simpson."

It was painful to be conscious again but Jessica thought that it would be rude not to listen. John looked at her anxiously, but she appeared to be wide awake now so he went on.

"I should tell you that Susan knows this story and she thinks it's funny too. You probably know that at Cambridge there are about ten times as many male undergraduates as there are female."

Jessica didn't know this; in fact she knew very little about Cambridge.

"Fortunately for the men there's also Addenbrooke's Hospital where there are lots of young nurses, one of whom I met at a dance on a June evening long ago—in fact I was quite smitten. Well, to cut a long story short, I agreed to meet Rosalind—it seemed such a romantic name—at Magdalen Bridge at half past seven and go punting on the river. I was a minute or two early but there she was already—only she was deep in conversation with another young man."

"Uncle James!" said Jessica, waking up a little.

"Yes, although I didn't know he was Uncle James at the time. So I coughed politely and as they turned to me I said, 'I do beg your pardon for interrupting, but I have an appointment with Miss . . .' only at that point I realized that I didn't know her surname. 'Funnily enough, so have I', said the young man. We both looked at Rosalind, who didn't seem to be in the least embarrassed. 'I'm sorry', she said. 'This happens to me sometimes. I met James at a party, and when I've had a couple I'm apt to become rather forgetful, so by the time I met you at the dance I had forgotten all about him.' I was rather shocked and disillusioned, but James said, 'I don't feel like punting. Let's go and have a drink and forget our sorrows.'

"So off we trooped to the Eagle. I was a penniless scholarship student, but James seemed to be very well supplied and every so often Rosalind insisted on buying a round. I have no idea what we talked about, but after an hour or two we all dried up—conversationally I mean—and I remembered that I didn't know Rosalind's surname. I mentioned this and James said, "You know, it's a funny thing but I don't either.' So we both looked at her and she said, 'Well, if you must know, it's Crump.' James sat there solemnly and said, 'Rosalind Crump' several times with different intonations. Then we both started to giggle and soon we were howling with laughter. Rosalind stood up and said, 'I don't think this is particularly funny. If you two are going to sit there making an exhibition of yourselves I'm going home.' I thought that we ought to make sure that she got home safely, but James said she was in better condition than either of us. So we stayed there and James started telling me his life story. By closing time he had got as far as telling me about a girl called Jenny he was in love with.

"The next day I wasn't feeling very bright but I thought I'd better go round to Addenbrooke's and see if Rosalind was all right. It wasn't the sort of place where you could just march in and start looking for someone, and the portress, or whatever you call her, told me something repressive about visiting hours. I was about to beat a retreat when a girl who had been waiting to talk to the portress asked me who I was looking for. When I asked her if she knew Rosalind Crump, she laughed and said, 'Everybody knows Rosalind Crump. Are you one of Rosalind's young men?' I didn't know what to say, so I muttered, 'Well, not exactly.' She laughed again and said, 'Don't worry, nobody is exactly.' She could see that I was a little confused so she explained. 'This morning Rosalind was making more noise than usual at breakfast, and being only a dozen places away from her I couldn't help hearing the tale she was telling about two men she had absentmindedly made appointments with at the same time. I must say she seems to have thoroughly enjoyed herself.' Well with that I realized that there was no need to make any further enquiries about Rosalind. Being a healthy young man, I began to take an interest in my informant, who turned out to have a perfectly normal name and was obviously very intelligent and attractive."

"Thank you kindly, young Sir", said Susan, who had just come into the room with a tray.

"Oh", said Jessica, "is that how you met each other?"

London before the war had always been alive at any time of the day or night, and in the small hours the unceasing rumble and the lights reflected on the ceiling of her room had been cozy and reassuring. Gloucester seemed somnolent during the day and perfectly dead at night—pitch dark and silent. It was very hard to sleep, so Jessica, who was always in danger of being overwhelmed by the past, tried to think about John and Susan. It struck her that she had never been treated so much like an adult before. Except for a few of her parents' younger friends and Miss Edwards, who was only twenty-three, grown-ups had never asked her to use their first names. She felt uncomfortable about the fact that John had told her that embarrassing story as if she were a friend and an equal, and a little upset that he had mentioned her Aunt Jenny as if her recent death were a matter of no consequence. It seemed safer and more comforting to think about Susan, so she fell asleep to a vision of freckles and golden hair.

John Berkeley, who had been educated in almost exclusively male establishments, had found Jessica's close proximity quite disturbing, and wondered whether this would be the case with all fifteen-year-olds or whether it was just this particular one.

Susan felt unaccountably euphoric and slept soundly.

CHAPTER IV

1965: Friday Evening December 17

"Margaret", Berry said in an awed whisper. "Just wait till we tell old Aggie."

Carter wasn't so sure. After a long pause he said, "I didn't know it would be like this. We ought to go and tell someone."

Davies had spotted something else.

"Look, there's a thing like a wallet there."

An oilskin pouch, held in a tight waterproof cylinder by several windings of copper wire, lay between the chin and the partly exposed breastbone.

"I think we should go to the police station", said Carter.

Berry objected.

"We're really going to get it in the neck from our parents. Couldn't we just telephone?"

"Now then, what's going on here?"

It was too late; the police had already arrived, in the person of Police Constable Albert Chard, whose evening round took him through St. Mary's Square. Hearing some odd noises coming from the building site, he had decided to investigate.

"It's Copper Chard", Berry whispered apprehensively.

Carter, however, felt relieved.

"Would you please come over here", he asked the constable. "We've found something."

Chard let out a low whistle when he saw what they had found.

"You're going to have to answer a lot of questions", he told them, "but first I have to get some help here. I'm going to telephone from the box at the end of Knave Street and I want you to stand in front of the fence for five minutes and make sure no one goes in. And no more digging—got it?"

"Where's that pouch thing?" asked Carter, as soon as the constable had gone.

"In my pocket", said Davies.

"We ought to give it to the police."

"I want to look inside first. I think it's something from Shakespeare."

"But Shakespeare wasn't here when she died. All that stuff that Aggie told us happened the year before."

"But he might have sent her a poem or something."

"And wrapped it in wire? It doesn't sound like Shakespeare to me."

"I'll hand it over when I've looked inside", Davies insisted.

"Look", said Carter, "We're in enough trouble already . . ."

But at that moment PC Chard reappeared and Carter bit his lip.

"Inspector Phelps and Sergeant Snipe will be here in a few minutes and they'll want to talk to you. Then he's going to send you home to your long-suffering parents, and you'd better not make up any fancy stories for them—unless you want them to find out what really happened by reading the *Citizen* on Monday."

But before leaving the police station Inspector Phelps changed the plan.

For most practical—and a few impractical—purposes, Bill had moved into Woodcock's flat on the lower slopes of Robinswood Hill shortly after the fire in St. Mary's Square, so while Constable Chard was phoning Inspector Phelps, she was sitting contentedly back in her chair and commenting on the meal just provided by her host.

"Well, that was the best leg of lamb I've had for a long while. Any woman would be glad to marry you just for your cooking."

"I have other talents too", replied Woodcock, looking around his apartment with a modest smile. "I can wash dishes and do a little dusting."

"And in spite of all that domesticity you are an excellent squire of dames. How you manage to combine all those things I can't imagine."

"Well, there's no need to leave it to the imagination. The night is still quite young . . ."

Unfortunately the telephone rang at that moment.

The headmaster picked it up and admitted that he was Colin Woodcock. A look of almost comical dismay came over his face as he listened.

"All right, I'll be there in a quarter of an hour", he told the instrument. Turning to Bill he asked, "What do you think they found under the foundations of the old labs?"

"A skeleton", Bill said promptly.

Woodcock was speechless.

"You mean it really was a skeleton? It was just the first thing that came into my head."

"Not only that—it was found by Carter, Davies and Berry, who were there with spades, trowels and flashlights digging up the subsoil—heaven knows why. I have to go and listen while Jack Phelps gives them the third degree."

"Can I come?" asked Bill. "I mean would it be seemly?"

"I don't see why not. Phelps is very tactful but I'm sure he put one and one together a long time ago."

By the time the headmaster's car turned into Knave Street it had begun to snow in earnest. The three boys had taken shelter in the back of the police car while Constable Chard guarded the entrance to the excavation, and Inspector Phelps and Sergeant Snipe took a close look at the remains. They emerged from the site just in time to greet the new arrivals.

"Well, there really is a skeleton or, at least, a skull and a sternum", said the inspector, a big, broad man with a rough brown face and a West-country accent. "I'll have to get it properly covered up until the morning. In the meantime I was wondering if we could talk to these boys in your office instead of taking them to the station."

"Certainly", replied Woodcock, "but it won't be very warm."

"Warmer than it is out here", remarked Sergeant Snipe, a slight, wiry man whose physique offered less protection against the cold than the inspector's burliness and the headmaster's rotundity.

Woodcock was right about the temperature of his office, so four adults and three boys sat huddled in a small circle in their overcoats, scarves and gloves.

Carter had become very silent and Berry appeared to be sulking, so Davies told the story as he had heard it from Mr. Bagwell, and explained how he and his friends had decided to conduct their own investigation.

"And what do you think about the result?" asked Woodcock.

"Well, Sir, there *was* a body there."

"Yes, son, there was", said Inspector Phelps, "and in your funny way you found something the might not otherwise have been discovered; but let me put you right on a couple of things. We don't know whose body it is, how it came to be there or how long it's been there. You think you found the old graveyard and proved that Mr. Bagwell's theory is correct, but that may not be the case. So the most important thing is to say as little as possible and let the police get on with the job of finding out why that skeleton happens to be where it is. You'll have to tell your parents about it and there's no way of keeping this out of the papers, but don't start telling people any fancy theories."

Turning to Carter he added, "You've been very quiet. Something on your mind?"

"We found something else", said Carter hesitantly. "Dai forgot to tell you."

Davies turned the color of beetroot and glared at Carter, but he fumbled in his pocket, brought out the object in question and handed it to the inspector.

"Well!" said Phelps. "You weren't thinking of doing a little investigation on your own, were you?"

"We had the idea that we might find Margaret and there might be something there from Shakespeare", Carter explained, trying to save his friend further embarrassment. "I know it was a crazy idea. We got a little carried away."

"All right", said the inspector as he slipped the pouch into his pocket, "no harm done."

"Couldn't we see what's inside" asked Davies plaintively.

"We shouldn't really, but I suppose we could stretch a point."

The Inspector took the pouch over to Woodcock's desk, unwound the copper wire and unrolled the oilskin. Inside was a sheet of paper. It appeared to be in good condition, so Phelps extracted it with the utmost care and flattened it on the desk. It was covered with firm handwriting.

"Poetry", he said.

"Shakespeare!" gasped Davies.

"I don't think so", said Bill who was looking over the inspector's shoulder and had already read half a dozen lines.

"No", Woodcock agreed, "definitely not Shakespeare."

"How do you know", asked Berry.

"Well, apart from the matter of the wire and the pouch, it's the wrong kind of paper, the wrong kind of writing, the wrong kind of pen and the wrong kind of poetry. You don't have to be an expert to see that."

"Could we read it?" asked Carter.

"Perhaps Mrs. Marjoribanks would read it to us."

This is what Bill read:

You asked how much I loved you,
And I said:
Let the Queen require
Five dozen shining snow-white lambs
With coal-black faces,
And let each single shining, snow-white strand . . .

But no; the Queen is dead,
The lambs are shorn
And love lies in the sheepfold dust.

You said:
To prove your love you must walk barefoot
To the lands beyond Byzantium,
And bring me a single perfumed rose
From the Caliph's palace garden.

At your command I walked barefoot
Around the world;
But the Caliph and his rose and its perfume
Were there no more.

If, in the deep soft spaces of the night,
You saw how gently
The bitter tears I weep for you
Fall, like rain, among the roses
In the garden that I keep for you,
You would not ask, you
Would not ask, would
Never, never, never
Ask.

"Not Shakespeare", said Woodcock, "but not completely without talent."

"No", Bill agreed, "and rather difficult to place as regards style. I suppose it's the vague flavor of pastiche . . ."

"Hmmm" said Inspector Phelps. "I think it's time we sent these young men back to their ever-loving parents. Now remember what I said: tell them exactly what happened, and otherwise keep your mouths firmly closed, especially when you get back to school on Monday."

"And", added the headmaster, "you'd better come and see me at break on Monday."

"Yes, Sir", said the boys, remembering previous occasions when they had given certain undertakings about their future behavior.

"Are we in very bad trouble, Sir?" Carter asked.

Woodcock suppressed a grin.

"I don't know. I'll have to think about it."

After the boys had left Inspector Phelps decided that it was time to put his cards on the table.

"There's something that fortunately the boys didn't see. I took a careful look at the skull and it appears to be pretty badly fractured at the base. We'll know better when the doctor sees it but I'm pretty sure that we're not dealing with a mystery over an old churchyard—we're dealing with a suspicious death, possibly a murder that took place about twenty years ago. Someone had a body that he wanted to dispose of and must have had access to that site when they started building the old labs."

"And", added Bill, "it was a very unusual murderer—if it *was* murder. I mean, they don't usually bury poetry with their victims."

"Yes, well that's another story, and we can't necessarily assume that the poet was the murderer. What we need first is some local history. I know that the labs were built just after the war, but it would be handy to know exactly when, and who built them"

"That building was put up in the summer of 1945 and old Johnson was the builder. I saw them working on it when I came home on leave. That was the beginning of September, and they were struggling to get it finished by the end of the holidays."

The speaker was Sergeant Snipe, who was usually very quiet in conferences of this sort, although in other circumstances he was apt to be quite loquacious. The others stared at him is if he were the Delphic Oracle.

"Well, Sir", he went on, addressing his superior officer, "as you know, I was a boy here at the Nave in the nineteen-twenties. Later on I joined the Force and when my turn came I went off to France with the B. E. F. I came back on a fishing boat from Dunkirk, but they soon sent me off to North Africa, so I didn't see much of Gloucester for the next five years. When I was on leave at the end of the war while I was waiting to be demobbed, I spent some time wandering about the town and looking to see if all the old places were still there. There was hardly anyone I knew here. I just about remembered Mr. Harescombe—he started the year I left, and Bob and Mr. Whitefield."

"Bob?" enquired Inspector Phelps.

"D. G. Roberts", explained Woodcock. "My predecessor in this position—highly respected, very much loved and a little vague at times."

"And a published poet", remarked Bill.

"Yes, but only in the local paper. His existentialist sonnets are a very different cup of tea from what we have here."

"Is he still alive?" asked the inspector.

"Yes, still riding his battered bicycle and publishing sonnets."

"I saw his last one", said Bill. "It was called *Sisyphus Unbound.*"

"Well, I think we'll have to talk to him—that is, if he can speak ordinary English."

"Oh, yes, very charmingly", said Woodcock, "but don't expect him to be very precise about dates and places."

"And", Phelps added, "we'll have to talk to Siggy Harescombe and anyone else who was around at the time. It's very unfortunate that old Johnson is no longer with us."

"But there's still young Johnson", Snipe remarked. "He was here in 1945."

"He was here today", said Bill, "driving that mechanical digger thing."

Woodcock looked quizzically at her.

"Johnson and Son used to do all the building repairs at the library", she explained. "Since old Johnson was getting a bit past it young Johnson did most of the work. Of course, he's not so young any more—he must be getting on for fifty."

"It happens to all of us", Phelps observed. "But he has his own business—why would he be working for Sandman? We'll have to have a serious talk with young Johnson and meanwhile we'll get the wheels turning on missing persons for the time in question. Presumably the medics will give us some idea of the age and sex of the victim. I don't think we'll do any more digging tonight—it would be too easy to miss something even with arc lights. And Snipey, we'd better put a watch on the site to make sure no one else decides to do a little investigating."

"Yes, Sir—what you might call a skeleton crew."

Police Constable Chard was sitting on an old chair in a canvas sentry box just inside the opening of the green fence, his face illuminated by the glow of a charcoal brazier. It would have been pitch dark inside the enclosure if it hadn't been for the brazier and the faint luminosity of the snow. He had forgotten that Gloucester had so many churches, and since none of their clocks seemed to agree about the time, the city took several minutes to strike twelve. Two hours to go before he would be relieved by PC Highnam, and he wasn't sure that he could stay awake that long. "Not a great night for a midnight stroll", he thought, "either for me or anyone else", but he decided that in order to avoid dozing off he had better take a walk around the site. He was about to push aside the canvas flap that covered the opening when he heard footsteps approaching. He got out his flashlight and stood with his back to the brazier. The flap opened and a faintly silhouetted figure appeared, looking rather like Aquarius with a burden in each hand. When Chard aimed his torch and pressed the switch the results were spectacular. There was a strangled scream and an enormous clatter as Aquarius dropped his load. The round white face that had appeared momentarily in the bright beam disappeared as the figure collapsed slowly to the ground.

"O God, I've killed him", muttered Chard as he tried to help his victim. "I hope he's only fainted."

Much to the policeman's relief, Aquarius soon began fervently to invoke the aid of St. Mary, although not the one the square had been named after, and within a few minutes Chard had him sitting in front of the brazier. His burdens turned out to be a spade and a bucket of gardening implements. He gave his name as Bagwell but he obstinately refused to explain the purpose of his nocturnal expedition, and unsuccessfully tried to insist on being told why there was a police guard on the building site. Having established that Mr. Bagwell was respectably employed as a teacher at the Nave, and lived almost next door to the school, Chard decided that it would do no harm to let him go home with a stern warning that he must be available to Inspector Phelps the next morning.

Chard was still awake when Highnam arrived. As the two stood in front of the fence, exchanging pleasantries, a car turned from Eastgate Street into Knave Street. When the beams of its headlights caught the two policemen it came to a slithering halt, backed round the corner into Eastgate Street and sped away.

"CRG569", said Chard.

"Right", agreed Highnam. "Now I wonder who the blazes that was."

"Someone else looking for skeletons, p'raps."

Inspector Phelps and Sergeant Snipe arrived in the square at seven o'clock the next morning, accompanied by two constables, the Police Surgeon and yet another set of gardening implements. PC Highnam was sent home for some rest, but not before he had told the tale of the night's happenings.

The tarpaulin that had been used to cover the burial ground was hidden under several inches of snow, but once it had been removed it didn't take long for the constables to expose the rest of the skeleton, a small pile of fragments of rotten wood and several brass screws.

"Young female, more or less fully grown, probably mid teens, somewhat taller than average", was the doctor's verdict. "Cause of death a severely fractured skull, unless she died of something else and then somebody hit her on the head. She has other injuries—a fractured radius, for instance, with no signs of knitting. She may have died in a fall or she may have been hit on the head and then fallen. I may be able to tell you more when I've had the opportunity to look at her under better conditions, but at a rough guess she's been here twenty or thirty years. Apparently she was buried in a coffin—unusual for a murderer. Furthermore, the skeleton was disarticulate, in fact rather higgledy-piggledy, suggesting that she might have been buried somewhere else and then put in a fresh coffin and rolled about a bit."

"It's not only the coffin that's unusual", Phelps remarked. "There was also a poem. Either this was an unusually fastidious murderer or she was buried by somebody else. Now I wonder who made coffins in this town twenty years ago."

CHAPTER V

1940: Friday, November 15

On the day after her arrival in Gloucester, Jessica, escorted by Susan Berkeley and properly attired except for the missing hat, arrived at Blenheim Hall to be interviewed by the headmistress, a large and buxom woman of ripe middle age.

"Let me see", said Miss Alderley after introductions had been performed, "You were in 5A at Greville's—a fine school and Miss Parker is an excellent headmistress. I was at Girton with her, you know. What a tennis player, and an expert with a punt pole!"

Miss Alderley indulged in a sentimental smile, and Jessica tried to imagine the spare and desiccated Miss Parker competing with this muscular academic.

"Miss Parker has written to me about you, and I gather that you have always been an excellent and industrious pupil. You will go into 5A here and sit for your School Certificate in July, just as you would have done at Greville's. We understand that this is a very sad and difficult time for you, but I have every confidence that you will live up to our school motto, *Labor vincit omnia*, and not allow your troubles to affect your school work."

Jessica was not so sure. She was sensitive to language and aware, if only subliminally, of the prefabricated quality of Miss Alderley's comments. Susan's internal commentary was a little more specific. *Labor*, she was thinking, might conquer everything, but it was a poor substitute for *amor*. There were, however, practical matters to attend to.

"Jessica is worried about her school uniform", Susan said. "It's a matter of coupons, of course."

"I don't think you need to worry. A few years ago we instituted the practice of asking departing students to leave their school clothing with us—provided, of course, that it was clean and in reasonable condition—for the sake of our poorer students. Now we find our clothing room extremely handy when there are difficulties about coupons. Now Jessica, I have asked Miss Thrower, who is form mistress of 5A, to speak to her class about you. The girls will be expecting you on Monday and I am sure that they will welcome you very kindly. First let me make sure that I have your address, Mrs. Berkeley and then we'll go to the clothing room and see what we can find."

"Jessica is only with us for a day or two", Susan explained. "She'll be staying with Mr. and Mrs. Simpson at thirty-two, St. Paul's Road."

"I expect the girls will be kind to you", said Susan as the bus carried them back to the house on Cheltenham Road, "but they'll probably bombard you with questions. They'll want to know all about London, the air raids and things that you won't want to talk about."

"I mean", she added as gently as she could, "exactly what happened to your family."

Jessica was hardly listening. The thought of starting at a new school and, in a few days, moving to another new home filled her with despair. She began to cry uncontrollably. Susan put her arms round her.

"I wish I were going to stay with you", Jessica whispered through her sobs.

"I wish you were, too. We could have had some wonderful times together. The trouble is I may not be here for more than a few weeks at a time, and John will be away for years between leaves."

"Our meals haven't got names any more", said John Berkeley ruefully, as he laid out plates and cutlery. "We just eat whatever we happen to have. Some people are so preoccupied with food that they spend their lives hunting and scavenging like our early ancestors, but Susan and I refuse to go traipsing round the shops and standing in long queues in the hope that something might be left by the time we get to the counter."

Jessica offered to help but John said, "No, my dear, I'm sure Mrs. Simpson will put you to work, but while you're here you can regard yourself as our guest."

"My father always says . . ." Jessica began.

"Try to tell us", said Susan, coming into the room at that moment with the tea tray. She put down the tray and sat with Jessica on the couch.

Jessica struggled for a moment. She couldn't stop her tears but she managed to speak.

"My father used to say that our main nourishment would have to be conversation and that it was much better than anything we could get from the grocer."

"Did it work?" asked John.

"Not really, we were always hungry. You see, before the war we had conversation *and* food."

"What kind of things did you talk about?"

"We used to talk about the war, but sometimes my mother would say that it was coming out of her ears, and then we talked about music and books and history and what we would do when the war was over . . ."

"I thought families always talked about what the children had been doing at school."

"My mother sometimes wanted to, but they were both teachers and my father used to say that he had had school all day and he didn't want it in the evening as well."

"What did your father teach?" asked Susan.

"He taught chemistry at the grammar school just down the road. My mother taught English at the girls' school, but she had to stop when they married. After the war started they needed an English teacher at Daddy's school so they taught at the same place. Mummy was the only woman on the staff there. They both really wanted to be musicians though. We had a piano and a whole room full of records and I had piano lessons. My father knew several real musicians and sometimes they used to come to the house and we used to stay up very late talking, singing and playing and listening to records. We still did it sometimes after the war started and everyone tried to bring something to eat, but not so many people could come and it wasn't the same."

"And they let you stay up?"

"Yes. You see my parents weren't quite like ordinary schoolteachers. For one thing, there was always so much to talk about and they always seemed to be interested in what I thought and didn't keep telling me where I had gone wrong."

"Forgive me for asking", said Susan, "but how did they manage to let you have piano lessons and send you to Greville's at the same time? I mean grammar school teachers aren't very well paid."

"It was because of Uncle James. He had a lot of money and he wanted to give us some, but my parents wouldn't let him. After the divorce he gave us his piano and they let him pay for my piano lessons, and he gave me my watch. I think he must have helped with Greville's too, but I don't really know."

"I stayed in touch with James", said John, "and I had the impression that he was not very upset about the divorce."

"I don't think he was. My father thought that he was rather relieved when Aunt Jenny left. He said that Uncle James had sown his wild oats while he was at Cambridge, and had become very respectable, particularly after joining the army, and Aunt Jenny was a bit too flighty for him."

"What did your mother think?"

"She thought the same as my father and they were both really on Aunt Jenny's side—they still liked Uncle James but they thought he had become a bit of a fuddy-duddy. You see, they were both a little bit envious of Aunt Jenny."

"Because she ran away and had adventures?"

"I suppose so. Only I don't think they would really have liked it."

"Just a nice romantic idea", remarked Susan.

"Something like that."

"What did you think?"

"I couldn't understand why Aunt Jenny left him. He's such a good, kind man and there are so many awful people in the world . . ."

Jessica bit her lip and struggled with her tears again.

"I'm sorry", she said after a minute. "Let's go on talking."

"Have you got any other aunts and uncles?" Susan asked.

"No, my father was an only child and his parents were quite old when they had him. They died when I was only a baby. And my other grandparents were living with us. It was really their house, you see."

"It's a funny thing", said John, who thought that a change of subject might be helpful, "but I was a chemist before I joined the navy. And I wanted to play the piano but unfortunately I was never very good at it."

"That's because you never practiced", remarked Susan.

John grinned.

"That's because practicing never seemed to make much difference. And Mrs. Mason always made me practice scales and arpeggios when I wanted to play Chopin."

"My teacher says that if you could learn to play Chopin you would find scales and arpeggios very easy. But he made me do them anyway."

"I'd ask you to play something for us", said Susan, "but the piano is hopelessly out of tune."

"This isn't our house", John explained. "The real owner is a physicist. He and his wife are somewhere on the east coast working on some very hush-hush anti-aircraft equipment. They've been gone for nearly a year, so it's not just the piano. When we got here practically nothing worked. The starlings had nested in the chimneys and it took us two days to get the gas and electricity switched back on. The telephone still hasn't been connected. Apparently the neighbors couldn't stand the way the front garden looked, so they got together and spruced it up a bit. But we're used to that sort of thing—since I joined the navy Susan and I haven't had a house of our own, so we just move from place to place hoping that when the war is over we can settle down and still be young enough to do the things that young couples are supposed to do. The higher-ups decided that Susan needed a sort of base of operations somewhere, and since she had worked at the Royal Infirmary at one time they decided to plonk her down in Gloucester, although it's not a very convenient place for a sailor's wife."

"You see", said Susan, "we were living in London and John was going to be some kind of industrial chemist, but he saw what was coming and joined up in 1935 so that when the war actually started he would be a naval officer instead of a mere conscript. A little later on I decided that I wanted to make myself useful too, so I trained as a military nurse instead of settling down and ending up as a hospital matron—it's such an awful word, for one thing. Now they send me all over the place to teach other nurses and muck in with the general nursing duties when necessary. When I'm here I work in the special ward at the Infirmary where we have seriously wounded soldiers who will probably never really recover. The irony of it all is that as it turned out, John wouldn't have had to go at all because what he was doing was a reserved occupation vital for the war effort, or some such phrase."

There was a note of frustration in Susan's voice and Jessica looked at her anxiously.

"Don't worry, I'm very proud of him. I'm glad we're doing what we're doing, but sometimes I can't help thinking about the young couple in the little cottage that we used to imagine."

"I think you're both perfect", said Jessica, and added, looking at Susan, "And I can't imagine you being a matron. You're much too young and beautiful."

Rather absurdly this remark caused John to experience a twinge of jealousy. It was encouraging to be considered perfect, but his wife had received a special accolade and he had not. Jealousy was succeeded by annoyance with himself that he should have allowed this child to have such an effect on him. He consoled himself with the thought that he would be leaving early on Sunday morning to return to his ship, and undoubtedly whatever was going on inside him would stop and he would return to normal.

The next day, however, was Saturday. Since Susan had to spend most of the day at the Infirmary she suggested that John should take Jessica for a tour of Gloucester, so in the middle of the morning the two of them set off on a bus and were duly deposited in King's Square.

"It smells like a farm today", said Jessica. "It's funny I didn't notice it before."

"It's the cattle market, conveniently situated next to the station. There probably aren't any cattle there today but the memory lingers on and how much you smell depends on which way the wind is blowing."

"It's an odd thing about cows, isn't it. If we made a smell like that we'd think it was awful, but somehow being from cows makes it all right."

They walked to the Cross, where the roads from the four ancient gates met in the center of the city, and saw the old pilgrims' inn, the Red Lion, with its courtyard and galleries, looking very much as it had for the past five hundred years.

"There's not much to drink these days", John remarked. "For the most part it's either bad Scotch or watery beer. Let's go and look at the cathedral."

"Yes, I'd like to, but could we just go and look at Susan's hospital first? She said it was in Southgate Street so it can't be far from here."

The Royal Infirmary had a redbrick front and a large glass door and was set well back from the street. Looking at the building and knowing that Susan was somewhere inside living her professional life gave Jessica a feeling, somewhere below her ribs, that she couldn't identify because she had never felt it before.

"All right", she said, "now we can go to the cathedral."

They stood for a while just inside the cathedral close, admiring the immense building.

"I don't really know much about architecture", Jessica remarked, "but they seem to have got everything exactly right. Our English teacher won't let us use words like beautiful, lovely and gorgeous, but when you don't understand how something is done that's about all you can say. The tower seems almost delicate, in a way, in spite of being so enormous. I suppose it would seem smaller if it were in London."

"Well it is enormous really. Seen from the west it absolutely dominates the city."

"It seems even bigger inside", said Jessica as they walked between the huge round pillars of the nave. "Do you think God likes this?"

John found this question difficult. It was hard to figure out what an agnostic should say to a young girl who asks a question about God.

Aloud he said, "I don't know. It's very hard to say what God likes."

"Well, he likes us to be good, doesn't he? I mean, to be honest and tell the truth and not hurt people."

"Yes, I suppose so."

"But does he want us to spend our time putting up these huge buildings when we could be doing something useful?"

"Well, I suppose it's useful to people who want to go to services and pray here."

"You don't sound very enthusiastic."

John was silent, so Jessica continued.

"You don't believe in God, do you?"

"No, I don't."

"Why not?"

"Because I've never found any compelling reason to. Some of my friends have had experiences that somehow made believers of them, but I've never had a religious experience of any kind."

"Perhaps you have but you didn't notice. Let's go outside—it's so cold and musty in here that I can't think properly"

"What about you?" asked John as they emerged into the thin sunlight. "Do you believe in God?"

"I'm not sure—it's all very confusing. When I go to church and sit with all the other people, I sometimes wonder what's the matter with me. Why can't I believe in God the way they do? I'd feel so much happier if I could. And then I think perhaps they're in the same boat I'm in. They're not really hypocrites, but they want it all to be true because it makes them feel better, so they persuade themselves that it is. I always wanted it to be true too, but . . . I don't know, perhaps I'm being unfair to them and it's really just a habit they got into when they were young. Or perhaps they're right and it really is all true. I suppose I'm a bit like you—it may be true or it may not, and I don't understand how anyone can tell. And it doesn't seem to make them any better. I mean the people who go to church aren't any nicer than the ones who don't, and sometimes it's the other way round."

"Do you still want it to be true?"

"I think so, but it's harder now because he let that bomb fall on my house. And I know that's a very childish way of putting it. The Rector didn't say so in so many words, but when he came to see me while I was staying with Miss Edwards he told me that God works in a mysterious way, and it was all for the good in the long run. He said in the end I would understand. But I don't think anybody understands. Have you read the Bible?"

"Not all of it, but I've read the New Testament pretty thoroughly."

"What do you think of it?"

"Well, it depends which bits we're talking about", said John, who was beginning to feel like a candidate taking an oral examination. "I find St. Paul very difficult and the Acts of the Apostles reads like a political tract, but in some places the Gospels are so vivid that you feel it must have happened like that. But they don't make comfortable reading."

"I know. We sing all these 'Jesu meek and gentle' hymns and then . . ."

"And then he says that he came not to bring peace but a sword, and to divide parent from child, and that those who don't believe are eternally damned and so on. Not exactly the way it usually comes across. It really sounds as though being a Christian would be so burdensome that no one could stand it."

"What I don't understand is, if he wanted us to be good, why did he make it so difficult?"

"Do you really find it so difficult? I mean, Jessica, you strike me as being a thoroughly good person."

"Well, I don't think I've had the opportunity to do anything really bad yet, but people do so many bad things when they get the chance, and I can't imagine that I'm any better than anyone else. And sometimes it's hard to tell whether something is bad or not. Don't you find it hard to be good all the time?"

"It's not just hard. It's impossible."

Jessica sniffed the air and said, "You know, it's the difference between cows and people. Cows make a little bit of a smell all the time but they can't do anything really bad, I mean really wicked. We wash ourselves with soap and water every day and try as hard as we can to smell nice, but when we do something bad it really stinks."

John and Jessica laid the table for tea with the inevitable bread and margarine, a precious jar of plum jam and a distressingly small piece of cheese. John was very efficient and talked cheerfully about nothing in particular, but now that they were back in the house Jessica felt a return of the slight discomfort in his presence that she had experienced on the previous day, so she was glad when Susan got home. There was a momentary awkwardness when Susan, having kissed her husband, turned and found herself facing Jessica. Each one wanted to hug the other but wasn't quite sure whether the feeling was reciprocated, and it seemed to Susan that having just given her husband a casual peck on the cheek it would be out of proportion to make more of a fuss over their visitor. So the moment passed with a smile and greeting.

Susan wanted to hear all about the day's adventures, and Jessica was quite happy to talk about the cattle market, the Red Lion, the cathedral and the brief visit to the Infirmary, but she felt rather shy about repeating her thoughts about God, people and cows. John was less inhibited.

"Jessica has doubts about the value of cathedrals—at least, in God's eyes."

Jessica had always found it embarrassing to have her opinions repeated by anyone else as though she were a bright child being shown off by a teacher. Her parents had been very tactful in this respect, and she was so taken off guard by John's remark that she blushed visibly. Susan looked at her sympathetically and it occurred to John that he might have blundered.

"Well, I don't blame her", said Susan, coming to the rescue. "The Church is sometimes a bit like the government, which is always spending huge amounts of money on things that nobody really needs."

"I don't know whether anyone needed it then", said Jessica, pulling herself together, "but I don't believe it does much good now, except as something beautiful to look at. Everything inside is so dusty and musty, as if no one ever goes in there. There are painted statues of virtuous couples and their children, and memorials to kings who died hundreds of years ago, and nobody who's alive now has any idea what they were really like. It must be nice for historians, but it doesn't seem to have much to do with us. Isn't the cathedral like all those things that you don't need any more but can't bear to throw away?"

"Well", remarked Susan with a twinkle, "I can see the difficulty of throwing a cathedral away."

Jessica smiled but John wasn't quite ready to let go.

"Especially since it would mean throwing away a big slice of the past. People do love to dig into the past and find out where they came from. In a sense it's all we have, apart from a tiny sliver of the present."

Susan looked reproachfully at John as tears came into Jessica's eyes.

"It's all right for you, John", said Jessica, with an effort. "You probably have a nice past that you can go back to whenever you want to. I have a nice past too—in fact it was more wonderful than I can ever say—but I can't go back there any more. It hurts too much."

But John still wasn't done.

"One day you'll be able to, Jessica. After a while it will be different—you'll see."

Jessica stamped her foot.

"No, I won't! It will never be different. And you sound just like the vicar!"

Tea was over. Jessica and John had apologized to each other very prettily and sincerely.

"I hope you can believe that I'm not usually such a bull in a china shop", said John.

"I know it", replied Jessica, "and you're not a bit like the vicar. And I'm sorry about stamping my foot. I don't think I've done it since I was about three. I'm usually quite well behaved."

There were several other things that John would have liked to say, but he felt as tongue-tied as ever he had as a teenager, and, in any case, they weren't things that a man can say to a girl in front of his wife. So they sat peaceably in front of the fire talking about nothing in particular until Big Ben and the nine o'clock news, after which Jessica decided that she would like to go to bed.

"May I look in and say goodbye in the morning?" asked John. "It will be about half past six."

"Yes, as long as you don't mind if I'm too sleepy to say much."

Susan looked as if she wanted to say something but when she did speak it was not what she had originally intended to say.

"Would you like me to come up and tuck you in?"

"Yes, please", said Jessica.

CHAPTER VI

1965: Saturday, December 18

Before leaving his office on the previous evening Woodcock had telephoned Charles Ferrier and arranged to meet him at the school at nine o'clock in the morning. This was a cause of some concern for Bill, who wanted to follow all the action. Inspector Phelps seemed quite happy to turn a blind eye to her liaison with her boss, but Ferrier might well be suspicious and censorious.

"This time I'd really better stay out of it", she remarked while Woodcock was shaving. "So far I think Jack Phelps is the only one who's really caught on. Ferrier still thinks I'm a respectable resident of Hartpury, so it'll seem strange if we arrive together early on a Saturday morning."

"It's an awful nuisance", agreed her companion, his red dressing gown and well-lathered chin making him look like a plump and balding Father Christmas, "but I'm afraid you're probably right."

"Unless . . ." began Bill hopefully.

"Yes?"

"Unless you drove me out to Hartpury first. Then I could drive in a little later and pretend I was drawn by simple curiosity."

"That's a very good idea, but what *will* the neighbors say?"

"Very little, probably. The Smithsons are only just back from their honeymoon and never emerge from their bedroom until tea time, and Mr. Storer undoubtedly spent last night at the Rising Sun and is still sleeping it off."

"*O felix culpa*", remarked Woodcock. "We'd better get a move on then."

The headmaster's Morris Minor was not built for speed, but as he had a tendency to drive it ferociously along the country roads and its exhaust pipe had other holes besides the one at the end, the inhabitants of Maisemore and Hartpury occasionally found themselves awakened at odd hours. On this occasion, however, he was forced to drive decorously over the snow-covered surfaces, and Mr. Storer snored in peace while the Smithsons remained oblivious of everything except each other.

It was a quarter to nine when Woodcock arrived at the School, greeted Inspector Phelps and was told how things had developed.

"I'm very surprised to hear about Bagwell", said the headmaster, "although he is a bit of a fanatic about local history. I believe he was appointed immediately after the war, so he arrived about the same time as the science building."

"Do you think his interest in archaeology is genuine?"

"I believe so—it's hard to imagine that anyone would keep up such a pretence for twenty years. I gather from my colleagues that he has always had the habit of giving impromptu lectures to anyone who would listen—and he certainly has a bee in his bonnet about the graveyard. Ah, here comes Ferrier."

Ferrier didn't enjoy weekends. His office was quiet and comfortable and so was his secretary, Mrs. Smail, whose mission in life was to protect him from all bother and annoyance and to make sure that he had a nice fresh cup of tea whenever he wanted one. Mrs. Ferrier was less tolerant, expecting her husband to help with the chores and their three children, who had all arrived simultaneously at the awkward age and remained there. So Ferrier was quite relieved to receive a call from Woodcock at ten o'clock on Friday evening and to inform his wife that he would have to confer with the headmaster and Inspector Phelps on the following day.

Saturday morning was bright, clear and cold after the snow, and there was a spring in Ferrier's step as he crunched his way along Eastgate

Street. He was not a religious man, but he enjoyed the Christmas atmosphere. By the time he joined the party in St. Mary's Square he was feeling quite relaxed.

"Merry Christmas!" he said, with a note of irony in his voice.

"The same to you", said the headmaster and the inspector, mechanically and without enthusiasm. Neither of them liked the director very much. Everything about him was quite ordinary—brown hair, brown eyes, average height and build, average intelligence—except his sense of self-importance, which was unusually highly developed. Leaving one of the constables to pack up the meager fruits of the search, and the other to remain on guard duty, the three men adjourned to Nave House. At Woodcock's suggestion they moved into Bill's office, since it had only a small window and one outside wall and might be slightly warmer. Privately he was thinking that it would be more natural for Bill to appear at the door of her own room than to walk in on a conference in the headmaster's office.

For Ferrier's benefit Inspector Phelps gave a brief recapitulation of the story, starting with PC Chard's interruption of the digging party.

"So", he concluded, "we have to investigate an accident or a murder that took place at least twenty years ago with an unidentified—and maybe unidentifiable—body and very little to go on except a piece of poetry, the remains of a coffin and the choice of burial ground."

"How long do you think it will be before the builders can start work again?" Ferrier asked.

"However long it takes to make sure that there's nothing else to find here."

"But Inspector, the building has to be finished by the time the boys come back on the tenth of January. Our plan was to finish preparing the site today and to start on the new building on Wednesday after the boys leave at noon. Now it looks as if they won't be able to start until after Christmas and they probably won't be finished by the time the Lent term begins. Imagine trying to teach a class with a building going up just outside your window."

"I'm sorry, Sir, but the teachers are going to have to put up with it. We can't risk losing any evidence that may still be there."

Ferrier was not particularly concerned about the comfort of the teachers or the pupils; he merely resented the fact that the police could pre-empt the activities of the Local Education Authority. Woodcock knew this and did his best to avoid a territorial squabble.

"Now that the area is fenced off they could continue with the preparation of the site on Monday or Tuesday if you can finish your investigation over the weekend."

"I think that's possible", said Inspector Phelps, getting the idea but unable to resist taking a dig at the Director of Education. "Policemen are used to working on Saturdays and Sundays—and Christmas Days and Boxing Days if it comes to that."

While Ferrier was trying to think of a suitable retort Bill opened the door and said, "Oh."

All three gentlemen rose to their feet with a chorus of good-mornings and Woodcock said, "Sorry to have taken your office, Mrs. Marjoribanks—we thought it might be a little warmer here."

Ferrier was the only one of those present who regarded Bill's secretarial role as placing her in a lower social and professional stratum. He would certainly have questioned the propriety of her joining the conference if Inspector Phelps hadn't quickly settled the matter.

"Please come and join us—your local knowledge may be very helpful."

So Bill sat down between Woodcock and Phelps, a position where she felt extremely comfortable, looked Ferrier in the eye and said, "Shocking business, this!"

Ferrier, ill-at-ease in the presence of an underling, especially one whose manner and personality had always tended to put him out of countenance, muttered, "Yes, indeed, quite shocking."

"Now", the Inspector went on, "to get to the actual case. We have the remains of a young female, with a fractured skull and various other injuries, buried in a coffin with a quite respectable poem by an unknown author. We assume that the burial took place in 1945, after the ground was prepared and before the concrete slab was laid for the science building. This gives us a fairly precise date and suggests that the builders must have known something about it. We think that whoever did the burying may not have been the murderer—again, if it *was* murder—and although we know when she was buried we don't know when she was killed. We know that the Johnsons, father and son, were responsible for the building and, oddly enough, that young Johnson was driving Sandman's excavator yesterday. That just about covers it but there are some other matters that cropped up and probably have nothing to do with the case.

"Yesterday Mr. Bagwell told his pupils about his theory that the labs were built on part of the old churchyard, and he gave them the idea that one of Shakespeare's girlfriends might be buried there. That was how the skeleton came to be discovered—three of the boys decided to do a little investigating of their own. PC Chard happened to come along at the crucial moment, but I think the boys would have come to the police anyway. Later on Mr. Bagwell arrived with his own equipment and was sent on his way by Constable Chard. It's also possible that another interested party arrived in the small hours and turned tail when he saw the police on duty. That's about as far as we've got. Sergeant Snipe is interviewing Mr. Bagwell, but we don't seriously expect to get anything out of him. We're checking on missing persons and we'll be having a serious talk with young Johnson. We'll also want to find out who else was working for old Johnson in 1945."

"There's something odd about this business of Johnson and Sandman", said Bill.

Ferrier seemed to have dozed off, but Phelps and Woodcock made encouraging noises, so Bill went on.

"Well sometimes, having nothing better to do, I read the local government news in the *Citizen*. The main reason why it took so long to start work on this project was that there was a tremendous wrangle about who should get the job—Johnson or Sandman. It seems that some of our councilors thought that since old Johnson had put up the old building, they might as well get his son to pull the remains of it down and do the new one. Others said that Sandman was better and more efficient and had given a lower estimate, and that they'd heard that old Johnson had made rather a mess of the first building. Sandman got it in the end, but there was a lot of nastiness. According to some of the scuttlebutt, young Johnson was using underhand means to get the councilors to vote for him. And now he turns up working for Sandman."

"What kind of means?" Inspector Phelps asked.

"Well, he inherited quite a big business from his father and he buys most of his raw materials locally—sand, gravel, timber and so on. Apparently certain of our city fathers got the idea that if they didn't toe the line, Johnson might go elsewhere and their businesses might suffer."

"It would be interesting", remarked Woodcock, "to find out whether Johnson has a reputation for such practices or whether he resorted to them only in this particular case."

"Just what I was thinking", said the inspector. "And I'd like to know how much of a mess old Johnson did make of the first building."

"You should talk to Siggy Harescombe about that", put in Bill. "I think after a while people got used to it, but in the earlier years there was a lot of frustration."

Ferrier stirred and asked, "Do you have inside information, Mrs. Marjoribanks?"

"Well, my sons were pupils here in the 1950's and there was still a lot of talk about how awful the building was, and if someone had given Siggy a gun he might have gone out and shot old Johnson."

"Really?" said the inspector, his professional interest aroused.

"Well, you see, after the war Siggy was the only science master left from the old dispensation. He worked for months on the design of the labs, only to find that through laziness, stupidity or sheer bloody-mindedness Johnson had got everything slightly wrong—not glaringly so, but just enough to wreck practically everything that Siggy had planned. Electricity, gas and water, fume cupboards, storage and that kind of thing. It all ended up as a sort of ad hoc jungle instead of the systematic design that Siggy had worked out. I came here to see him one day about Johnny, and he was practically apoplectic, so I let him tell me all about his troubles before getting on to mine."

While this conversation was going on Sergeant Snipe entered quietly and sat by the door. When Bill finished he cleared his throat discreetly. Inspector Phelps looked at his colleague and nodded.

"Well, Sir, as I was telling you yesterday, I was here when the old labs were being finished. Old Johnson was here and he had some rather unpleasant things to say about schoolmasters and their funny ideas. I gathered he had quarreled with Mr. Harescombe."

"Did he say what it was about?"

"Not exactly, but he was muttering about the furnace and the boiler. I remember that he said that just because Mr. Harescombe had M. A. after his name it didn't mean he knew everything."

"Of course, Sir", Snipe added, looking at Woodcock, "that was long before your time."

"Never mind, sergeant", said the headmaster kindly, "schoolmasters do have a lot of funny ideas. Mr. Harescombe is a very practical man, however, so it's hard to imagine what Johnson was complaining about."

"How about Mr. Bagwell?", Inspector Phelps asked his subordinate.

"Nothing much there, Sir. His story is that he wanted to do an archaeological exploration before the excavator got to work. His wife backs him up. Apparently she's just as crazy—I mean she believes as strongly in the graveyard theory as he does. They discussed it and she sent him off with her blessing just before midnight."

"Why didn't he tell that to Chard last night?"

"He said he was completely unnerved by the flashlight. The first thing that came into his head was that he had trespassed on consecrated ground and was having some kind of religious experience like St. Paul on the road to Damascus. Then he felt so foolish that he didn't want to say anything about why he was there. It seems that he and his wife are devout Roman Catholics and they have strong feelings about graveyards."

"Not only Roman Catholics", said Woodcock. "I should be very disturbed at the thought that we were digging up an ancient graveyard. After all for the first four hundred years of St. Mary's existence—I mean the building, not the saint—we were all Roman Catholics. Fortunately all the evidence indicates that the graveyard was on the other side of the church. It's also fortunate that it looks as if we can absolve Bagwell of any complicity in the death of this young woman."

Charles Ferrier, however, had reservations about Bagwell's absolution.

"It seems to me that this was extraordinary conduct on the part of a responsible member of the staff. He must know that there are proper channels for such explorations. He may not have done anything criminal, but he ran a serious risk of bringing the education department into disrepute."

Woodcock groaned inwardly. There was some truth in what Ferrier had said, but why must he always be so much more concerned with appearances and reputations than with education?

"I'll talk to him", he said. "As far as I know this is the only bee in his bonnet, so I don't think we need worry about any future escapades."

Inspector Phelps, realizing that all the vital ground had been covered, rose and announced that he and his sergeant would have another look at the scene of the crime, supposing that it was a crime, and then make their way back to the station. Woodcock said that he had a few things to attend to in his office and Bill, with a purposeful air, removed the cover from her typewriter. Ferrier, having a vague notion that he was not needed, murmured, "Well, good morning", and wandered out into Knave Street. Feeling somewhat unsettled, he decided to spend a little while in his office before going home. Mrs. Smail wouldn't be there, but he knew where the tea things and the digestive biscuits were kept. He was also thinking that it might be a sound move to telephone a old friend of his who happened to be the managing editor of the local paper. It was always a good idea to keep the press in one's debt.

Bill waited until he was safely gone, replaced the typewriter cover and went into the adjacent office, where Woodcock was standing at the window, gazing absently into Knave Street.

"What do you think?" she asked.

"I think that the young woman was killed by accident in circumstances that made it impossible to report the matter to the police, and that whoever buried her was in love with her—and I don't claim any great detective ability in saying that. There's something about this business that doesn't feel like murder."

At the police station, Sergeant Bunn had done a little research.

"CRG569 belongs to an Arthur Williams who lives in Longbridge Lane", he announced to Phelps and Snipe. "Not known to us in any way."

Snipe knew the whole area better than the back of his hand. "That's just round the corner from Johnson's place on the Tewkesbury Road. Funny thing, though—that name rings a bit of a bell with me, only I can't think where from."

"I think I'll pay a surprise visit to young master Johnson", Phelps told Snipe, "and you can drop in on this Williams character and find out what his story is about last night. Then I want you to go and see your old friend Siggy Harescombe, while I have a few words with Bob. If he's as vague as he's made out to be it's probably better not to confront him with two policemen at once. They live within shouting distance of each other in Brookethorpe, so we can go out there together after we finish with Williams and young Johnson. I suspect that I'll be longer than you are so you can leave me at Johnson's place and come back when you're done."

In spite of old Johnson's death the smartly painted sign above the door of the big shed on the Tewkesbury Road still proclaimed WILLIAM JOHNSON AND SON, BUILDERS. In the yard in front there were several large pieces of machinery, including a mechanical digger very much like the one in use at The Nave. To the right of the shed there was a big, well-kept house, and between the two buildings a private lane led down a gentle slope past a large back garden and up to a summerhouse on a little knoll. Finding no one about, the inspector went to the front door and used the knocker. After a long pause the door opened and a middle-aged man with the remains of a mop of red hair appeared. He was fully dressed with a jacket and tie, but a slight air of dishevelment suggested that the process had been rather hastily completed.

"Mr. Johnson? Good morning, Sir. I am Inspector Phelps from Gloucester Central Police Station. We are making enquiries about something that has been found in St. Mary's Square and I'd like to ask you a few questions."

"Really? I'm rather inclined to say, 'Lord, why me?' but I suppose you'd better come in and explain what this is about."

Phelps had already summed up his host. There was caution, even anxiety, in his eyes, but he was quick on the uptake and ready to spar a little if he thought it necessary. "Might as well come straight to the point", was the inspector's verdict.

"Last night a skeleton was discovered in the ground where the old science building used to be."

"How extraordinary! But what exactly does this have to do with me?"

"You were working on the site yesterday, and we thought you might have seen something."

"Good heavens, Inspector, your spies must be everywhere. Yes, I was there, but all I saw was a great deal of concrete and a certain amount of gravelly subsoil."

"Which I noticed you had been extremely careful not to disturb—was there a reason for that?"

"Just a matter of keeping the concrete as clean as possible."

"Is that important?"

"It may be, depending on what it's going to be used for. Why, do you think I was trying to avoid digging up a skeleton?"

"It certainly crossed my mind, Sir. But what really puzzles us is why you were working for Sandman. I wouldn't have expected you to be on the best of terms with him, after all the fuss there was about getting the contract."

"Just doing a little slumming, Inspector. His driver is ill and business is a bit slack at the moment, so I thought I might as well earn fifteen bob an hour doing this as kick my heels in the office waiting for a job to show up."

"I thought perhaps you wanted to keep an eye on things."

"Like stray skeletons? Really, Inspector, you do have a nasty suspicious mind."

"Well, Sir, you must admit that there are some odd things about this case and you seem to be involved in several of them. The police surgeon estimates that the person whose skeleton we found yesterday was buried twenty or thirty years ago, and it seems highly probable, if not quite certain, that the burial took place just before the foundations of the science building were laid. Just imagine someone with a body to dispose of, someone who had access to the site and could make a shallow grave and pour a few inches of concrete on top of it—the sort of thing that most murderers would die for. Now, Sir, you were involved in the erection of that building and we'd like you to give us some details—when you started, what, if anything, was there beforehand, how deep the preliminary excavation was and anything else that strikes you."

"All right, I'll do my best—you have to remember this was a long time ago. We started in July, hoping to get most of the work done before the boys came back to school in September. Part of the site was a garden that had been completely neglected during the war. The rest of it was a sort of summerhouse affair that I suppose the old people used to sit in in better days. It had gone to wrack and ruin and it more or less fell over when we gave it a mild push. We dug the whole thing down about two feet, put in a layer of gravel and poured the concrete on top.'

"How long elapsed between digging the hole and putting in the concrete?"

"I don't remember exactly but it might have been a day or two."

"Was the site protected in any way?"

"Just a rope and a few red oil lamps at night."

"So someone might have sneaked in at night and buried a body. Wouldn't you have noticed that the ground had been disturbed?"

"Not if he had done the job carefully enough."

"Forgive me for asking, Mr. Johnson, but I can't help wondering why you weren't in the forces somewhere while this was going on. You must have been in your twenties at the time."

"So you're politely handing me a white feather. Why wasn't I serving King and Country? Well as a matter of fact I was in the navy. I was a radio officer and I happened to be on the bridge one day when the ship was torpedoed. We managed to launch one or two boats but I was floundering in the sea for a long time before someone took me by the scruff of the neck and hauled me onto a raft. We were picked up eventually but I caught pneumonia, nearly died and never made it back to active service. Don't bother to give me a medal."

"I beg your pardon, but if we didn't ask questions we'd never find anything out."

"That's all right, Inspector, just doing your job. Well, now I have to do mine, so if there isn't anything else I'd like to get on with it."

"Just one more thing—do you know a man called Arthur Williams?"

Johnson's answer was not quite so ready.

"Yes, as a matter of fact I do. We play golf together every Sunday morning. How does he come into this?"

"Just a routine question, based on information received. Now, perhaps you can tell me where you were at two o'clock this morning."

"Really, Inspector, you ask the strangest questions. Well, if you must know, I was at home in bed. Now you ask me if I have any witnesses."

"All right, Sir, have you?"

"Just my wife—and now you say, 'That doesn't count.'"

"And when did you last see Mr. Williams?

"Last Sunday at the Longlea Golf Club."

"So you weren't with him when he drove into Knave Street last night."

"No, Inspector. As I believe I mentioned, I was in my conjugal bed."

Longbridge Lane had once been a cart track that led from the Tewkesbury road to Longlea Farm and its surrounding meadows, and thence to the Cheltenham Road. The farm was long since gone, the meadows had been turned into a golf course, and the lane had acquired a row of desirable residences for the upper middle class, the price tags of which were roughly proportional to their distance from the main road. Arthur Williams's house was the third one along, so Snipe concluded that he must be well off but not stinking rich.

There seemed to be plenty of room in the driveway, so Snipe turned in and found himself staring at the rear end of a black Humber Snipe with the number plate CRG 569.

"Oldish car", he thought to himself, "But luxurious and very nicely looked after."

While Snipe was looking at the Humber, the front door of the house opened and a large man wearing a long overcoat and heavily muffled against the cold appeared.

"I'm afraid you're going to have to move your car, whoever you are. I'm about to leave."

"Sergeant Snipe from Gloucester Central Police Station, Sir. If you are Mr. Arthur Williams I'd like to have a few words with you before you go."

"Then you'd better get into my car. We can talk while I warm her up a bit."

The engine started so readily that Snipe thought it must have been warm already, but he admitted to himself that this might simply be the result of good maintenance.

"What's it all about, Sergeant? I can give you about five minutes so you'll have to talk fast."

"Well then, to put it as briefly as possible, we'd like to know the reason for your visit to St. Mary's Square last night."

"On what grounds? Or do you enquire into the comings and goings of everyone who drives at night?"

"On a number of grounds, Sir. In the first place this may be the beginning of a murder investigation. Secondly, when a driver turns tail and bolts at the sight of a couple of policemen it's apt to make us wonder."

"All right, Sergeant, I suppose I'll have to tell you the truth, even though it is rather disreputable. First, though, I should mention that I recognize you even though you apparently don't remember me."

Something clicked in Snipe's memory.

"Got it", he said. "You were a prefect when I was in the Lower Fourth. In fact, you were responsible for getting my hide tanned after we immobilized Bob's bicycle."

"Yes, the famous bicycle. I heard that it wasn't much of a tanning."

"Just a token. I think he was really rather amused, only he didn't want to show it."

"Well, what a charming situation—two Old Navians thrown together by circumstances, and now you have the upper hand."

"Yes. Now I believe you were just going to tell me about last night."

"Yes, I was, but these recollections are, in fact, apposite. Do you remember Goofy Thomas?"

"Vaguely—tall chap with fair hair and a vacant expression."

"That's him. Eccentric and highly intelligent. He lives a little further along the lane and we sometimes meet at the local pub on a Friday night and do a bit of reminiscing. Last night we were at the Hare until throwing-out time. Then we went to his house for a nightcap, and about one o'clock, not being very sober, he was overcome by a fit of sentimentality and announced that he wanted to go and look at the Dear Old Place. I have to admit that I was a little merry myself, but I was in better condition than he was so we got my car and drove down to St. Mary's Square. When we saw your two bobbies we realized that an interview with the law was not a very good idea so, as you put it, we turned tail and bolted. Now perhaps you would satisfy my curiosity as to what has been going on there."

"In a moment, but first may I ask what your wives were doing at the time. I mean, do they approve of that kind of expedition?"

"My wife died twenty years ago, Sergeant, and I have lived here with a housekeeper ever since. All very respectable I assure you. Goofy never married but he maintains a large house so that he can entertain his innumerable friends, brothers, sisters, nieces and nephews. He's extremely sociable and has plenty of money, so he's very popular. Now, am I going to get an answer to my question?"

"Yes. Yesterday evening a skeleton was found at the site where the new science labs are going to be built. The two constables you saw last night were keeping an eye on things and it appears that several people were interested enough in what was going on there to make late night calls. Naturally we'd like to know whose skeleton it is, how it got there and whether any of these callers know anything about it."

"Well, I can assure you that Goofy and I know nothing whatsoever about it. I'm afraid you'll have to put our visit down to the long arm of coincidence. Now I really must run."

"Just one thing—when did you last see Henry Johnson?"

If Snipe had been hoping to surprise Williams with this question he was disappointed. The answer was perfectly timed.

"Another of your odd little questions. I saw Henry last Sunday morning—we played a round of golf together. Now I really must go. Goodbye Sergeant—it's always a pleasure to meet a fellow Old Navian."

Unable to think of a suitable reply, Snipe returned to the police car and went on his way. He kept an eye on his mirror but saw no sign of the Humber entering the lane. It occurred to him that Williams had shown remarkable restraint in not commenting on the coincidence of the car's name and his own.

Snipe got back to Johnson and Sons just in time to see his superior emerging from the front door. After a brief exchange of information they set off again along Longbridge Lane. It wasn't the quickest way of getting to Brookethorpe but the sergeant wanted to see whether the Humber Snipe was still where he had last seen it. It was.

"He didn't want you in the house", commented Inspector Phelps.

"No, Sir—I wonder why."

"And Henry Johnson looked as if he'd just dressed in a hurry—maybe because he was up very late last night. Now tell me, Snipey, what you could possibly use a load of old concrete for that would involve keeping it clean?"

CHAPTER VII

1940: November 15

Between anxiety about returning to his ship and the realization that he was in love with Jessica, John Berkeley found sleep very elusive. He was amazed at the power of the physical attraction, and thought, perhaps, that it was characteristic of the recently nubile, although he had a feeling that he would find the typical Gloucester fifteen-year-old rather repulsive. It wasn't just a matter of the difference between the metropolis and the market town. There was something about Jessica, a combination of intelligence, innocence and experience that must be unusual even for a Londoner. He told himself that this was merely a passing infatuation. When it was all over he would see that Jessica was just an ordinary girl and smile at his own naivety; but since common sense had little effect on the uncomfortable things that were going on inside him, his main hope was that a year or so of hunting submarines and dodging torpedoes would do the trick. Susan was in a strange mood too, seeming preoccupied and distant. "I think perhaps she knows", John thought. "Well, by the time I get back it will all be over."

Jessica, falling asleep with Susan's goodnight kiss on her lips, slept better than she had on any night since the air raid. When John knocked on her door the next morning it was still dark. She was too sleepy and confused to say anything, so he opened the door a little and said, "May I come in. I'll be leaving in five minutes"

Jessica was conscious enough by now to sit up and say, "Yes", so John went in and sat on the edge of the bed.

"I hope everything will turn out all right for you at the Simpsons'. Perhaps by the time I get back the war will be over and you'll have gone back to London."

"Yes", said Jessica, who was gradually waking up and feeling slightly stumped for something to say. "But we could still be friends."

"I hope so", said John, trying sound matter-of-fact. He took her hand and kissed her on top of the head. "Be good and take care of yourself."

As he made for the door Jessica jumped out of bed and ran after him.

"Thank you for being so kind to me."

John had been disappointed at Jessica's cool response, but the resulting hug changed all that, so that what he carried away with him was the feel of her young body experienced with great immediacy through her thin nightgown, a sensation that was to keep him awake at night for many weeks to come. He was feeling so dazed that he almost fell down the stairs and had to make a considerable effort to appear normal to his wife, who was waiting by the front door.

An observer would have thought that it was a strange goodbye, between two pre-occupied people who did not seem to be fully conscious of each other. Meanwhile, Jessica got back into bed, fell asleep and dreamt that she and Susan were getting breakfast ready in the kitchen.

On Saturday Susan had learnt that Mr. Simpson had made an unexpectedly quick recovery, but she hadn't had the heart to tell Jessica. So it was a very subdued Jessica who struggled with her breakfast after receiving this dreaded piece of news.

"Do you think I'll still be able to see you sometimes?" she asked.

"Yes, my darling. All you have to do is catch a bus, and when I'm going to be away I'll tell Mrs. Simpson, so you won't have any wasted journeys."

The endearment dropped quite naturally from Susan's lips and helped to ease Jessica's pain.

"Susan, could we go for a walk together or something before I have to go?"

"Yes, I'd like to very much."

The air was chilly and misty but not terribly cold as they wandered through the nest of unspoiled country lanes between the main roads to Cheltenham and Tewkesbury. The sun gradually penetrated the mist and gleamed on the drops that clung to every twig. Susan and Jessica held hands as they walked like a pair of children through a magic world in which everything seemed to sparkle with life in defiance of the approach of winter.

Later that day Susan lent Jessica an extra suitcase to accommodate some of her newly acquired clothing, and accompanied her on the bus to St. Paul's Road, where the Simpsons lived in a semi-detached house not far from the center of Gloucester, and within walking distance of Jessica's school.

Susan had originally thought of Jessica simply as an orphan who needed a place to stay until the blitz was over, but now that she had met her she had grave misgivings about sending her to the Simpsons. There was nothing wrong with the neighborhood, which was occupied by a mixture of working class and lower middle class families. The problem was that Jessica would have nothing in common with the Simpsons, whose most important activity seemed to be keeping up appearances—"holding one's head up", as Mr. Simpson, elderly, retired and grumpy, often put it. His wife was twenty years younger, plump, hearty, and the sort of nurse only a healthy patient can tolerate. In spite of her frequent tears Jessica seemed quite resilient, but unfortunately she had rather a lot to be resilient about. Susan also had some anxiety about Jessica's reception at Blenheim Hall. She was much more grown-up than any of the girls she was likely to meet at school, and this might set her apart from her classmates and arouse the suspicions of her teachers, many of whom were elderly, single and somewhat frost-bitten in their view of life.

"The trouble with these old maids", Susan said to herself, "is that they're preoccupied with sex."

Then, being strictly honest with herself, she recognized that her reluctance to let Jessica go was not just a matter of concern about her welfare. Having her in the house had given Susan a sense of inner contentment and well-being that she hadn't experienced for a long time. "I ought to have had some children of my own by now. Then I wouldn't be having these complicated feelings . . . Or would I?"

Although Jessica was full of trepidation about the move, she had decided that the time for tears was over. If Susan thought that the Simpsons were all right that would have to be sufficient, and if things turned out to be difficult she would just stick out her chin, as her mother used to say, and deal with situations as they arose. With the clothes she stood up in, her new school uniform in a borrowed case and a few shillings in her pocket, she set out to meet the world.

The world manifested itself in the shape of Mrs. Simpson, who opened the front door with a flourish and a hearty, "Well, here we are then!"

Susan decided that it would be better not to go in, and this resulted in an awkward goodbye on the doorstep with Mrs. Simpson looking on. Jessica had been thinking about what she wanted to say to Susan when they parted, but in the circumstances very little of it came out. Susan, surprised at the strength of her feelings, could say very little, but managed, in the course of a brief hug, to whisper in Jessica's ear, "You know where I am if you want me. I'll be there for at least another three weeks."

While Susan was going home on the bus, Mrs. Simpson was showing Jessica her room, which was in the back of the house on the second floor and suffered from the disadvantage that in order to get to it she had to pass through another bedroom. It was rather long and narrow, and had a single window looking over the back garden.

"We haven't got what they call 'all mod cons' in this house, dearie. There's no running water upstairs and when we want a bath we have to light a fire under the copper and get the water into the tub with a bucket. The bath's with the copper in the little scullery behind the kitchen next to the back door, but it's as cold as charity in there so we fill the tin bathtub in front of the living room fire. Course we'd have to get Mr. Simpson out of his chair and he doesn't like to do that."

Mrs. Simpson rubbed her nose thoughtfully.

"Then there's the lavatory. It's not really in the house—you have to go out of the back door and turn left twice."

The reason for the shape of Jessica's room was that it was built over the kitchen and the "little scullery", which formed a narrow extension behind the main part of the house. Just below her window was the roof of the further extension that contained the lavatory.

Mrs. Simpson prattled on, unaware of the cold lump of lead that seemed to be forming in the pit of Jessica's stomach.

"The last lodger we had here used to pop out of the window, cross the roof and climb down the drainpipe on the corner when he wanted to go to the lavatory at night. He was a caution if ever there was one. He started that when my sister and brother-in-law came and stayed in this bedroom next to yours. He said he didn't want to walk through their room in the middle of the night. 'You never know what they might be doing', he said."

Mrs. Simpson passed this information on with a knowing wink.

"Listen to me, talking to you like that. But then, young girls know everything these days, don't they. Anyway, he found it was quicker and more convenient even when there wasn't anyone else here, so he kept on doing it until one night the drainpipe broke and he fell into the rainwater tank. There was quite a piece of work about that. Mr. Simpson tried to make him pay to have it put back together, and Alfred, that was the lodger, said he was going to see his solicitor about compensation for injuries caused by—what was it he said?—'inadequate means of egress', or some such bit of nonsense. Mr. Simpson told him he should have used the chamber pot like everyone else, but Alfred said he couldn't sleep with that under his bed. By the way, have you got your ration book?"

Jessica produced the book and Mrs. Simpson clutched it eagerly, flipping through the pages to make sure that everything was still there.

"Your Uncle James is sending us the money for your room and board—leastways, it's coming from his bank—but this is the most important thing unless you're one of those rich people who can get whatever they want. We can't afford the black market—not that we're poor, mind you, we can hold up our heads, but black market stuff costs ten times what it does in the shops. Now you'd better come downstairs and let me show you to Mr. Simpson. Don't worry if he's a bit grumpy—he says a lot but mostly he doesn't mean anything."

George Simpson, clad in a long, dun-colored dressing gown and slippers, sat in a dilapidated armchair in front of a small coal fire. His woolen cap, pulled down over his ears, and the high collar of his dressing gown combined with the actual shape of his red face to give the impression that his chin, nose an eyes were all much too close together.

"Bring her over here so I can see her properly", he commanded in a raspy bass voice.

At a nod from Mrs. Simpson, Jessica went and stood next to the fire.

"Can you cook and do housework?"

"George . . ." began Mrs. Simpson in a timid voice quite unlike the one she had used upstairs.

"You don't think she's going to sit about doing nothing all day, do you? Young woman, if you thought you were going to come here with your London airs and graces and be a lady of leisure, you've got another think coming."

Jessica was never far from tears, but the effect of this assault was to awake a tinge of anger and stiffen something in her spine.

"I didn't know what to expect, Mr. Simpson, and I don't know what you mean by 'London airs and graces.' Yes, I can cook and do housework."

"Don't forget she has to go to school and do her homework", put in Mrs. Simpson nervously.

"In my day girls of her age didn't go to school. What do they need all that book-learning for? They should go into service or get married. While you're here, young woman, you'll toe the line or you'll find yourself on the next train back to London."

"George", implored Mrs. Simpson, "don't forget . . ."

"All right, Jill, that'll do!"

Mr. Simpson paused, aware that his wife was referring to the prospect of generous monthly payments from Uncle James's bank, which, unknown to Jessica, included pocket money for her.

In the pause Jessica remarked, "I can't think of anything I'd like better," and, her anger getting the upper hand, added, "This is a horrible house and you are a horrible person. I'm sorry, Mrs. Simpson."

Jessica left the room with all the dignity she could muster, followed by the beady eyes of a startled George Simpson.

Having gained the relative safety of her bedroom Jessica realized that she badly needed to go to the lavatory and that her feelings about the chamber pot were the same as Alfred's. There were three ways of getting there. The obvious one was out of the question since it would have meant going downstairs and walking through the living room to the back door. Another possibility was to go out of the front door, which was actually at the side of the house, and thence to the back. This would mean passing in front of the living room window, and, in any case, she doubted whether she could manage the front door without being heard. The third possibility occurred to her as she gazed distractedly out of her window. Alfred the lodger had found a way. He had not been hampered by a skirt, but Jessica, smaller, lighter and more agile, found the trip easy and a little exhilarating. The window was only just big enough and she wondered how Alfred had managed it. The roof sloped quite gently away from the window and the gutter ran from left to right until it found the drainpipe at the corner next to the garden path. Jessica crawled across the roof, maneuvered herself into position on the corner, climbed down the drainpipe, which seemed firm enough, put one foot on the edge of the steel rainwater tank and hopped lightly to the ground. Tiptoeing round the corner she found herself facing the living room window. It was getting dark and the blackout curtains had been drawn, but she heard the angry voice of Mr. Simpson and, faintly, the tremulous protests of his wife. Jessica turned into the passage leading to the lavatory, which was plain, simple and clean. It fulfilled its basic purpose with no pretence at any niceties such as provision for the washing of hands.

On the way back she stopped and listened again. Mr. Simpson's voice was louder still and, having noticed a crack in the living room blackout, Jessica crept up to the window and looked in. Mrs. Simpson was standing with her hand on the knob of the door that led to the stairs and speaking a little more vehemently.

"It's not honest, George, it's not honest and I won't have it."

"Oh, so that's how it is, is it? Listen to me, my girl, I may be old and ill but I'm still master in my own house, so don't start telling me what you will or won't have. You heard how she talked to me. There'll be no pocket money for her until I find out whether she can behave herself properly. Now go upstairs and bring her down."

"But George . . ."

"Now! At once! Do you hear?"

Mrs. Simpson opened the door and started up the stairs. Jessica knew that she would have to be very quick to get back through the window of her room before Mrs. Simpson arrived at the door, so she ran to the back of the house and tried to pull herself up on to the water tank. Finding that her skirt made it very hard for her to get her knee on to the edge of the water tank she loosened it at the waist, pulled it over her head and threw it onto the roof. Getting onto the tank and up the drainpipe was easy, but in scrambling over the gutter she dislodged her skirt, which fell back into the water. She was about to go back down the drainpipe when she remembered that her new school skirt was in her suitcase and she could rescue the old one later. She was halfway through the window when she heard the door open.

"Sitting here in the dark, Dearie? Just draw the blackout curtains so we can put the light on. Oh my God!"

The final exclamation was caused by Mrs. Simpson's having seen, in the remaining dusk, a figure silhouetted against the window and apparently climbing in. She shouted, "George" and quickly turned on the light.

Jessica thought that even in the most favorable circumstances the discovery of her escapade would have landed her in serious trouble, and that her appearance wearing only a blouse and what the Simpsons would undoubtedly consider to be highly inappropriate underwear would make matters considerably worse. What she didn't realize was that her encounters with the drainpipe had left damp sooty deposits all over her arms and legs, some of which had been transferred to her face. She started to try to explain but made little progress because Mrs. Simpson was sitting on the bed rocking herself back and forth and crying, "Oh dear, oh dear, oh dear . . ."

Mr. Simpson was perhaps less of an invalid than he made out, since he appeared at the door in less than half a minute. One might have expected that his Victorian frame of mind would have led him to withdraw immediately at the sight of a girl in her panties, but he stood and stared for several seconds before turning to his wife.

"Stop bawling, woman, and pack her things and send her back to where she came from."

"But George", whimpered Mrs. Simpson.

Simpson's eyes returned to Jessica.

"No, perhaps you're right for once. I'm going to light the fire under the copper. Then you can bring her downstairs and give her a bath and we'll see."

What he was hoping to see he didn't make clear.

As soon as Mr. Simpson had disappeared Jessica opened the suitcase given her by Susan and took out her new skirt.

"What are you doing?" asked Mrs. Simpson, who was still sitting on Jessica's bed and rocking herself in anguish, while noises of someone fueling the copper and sloshing buckets of water into it floated up from below.

"I'm leaving."

"But you can't do that. You're supposed to stay with us and you haven't got anywhere to go."

"I'm leaving", repeated Jessica, unequal to the task of explaining to this well-intentioned woman why she couldn't possibly live in her house.

"He's not as bad as all that", said Mrs. Simpson, grasping part of the problem.

Jessica closed the suitcase and started to put on the skirt.

"You can't put that on, on top of all that dirt."

"What do you expect me to do—wait until your husband gives me a bath?"

Seeing that Jessica was still intent on getting dressed, Mrs. Simpson said desperately, "Wait a minute, won't you", and rushed from the room. She returned a few moments later carrying a china basin, a flannel, a towel and a soap dish.

"It's what we keep in our bedroom. The water's cold but it's better than nothing."

Jessica did her best to remove the dirt from her arms and legs, but it was difficult with cold water and a great deal of it ended up on the towel.

"It's on your face, too. Here, let me help you."

Jessica submitted to having her face washed and was surprised to find her hostess gentle as well as expert. An older Jessica might have enjoyed this childlike submission, but being fifteen she endured it and was thankful that it wasn't worse.

"Where's your other skirt?" asked Mrs. Simpson, who was gradually regaining her equilibrium.

"It fell into the rainwater tank."

"And you just left it there? What were you doing on the roof, anyway?"

"I had to go to the lavatory and I didn't want to go through the living room."

"You mean to say you climbed down the drainpipe?"

"Yes, it was easy. But climbing up was more difficult and I had to take my skirt off."

Mrs. Simpson sat down again with a thump.

"You're too much for me", she said. "But listen—Mr. Simpson always goes to bed early on account of his heart. I'll tell him you'll have your bath later. I'll put it in the living room and you can be private there. I'll sit in the kitchen until you've finished. You'll see—it's not as bad as you think it is."

"All right", said Jessica, not mentioning the plan that was forming in her mind. It would be nice to be really clean, but it would be much nicer not to have to stay in this house at all.

Mrs. Simpson went downstairs and soon Jessica heard the murmur of voices. The conversation got louder and Mr. Simpson's repeated shouts of "I won't have it in my house" became clearly audible. Eventually the noise died down and a few minutes later Mrs. Simpson appeared at Jessica's door.

"Well, that's settled", she said. "Now you'd better come down and have some tea. And Mr. Simpson is expecting an apology."

Jessica might have refused to go down but by now she was extremely hungry and, in any case, the temporary appeasement of Mr. Simpson was part of her plan. One thing she was clear about, however: she had no intention of apologizing.

Jessica sat in the steaming galvanized bathtub in front of the living room fire. Mr. Simpson was, she hoped, safely in bed, and Mrs. Simpson was in the kitchen reading the Sunday paper. Tea had been an ordeal which she had survived by being as quiet as possible, passing things when requested and agreeing with everything that George Simpson said. As she had expected, she had been grilled about London, the blitz, her parents and her school, but she had found a formula that enabled her to turn some of the questions aside, namely that she was still too upset by recent events to be able to talk much about them.

What she had not expected was that as the meal progressed, Simpson had made an effort to put his prejudices aside and express some sympathy. As they rose from the table, he put his arm around Jessica's waist and told her that he was sure that they would soon be great friends—not, he said, that anyone could ever take the place of her parents, but there were other kinds of friends besides parents. Jessica couldn't see his face when he was saying this, but she did feel the little nip from his thumb and forefinger. As she left the room after tea she had a glimpse of his eyes following her, and she had to restrain an impulse to sprint up the stairs and leave immediately by the back window.

Having completed her ablutions and put on the huge dressing gown which Mrs. Simpson had lent her, she knocked on the kitchen door and said, "I've finished, Mrs. Simpson. Can I help you with the bathtub?"

"No, dearie, I'll empty it with the bucket. It's easy enough when you're used to it. You can just run along to bed now and I'll give you a knock at seven o'clock. There, I'm a poet. By the way, your other skirt is hanging up in the scullery—it's warm from the copper so it'll probably be dry in the morning."

Jessica was taken aback to find that Mrs. Simpson was expecting a goodnight kiss. As the large face approached her she involuntarily recoiled, but seeing a hurt look quickly appear she forced herself to submit. The kiss was rather wet and Jessica would have liked to wash her face again.

"That's right, dearie. Us girls have to stick together."

Before getting into the bathtub, Jessica had checked that the door leading to the staircase was firmly closed, but now, as she turned away from Jill Simpson, she saw that it was partly open, leaving a crack through which the tub was clearly visible. With the blood surging to her face she crept up the stairs. As she reached the top, she heard a door close softly and drew the obvious conclusion. Getting into her cold bed, she looked at the watch that Uncle James had given to her and thought, "I mustn't oversleep."

CHAPTER VIII

1965: Saturday, December 18th

Most people were unaware that Siggy Harescombe's Christian name was really Siegfried. His parents had caught the Wagnerian fever of the late nineteenth century, and when he was born in 1901 it had seemed natural to call him Siegfried. At first the name had merely been an embarrassment, but as relations with Germany worsened, he and his parents began to think that it might be a good idea to use his second name instead. Unfortunately this was William, so not wishing to foster any associations with the Kaiser they decided to stick to the abbreviated form of Siegfried that he had adopted in childhood and hope that no one would make the connection. Nothing, after all, could be more English-sounding than Harescombe.

By the time Inspector Phelps dropped Sergeant Snipe in front of the Harescombes' cottage and went on his way the two men had given each other verbatim accounts of their respective interviews.

"Looks like a picture-postcard", the Sergeant muttered as he opened the front gate. English country cottages may not be at their best in the winter, but the vine-covered walls, windowboxes and dainty curtains suggested the presence of someone who knew how such a residence ought to look.

By the time Snipe reached the front door it was already open and Siggy was standing on the doorstep. With his slender, stooping figure, thinning gray hair, old tweeds and briar pipe, he looked the archetypal English academic.

"Good morning, Sergeant, come in out of the cold."

As Snipe crossed the threshold he found himself face to face with a short, stocky woman with a face the color and shape of a russet apple.

"This is my wife, Mabel. Mabel, this is Sergeant Snipe."

"Oh dear, I hope he hasn't come to arrest us."

"No, Ma'am, I'd just like to ask Mr. Harescombe a few questions about something that has cropped up at his school."

"There, Siegfried, I told you that fire business wasn't over by a long chalk. There'll be more bodies, you mark my words."

"Yes, dear, you did say so. Now run along to the kitchen and make us some tea and then the Sergeant will tell us all about it."

Mabel disappeared promptly and Siggy escorted Sergeant Snipe into a small parlor. Whoever had furnished it had an eye for old hunting prints, rustic bridges, September evenings and willow pattern plates, but it had been done with decent economy, so that the visitor could actually breathe without fear of upsetting something. Snipe, whose tastes were simple and wholesome, looked around appreciatively.

"Very nice", he said.

"You must tell Mabel. She has undertaken the responsibility for everything to do with the cottage and the garden. She sends me out to work every weekday with a good breakfast inside me and on Friday evenings she gives me a list of tasks to be performed the next day."

Snipe was anxious to get down to business but he couldn't help asking what happened on Sundays.

"Mabel goes to Morning Prayer and Evensong and spends the afternoon in contemplation. I occasionally go with her, but she has realized that I am really an old atheist, so she generally lets me stay at home and catch up with my schoolwork. It is in many ways a satisfactory arrangement."

The last comment was accompanied by a mild grimace that cast some doubt on its validity and on whether it was intended to apply to the whole *modus vivendi* or only to what happened on Sundays.

"Well, Sir", said Snipe with a polite cough, "the fact is that we have found a skeleton under the foundations of the old science building."

"Really, Sergeant? What an astonishing thing!"

Snipe noticed, however, that after the initial reaction Siggy looked more thoughtful than astonished.

"Yes. It appears that the burial must have taken place just before the foundations were laid. Since you were involved in planning and supervising the work you might be able to help us to find out how the skeleton got there. Not meaning, of course, to imply that you had anything to do with it."

"Well that's nice to know. I should hate be the well-known man 'assisting the police with their enquiries', although as a matter of fact I think I may be able to help. Some very odd things happened at the time which would be easier to explain if someone was trying to dispose of a body. Could you tell me a little more about what you found?"

D. G. "Bob" Roberts, the former headmaster of the Nave, lived in a small cottage a few doors down the village street from the Harescombes. At the age of seventy-two he was still very fit, and when Inspector Phelps found him he was kneeling in the snow by his front door doing something to an elderly bicycle which was standing upside down on its saddle and handlebars. The front wheel, minus its tire, lay on the ground, and Bob was carefully cutting a patch from a piece of stout canvas. As the inspector approached he looked up and said, "It's over there Mr. Pettigrew. It overflowed again yesterday and the smell is getting worse."

"No, Sir, as a matter of fact I'm not Mr. Pettigrew and I haven't come about the drains."

Bob looked intently at Phelps.

"No, you aren't Mr. Pettigrew. What a pity. But perhaps you've come about the geyser. I don't really mind a cold bath, but it would be pleasant to have hot water sometimes."

"I'm afraid not, Sir. I'm a policeman—Inspector Phelps from Gloucester Central Police Station."

While they were talking, work on the bicycle continued. There was a split in the tire, and the method of repair was to stick a canvas patch on the inside. In addition to this Bob cut a larger piece of canvas and wrapped it round the inner tube for several inches on each side of the weak point. Inspector Phelps was very impressed.

"I used to do that sort of thing when I was boy", he said, "but you do it much better than I ever did."

"My weekly woman says that things aren't what they used to be", said Bob as he began to replace the tire. "I think she must be right. The tires that were on this bicycle when I bought it lasted for twenty-five years."

"When was that, Sir?"

"Let me see—yes, I believe it was 1928 when I came here. I was told that a headmaster really ought to have a car, but I have never liked cars and I am quite certain that I should never have been able to drive one. Rather than becoming a public menace I decided to stick to the bicycle."

Having replaced the tire and the wheel, Bob stood up, righted the bicycle with very little effort, leaned it against the corner of the cottage next to the offending drain and set about pumping up the tire.

"There", he murmured to himself, "I think that will do quite well."

Inspector Phelps coughed politely.

Bob turned and seemed slightly surprised to see that he had a visitor.

"Oh, Mr. Pettigrew, it was kind of you to call."

"But . . ." began the inspector.

"Oh, I was forgetting. And you're not the geyser person either . . . Something about the police . . ."

"Yes, Sir, Inspector Phelps."

"Oh, yes, of course. Now what was it about Inspector Phelps?"

"No, Sir, I *am* Inspector Phelps."

"Oh, I see. How do you do?"

The two men solemnly shook hands, in which process a certain amount of oil was transferred from one to the other. Seizing on the moment of silence, the inspector hurriedly broached the subject of his visit.

"You probably know that a new science building is being erected in St. Mary's Square. In the process of clearing the site a skeleton was discovered under the old foundations. Circumstances suggest that it was buried there just before the old labs were built. Naturally the police would like to find out whose skeleton it is, how it got there and whether foul play was involved."

Now that he understood his visitor's purpose Bob became quite attentive. It seemed that his habit was to focus firmly on one thing at a time. While working on the bicycle he was hardly conscious of anything else. Now that his attention was fixed on the inspector's problem, it didn't occur to him that they were standing outside on a very cold day a few feet from the warm interior of a cottage. Phelps was perfectly willing to endure a little discomfort for the sake of some hard information, but unfortunately there wasn't much information to be had. Although Bob remembered the construction of the building quite clearly and recalled speaking with old Johnson, all he could do was to confirm what the police already knew.

"I had very little to do with it, you know. You should really talk to Mr. Harescombe, who worked with Mr. Johnson on the design. However, saying that does remind me of something rather peculiar. Johnson came to me one day with a sad tale about water getting into the basement."

"Why was that peculiar?"

"Well, you see, it was the only occasion on which he ever spoke to me, and I could not understand why he should have wanted my advice on a subject about which I knew nothing. Later on I was informed that the building had no basement, and that made the incident even more perplexing."

"Do you know of any disagreement between Mr. Johnson and Mr. Harescombe?"

"Mr. Harescombe had rather a low opinion of Mr. Johnson's capacities. He told me that with a squad of boys to help him he could have made a better job of it himself. But I believe Mr. Johnson is dead and decently buried, so it could hardly be his skeleton. And, of course, he was still alive at the time you are asking about."

"Yes, Sir. Perhaps I ought to have mentioned that the skeleton is that of a young woman. One more question—do you know whether any of your teachers have written poetry in their spare time?"

The question didn't strike Bob as incongruous. He turned it over in his mind and replied, "I believe that some of them have circulated scurrilous verses about their colleagues and, on occasion, about their headmaster, but I know of no serious poetic ambitions. Some, I understand, have poked gentle fun at my foolish habit of contributing poetry of a sort to the local newspaper."

"Well, that's been very helpful", said the inspector insincerely. "But I do have one other question. Do you remember a pupil called James Snipe?"

"Yes." The answer came without hesitation. "A very likeable boy—intelligent but not inclined towards academic pursuits. Why—has he got into trouble again?"

"No, Sir. He's my sergeant and he's been telling me about an incident with your bicycle that took place more than thirty years ago. I gather that this is the bicycle in question."

"Yes. He and his friends removed the chain and locked the brakes in position so that even if the chain had still been there I should not have been able to make much progress. It was that incident that moved me to become my own mechanic, since at the time I had no idea how to deal with the situation."

"Snipe told me that you were quite merciful."

"Within reason, Inspector. As far as boys are concerned it is often a question of administering enough punishment to maintain one's dignity, without losing sight of the humor of the situation. I imagine that it is different with criminals."

"Unfortunately it usually is, and I must say that most of my teachers seemed to be more interested in their dignity. If I may say so, I begin to understand why everyone speaks of you with such respect and affection."

"You are very kind, Inspector."

Bob continued to gaze sorrowfully at his malodorous drain while Phelps got back into his car to drive the hundred yards to Siggy Harescombe's cottage, where Snipe was sitting among the teacups with an attentive audience. Mabel immediately brought another cup, which its recipient, still feeling the effects of his long outdoor conversation, accepted gratefully.

"I think I've covered all the ground, Sir", said Snipe, "and Mr. Harescombe was just telling me about some of the difficulties with the old building."

Encouraged by Phelps, Siggy started his story again.

"I won't go into the whole history of the building, but there are certain points that seem to me to be of considerable interest. In the nineteen-thirties, when it was already clear that we needed new science facilities, we started making some plans, but of course no building was possible until after the war. Towards the end of the war it emerged that the building would be needed in rather a hurry because the Local Education Authority was planning a large increase in the grammar school population. We were told, in fact, that speed was of the essence and that we had better put up a temporary prefabricated building. They thought that after a few years, when the country had recovered from the war, we should have a much better chance of getting what they referred to as a 'really fine building'. Having already experienced the aftermath of one war and spent fifteen years struggling with the local authorities, I was very sceptical, and we—that is, the architect and I—designed a building that we thought would be ready in time and would last for the foreseeable future. We finished our plans by the beginning of 1945 and took them immediately to Mr. Johnson. He hummed and ha'd a bit and said that as things were, with the shortage of labor and the difficulty of getting everything from bricks and mortar to electrical supplies, it was going to be impossible to get anything done until the war was over, and even then it would be extremely difficult. But he did give his blessing to the plans and he thought it was a good idea to try to make a building that would not have to be replaced after a few years.

"Well, the war in Europe ended in May and in spite of all the difficulties Johnson started work in St. Mary's Square in July. I won't try to describe the whole process—it seemed that almost every day something went wrong and Johnson was after me to change this, that or the other. There always seemed to be a good reason, and it wasn't until some time later that I began to wonder if he was just trying to make things easier for himself. What interests me in relation to this present business is the matter of the basement."

Phelps visibly pricked up his ears and Siggy said, "Ah, I see you've already heard something about it."

"Yes, I was just down the road talking to Mr. Roberts and he said something about the basement. Apparently it never happened."

"Yes, it never happened, and that was the biggest bone of contention between Johnson and me. It was only to be a small basement, just big enough to hold the furnace and the boiler, but it was essential to the whole design. However, a day or two after starting work he told me that in digging the hole for the basement they had come upon a shallow watercourse and that there were several feet of water in the hole. He invited me to go and have a look, which I did. It was certainly true that there was water in the hole, but I told him that builders must have been dealing with such problems for centuries, and I was sure there were ways of making a basement watertight. He was adamant, however. He said that he wouldn't take the responsibility for putting a basement in a place like that, and if we must have one we'd have to build somewhere else. He maintained that with some minor alterations everything that was supposed to be in the basement could easily be accommodated above ground. This was sheer rubbish since what he was proposing to do would have completely disrupted the original design. This was on a Friday. I told him that I wanted talk to the architect before he went any further and that I'd see him on Monday morning. But when I got there on Monday I found that he had already filled in the hole and concreted over the whole thing. Johnson said he thought that was what we had agreed to. I told him that was nonsense and that I had made myself perfectly clear, and we had a flaming row. The upshot was that the furnace and the boiler and whatever else was supposed to be in the basement had to be accommodated upstairs, which really jiggered the whole works.

"Do you think that Johnson's concern about the basement was genuine or did it seem more like a pretext?"

"It's very hard to say. I must admit that it crossed my mind that he might have had some reason for not wanting a basement, and just pumped some water into the hole for me to see. But I asked a local geologist and he told me that there really are watercourses under various parts of the city, so it may have been true."

"Now here's a very important question", said the inspector. "You said that you believed that in spite of the official policy of having a temporary structure, you thought you could construct a building that would be as near permanent as any building is likely to be. What I should very much like to know is whether Johnson had that opinion even after the alterations in the design."

"You mean that if he had expected the building to be replaced after a few years he would hardly have buried a body under it. It's hard to say, but I do think there was a change of attitude somewhere along the line. In spite of our differences he seemed quite painstaking and conscientious at first but later on he appeared to be anxious just to get the job finished and get away. I'm not sure if that fits in with what you're thinking."

Mabel stood up to collect the teacups and paused in the act of taking out the tray.

"If I had a body that I wanted to get rid of and there was a convenient place to hide it, I'd just put it there and run away as fast as my legs would carry me."

"That's a very good point, Ma'am", said Inspector Phelps. "The fact is that we know very little about it. Johnson may have taken the opportunity to dump the body and then felt that he couldn't bear to be in the vicinity any longer than he had to. Even if that's true it doesn't mean he was the murderer. Or it might have been someone else who buried it. But it does seem clear that whoever it was must have had some connection with Johnson and the building—which, I suppose, brings us to young Johnson."

"Yes, young Johnson. A very pleasant young man, not in the best of health I seem to remember, but a hard worker and very intent on getting things right. As his father faded, so to speak, he became more responsible. Things would have been much more of a mess without him."

CHAPTER IX

1940: Monday, November 18

At six o'clock on Monday morning Mrs. Simpson rose, contemplated her sleeping husband with little satisfaction, went downstairs and put the kettle on. There wasn't much for breakfast, only the usual bread and margarine, but at least she would have a decent cup of tea before facing the day's work. Of course, things might be just a little easier now that she had Jessica's ration book. Looking at the shelf over the kitchen table where she had left it, she was surprised to see that it wasn't there. She searched the kitchen without success and was about to start looking in the living room when an awful thought struck her. A quick glance into the scullery showed her that Jessica's skirt had gone too. It was only twenty past six but she ran up the stairs as fast as her thirteen stone would allow her and knocked loudly on Jessica's door. Getting no reply she marched in and found the bed neatly made and no sign of Jessica or her belongings. On the chest of drawers was a note in Jessica's well-formed handwriting.

> "Dear Mrs. Simpson,
> Thank you for being kind to me. I can't explain why, but I simply can't stay here.
> Don't worry, I'll be all right and I'll write and let you know where I am.
> Yours sincerely,
> Jessica.

P. S. I took my ration book because the people I stay with will need it, but you can keep my pocket money for this month."

Mrs. Simpson's first impulse was to go and rouse her husband, but after sitting on Jessica's bed for a few moments she thought better of it. He, she was sure, was the main reason why Jessica had left. Let him go on snoring for another hour before the eruption—a blessed hour of peace and quiet and another cup of tea. At that moment, however, a less comforting thought struck her: how did Jessica know about the pocket money and how were the Simpsons going to manage without the extra income that they had counted on? It was a very worried Jill Simpson who sat down at the kitchen table to wait for the kettle to boil.

It was still dark when Jessica left the house a little before six o'clock, so it took her a long time to find her way to King's Square and it wasn't until half past six that she was sitting on a bench waiting for a bus. She had done this part of the journey several times in the daylight, but she was a little nervous about missing her stop in the darkness. Fortunately, by the time the bus arrived there was a little grey November light in the sky. The bus was almost empty and the elderly conductor, intrigued by the sight of a young girl with two suitcases getting on at that hour, was inclined to be talkative.

"Running away from home, Ducky?" he asked in a wheezing voice.

It occurred to Jessica that the Simpsons might report her disappearance to her school or even to the police, so, with as much confidence as she could muster she said, "No, I'm just going home. I was staying with my grandmother."

"She must be an early riser."

"Well, I have to go home and then go to school."

The bus stopped and some more passengers got on, so Jessica was left in peace for a while. A man with a newspaper sat down next to her and she saw the headline—something about battles in North Africa.

She had a feeling that that was where Uncle James was going and she remembered that she hadn't given him a thought for the past three days. She prayed fervently that he would be all right, forgetting for the moment her doubts about God.

Now she had to keep a careful watch. She could only just make out the outlines of the houses and they all looked very much alike, so it was more by instinct then by good judgement that she got off at the right stop. When she opened the front gate, a few minutes before seven, the light was still quite dim and she wondered whether she ought to wait until a more reasonable hour before knocking on the door. She hesitated for a moment, but there was nowhere to wait inconspicuously so, suddenly feeling very timid, she approached the front door. To her vast relief, it opened before she could touch it.

"Oh, Susan", she said, and was for a few moments unable to maintain her resolve that there should be no more tears.

Susan pulled her inside and held her tightly in her arms.

After a while Susan said in a muffled voice, "We can't stand here for ever, you know. Come and sit down and I'll bring your cases in. Then you can tell me what's happened."

Jessica wasn't very coherent, but with a little prompting from Susan the whole story came out.

"You were right", said Susan at the end. "He *is* a nasty old man. But you must admit that the thing has its funny side."

Jessica considered this idea for a moment.

"Yes", she admitted with a rueful smile, "I suppose it has. Do you think I ought to have just grinned and born it?"

"Well, I'm not really a very good judge of the situation, but now that you're here I'm certainly not going to send you back—I want you here with me as long as I can have you."

"That's what I want too. I never want to go anywhere else."

This remark led to another prolonged hug.

"I wish we could stay like this all day", said Jessica.

"I know, darling, but I have to go to work and you have to go to school."

"Oh, I'd forgotten about that."

Susan gave Jessica an extra squeeze and kissed her on the forehead.

"We'd better have something to eat. We can go on the bus together and I'll show you where we hide the spare front door key as you'll probably be home before I am."

"I like it when you say 'home'", said Jessica, "even if it's only for a few days".

"Well, as far as that goes, I have an idea. I think it's going to be more than a few days but I'll explain it to you later—when we're both home."

Susan worked very hard to make Jessica look like an utterly respectable schoolgirl with correct shoes, the inevitable lisle stockings, and her hair properly put up and largely hidden by her new hat. When she had finished she stood back and admired the result. Jessica had been lucky enough to find a blazer that fitted her perfectly. It was dark blue with shiny brass buttons and a matching skirt, and was set off nicely by the new white blouse which Miss Edwards had given her and which Susan had carefully adjusted so that exactly an inch of sleeve showed below the cuffs. Susan clapped her hands.

"If I met you in the street I'd salute and say, 'Aye, aye, Cap'n.' Don't worry, I don't usually make such a fuss—it's just that you look so adorable I can't help it."

Jessica smiled. She had never been tremendously interested in clothes, but she liked her blue uniform much better than the old green one and, more to the point, Susan had said she looked adorable. Susan looked adorable too, in her nurse's uniform, and it seemed a pity that they had to put on overcoats. The bus service was not very reliable and it was a raw November day. By the time their transportation arrived their faces were flushed with cold as well as excitement, and the conductor said, "Well you're the cheerfullest people I've seen for a long time."

School turned out to be no better and no worse than Jessica had expected, but something disconcerting happened almost as soon as she set foot in the building.

"Good morning, Jessica. I hope you are comfortable with the Simpsons—such good people. Jill Simpson was a pupil here you know—most worthy and industrious."

The voice was Miss Alderley's and Jessica remembered that at the interview Susan had given her address as 32 St. Paul's Road.

"Yes, thank you, Miss Alderley", said Jessica, as brightly as she could manage. Since it was out of the question to explain what had actually happened, there didn't seem to be anything else to say. Fortunately the headmistress's attention was caught by the sight of a girl whose hair had escaped from prison and flopped all over her face.

"Oh, do come here, Elspeth, if you can see where you are going. If you cannot keep your hair in better order than that we shall have to have it all cut off."

Miss Alderley chuckled at her little jest.

Jessica escaped and went to her classroom. As she had expected, she was subjected to rather a lot of staring, but compared to most of the Gloucester girls, who tended to be rather stocky and to run to puppy fat, she was tall, slim and curiously imposing, so students whose eyes she caught tended to look away.

Penelope Thrower, a no-nonsense kind of person who was Jessica's form mistress and mathematics teacher, said, "Hello, Jessica. Everything all right?"

"Yes, thank you, Miss Thrower."

"Good. Here are some books for you—algebra, geometry, trigonometry—make sure you put your name in them and don't on any account lose them. They may be old and tattered but all the pages are there and we can't get any new ones."

Miss Thrower turned to her class.

"Girls!" she said, producing instant silence, "this is Jessica. She's been bombed out of her house in London and she'll be with us for the foreseeable future. Treat her as one of yourselves and don't ask too many questions. It's hard enough to lose everything, without having to keep on talking about it. Time to go to assembly now."

So 5A lined up and marched in good order to the school hall where they sat and listened to morning prayers conducted by Miss Alderley, and sang "Through the night of doubt and sorrow", which was one of that lady's favorite hymns. Unfortunately she was considerably more loquacious than Penny Thrower. After the hymn she made a little speech about the newcomer from London who had lost her home and her parents, and was now living far away from everything that was familiar to her.

"You must all make a very special effort to treat her with friendship and kindness. This is part of the spirit of our beloved school, and I know that I can count on you not let her feel lonely or neglected."

Jessica, happening to glance along the row she was sitting in, saw the curled lip of Miss Thrower and wooden expressions on the faces of most of her classmates.

As she was leaving the hall on the way to her first lesson Miss Thrower buttonholed her.

"Good luck, Jessica. Don't take too much notice of all that. The last thing you want is a lot of people being excessively kind to you. It may take a few days but you'll soon settle in."

"Yes", Jessica thought, "I really wish people would just let me alone."

But she made a mental reservation in the case of Susan.

CHAPTER X

1965: Saturday, December 18

On the way back from Brookethorpe, Phelps and Snipe made a detour and called on Andrew Thomas, known to his friends as "Goofy". As they had expected, he confirmed Williams's story in every detail, and by five o'clock in the afternoon the two policemen were back at the station, refreshing themselves with cups of tea provided by Sergeant Bunn.

"I thought you might like to see what the *Citizen* has got hold of", said Bunn, flourishing a copy of the local paper. "There's a picture of the building site and it says, 'Remains of young woman found in St. Mary's Square.'"

"Good God!" exclaimed the inspector disgustedly, "How the hell did they get that? I thought it would take them at least until Monday."

"One of those boys, I should think", said Bunn, who had been kept well informed about the case.

"The boys didn't know it was a girl", said Snipe.

"But they were pretty certain that it was—or, at least, Davies was. Carter wasn't so sure."

Meanwhile Phelps was reading the article. In addition to describing the exact circumstances in which the skeleton was found, it gave the names of the boys who found it and a brief history of the old science building. It said that the police were very interested in the origins of the building and were expecting to interview Mr. Henry Johnson, the well-known contractor. Near the end there was a subsidiary headline,

"Shakespeare's girlfriend?", followed by some remarks about a highly romantic poem which had been found with the skeleton, and some speculation about the original graveyard of St. Mary's church.

"I shouldn't be surprised if Bagwell had a hand in it", said Snipe, who was looking at the paper over the inspector's shoulder, "although there's a lot of stuff here that he didn't know either."

"What about Chard and Highnam?" asked Bunn.

"I really don't think so—at least, I hope not."

"I hope not, too", said Inspector Phelps grimly. "Get them in here as soon as possible, Bunny."

But the two constables strenuously denied any connection with the article, and the inspector and the sergeants believed them.

"And, by the way, Sir," Bunn added as he was leaving the room, "no one in this town makes coffins any more. They just order the style and size that they want from a place in Birmingham. One of the undertakers told me that he didn't think there'd been a local coffin maker since before the war."

"Thanks a lot, Bunny", grunted the inspector morosely. "Don't come back until you have some good news."

"If you say so, Sir", Bunn replied with a grin. "It was nice working for you."

"Well, Sir", Snipe asked his boss, "What do you think? About the *Citizen* article, I mean."

"If we think about people who knew all the details there are three possibilities, and two of them are people I'd trust a long way, so that only leaves . . ."

"Ferrier."

"Right."

"I suppose we couldn't run him in for interfering with a police investigation."

"I'm afraid not, but we'll have to find some way of putting a spoke in his wheel. Meanwhile we still have to find out somehow who this young lady was. I'm pretty sure Johnson knows something about it and maybe he could tell us—but he won't unless we can find some way of twisting his arm. Williams and Thomas are probably just helping out a pal and they won't talk either. Then there's the matter of the poem and the pouch it was in. That ought to lead somewhere, but they used to sell pouches like that at Woolworth's for tuppence-ha'penny, and I doubt whether we're going to find an English professor who can identify the murderer on the strength of one poem. There's something odd about that bit of copper wire, however."

"I know", said Snipe. "Somehow it doesn't seem to belong. But it does remind me of something."

"Oh, what's that?"

"It's the sort of wire we used to use in physics lessons. And in my last year at The Nave my physics master was . . .'"

"Siggy Harescombe"

"Yes, but . . ."

"If you were going to say you can't imagine him being mixed up in this, I agree with you. But there have been other people teaching physics and presumably almost anyone could wander into the lab and help himself to a piece of wire. Of course it would have been the old lab, wherever that was."

"It was a big room in the older part of the school—not really meant to be a lab, but good enough in my day when there were only a couple of hundred boys in the whole place. And, you know, it was only an idea. That piece of wire might have come from almost anywhere."

"I know—so might the skeleton."

After Snipe had gone off duty, Phelps sat at his desk for several minutes, chewing things over. Finding that his mind was gradually going blank, he picked up the telephone and rang the headmaster's number.

"Sorry to disturb you again", he said when Woodcock answered, "but I thought I ought to tell you that I'm going to give Sandman and his men permission to start work again tomorrow."

"Thank you for letting me know."

"They'll be finishing the hole for the basement, After that I suppose the cement mixers will arrive and it will get pretty noisy."

"Well fortunately it's only for three days. I'm sure we'll be able to tolerate it."

"And", Phelps continued, "I was wondering if you had had any further thoughts about the poem. I mean it would be very handy, for instance, to know whether it came from somewhere or it was written specially for the purpose."

"As a matter of fact, Mrs. Marjoribanks and I have been giving some thought to that question. She mentioned the flavor of pastiche, but it's hard to say what it's a pastiche of. It really doesn't remind me of anyone in particular, although most of the imagery is very old-fashioned—the lambs, walking barefoot, the palace garden and the garden of roses. But it also has elements of modernity, in the layout of the last stanza for instance, and might be read as a lament for something irretrievably lost. On the whole I think that it was written especially for the girl, and not by her murderer—if there was one. All of which is not very helpful, I'm afraid."

"Well, no, I don't suppose it is, but you never know. You said yourself that the poet was not without talent, so maybe this isn't the only poem he ever wrote."

"You mean we might eventually catch him by stylistic analysis."

"Something like that. It's a bit far-fetched of course. But then, the whole thing is far-fetched."

Phelps put down the phone and went over the case again in his mind. There was one outstanding oddity that he had not yet investigated, and that was young Johnson's presence at the building site and his unconvincing explanation of it.

"It might have happened that way", he thought, "but I don't believe it did—specially not with the coincidence of his pal Williams turning up in the middle of the night."

He picked up the telephone directory and was gratified to find that Sandman was both listed and at home. He was in for a disappointment, however, Sandman claiming to have been just as surprised as the inspector by Johnson's presence.

"I don't do much on-site work these days", he explained. "I have several crews out on jobs and I go round regularly to check up on them, but as far as hiring labor is concerned Charlie King does most of that and he knows he'll get a rocket from me if he falls down on the job. I asked him about Johnson—I expect you know that Johnson and I are not on the best of terms since I got this contract—and he said it was true that he needed a driver and Johnson said he had heard about it on the grapevine and needed some work. Seems it turned out all right as far as it went—he did the job and didn't cause any trouble. What I'd really like to know is when we can start up again."

"You can start again tomorrow if you don't mind paying time-and-a-half."

"Not me, my friend. It's the City Council that will be doing the paying."

"Do you think it's true that Johnson is short of work?"

"I'd be surprised, but he'd know better than me."

"I expect he would. Well, thank you, Mr. Sandman. Do you know where I could get hold of Charlie King?"

"I'd suggest by the scruff of his neck—otherwise he'll be at home watching the telly and pretending that he can't hear his missus nagging him. 37A New Street. Telephone 24371."

"Thanks—I think I'll call on him personally, and I'd be grateful if you would wait an hour or so before contacting him."

"Aha! OK, if you say so."

New Street was only a fifteen-minute walk from the Central Police Station. Phelps's route took him down Southgate Street past the Royal Infirmary, along Spa Road, and through the park. By this time the snow on the pavements had degenerated into grimy slush but the park still looked pretty enough for a Christmas card, complete with pink-faced children with flying scarves, energetically hurling snowballs at one another. Crossing the footbridge over the railway on the southern side of the park, he found himself in Weston Road, a residential street of well-kept semi-detached houses with trim front gardens. A few more paces took him to the corner of New Street, which was quite a different proposition, an anomaly, in fact, situated between the well-heeled Weston Road and the eminently respectable St. Paul's Road, with disheveled children playing on the pavements in front of ill-favored row houses. The inspector was familiar with New Street, having had to interview some of its residents in connection with various misdeeds. 37A looked a little tidier than its neighbors, having clean windows and neat curtains and lacking the assorted debris of wrappers, cigarette cartons and abandoned toys that adorned the fronts of most of the houses.

Mrs. King, who opened the front door, was fiftyish, tall, thin, bespectacled and studious-looking. With her tight bun and her habit of peering over the top of her glasses she might have been mistaken for an old-fashioned schoolmistress—until she opened her mouth.

"Charlie", she yelled after Phelps had introduced himself, "come 'ere. It's the pleece."

Phelps was amazed at the volume of sound produced by such a skinny person, but there was no response from the interior of the house.

"You better come in. I'm just getting 'is lordship's tea while 'e watches the football. You can't get 'im away from it no matter what you do. 'E never 'ears a word I say, but maybe you'll 'ave better luck."

"Inspector Phelps to see you", she said with mock formality as she led the way into the living room. "You better turn that off and listen."

"Can't", said her husband from the depths of a well-upholstered sofa. "It's one-all with five minutes left."

"You talk to 'im", said Mrs. King to the inspector as she flounced out of the room, "I might as well be chewing a brick."

"Chelsea versus Charlton", Phelps remarked, looking over Charlie's shoulder. "Local Derby—everybody's choice for a draw. Got them in the treble chance?"

"Yeah—like ten million other people."

"I know—when the games turn out according to form everybody gets them right and you win twenty quid if you're lucky. I've often thought of putting down the eight unlikeliest matches and praying for a £75,000 miracle."

"That's a good idea, only miracles don't happen to the likes of me. My God, look at that. See what I mean—miracles do happen but it's always the wrong way round. Looks as if I'll have to work another week."

One of the Charlton forwards had shot from the edge of the penalty area and the ball, after hitting the crossbar, had bounced off the back of the goalkeeper's head and into the net.

A moment later the referee blew the final whistle and Inspector Phelps said, "Speaking of work, I have a couple of questions I'd like to ask you."

Charlie's head jerked round.

"Work? What for? I haven't done anything wrong."

Something about this response prompted the inspector to improvise a little.

"I didn't mean to imply that you had, but I must say that's a very nice TV set you have there. Must have cost quite a packet."

"Got it on the never-never", protested Charlie. "You don't suppose I could afford to buy something like that straight out."

"Exactly. Where did you get it?"

"Just you wait a minute, Mr. Bloody Inspector." The voice came from Charlie's wife, who had been listening at the door. "'E may be a lazy bugger but 'e's an honest one for all that. Brings 'ome 'is pay packet every week regular as clockwork. If you want to know, we got that TV from Sam Williams in Southgate Street. You know Sam Williams. 'E'll tell you. 'Ten quid down and five half-crowns a week for the rest of your life' 'e says, thinkin' 'e's bein' funny."

"Now then, just hold your horses", protested Charlie, standing up and revealing himself as a genuine five-by-five almost as well covered as the sofa. "Don't encourage this bloke to go sticking his nose into our affairs any more than he has already. You know the police—if they can't find anything to pin on you they'll imagine something"

"What have we been imagining about you?" enquired the inspector. "Anything in particular?"

"Not that I know of, but you've only been here five minutes and you're on about my TV."

"All right, let's forget about the TV—for the moment. What I really want to know is why Henry Johnson was driving your digger on Friday."

"Why shouldn't he? He said he needed the money and he'd been driving the exact same machine for years. So I took him on—anything wrong with that?"

"Not a thing. How much did he pay you?"

Charlie sat down with a bump, and his wife emitted a low growl.

"So he did grease your palm, and you forgot to tell the missus, huh?"

"Nothing criminal in that, is there?"

"Maybe not, but there would be something criminal if you obstructed the police in the execution of their duties, so you'd better come clean. And after that I'd advise you to buy your wife a new hat or something."

"All right, don't get shirty. He came to me the middle of last week and said he wanted to drive the digger when we started on the old foundation. I told him we already had a driver but he said he'd take care of that and asked for the driver's name and address. I couldn't understand why he wanted to do it but he said he was professionally interested as he laid that concrete twenty years ago and wanted to see how well it had lasted."

"Did you believe him?"

"I don't know. To tell the truth I thought the whole thing was a bit fishy. But then, the ten-pound notes were real enough so I didn't ask any more questions."

Mrs. King was staggered.

"Ten-pound notes! What happened to *them*, that's what I'd like to know."

Phelps decided to make a quick exit before the family quarrel started.

"Well, I think that's all I need to know. You can explain the rest to your wife, and good luck! But watch your step or we may have to take a closer look at your personal finances. And by the way, you're starting work again tomorrow, so you'd better find out if your driver has recovered from his so-called illness. Mr. Johnson won't be working for you any more."

It was getting dark when Inspector Phelps closed the front door of the Kings' house on the pitched battle that was going on inside. It was at times like this that he was thankful that he had never married. Sergeant Snipe was remarkable, being a good policeman, a good husband and a good father. His wife was remarkable too, having made a good thing of the difficult role of being a policeman's wife. Arthur Williams's wife was dead, Goofy Thomas was making the best of a bachelor existence, Siggy Harescombe had a working arrangement that he seemed to be able to tolerate, and Henry Johnson's wife had so far remained invisible. Bob Roberts pottered happily about on his own in his little cottage. Meanwhile it looked as if Colin Woodcock and Bill Marjoribanks were enjoying all the perks of married life without any of the responsibilities. "Well, good luck to them", he said to himself, "but it can't possibly last." Tongues must be wagging already—either they'd have to tie the knot or they'd face a public scandal. Fortunately they were both single, so the eternal triangle didn't apply. Perhaps this unfortunate girl whose skeleton they had dug up was part of a triangle. He somehow didn't think that she had been killed for her money, and whoever wrote the poem was obviously in love with her. Johnson must know something—he didn't finagle his way onto the site just to look at the concrete. He must have been so anxious to see what was under it that any excuse would do. The impulse to go straight out to Johnson and Son and confront its proprietor was hard to resist, but Phelps wasn't quite sure that this was the time to do it. Johnson's behavior had been highly suspicious, but there was no actual evidence that he knew anything about the girl who had died twenty or thirty years ago. All he had to do was to deny it.

The park was almost deserted, its snowy surface sparkling in the lamplight. As he made his way to Spa Road he was suddenly assailed by volleys of snowballs from among the trees on both sides of the path. Here he was, an anonymous muffled-up middle-aged pedestrian, an obvious target for high-spirited kids who rarely had such an opportunity and had no idea that they were shooting at a police inspector. Counting on poor marksmanship he ignored the barrage and kept on walking, with a line or two from Hamlet's famous soliloquy stirring in his memory. "Whether 'tis nobler in the mind to suffer the slings and snowballs of outrageous fourteen-year-olds . . ." There certainly seemed to be no point in taking arms against this sea of invisible hurlers when he could simply rely on his legs. Tennyson vied incongruously with Shakespeare for his attention. "Was there a man dismayed?" he asked himself as the snowballers from the left and the right volleyed and thundered. Almost certainly, and probably a lot more than one. The difference between Hamlet and General What's-his-name at Balaclava was that the general had made up his mind. The similarity was that in both cases the results had been disastrous. Well, at some point he was going to have to make up his own mind and he didn't want a disaster. There was nothing criminal he could charge Johnson or anyone else with at the moment. Johnson had merely crossed a foreman's palm with silver in order to obtain a day's employment. He had done his work well, earnt his pay and gone home at the end of the day. He would undoubtedly stick to the story he had told Charlie King and apologize for misleading the police in the matter of the "sick" driver. Phelps wished he had Snipe with him to help mull these things over, but Snipey was probably sitting in front of the fire at home while his admirable wife made his tea in the kitchen. The occasion didn't seem to warrant disturbing his domestic tranquility.

Arriving at the station, Phelps was greeted by Sergeant Bunn, a monument of good-humored rectitude, but somewhat lacking in imaginative penetration. Nevertheless, it seemed worthwhile to outline the situation for him and get his response.

"So the question is, do I go out and give him a good grilling now, or do I save it until we have a bit more to go on."

Sergeant Bunn scratched his head and paused for thought.

"That's a very good question, Sir", he remarked eventually.

"Thank you very much, Bunny, but could you give me a very good answer?

"Well, Sir, I don't know that I rightly can. I've never met this bloke Johnson, so I don't know whether or not you could shake him. I think maybe I'd go after him, but you know much more about it than I do. You see, Sir, I've never had much to do with interrogations and that kind of thing."

"Put in my place", the inspector muttered as he made for his office. "'You do your job and I'll do mine.' Well I suppose it's fair enough."

"Oh, Sir", Bunn called after his retreating superior. "Mr. Woodcock phoned half an hour ago. He asked me to ask you if you would like to go up to the Dower House for dinner. He said to tell you it would be a bit of real home cooking."

"Did he say anything else?"

"No, Sir, only to give him a buzz when you got in."

Phelps suddenly felt a hundred pounds lighter.

Bill Marjoribanks sipped her glass of red wine and sighed appreciatively. "Nothing like a good old-fashioned steak and chips, is there?"

Phelps agreed.

"Very satisfying and cooked to perfection, if I may say so, Sir."

"Thank you very much", replied Woodcock, "and I think it's time to drop the 'Sir'".

"Yes, Jack, if I may make so bold", Bill chimed in. "As far as I know I'm the only one who ever calls Colin by his first name, and I need company. The most familiar anyone gets at school is to address him as 'Headmaster'. Usually they either say 'Sir' or don't call him anything at all—not even 'Hey you'."

"That is unless you include what they call me behind my back", added Woodcock, referring to his nicknames; "Pegleg" for the more polite and "Prick" for the less.

"Well, Sir—I mean Colin—we don't need to go into that. 'Sirring' people is a bit of a habit with policemen and you decide instinctively who gets it and who doesn't. Something to do with money, position or education, but I couldn't really define it. Sometimes it's a way of keeping people in their place—like young Johnson, for instance—whereas with you it just seems natural. To someone who left school at sixteen and worked his way up through the ranks, a headmaster or even an ordinary schoolmaster of the old-fashioned sort is a person with authority. And as for you, er, Colin, your way of talking and the fact that you seem to know everything would do the trick even if you weren't a headmaster."

"That's right", said Bill, "and there's no need to blush. It's all true, but we love you anyway. Have another drink and tell Jack what we've been thinking about this 'ere skellington."

"All right, here goes, but with the proviso that some people who leave school at sixteen learn more than others who go to universities. Anyway, we were thinking that you must have records of missing people, but that that must open a huge field since you don't know within a few years when this young woman disappeared. In any case, it was wartime and people were disappearing in large numbers all over the country—some killed in the blitz, some going off to the war, and some disappearing from one place and reappearing in another. May I take it that you haven't found anything in the police records that jumps out at you?"

"We haven't finished looking, but that's true as far as the immediate locality is concerned, which suggests that she wasn't a local girl. She was at least fifteen and maybe sixteen or seventeen, so if she was still at school she would have been in the fifth or sixth form at one of the grammar schools, but we haven't been able to find any reports of sudden disappearances. And if she wasn't at school—well, talk about needles and haystacks! Unfortunately for us she also had a perfect set of teeth, so even if we did get a line on her, there wouldn't be any chance of a convenient dentist popping up and identifying her."

"Well then, to speculate a bit further, we wondered whether we could deduce something from the way she was buried. Am I right in thinking that the condition of the skeleton and the absence of clothing suggest that she had been buried elsewhere several years previously and moved to St. Mary's Square in 1945?"

"That's right, up to a point. The bones look as if they rolled about a bit after being placed in the coffin, and people are usually properly dressed when they're buried—but maybe not if it's a hurried or improvised burial after a murder. It would depend on what she was wearing when she died."

"We hadn't thought of that", said Bill. "Perhaps she wasn't wearing anything."

"It has been known to happen", Woodcock commented. "The enraged husband comes home to find his wife in bed with his best friend—although in this case it would have been the enraged wife. Anyway, it seems quite likely that St. Mary's Square was not the original burial place and that she had died several years previously."

Phelps smiled indulgently.

"It's very speculative, but on the whole I agree. By the time that building was going up our bit of the war had been over for a couple of months, and the disappearance of a young girl would have been far more noticeable."

"Good, then I'll go on to the next item—as far as all of the above goes, the girl might have come from anywhere, but the choice of burial place and the unaccountable presence of young Johnson at the building site on Friday suggest that local people were involved. If we assume that she died at some time in the middle of the war and that she was fifteen or sixteen it would mean that at the outbreak of war she was about twelve or thirteen. It occurred to Bill that at that time children were being moved about the country in large numbers and that under certain circumstances the disappearance of one of them might have been quite easy to cover up."

"Evacuees", said the inspector. "Now that's an idea."

"Yes", said Bill. "My parents had some for a while—twelve-year-olds from London. Of course, if one of them had disappeared they'd have told the police and got in touch with the parents—but suppose something had happened to the parents."

"There would still be uncles, aunts, cousins and whatnot. And what about the school they were going to?"

"It would have been easy enough to tell the school that the child had gone back to London. They would simply remove the name from the register, and if the child had been billeted on a respectable citizen, what do you think of the chances that any further enquiries would have been made?"

"So then Uncle Joe starts asking whatever happened to his missing niece!"

"Perhaps Uncle Joe doesn't exist."

"All I can say is it's possible and it's an interesting idea, but I don't quite see where it gets us."

"Certainly it's all speculation", Woodcock admitted, "but if we take it as a working hypothesis we may want to ask why a sixteen-year-old evacuee would still be in Gloucester. By that time the worst of the blitz was over and, in any case, children usually went home before reaching that age. I can think of two possibilities; she may have been a land girl rather than an evacuee or she may have still been at school here. In the latter case it may have been because she was doing well and wanted to take her Higher School Certificate and university entrance exams before leaving."

"That would have meant that she got on very well with the family she was staying with. Most people wanted to get rid of their evacuees as soon as they possibly could."

"Maybe she got on with them too well", said Bill. "Or one of them, at any rate."

Woodcock stuck to his point.

"If she was at school here it would have been Blenheim Hall or Finland Close, since they were the only girls' schools with fifth and sixth forms. So we would be looking for a fifth or sixth former who was an evacuee and who left abruptly a couple of years or so after the start of the war, and whose disappearance might have been explained away without arousing anyone's suspicions. I don't know anything about land girls, but I suppose there may be records of them somewhere. It also struck us, by the way, that she must have had some unusual qualities to inspire that poem, although I admit that there's no accounting for taste in that regard."

"We'll be getting on to the schools first thing on Monday, and this idea of an evacuee may help narrow it down a bit. We mustn't be too hopeful, but I will say that even when the speculation is completely up the pole it sometimes puts us on the right track. One problem is that we may have some trouble finding those old school registers. I mean if someone asked you for records of your school for 1942 and 1943 would you know where to lay your hands on them?"

"Frankly I wouldn't. For all I know they may have rotted away or been burnt. Ferrier is supposed to know that sort of thing."

"Ferrier!" growled the Inspector. "We think he was responsible for the report in this afternoon's *Citizen*."

"Which we haven't seen yet", said Bill. "It's down by the front door and we've been too lazy to go and get it."

"Don't bother—it has a picture of the site and a slick article revealing practically everything we know except the fractured skull. It even reports that the police intend to interview Henry Johnson."

"How do you know it was Ferrier?" asked Bill.

"Well, you see, apart from the police there were only three people who knew all those details."

"And you assumed it wasn't one of us"

"Right."

"Well, thank you very much. I hope you're going to tell us what he said."

"Who?"

"Young Johnson."

"Oh, yes—I was going to, as a matter of fact. You may be able to help me make up my mind about something."

So Phelps launched into an account of his dealings with Johnson and his associates and also of his visits to Bob Roberts and Siggy Harescombe.

"The thing is", he concluded, "it's obvious that Johnson has been up to something and that he knew what was under that concrete, but he's a sharp fellow and as far as we know he hasn't committed a crime. He's not going to give anything away. The problem is that I don't have much hope of getting anything from the school records, so maybe the only way of finding out who this girl is is through Johnson."

"It strikes me", said Bill, "that this *Citizen* article may be a blessing in disguise. It may ring a bell in somebody's head. Perhaps if you wait a little while something will turn up."

"Wilkins Micawber", commented Woodcock, "but I agree. Johnson must be on tenterhooks waiting to see what happens next, so perhaps he'll improve with keeping. Meanwhile, in view of some of the things you've been hearing, there's something I'll be very interested to see when they dig that hole."

"Whether it fills up with water?"

"Exactly."

Chapter XI

1940: Monday, November 18th

Susan had a rather difficult day at the infirmary. For all she knew Jill Simpson might already have reported Jessica's disappearance, so the first thing was to see her and find out how the land lay. Fortunately Jill was on the early shift, which made it more likely that she would want to talk to Susan before doing anything else. So at nine o'clock that morning Susan was in the nurses' room listening to Jessica's story told from a different point of view. She was very relieved, although not surprised, to find that in spite of the changed perspective the story sounded exactly the same. Jessica had told her the full and unembellished truth, which would seem remarkable to anyone who hadn't met Jessica. Susan, however, had to invent something, at least for the time being, and Mrs. Simpson's closing remarks gave her what she thought might turn out to be the key.

"And it's not just the embarrassment of having this girl come and after a few hours decide that we're not good enough for her. That's hard to bear, Mrs. Berkeley, but we were counting on that little bit of extra money. It wasn't much, but what with Mr. Simpson not being able to work and everything being so difficult, it would have helped a lot. What I want to know is who decides what's going to happen next. Apparently all she has is this Uncle James, and he's in the army and God knows where."

"I think", said Susan, "that it will be best if she stays with us for a few days while we get things sorted out. My husband knows her Uncle

109

James, and will probably be able to get in touch with him, so I don't think that you need feel any further responsibility for her. You did your part and what happened certainly isn't your fault."

"You don't think we could persuade her to try again? I have to tell you, Mrs. Berkeley, in spite of everything, I like that girl. She was really very polite to me and I admire a young woman with spirit. I mean when I think of her climbing out of that window and down the drainpipe and losing her skirt on the way back, I really have to laugh. And the way she talked to George. I wish I had the nerve."

Susan, who was not a natural prevaricator, was aware that her motives were confused, so it was with growing discomfort that she continued.

"I don't think so. She's a very determined young woman and at least we know where she is now, whereas if I tried to make her go back to you we might lose her altogether. As far as the money is concerned there's no need to do anything about it until we get Jessica settled. You've been put to a lot of trouble and inconvenience, so I think you've earnt it."

If Susan was hoping that the financial carrot would pacify the Simpsons and keep them quiet, her plan looked like being a success. Jill's anxious expression resolved into a revealing smile.

"Well, I can't say it won't help. And I'll be very relieved if I can just leave it all to you to settle."

That was how it was left, and Susan felt that she had accomplished the first part of her plan.

When Jessica got home from school it was almost dark, so she closed the blackout curtains, lit the living room fire, as instructed by Susan, and sat and watched it for a while. It would have been a good time to start on her homework, but she felt too restless to concentrate on algebra or French. She wandered about the house, looking in all the rooms, wishing that Susan would get home and, at the same time, feeling strangely apprehensive. She sat in front of the fire again but couldn't keep still, so she went into the front room and looked out of the window to see if Susan was coming. It was pitch dark, inside and out, and although Jessica knew that Susan must have done this journey scores of times, she worried about whether she would be able to find her way home. Groping her way back across the room she bumped into the piano, so she lifted the lid of the keyboard and played a few chords. It really was horribly out of tune, and she wondered how hard it would be to tune a piano. Back in the living room she sat down at the table and opened her algebra book. "Tom has 200 feet of fencing and wishes to make a rectangular garden with an area of 2,400 square feet. Calculate the dimensions of the rectangle."

Questions of this sort seemed very silly to Jessica. It was easy enough to get the right answer in ten seconds just by looking at the numbers, but this wasn't allowed. Naming a variable, setting up an equation and solving it took much longer, and nobody ever made a garden like that anyway.

It seemed to Jessica, in her young wisdom, that this was one of the problems of the world. In order to do what you really needed, or wanted to do, or even to say what you really meant, you always had to go through a lot of meaningless formalities. Why not just say, "If x plus y equals a hundred and x times y equals two thousand four hundred, find x and y"? As far as algebra was concerned she knew the official answer—you had to be able to change verbal relationships into symbolic equations—and presumably there might similarly be reasons for observing social formalities and distinctions that often seemed pointless and artificial. Susan, however, seemed unusually free of social red tape. In fact she seemed to be admirable in every possible way. Jessica had always been amiably contemptuous of her classmates when they developed crushes, but this was different; she was sure that none of them had ever met anyone like Susan. She wished that Susan could be there now, holding her in her arms, and it was with this picture that she suffered a sudden loss of confidence. Was it really possible that Susan, calm, efficient, responsible, worldly-wise and almost twice her age, loved her as much as she loved Susan? First names or not, Susan was part of the adult world whereas she, Jessica, was just a child doing her algebra homework. Susan was a good person and a nurse. Wasn't it much more likely that she was just being kind to a young schoolgirl who had lost her home and her parents, had been assaulted on the train as it carried her to a strange city, and had been leered at and bullied by the old man in whose house she was supposed to live? It hadn't felt like mere kindness, but now she wasn't so sure.

Jessica heard the front door key begin to turn. She got up and started to run, but abruptly stopped. It would be much more reassuring if Susan would run to her rather than her running to Susan.

Sitting in the bus on her way home, Susan knew exactly why she felt so unsettled and nervous. The object she had in mind was so compelling that she was using devious means to achieve it, even though she knew very well that she had not thought out all its implications. She was in love with Jessica, but she couldn't even begin to grapple with the questions of where it would go, what it would mean for her husband, and what would happen when her superiors decided to send her somewhere else. What she was doing was wrong and might well end in disaster, but she couldn't think about this either. What possessed her whole being, to the exclusion of all other considerations, was her vision of what was going to happen when she opened the front door—she and Jessica running into each other's arms.

When the bus stopped in front of the house Susan had her key ready. The darkness was not a problem, but as she was turning the key she was assailed by a wave of doubt, almost of panic, and a picture of the misery that her planned course of action might lead to. She stopped for a moment with the key half turned. Was there any way in which she could turn things back and restore commonsense ordinariness to her life? Could she bear to make the effort? She had committed herself that morning to keeping Jessica with her. She ought to be doing it in the capacity of a surrogate parent, but she doubted very much whether she could. For a moment she considered the possibility of finding another home for Jessica and somehow getting out of this mess; but the thought of losing her caused such an inner upheaval that she banished it immediately. Jessica would have to stay and Susan would have to do her best to survive her inner turmoil and behave like a responsible foster-mother. She stepped into the dark hall and saw Jessica standing at the door of the living room.

"Hello, Jessica", she said.

"Hello, Susan. I've lit the fire."

CHAPTER XII

1965: Sunday, December 19

On Sunday morning Inspector Phelps visited Miss Norbury, the headmistress of Finland Close for the past fifteen years, and was not surprised to find that nobody knew the whereabouts of the school registers from the wartime years. There was nothing more than twenty years old in the school, and Miss Norbury understood that everything from the years before her arrival had been stored in the basement of the Gloucester Public Library, where, she thought, it had probably rotted, since such places were notoriously damp and no one really cared about old school records anyway.

"Of course, we have all the Yearbooks back to the year dot", she said brightly, "but they probably won't be of much help since they give only the child's name, date of birth and House."

"House?" queried the inspector.

"Well, perhaps it's a quaint habit, but my late predecessor wanted to foster a sort of public school atmosphere here, so she divided the pupils into four houses, named after famous Old Girls. They competed against each other in sports and had little meetings but it was really meaningless. Frankly, the backgrounds of most of our girls make the idea of a public school atmosphere ridiculous. And they're none the worse for it. The best ones work much harder and achieve more than most public school girls. I understand that they still have Houses at Blenheim, but I stopped the practice here a few years ago. But there, I mustn't let my hobbyhorse distract you."

"Thank you, Ma'am. Could you tell me how many teachers you have who were here throughout the war? It's just possible that someone may remember a girl who suddenly disappeared."

"There are at least half a dozen, but only one or two whose memories I should trust. You could talk to Miss Bentley and Mrs. Ferguson. They were both in their twenties at the time and are not given to the kind of sentimental wool-gathering that afflicts some of our more elderly mistresses."

"That sounds like a good idea. Perhaps you could arrange for me to see them in the morning break tomorrow."

"Certainly. You can talk to them in my office at eleven o'clock—I expect you understand that I should prefer to keep you out of sight as far as possible."

"Yes, Ma'am. Tongues *will* wag, won't they."

Meanwhile, Sergeant Snipe was having a similar conversation with Miss Dwight, the headmistress of Blenheim Hall, and her colleague, Miss Evans, both of whom were dressed for badminton. Snipe noted that for a pair of middle-aged school teachers they looked unusually young and athletic, and tried to avoid staring at their legs.

"We're due at the court in ten minutes, Sergeant", said Miss Dwight, "but tell us what this is about so we're not left in suspense. I hope it's not Baker again."

Beryl Baker was a well-endowed fifth former who had been surprised *in flagrante delictu* with the groundsman in his hut at the Spa cricket ground adjacent to the school. The popular version of the story was that the groundsman had been putting a bun in Baker's oven.

"Well, I've only been here for two years", said Miss Dwight after hearing the nature of Snipe's errand, "but you were here throughout the war, weren't you, Gwynny?

"Yes, but that was a long time ago. Offhand I can't remember a girl simply vanishing from one day to the next. You see, I'm the physical education mistress and I see almost every child in the school for just one lesson a week, so it's very hard to remember a particular one from twenty or more years ago. Of course, there were a great many comings and goings during the war, but we usually knew where they were coming from or going to. By the way, we read the report in the local rag, but we thought they were probably making most of it up, so we didn't pay very much attention to it"

"Well, Ma'am, the factual stuff was pretty accurate, but we have some ideas that the reporter didn't get hold of. We think that this girl may have come to Gloucester near the beginning of the war as an evacuee. We don't know any of this for certain, but she might have been about thirteen then, which would mean that she probably died between 1941 and 1944. The most helpful thing would be to find the school registers from the wartime years. Otherwise we'll just have to rely on someone remembering something."

"I have to confess", said Miss Evans, "that when you put it that way my mind goes completely blank. Perhaps if I sleep on it I'll remember something."

"I doubt whether you'll have any luck with the registers", added Miss Dwight. "I wasted a great deal of time trying to put together the records for the past ten years and now you want us to look for something that happened twenty-five years ago. We'll do our best, course, but I'm not very optimistic. But I think it would probably be a good idea to talk to Miss Thrower. She was here throughout the war and may remember something helpful."

Snipe arranged to see Miss Thrower on the following day, and the two ladies slipped into their overcoats before disappearing with a roar in an old MG.

"Well", said Inspector Phelps to his sergeant an hour or so later, "it looks to me as if we'll have to do what Mrs. Marjoribanks said last night."

"What was that, Sir?"

"Wait for something to turn up."

"I suppose so, but it's very annoying."

"I know what you mean, but tell me your version."

"Well, as you were saying yesterday, there are people we've talked to who obviously know something, and we haven't got any way of getting it out of them."

"Meaning Johnson and his pals."

"Yes, Sir. I'm still wondering whether we ought to give them another grilling."

"So am I, but I'm hoping that whatever it is that turns up will give us a bit of leverage. That report in the *Citizen* may possibly stir something up. And then there's the funeral tomorrow. Somewhere there's someone who was in love with that girl, and I don't believe it's

Johnson. It's possible that whoever it was will be at the funeral and there may be some indication."

"Perhaps, but I'd call it a long shot at best."

"Before I make any comments I'd very much like to know what your parents thought about your escapade on Friday evening."

It was eleven o'clock on Monday morning, and Carter, Davies and Berry were standing in front of the headmaster's desk instead of letting off steam in the playground.

"You go first, Berry."

"Yes, Sir. My father was very angry. He said I had lied to him and then got mixed up with the police. And my mother cried. Oh, and he stopped my pocket money for three weeks."

"Davies?"

"They were very upset at first but I told them it had been very interesting and the police were very nice about it. My father said perhaps we could sell the story to the *Citizen*, so I told him we weren't allowed to do that and he got angry again. And I'm not allowed to go to the pictures until further notice."

"Carter?"

"My mother was a little bit nervous in case we'd been breaking the law, but my father laughed and said that if he'd known about it he'd have come and helped."

"So two of you have been punished and one hasn't, and that strikes me as being fair up to a point, since Carter seems to have been the most responsible member of the party in this episode, at least in the matter of the pouch containing the poem."

"Sir", said Davies, "may I say something?"

"By all means."

"Well, Sir, Carter wanted to go to the police even before Copper—I mean Constable Chard got there."

"Thank you. I'm glad to hear it. Now, I seem to remember that last time we had an interview like this I told you to be good citizens and not to get into any more mischief."

"That's what Mr. Hume said, Sir", remarked Davies. "I'm sorry, Sir, I didn't mean to interrupt—it's just that he said it when we were looking at the building site on Friday, and I just remembered."

"Well, it was very good advice, but I'm not sure that it would have been a good thing if you had taken it. I believe that you acted with good intentions and found something important, and that if you had asked for permission to do your investigations you probably wouldn't have got it. I strongly disapprove of your lying to your parents but as far as that goes it was up to them to decide what to do. I have decided not to take any further action—but just remember Mr. Hume's advice next time you're cooking up one of your little schemes."

Davies started to speak, got as far as saying, "Sir", and then became completely tongue-tied. Carter helped him out.

"Sir, I think what he wanted to say is that we are very lucky to have you for our headmaster."

Now it was Woodcock's turn to be tongue-tied. He had a high opinion of these particular boys and was quite touched at receiving such an unusual compliment, which he thought was probably not just soft soap. He quickly pulled himself together.

"It's kind of you to say so. I feel very lucky to be here. Now run along before I change my mind."

Inspector Phelps's visit to Finland Close proved frustrating, not because the two women were unable to think of anyone who might have answered the given description, but because there were too many possibilities.

"You seem to remember practically every pupil who ever came here", he remarked when he had finished writing down the list of names, forms and ages that he had been given. "But it's going to be hard to track these young ladies down since it seems that you don't know where any of them lived."

"Well, that's the way it usually is", said Miss Bentley. "We work very closely with the girls, especially when they get into the upper forms, but we have very little to do with the parents. And, you see, we both threw ourselves very deeply into the work here because in the first year of the war Jane lost her husband and I lost my fiancé."

"I'm very sorry. I can only hope that you have found your work rewarding."

"It is and it isn't", said Jane Ferguson. "Many of the girls are wonderful, of course, but I'd rather have worked with a few of my own children than with hundreds of other people's. Every so often one comes along that you wish had been your own daughter, but then after a few years she's gone and you know that to her you're just her old History teacher. Forgive me, Inspector, I shouldn't be going on like this."

"That's all right, Ma'am. Life must have been very hard for the thousands of women who lost their menfolk in the war."

"Yes", said Miss Bentley, "and by the time it was over most of us felt that we were pretty firmly on the shelf."

Meanwhile, Snipe was having a rather different kind of interview at Blenheim Hall. It appeared that Miss Dwight was less concerned than her colleague at Finland Close about the possible effects of the sight of a policeman wandering through her school, so the talk took place amid a buzz of conversation in the common room, where tea was served in thick mugs. Miss Thrower, tall and wiry, with dark, greying hair and a pugnacious expression, looked like an alert sort of person who might be expected to have a good memory, but she turned out not to be very helpful.

"I'm sorry, Sergeant. No one in particular springs to mind. We certainly had evacuees here but I can't recall anyone disappearing in unusual circumstances."

"The circumstances would not necessarily have seemed unusual."

Miss Thrower thought a little longer.

"No, I'm sorry, I really don't think I can remember anything helpful."

"All right, Ma'am. If you do think of anything please let us know."

As Snipe rose and turned away he almost bumped into Gwyneth Evans, and had the impression that she had been listening to the conversation.

"I'm sorry", he said. "I don't suppose you've remembered anything since yesterday."

"No, I'm afraid not."

At a quarter past four on Monday afternoon the funeral service for the unknown victim was held at St. Mary's Church. That hour was chosen so that Woodcock, Bill and any other interested members of the school staff could attend. Phelps, Snipe and Ferrier were also present. By this time most of the inhabitants of Gloucester had read the *Citizen's* romantic story of the remains of young girl found amid the snows of Christmas, with a poem from her mysterious lover.

Phelps was not surprised to find the church crowded.

"Wonderful thing, curiosity", he remarked to his sergeant as they looked for a vacant pew. "I'd be willing to bet that most of these people don't see the inside of a church from one year's end to another."

"Maybe it's not just curiosity", replied Snipe. "Look who's just come in."

The inspector gave a low whistle.

"Johnson", he said. "And do you suppose that's Mrs. Johnson?"

"I don't know. She looks a few years older than he does."

Johnson's companion was heavily muffled and did not remove her hat. The impression of age came more from the way she walked and leaned on Johnson's arm than from her actual appearance. They were followed by another man whom Snipe identified as Arthur Williams.

Meanwhile, Woodcock, who had arrived early and was seated discreetly at the back of the church, was remarking to his secretary that apart from Siggy Harescombe, who was sitting in obscurity by one of the side aisles, the school didn't seem to be very well represented.

"No", said Bill, "so far I've only seen Aggie Bagwell and his wife—oh, and there's John Hume and Dotty."

Dotty and Hume were standing by the church door, having apparently decided that there was no longer any chance of finding a seat.

The plain coffin, statutorily provided by the City of Gloucester, was topped by three wreaths, one from the Rector, one, as Bill found out later, from the headmaster, and one of unknown origin. The choir being unavailable at this time, there was no music except for the *Nunc Dimittis*, and in the absence of regular church-goers it might well have become an organ solo if it had not been for the combined efforts of Bill,

Woodcock and the sexton, whose voice resembled that of an amplified gnat. After the service, as the headmaster descended the church steps into the chilly dusk he found that Thomas Hardy's *Choirmaster's Burial* was running through his mind.

> *'I think', said the Vicar,*
> *'A read service quicker*
> *Than viols out of doors*
> *In these frosts and hoars.'*

The steps were icy and, having slipped on the bottom one, he was saved from a nasty fall by the long arms of John Hume.

"Thank you very much", he gasped. "It just shows that it's better not to be thinking about poetry when one is on a slippery staircase."

"Oh? What were you thinking about?"

"The Choirmaster's Burial"

"Hardy, and *Winter Words* at that—how extraordinarily appropriate. Yes, Hardy would have understood."

Hume turned abruptly and walked away.

"Now what did he mean by that?" asked Dotty.

"I don't know", replied Woodcock, but he looked very thoughtful.

"It was good of you to come, Dotty", said Bill.

"Well, according to what I read in the paper she was about the same age I am, and I thought she might like to have someone of her own age here. Of course that's silly, she's much older now, but somehow . . . I don't know, it seems like something you might read in a book, with that poem being in the coffin. I wish I could read it."

"I'm sure you will eventually, when the police have finished investigating."

"You saw it, didn't you Mrs. Marjoribanks?"

"Yes. It was very touching—and very mysterious."

"Very mysterious indeed", remarked Inspector Phelps, who, with Snipe at his shoulder, had been standing just behind Dotty and listening to the conversation.

"Oh, Inspector, you startled me", exclaimed Dotty, "creeping up on me like that."

"He didn't creep", said Bill. "He was just standing there waiting to get a word in edgeways."

"I'm sorry, Miss Ayers. Sometimes the police do have to creep up on people, but I really didn't intend to this time. If I may, I'd like to have a word with Mr. Woodcock and Mrs. Marjoribanks."

"I've got something to show you", said the inspector after Dotty had politely departed. "I think it calls for another session in the headmaster's office."

Much to the relief of the policemen, Nave House was warmer than it had been on Saturday morning. Phelps took an envelope from his pocket.

"I want you to look at this", he said. "The Rector found it with one of the wreaths on the coffin at the end of the service when they were about to take it off to the cemetery for the burial. That's where he is now, but he'll be back in an hour or so in case we want to talk to him." Handling the envelope very carefully he removed a piece of typewritten foolscap which he held by the corners and unfolded on the headmaster's desk.

"You're our official poetry-reader, Bill", said Woodcock.

So Bill read:

She dances o'er the gentle springing grass,
And feels the leaves caress her dainty toes.
The daffodils and bluebells see her pass,
And nod and curtsey to her as she goes.
At evening, when the light is dim and dying,
At morning, when the dewdrops shyly glisten,
She sings her song and sets the world to sighing,
While all the songbirds hear and pause and listen.
Now by her tender magic held in thrall,
The woodland creatures worship at her feet,
And follow her, obedient to her call,
High and haunting, soft and strange and sweet,
While swaying branches stir the scented air
To kiss her and caress her golden hair.

"There", Bill couldn't resist adding, "I told you something might turn up."

"What do you think?" asked Phelps, who had come to regard Bill and Woodcock as literary authorities.

"Well", said the latter, "It's in Shakespearean sonnet form—three quatrains and a couplet—but it's plainly not Shakespeare, if that's what you were wondering."

"That's what I thought. It just doesn't sound like Shakespeare."

"It sounds like someone who's been reading too much Victorian and Edwardian poetry", remarked Bill. "With a little bit of Tolkien thrown in, perhaps. It's quite neat in its way, but it's not in the same class as the other one."

"So you think it wasn't written by the same person?"

"That's a hard question. What do you think, Colin?"

"It *is* a hard question. Let's put it this way: if this had been very similar in style and accomplishment to the other one, it would have been natural to assume they were written by the same person. They do have a certain amount in common—that predilection for old-fashioned imagery that we noticed in the earlier one—but this one simply accepts a sort of fairyland convention and sticks to it, whereas the other one seems much more knowing or world-weary. That doesn't mean it couldn't have been written by the same author, but it does make one wonder. Incidentally, I think Bill was a bit hard on it. You have to admit that of its kind it's pretty well done—the little conceit at the end, for instance, as if the branches were stirring the air instead of the air stirring the branches."

"I know", said Bill. "It's just that I don't like the kind. But then, I have the same reaction to some of Shakespeare's sonnets."

"You're not saying that this could be by Shakespeare after all, are you?" asked the inspector.

"Oh, no, not at all. It's really the other way round—I've always found it difficult to believe that some of Shakespeare's sonnets are by Shakespeare."

Phelps digested this remark for a moment before returning to the chase.

"What I'd really like to know is whether there was anyone at the service who we think might—or could—have written this. I'd like us to put our heads together and make a list of everyone we saw there who has any conceivable connection to this case. I suspect it's less than a handful even if we stretch our imaginations a bit. The only ones I saw were Johnson, his friend Arthur Williams, and Mr. Bagwell."

"Well", said Bill, "if you're really going to be imaginative you might as well include Siggy Harescombe, but I can't think of anyone else."

Inspector Phelps looked enquiringly at Woodcock.

"I didn't see anyone else who has any association with the case that I'm aware of", said the headmaster. "I don't know anything about Williams, but from your descriptions Johnson doesn't sound like a likely poet. Apart from his archaeological passions Bagwell has always struck me as a prosaic soul. Harescombe is a different matter, but I can't help feeling that if he had written a sonnet it would have been . . ."

"Better" suggested Bill.

"Not exactly—more grown up, perhaps, and totally different in tone. Siggy has a tendency towards sardonic humor which is never absent for long at a time. I doubt whether he could write as many as fourteen lines without a hint of self-mockery showing through, whereas our unknown friend clearly takes himself much too seriously. Not very helpful, Jack, but it's the best I can do."

"On the whole then, the appearance of this sonnet suggests that there's someone else involved who is still unknown to us and was present at the funeral."

"It certainly looks like it", said Bill.

After the policemen had left, Bill looked accusingly at Woodcock and said, "You've got something up your sleeve, haven't you."

"It's nothing very much—just a vague idea."

"Something to do with poetry?"

"In a way."

"Yes?" said Bill hopefully.

"Not yet—I have to think about it first."

Meanwhile, Phelps had a question for his sergeant:

"Why would young Johnson come to the funeral if he has no connection with the dead girl?"

"Beats me, Sir. Maybe we should go and ask him."

"Maybe we should. 'Into the valley of death rode the six hundred.'"

"I beg your pardon?"

"Oh, nothing—just something I was thinking about."

Chapter XIII

1940: Monday Night, November 18th

Susan sat up in bed. She obviously wasn't going to be able to sleep, so she might as well try to think things out. The trouble was that thinking had become almost impossible. In the morning she had felt that she and Jessica had made a commitment to each other. She wanted Jessica to stay with her, Jessica wanted to stay, and they had hugged and kissed each other, not like an adult and child but like a pair of lovers. Susan hadn't experienced this kind of attraction since she had been Jessica's age and had fallen in love with the precocious blonde next door. She remembered this episode with shame and embarrassment, not because of any particular scruples about same-sex attractions, but because the precocious blonde had used her, while secretly laughing at her. That was long ago, but the present situation brought it back vividly and painfully. She was in love with Jessica and had thought that Jessica felt the same way about her; but now she was scared that this had simply been wishful thinking.

Wishful thinking or not, the picture of herself lying with Jessica in her arms wouldn't go away, and the only surprising thing was the speed at which the situation had developed. There was no repugnance at the thought of feeling that way about someone of her own sex. What offended the moral and rational sides of her makeup was that she was thinking of this fifteen-year-old girl as a potential lover when she was really supposed to be acting as a parent. And the thought of living with her in the same house as a parent when she wanted to be a lover was intolerable. Yet that was what the arrangement now was. The idea that Jessica would stay in the house by herself when Susan was away from Gloucester had been an essential part of Susan's plan for keeping her. Before going to bed that evening they had agreed that that was what would happen, since Susan did not see how she could retract the offer. Now it seemed totally irresponsible, for she could imagine all kinds of situations—illness or difficulties at school, for instance—in which the absence of a parent or guardian would be a serious problem.

Susan's preoccupation with Jessica didn't prevent the figure of her husband from hovering tenuously around the edges of her thought. Was it possible that she no longer loved him? He was still the same person, and the only thing that he had done wrong was to join the navy five years ago when he could have stayed with her. She couldn't really blame him; it had seemed to him to be the best thing at the time, and she had allowed herself to be persuaded. She tried to convince herself that if he had stayed they might be living in their little cottage now, and she wouldn't have got herself into this situation—but now that it had happened she wasn't sure. It was possible that something like this had been inevitable, and it left her with a question that she couldn't answer; how would she respond to John when he finally came home? Well, the only way out of it was a strait and narrow path which she would have to follow if she could. She would do her best to behave like a parent, and perhaps after a while she could find somewhere else where Jessica would be able to live. She believed that she had made a decision and that doing so ought to bring her some repose, but as soon as she lay down and tried to sleep, her desire for Jessica silenced the voice of reason and left her with the most painful perception of all: that almost certainly Jessica loved her simply as a warm and comforting adult presence, a substitute for her mother.

After so many tumultuous days Jessica was bone weary, but she, too, was unable to sleep. Susan had been so warm and loving in the morning, and now she seemed cold and distant. Jessica thought perhaps it was her own fault, and blamed herself for not running straight to the door and hugging Susan when she got home. She thought that her hesitation, her loss of confidence, had cost her a whole evening of happiness and perhaps a great deal more. She tried to dwell on the good things. Susan had told her that she could stay as long as she liked, so she no longer had to face the prospect of an endless succession of days and nights with the Simpsons. She had got through her first day at school, without anything awful happening. Miss Thrower seemed to like her, and some of the girls had been quite friendly. It came as a shock to realize that the events of the last day-and-a-half had almost driven her parents out of her consciousness, and she was momentarily overwhelmed with remorse and a sense of irremediable loss. They were gone, and now Susan seemed to be gone too. The thought finally crystallized in her that she was in love with Susan and that her mother had been right about being in love, except for the hopeless inadequacy of the word she had used. "Uncomfortable" was a bad joke. The only cure for the excruciating pain that filled her soul and body would be for Susan to hold her tightly in her arms as she had done early in the day, sending her off to school in a mood in which she could have conquered the world with one hand tied behind her back. Her resolution that there would be no more tears broke down again as exhaustion gradually carried her across the borderline of uneasy sleep.

Jessica was floating in a huge void. It was very dark, warm and blessed. Now there were grass and trees and a gentle breeze, and there was Susan, dressed in a long white gown, open at the breast. Her arms were outstretched and welcoming, and Jessica ran into her strong embrace. She looked at Susan's face and screamed because it was the face of Jill Simpson. Jessica sank to the ground and as Mrs. Simpson ripped the clothes from her a rasping voice said, "Hold her down for me." It was George Simpson, but he was dressed as a soldier and he had a rifle in his hand. He aimed the rifle at Jessica and pulled the trigger. Jessica didn't feel anything, but she thought she must be dead. It was a very strange feeling, as if her lungs had stopped working. It felt good to be dead, but now someone was shaking her. Reluctantly she stirred.

"Jessica, Jessica, darling, wake up!"

Jessica was terrified and it took some time for her to realize that she was in bed. The room was completely dark.

"Susan? Is it you?"

"Yes, my sweet, it's me."

"I think I must have been dreaming. I thought I was dead."

"I know—I heard you screaming."

Jessica sat up and Susan knelt by the bed and put her arms round her.

The miseries of the previous evening came flooding back into Jessica's mind.

"Do you love me, Susan?" she asked.

"Yes, my darling, I love you very much."

"Why didn't you love me when you came home?"

"I did love you and I'll always love you, only I was afraid that I was getting it wrong."

"I love you and I was afraid too. I'm sorry. Now I know you love me I'll be all right."

"But my poor darling, you're soaked in perspiration."

"It was very hot."

"Come with me."

Susan took Jessica's hand and guided her to her own bedroom, stopping on the way to get a towel from the linen closet. She was about to switch on her bedside lamp, but thought better of it and lit a candle. She helped Jessica to take off her nightgown and gave her an expert rubdown. She told herself that she was doing what any nurse would do in the circumstances, but she knew it was a lie. She was the lover, not the calm, competent nurse. The towel slipped from her hands and she kissed Jessica's breasts.

"Is it all right, Jessica?"

"Yes, I like it. I like it very much."

"Slip into bed and I'll find you something to wear."

Jessica did as she had been told but said, "Don't bother—you made me feel so warm and lovely I want to stay like this."

Susan slipped off her own nightgown and got into bed.

"I wanted to be like you, Jessica", she said, her voice shaking a little.

"And I want to be like you."

"Do you think you can sleep now?"

"I don't think so, but not because of the nightmare. I want to tell you something first—something that happened on the train. It was in my dream somehow, all mixed up with Mr. Simpson."

"I thought there was something."

"Put your arms round me and I'll try to tell you."

Lying in Susan's arms Jessica told her about the assault by the three soldiers and her rescue by Sergeant Willis.

"I've never been so frightened", she went on, "only it wasn't like being frightened in the ordinary way. I mean, you know what it's like when you nearly fall down the stairs or when you nearly get run over. It takes some time for your tummy to turn the right way up again. But the worst thing that could happen is that you would be dead, and if you're not dead you soon feel all right again. Now I can understand those stories about Lucretia and Susannah. You would never feel all right again and you would *rather* be dead. And while I was being so frightened my body was all churning inside, as if it knew what was going to happen to it. It was all very beastly, but somehow I've been managing not to think about it. Sergeant Willis was very sweet to me and then I met you and John. But yesterday there was Mr. Simpson. The way he looked at me was really horrible. I know he watched me having my bath. I couldn't bear it. But, Susan, now I'm here with you like this and it's the most heavenly thing I've ever known. You could do anything you like and I wouldn't be afraid. The way I feel inside is sort of like a car with the engine running, all ready to go. I didn't know it could be like this and I want it to go on for ever. I don't want to go to sleep."

"My poor darling, I didn't know either. You've made my engine run so fast I can hardly stand it, so let's make the most of now and not worry about for ever."

"The only thing is", said Jessica, "I don't really know how to drive."

"I don't think I know much more than you do, darling. I've never done this before. We'll just have to do some exploring."

"I'm so glad, Susan. We can learn together."

So they made the most of now and then they slept in each other's arms for a long time.

"I suppose we ought to get up", Susan said dreamily.

"I suppose so", said Jessica.

It was seven o'clock and the reluctant November daylight was seeping into the outside world. The blackout curtains were still drawn, so Jessica switched on the bedside light.

"Susan, do you think I look different?"

"Not really—just a little more beautiful."

"I feel so different that I'm sure people are going to notice."

Susan sat up and asked anxiously, "Is it all right? I mean you don't hate me or anything, do you?"

Jessica smiled, put out the light and took Susan in her arms again.

"Why? Because you've corrupted me? But I wanted to be corrupted—only I don't believe it was corruption, not when we love each other so much. It would only be corruption if you seduced me just for the thrill of it. Besides, they could just as easily say that I seduced you."

"And I would just say, 'Well I wanted her to'. But it wasn't seduction any more than it was corruption. It was more like two little birds learning to fly together, it all seemed so natural."

"Yes", said Jessica with no trace of defensiveness in her tone, "it really is natural, no matter what anyone says. Do you think it's because I've been thrown out of my nest?"

"Perhaps. And I haven't really got a nest at the moment."

"Susan, may I sleep with you again tonight?"

"Of course—only let's light a fire in here. Well, come to think of it, I suppose we already did, but I mean in the fireplace."

"Yes—it's so inconvenient when we have to stay under the blankets all the time."

Susan laughed.

"You have a most adorable way of putting things. Of course, it means we won't be able to have a fire in the living room, but we can keep warm in the kitchen."

"And we can go to bed very early."

Susan held Jessica in her arms a moment longer. She wasn't sure if her young lover realized how fragile this extreme happiness was.

"And Susan, one day soon I'll be able to call you 'darling'. I don't know why it is, but I can't quite do it yet. So every time I say 'Susan' it means 'I love you'."

"I know, darling. Now let's go and get you ready for school."

It was cold in the bathroom but neither seemed to notice. Soon there was a plentiful supply of hot water coming from the geyser, accompanied by the sounds of splashing, laughter and singing.

CHAPTER XIV

1965: Tuesday, December 22

On the day after the funeral something else turned up, in the shape of a letter from London. As Woodcock had predicted, it was a result of the report in the *Citizen*. Inspector Phelps read it, with Sergeant Snipe peering over his shoulder.

Dear Inspector Phelps,

In 1940 I was the physical education teacher at Greville's School in

London. In November of that year a pupil named Jessica Smith, who had lost almost her entire family in the blitz, stayed with me for three weeks before being evacuated to Gloucester. The only remaining person who was close to her was the divorced husband of her mother's sister, Major James Philips. Major Phillips arranged that Jessica should live with a Mr. and Mrs. Simpson, but unfortunately I do not know their address. Jessica was fifteen years old, tall, slender and, to my eyes at least, strikingly beautiful, with long black hair.

Jessica and I were on very friendly terms and we promised to write to each other. I received one letter in which she said that she would not, after all, be staying with the Simpsons and would write again shortly to let me know where she was. That was the last I heard from her, and I became concerned because Jessica had impressed me as someone who would not willingly break a promise. After several months had gone by I tried to get into touch with Major Phillips, only to find, after many enquiries, that he had been killed in action in North Africa. It then occurred to me that I might be able to find something out by writing to the headmistress at Blenheim Hall, Jessica's school in Gloucester. I learnt from Miss Alderley that Jessica had become a pupil there in November, had stayed for two months and had then gone back to London. According to Miss Alderley, Jessica had lived with the Simpsons and it was they who had informed the school of her departure. Everything seemed plain and above-board to Miss Alderley, and she told me that I was worrying unnecessarily. Girls, she said, tended to be flighty and to forget promises, and Jessica, in spite of her remarkable capacities, was, after all, really only a child.

I found Miss Alderley's account of things rather difficult to accept. If conditions had been different I might have gone to Gloucester to investigate, but I had recently decided to join the W.R.N.S. and the journey was impossible.

I am sure you will have realized that my letter to you is prompted by my having seen the report in the Gloucester Citizen, which a friend who happened to have been traveling through Gloucester showed to me yesterday. I have always hoped that Jessica was alive somewhere, for she was very dear to me, but at the same time there has been a conviction, which I have been unable to dispel, that something happened to her in Gloucester. I cannot believe that anyone would ever have deliberately hurt her but, in trying to think of her objectively, I realize that she had an unusual degree of what I believe is known as personal magnetism, the ability effortlessly to inspire personal devotion and, perhaps, poetry too.

I realize also that there is very little chance that the remains that you have found will be identified as those of my dear Jessica, but I hope that you will be kind enough to let me know if there is any such possibility.

Yours faithfully,
Veronica Edwards.

"What do you think, Snipey?"

"Well, she was a bit older than we thought—when she was evacuated, I mean—and maybe a bit younger when she died, but she was tall for her age, which fits, and so does that bit about losing her entire family—nobody much left to make awkward enquiries. I think we should go and talk to Miss Thrower straight away. I had a feeling that Miss Dwight thought her memory might be better than Miss Evans's, but we could talk to her too. If this rings a bell with either of them we could ask Miss Edwards to come down here and get them all to compare notes."

"Excellent. I'm beginning to get a feeling about this."

Phelps and Snipe arrived at Blenheim Hall just after the end of afternoon school and tracked Miss Thrower down in her classroom, where she was working on a large stack of end-of-term exam papers.

"Hello", she said with a rueful smile, "I hope you've come to distract me from my work for a little while."

"I'm afraid this won't take long, Miss Thrower", replied the inspector, "but I could lend you a match if that would help."

"That's a very interesting suggestion, particularly when it comes from a respectable policeman, but I'm afraid I'll have to stick to the path of duty. Are you still on the trail of the missing girl?"

"Yes, we are, and we'd like you to tell us whether you remember a girl called Jessica Smith who came to the school from London in November, 1940 and went back there in January or February of 1941."

Penny Thrower hesitated before replying in a troubled voice:

"You think it might have been Jessica?"

"We don't know, but there is a possibility and it would be very helpful if you'd tell us what you remember of Jessica's arrival and departure."

"Jessica made quite an impression on most of us here, so even though this was twenty-five years ago there's no difficulty in remembering. When she came here she had lost nearly all her possessions and had only the clothes she stood up in. I first met her when Miss Alderley took her to the clothing room, where we kept school uniforms and other articles given by pupils who were leaving. There was a young woman with her, who turned out not to be the person she was staying with, but I can't remember her name. There was some difficulty because Jessica was both taller and slimmer than most of our girls, but eventually we found some things that were a pretty good fit."

"It would be very helpful if we could identify the young woman you mentioned."

"All I can tell you is that she had red hair, seemed to be in her late twenties and was very self-possessed without being unduly assertive—a professional person of some sort, I should think. I'll do my best to remember her name, but I'm very much afraid that it's really gone."

"And did you ever meet the people she lived with?"

"Only at the very end, and Jessica was extremely reluctant to talk about them. One day in January a woman came to the school to tell us that Jessica had been called back to London and would not be returning. She said that some family friends were going to take her in. And for some reason I do remember her name. It was Simpson."

"What sort of impression did she make?"

"She was middle-aged, plump and bossy in a friendly kind of way. I didn't see much of her, though. She saw Miss Alderley first and then she came to the classroom to collect the few belongings that Jessica had left in her desk. Oh yes, the reason why I remember her name is that she was an Old Girl and after she'd gone Miss Alderley went on about her at some length."

"And you were given to understand that Jessica had been staying with the Simpsons throughout her two months here?"

"Not in so many words but, yes, that was my impression. Why do you ask?"

"Because we have information that Jessica wrote to a friend in London and told her that she would be living somewhere else. Unfortunately she didn't say where. We were hoping that you would know."

"No, she didn't say anything about it to me. I think she must have stayed with the Simpsons after all."

"Do you know where the Simpsons lived?"

"I'm afraid not. When we need a pupil's address we go to the office for it, but that usually only happens when there's a problem, and there weren't any problems with Jessica. But I'd have thought that the education office would have all that stuff somewhere."

Inspector Phelps sighed.

"Somewhere, perhaps, but nobody seems to know where. Tell me more about Jessica."

"Well, you know, she was always very hard to talk about because one never really knew what was going on inside. She was a very good child in every possible way—always neat, clean and very polite. She was attentive in class and always did her homework. You might have thought that she was going out of her way to be unobtrusive and yet she was nearly always the center of attention. I don't think she ever put herself forward in any way, but one was always conscious of her presence, and when a question came up people always wanted to know what Jessica thought."

"Did she have any special interests—anything she was passionate about?"

"She seemed to be interested in everything. She always wanted to know the truth and the reasons for things and in her quiet way she was very adventurous. Most of our girls are, shall I say, moderately gifted, so I have to teach in a slow, methodical way. Jessica did all that was required and never even hinted that she would like to go a little faster, but whenever I gave the class the opportunity to tackle a harder problem or try a different method she jumped at the chance. Well, perhaps 'jumped' isn't the right word. As I said, she was never in any way obtrusive. I do know that some of her other teachers had a similar impression."

"Did she make any particular friends?"

"I don't think so. Most of the girls seemed to be a little afraid of her, and I believe she made some of her teachers a little nervous—but that, again, gives the wrong impression. As far as I know, Jessica never did anything to frighten anyone. It's just the way she was—as if there was always something in reserve, as if she might have been able to blow you out of the water if she had wanted to, but she never wanted to. And, once again, that really overstates it. That's why I said she was very hard to talk about. You sensed all these things about her but when you tried to put them into words they never came out right. I am sure that Jessica was a very kindhearted girl and that her politeness and reserve were genuinely part of her character. I don't think she really knew how gifted she was."

"Were you aware of any problems in her life?"

"Only that she missed her parents very much. I thought she was amazingly happy, considering the circumstances."

"Could you tell me whether there are any other teachers still here who knew Jessica?"

"Not many. You see, 5A was always rather a privileged class. They were the top stream and they were preparing for the School Certificate, so they always had the best or, at least, the most experienced teachers. It was only by chance that I had them—the senior maths mistress, Miss Hoyle, was taken ill at the beginning of term and never fully recovered. Let's see—she had Miss Wenlock for English and Miss Rockingham for history. Unfortunately, Miss Rockingham died at least ten years ago and Miss Wenlock is in a nursing home somewhere. There was Miss Toddington for French, and she was the one teacher I remember who professed not to like Jessica. It was generally believed in the staff room that it was because Mlle. Bouvier, the French *assistante*, let it be known that Jessica's accent was better than hers. The only other person I can think of who might know anything is Miss Evans, her gym teacher—children do sometimes talk to their gym teachers in ways that they don't talk to others. She's probably still there, putting things away."

"Thank you—we've met Miss Evans and we would certainly like to talk to her again. I gather that you liked Jessica."

"I liked her very much", said Miss Thrower, with an undercurrent of feeling that was unusual for such a matter-of-fact person.

"Just one more question—could you describe her hair?"

"It was long and black, very soft and fine, but usually she kept it in a bun. May I ask why you think it was Jessica?"

"Because the friend who wrote to us thinks that Jessica never returned to London."

After a year or two of living near the border, Inspector Phelps had come to the conclusion that there were two kinds of Welsh people. One was small, redheaded and mercurial, and the other was tall, dark-haired and melancholic. Gwyneth Evans, however, was somewhere in between, being of medium height, and although she was in her late forties her skin was clear and her brown hair was untouched by grey. She looked immensely fit and Phelps was pretty sure that she could move like a greyhound if the occasion arose. Her description of Jessica, given in a voice that retained some of its youthful eagerness, tallied very closely with Miss Thrower's.

"She was absolutely fearless. You should have seen her on the vaulting horse. Of course, she was taller than most of our girls, but it was more a matter of attitude and, I believe, trust. She seemed to think that if I thought she could do it, she *could* do it, and she wasn't afraid to let herself go flying through the air. She trusted me to be there to catch her if she made an awkward landing. I thought she had it in her to become a very accomplished gymnast, and I remember asking her if she would like to do a little extra work after school, but she always seemed to want to get home as early as possible."

"Do you know why that was?"

"Not really, but it may just have been because she was so happy there."

"Did she tell you that?"

"Yes—I asked her one day whether the people she was living with were treating her well, and all she said was, 'Oh, yes', but the way she said it spoke volumes. Apart from that she was very reticent."

"So you don't know who she was living with."

"No, I'm afraid not."

"Well, that seems definite enough up to a point", said Inspector Phelps as the two policemen walked back to the station. "Miss Edwards's Jessica and Miss Thrower's Jessica were the same girl, and I have a hunch that it was Jessica who ended up in St. Mary's Square, but I'm not sure how much forrader that gets us. We're going to have to track down this Mrs. Simpson and the freckled redhead whose name we don't know. And we still have no idea how young Johnson comes into this. One thing I'm sure of is that that girl wasn't buried in St. Mary's Square in 1941. It's not impossible, I suppose, but there must have been thousands of more convenient places to put a body away."

"Yes, Sir. It would have been pitch dark in the square and anyone messing about with torches and shovels would surely have been spotted. In any case, we don't know when she died. She may have been living somewhere else and come back to Gloucester in 1945. She may really have gone back to London."

"Maybe, but I'm pretty sure she was already a skeleton when she got to the square, and I'm all but certain that it was young Johnson who put her there. But I don't think he killed her."

"No, Sir, and that means he's protecting someone."

"Grrr."

"I agree", said Snipe, and then maintained a respectful silence until they were sitting in the inspector's office.

"OK, Snipey, what do we do next, apart from hunting for those women?"

"Well, Sir, something struck me about both those ladies at Blenheim Hall and about Miss Edwards. I wondered whether it had struck you too."

"They were all in love with her?"

"Well, devoted to her, at any rate."

"Come on, Snipey, don't tell me you've never seen that kind of thing before."

"All right, Sir, but mostly in the villages where there's a lot of, hmmm, inbreeding, so to speak. I any case I don't think Miss Evans was in love with her and I'll bet whatever Miss Thrower's feelings may have been she kept things under control."

Phelps would have liked to hear Snipe's definition of 'inbreeding', but he stuck to the point.

"All right, let's settle for devoted then. And you were thinking that if we put them all together and let them talk, something might emerge. By the way, did anything else strike you about Miss Thrower and Miss Evans?"

"Yes, Sir."

"All right, out with it then!"

"Well, there's this girl who's an evacuee and who unexpectedly disappears overnight, and we have these two women who were devoted to her or in love with her and seem to remember everything about her—but it didn't occur to either of them to mention her when asked quite specifically whether they remembered any evacuees disappearing during the war."

"Exactly. So what's the explanation?"

"I don't know, but if they had something to do with Jessica's disappearance, we'd still have to explain why young Johnson has shown such an interest in St. Mary's Square."

"Grrr!"

Chapter XV

1940: Wednesday, November 20

Susan and Jessica were considerate lovers, and after a while the honeymoon settled down to a comfortable routine. The bedroom with its fire was very cozy, and Jessica discovered that she liked to do her homework sitting up in bed with a tray on her lap. Susan had paper work to do to, so she did likewise, and when they weren't out at work or school they spent most of their time in bed. On their third evening together Susan opened a drawer under her dressing table and took out four nightgowns, all neatly folded and wrapped in tissue paper.

"Look", she said. "It's delicious going to bed like Adam and Eve but maybe it would be nice to dress up sometimes. And anyway, they don't hide very much. What do you think?"

"I think it would be fun. Oh, look, this one is for you."

It was a pale diaphanous green, quite short and cut very low, with slender straps.

"Look, it goes perfectly with your hair. Do put it on."

Susan hesitated.

"I'm sorry, darling," she said in a troubled voice. "I had forgotten. It has . . . associations. One day when we've been together a little longer I'll wear it for you, but I don't think I can yet. Please don't be upset—it's just that you've made my life so wonderful and I don't want to think about the time before you came to me. Wouldn't you like me in black? I'll be very mysterious and seductive."

The exchange reminded Jessica of something that she would rather have kept out of her thoughts—that Susan was an experienced woman.

"I'll be all right", she said, putting down the green nightgown. "I try not to think about it, but when I do something happens inside me. But I'll love you just as much in black. Show me."

The nightgown was long, covering the arms and shoulders with dark transparent gauze and small areas of comparative opacity. Since red hair, freckles and an impish grin don't conduce to an air of mystery, Susan looked more like a child in dress-up than a seductress.

"O Lor'", exclaimed Susan, as they stood side by side in front of the long wardrobe mirror, Susan the mischievous schoolgirl and Jessica tall and elegant in her nakedness. "This was a present from an old friend when I was married, and I've never worn it. Do you think I look too silly?"

"No, you look adorable and I want you to wear it tonight. And I'm sort of relieved that you don't look like a seductress. The only thing is that it might be hard to take off."

"You'll do it very nicely, my love, as long as you're patient."

"You're making me feel very impatient now."

"Well just try the red one on and then we can both feel impatient."

The red nightgown had a deep V-neck, left the shoulders bare and consisted mainly of a few layers of gauze.

"It suits you much better than it does me", said Susan as they stood once more in front of the mirror, red hair above a black dress and black hair above a red one. "And it's much better than fig leaves."

"Le Rouge et le Noir", said Jessica.

"I never did like that book, but of course, I only read it in English."

"Me too, but Mlle. Bouvier told me it's not much better in French. She thinks that if people want to go to bed together they should just do it and not make such a song and dance over it. Susan, which one of us is Adam?"

"I don't know. Maybe we're both Eve."

"And what about the serpent?"

"We seem to have managed very well without one."

Jessica laughed, but was immediately serious again.

"And Susan, I think when we slept together the first time you were still a virgin—in a way, I mean."

Naivety, wishful thinking or a valid observation, there was something about Jessica's remark that sent a pang through Susan's body and brought back all her old doubts about what she was doing. No one in her own age group could possibly have said anything like that—but it was much too late to turn back now.

"I hadn't thought of that but I think perhaps you're right—it was all so completely new. It's wonderful the way you think of things that would never occur to me. Are you still feeling impatient or would you like to try the white one?"

"I'm feeling very impatient."

"So am I, so I'll put the others away and you can try the white one another time."

The nightgowns were a great success.

One fly in the ointment was Mrs. Simpson, whom Susan saw every day at the infirmary and who often asked about Jessica. As time went by Susan realized that there was a limit to how long she could keep on saying that Jessica was staying with her for a few days until another home could be found. One day, when Mrs. Simpson expressed some anxiety about the money she was receiving on Jessica's behalf, Susan saw the opportunity to encourage her colleague to be less talkative.

"I really don't think you need worry about it, Jill. As long as I'm taking care of Jessica there's no need to say anything, and I'll let you know when the situation changes."

Susan's unaccustomed use of her colleague's Christian name was as good as a nod and a wink, and Mrs. Simpson never brought up the subject again.

When Jessica's Christmas holidays started, Susan managed to wangle a few extra days off. Thinking that it probably wasn't a good idea to stay in bed all day, they took to going on long, slow bus rides through the villages surrounding Gloucester, while avoiding the city center, so as to reduce the probability of meeting anyone from Blenheim Hall. In the evenings they listened to news and music on the radio, which Susan had moved into the bedroom, and since they were both curious and imaginative there never seemed to be any danger of their running out of things to talk about.

Most of the war news was bad. On some evenings reports of devastating air raids, losses at sea and fears of an imminent invasion produced a sense of deep foreboding, which they fought off by making love with a kind of desperate concentration, as if the intense focus on each other's souls and bodies could provide a shelter against all intrusions. They had not forgotten that at some point this episode in their lives might end abruptly and painfully, but for a few weeks their paradise remained intact in spite of the sea of troubles that surrounded it. Susan had achieved this state by coming to an agreement with herself; she would accept this period of unexpected bliss and shut off all thoughts of the future for as long as she could. Then, if or when the blow finally fell, she would pay whatever price was to be exacted for her spell of sublime happiness. She justified herself with the thought that if trouble came it would hit her far harder than Jessica, who would almost certainly be regarded as a young orphan girl who had been led astray by an unscrupulous woman. But her real justification was her intention to stay with Jessica permanently or, at least, as long as Jessica wanted her, if only the rest of the world could be persuaded to mind its own business. To Jessica, badly hurt by the loss of her parents and still recovering from her encounters with the soldiers and the Simpsons, the affair seemed to be both a great adventure and the end of all adventures. Like Susan she felt that, against all normal probabilities, she had met the person with whom she wanted to spend the rest of her life. And each one nursed the hope that the blow would never fall.

"Most people would say it was really silly, wouldn't they?" said Jessica one night as they lay on their backs looking at the remains of the firelight on the ceiling.

"What, darling?" asked Susan.

"Well, I'm fifteen and I've never had a love affair before and now I think this is the only one I'll ever have. I mean, to anyone who didn't know it would seem very improbable."

"Well, when you come right down to it, it *is* very improbable."

"Susan . . ."

"No, my darling love, I don't mean the bit about staying together for the rest of our lives—I want that more than anything else in the world. It's just that *everything* that happens is very improbable. That's what the Vicar said in his sermon the last time I went to church. I had never thought of it before but I think it's true. Have you ever thought about what it took to bring you here to me?"

"You mean the bomb falling on my house? No, if it had just been that you wouldn't have said it."

Susan rolled over and kissed Jessica.

"No, if that bomb could somehow be taken back and you could still be living happily with your parents I would say, 'Yes', even though it meant losing you."

"But somehow we would still have found each other, wouldn't we?"

"I don't know, but I want to think so. All I know is that we have met and we've discovered a new world. And it's much better than the one Columbus discovered."

"And", said Jessica, "you were going to say that it wouldn't have happened if John hadn't met Uncle James ten years ago."

"And that wouldn't have happened if a silly girl called Rosalind Crump hadn't got tipsy and double-dated herself."

"And you wouldn't be here if you hadn't happened to walk by when John was asking about her."

"And you wouldn't be here if Mr. Simpson hadn't happened to fall ill."

"I can see what the Vicar meant. It sounds as if someone up there is arranging things."

"Yes—he said that it was one of the reasons why he believes in God."

Jessica thought for a moment before saying in a relieved tone, "If that's true it means that God wants us to be together."

"I think He must—that is, if He's really there."

"But", Jessica added as her thought kept rolling on, "perhaps he put us together just to see if we could resist temptation. Do you think he would be so cruel?"

"Well, he did it to Adam and Eve."

"Yes, but he told them exactly what they weren't allowed to do, and they did it anyway. And that was just eating an apple. I think I could have resisted eating an apple when there was so much other fruit about, but he's given us something that's absolutely impossible to resist and it doesn't seem quite fair. And I know people say that the apple really means sex but that isn't what it says in the bible."

"I know—it was the tree of the knowledge of good and evil—*and* he actually told them to multiply."

"And I don't think he was talking about arithmetic. So it means that now we are supposed to know good and evil, and I don't believe what we're doing is evil. And I think if you're tempted to do something that isn't bad it doesn't really count as temptation."

"Most people think that what we're doing *is* bad."

"But it only matters what *we* think, and God didn't tell us—at least, I don't think there's anything about it in the Gospels, only in the bits of the Bible that other people made up—so we don't really know whether he thinks it's evil or not. You know, for all the good he does he might just as well not be there—if he *is* there."

Susan couldn't help laughing and after a few moments Jessica started to laugh too. Soon they were holding on to each other and giggling uncontrollably

"You're a wonderful theologian", Susan gasped when she was finally able to speak. "You've got the Vicar beaten into a cocked hat."

She paused to get her breath back before speaking again.

"There's something I want to tell you and it will be easier if you lie here with my arms round you and your head on my shoulder. I don't know why, it just will."

"Is it something bad?" asked Jessica apprehensively as she obediently snuggled into Susan's arms.

"It seemed bad when it was happening, but now I think in a way it's actually good. Do you remember on our first night I told you I had never done anything like that before and you said we would be learning together?"

"Yes", said Jessica, wishing that her heart would stop thudding so painfully.

"Well, it was perfectly true. It was all new and wonderful. But when I was a child I had a friend called Elizabeth, who was a year older than I was. We grew up practically next door to each other and always played together, but when she was twelve her family moved away and it made me very unhappy. Well I had other friends and I got over it, but when she was sixteen they moved back, and when I saw her I thought she was the most beautiful creature I had ever seen, with long blonde hair, blue eyes and the sort of figure that a Greek sculptor might have given her. So we started being friends again and I fell in love with her, or, at least, I thought I did, and I tried to do everything I possibly could to please her. It went on like that for a year or so, but she was just an ordinary girl looking for a boyfriend, and when I tried to tell her how I felt about her she thought it was funny. She told her parents about it, and they thought it was disgusting, so they told my father and said he ought to get me psychoanalyzed. He was furious and told me if there was any more nonsense he would throw me out of the house. I was absolutely mortified, but after a day or two I started getting angry. I was angry with Elizabeth and her parents and my father, but mostly I was angry with myself for getting into that position—I don't just mean being in love with Elizabeth, but demeaning myself and letting her treat me almost like a servant—and I decided that I was going to leave home and get a job and a boyfriend. When I told my father what I was thinking, he laughed and asked me what kind of work I thought I was going to do, so I said the first thing that came into my head, which was nursing. And he said, 'Oh, I suppose you want to live in a hostel with a lot of other young girls.' But I think he was quite happy to get rid of me, so he let me apply to Addenbrooke's, and when I got in he supported me until I qualified."

"Did you ever go home again?"

"Occasionally, but it was very uncomfortable. He couldn't resist making comments, like asking me if I had a nice girlfriend I'd like to bring home, and when I got upset he would say he was just teasing me, only, of course, he wasn't. So eventually I stopped going home."

"What about your mother?"

"My mother died when my younger brother was born, and I was only two so I hardly knew her. After that my Aunt Ruby—my father's younger sister—came to live with us. She was very different from my father, always singing songs and telling stories and making us laugh. But when I was about ten she got married and went away, so my little brother and I more or less looked after ourselves. After I stopped going home he used to come and see me in Cambridge sometimes and by then I had met John. When John joined the navy I decided to try again, and I got a job here at the Royal infirmary. But it didn't do any good. My father said that if I had been a proper wife John would have stayed with me."

"Susan?"

Jessica was unable to articulate her question and Susan answered it obliquely.

"Well you know the story of how I met John. Things being what they are in Cambridge I had met quite a lot of undergraduates. Most of them only had one thing in mind, but what I was after was something slightly different. I wanted to find out if I could be like most of the other girls and fall in love with a boy. I was more interested in love than in sex, and with most of the boys it was the other way round. Then I met John and he was different and seemed to like me, and I think what happened was that I somehow talked myself into it. It seemed real enough at the time, but now that I look back I have the feeling that there was a lot of kindness and consideration instead of the sort of gay abandon that you and I have."

"But we're kind and considerate—at least, you are, and I try to be."

"You are, my darling. I think this is too hard to explain—I did try to be a proper wife, and I thought I was, but now I'm not sure and I suppose it's possible that my father was right. Does it upset you very much that John and I slept together?"

"I don't think it upsets me—it just makes me feel very funny inside and it makes me want you even more, as if what we do together somehow wipes out what you did with John. Susan, when two people are in love does each one always want to do all the same things that the other one does. I mean, is that sort of normal?"

"I don't know—this is the only time I've been properly in love—but I know what you mean. When you go off to school and I think of you spending the day with all those people that I've never met, I get butterflies in my tummy.

"Yes, but at least you've been to school and you know what it's like. I've never slept with a man and I never want to, but I do so want to know what it was like for you . . ."

"But, darling, that's all in the past. It's not like that now. And think what you would have to do if you really wanted to be like me—for a start you'd have to dye your hair and make yourself two inches shorter and twelve years older."

Jessica smiled and let the matter drop but she couldn't get the images out of her mind—Susan in the green nightie, or nothing, in John's arms. What she wanted to know more than anything else, and couldn't ask, was whether Susan had enjoyed it.

"I'm sorry. Dearest Susan, please forgive me—I won't do it again. And talking about it makes me want you so much I'm afraid I might burst."

Some time later Susan spoke again.

"The real problem is that John is a wonderful person and I care for him very much, and it's only now when I know what being in love is really like that I begin to doubt whether I was ever in love with him. And I know that I could never be a wife to him again."

"Susan, can we somehow make it all right for him?"

"I think the only thing I can do is to tell him the truth, and I'm afraid it will make him very angry and unhappy."

"Are you going to write to him?"

"I don't think I could do it in a letter. Can you imagine him getting a letter like that when he's hundreds of miles away, and not knowing when or whether he'll see me again? I think I'll have to wait until he comes home on leave, or perhaps it would be better to go and see him next time his ship is in port. Then I think I might be able to do it without bringing you into it."

"I'm glad we don't have to do it at once. I just want to be with you like this a little longer before the hard part comes. And I'm not sure whether I want you to take all the blame. If he knew about me he might not be so angry with you."

The conversation made them feel very solemn and they fell asleep thinking about John instead of each other.

Susan woke up the next morning with the feeling that she had accomplished something. Of all the ramifications of her love affair with Jessica, the one that had most deeply troubled her conscience was her betrayal of the man to whom she had made a lifelong commitment. Now that she knew what she would have to do, she thought that although it would be very difficult it was within her powers. It would be very hard on John, but she sincerely believed that in the long run it would be better for him to know exactly how things stood. She looked at her partner, who lay curled up on her side with her arm around Susan's middle.

"It's going to be all right", she murmured. "Everything's going to be all right."

"Dearest Susan", said Jessica, apparently without waking up, "you always make everything all right."

CHAPTER XVI

1965: Wednesday, December 22nd

Miss Edwards traveled to Gloucester on the tracks that had carried Jessica there twenty-five years previously. Inspector Phelps and Sergeant Snipe met her at the station in the middle of the afternoon and took her straight to Blenheim Hall, where Miss Thrower and Miss Evans treated them all to tea and crumpets. The first thing that the policemen noticed about Miss Edwards was that she had the fading remains of a fine set of freckles, and that although she was greying she must once have possessed quite a mop of red hair. There was, however, no sign of recognition between her and Miss Thrower.

Inevitably the conversation began with a question about Miss Edwards's journey and a discussion of the parlous state of British Railways. It turned out that as a member of SRUBLUK (The Society for the Reinvigoration of Unremunerative Branch Lines in the United Kingdom), she held very strong views about the government's cost-cutting activities. Ten minutes elapsed before she remarked with sincere contrition,

"Oh dear, here I am running on and on about my hobby horse and forgetting all about my dear Jessica. I should very much like to hear all that you can tell me about her stay at Blenheim Hall."

"Well, first of all we can tell you the things we told Inspector Phelps", said Miss Thrower. "Then I have something to add, and so does Gwyneth."

So the inspector heard the story for the second time and a tailpiece that was new to him.

"Now I said that Jessica was reticent and it was hard to tell what was going in inside, and that's true, but it wasn't a dull or even a shy kind of reticence. I mentioned that she was surprisingly happy. Something seemed to be bubbling just below the surface, something that filled her with secret joy and was too precious to be allowed out for others to see."

"I had a similar impression", said Miss Evans, "although I don't think I saw it as clearly as Penny did. As I told Inspector Phelps and Sergeant Snipe yesterday, Jessica was absolutely fearless in the gym. Most of our girls are quite reluctant to throw themselves about, but it was as if Jessica had simply given herself up to her surroundings and was ready for anything. Then, after she had gone flying through the air in the most abandoned way, she would be her usual calm, obedient self. I think most of the other girls found her completely incomprehensible."

"Was she older than the others?" asked Inspector Phelps.

"Her birthday was in July", said Miss Edwards, "so she was a good age for the class. Now, perhaps, it would be helpful if I were to tell you about my recollections of Jessica.

"I was appointed in 1939, so I knew her for just over a year. Greville's, if I may say so without causing offence, draws its pupils from a wealthier section of society than Blenheim Hall and, in any case, I understand that London girls are apt to be considerably more sophisticated than their more rural counterparts. My point is that she didn't stand out in quite the way that she evidently did here. Nevertheless, she was clearly in some ways out of the ordinary, and that had something to do with her parents, who were both teachers, but not exactly typical members of their profession—at least as teachers are usually imagined to be. Her father was a chemistry master at the boys' grammar school, a few minutes' walk from their house, but he seemed to be more interested in music than in chemistry. Her mother had been an English teacher, and after the war broke out she went to teach at the grammar school because many of the men had gone into the army. People used to say that the Smiths had rather advanced views. I don't think they believed in free love, but they did invite artists and musicians into the house and they stayed up all hours of the night, not exactly carousing, but singing, playing and talking."

"Were you ever invited to one of these parties?" asked Phelps.

"No, but some of the mistresses had been there occasionally before the war. Apparently there was a certain amount of smoking and drinking, but most of the time was spent on music and talk. What surprised them was that Jessica, who was a child of twelve or thirteen at the time, was allowed to stay up until the small hours. She didn't smoke or drink, but she took part in those long conversations about life and the world that are apt to take place in such circumstances. Jessica told me that after the war started there weren't so many parties and only a few close friends were invited."

"Did you know Jessica very well?"

"Not during my first year. Of course one couldn't help noticing her, but one gets into the habit of treating all one's pupils exactly the same, even the ones who are very different, and in any case, I don't think that Jessica would have wanted familiarity on the part of her teachers. But a few weeks before . . . before the bomb fell, she sprained her ankle. Not in the gym, I should mention. There she was a model of care and precision. Apparently someone pushed her as she was getting off a bus and she landed awkwardly. Since she couldn't take part in the exercises for a week or so, she helped me with my lists and other odd jobs, and we talked a little sometimes. I think that she became quite fond of me, which is one hazards of the teaching profession because when that happens it is hard not to reciprocate. I'm not talking about gross crushes, of course, which tend to be comical or nauseating. I have always felt it best to keep the girls at arm's length, and I mention it only because we are trying to make a picture of Jessica, presumably in the hope that something will emerge that will help us to find out what happened to her.

"I was living in a flat at the time and I had a spare room, so after the air raid I suggested that she should come and live with me until a decision could be made about her future. Miss Parker, the headmistress at that time, knew of my suggestion and gave her approval before I took any action."

"May I ask you, Miss Edwards, whether you would have done that for any other student who had been bombed out?"

"Yes, Inspector, you may," replied Miss Edwards, looking rigidly through the space in front of her, "and the answer is, 'No, I would not have.' I had become extremely fond of her. In spite of the appalling circumstances, it gave me great joy to have her in my house."

"I can understand that, Veronica", said Miss Thrower quietly. "I was extremely fond of her too. I was broken-hearted when she left."

"I knew that." The speaker was Miss Evans, who was looking compassionately at her colleague. "You were utterly professional about it, and I don't think anyone else noticed. But we were friends, you see."

The pain in Gwyneth Evans's voice was so apparent that everyone looked at her for a moment and then looked away.

"I'm sorry Gwynny, really sorry."

Inspector Phelps cleared his throat. He had hoped that these ladies would give him something to work on, and he was glad that they were talking so freely; but enough, after all, is enough.

"Jessica seems to have inspired great affection wherever she went", he said, "but it seems to have been generally among women considerably older than herself. Do you know whether she had any male friends?"

"Not to my knowledge", said Miss Edwards. "There would have been very little opportunity for her to develop such friendships unless she met someone at one of her parents' parties."

"I don't know either", added Miss Thrower. "She may have had a boyfriend, but we have no idea how she spent her time when she wasn't in school."

"So there was no known boyfriend and there were, in fact, no close friends of her own age at all. The reason I asked is that more often than not murders are connected with money or sex, and there doesn't seem to have been any money to speak of in Jessica's background. We must all bear in mind, however, that we have no proof that Jessica was murdered or even that the remains that were found are hers. All we know for sure is that at some point someone illegally disposed of a body. If, however, we are on the right track it looks as if whatever happened had to do with goings on with the people she lived with."

Surrounded by schoolmistresses and conscious of a degree of syntactical infelicity, Inspector Phelps paused for breath.

"I would agree with that if it weren't for the fact that I actually met Mrs. Simpson", said Miss Thrower. "She was so perfectly ordinary and prosaic—mid-forties, plump, comfortable and probably not particularly bright. She may have fallen for Jessica the way Veronica and I did—forgive me for putting it so crudely, Veronica—but it's hard to imagine Jessica having any feelings for her or for the kind of husband or son she was likely to have had. And I ought to add that although Jessica seemed to be fond of me it was in due proportion—the sort of fondness that a child often feels for a teacher."

Miss Edwards was silent, so Phelps continued.

"As far as the police are concerned the most obvious course is to track them down and find out, but there are a lot of Mr. and Mrs. Simpsons in the city and it's fairly likely that none of them have ever heard of Jessica. Her Mrs. Simpson must be about seventy now and it's quite possible that she or her husband or both are no longer with us. Furthermore, if there was any dirty work and we do happen to find the right people, they'll deny all knowledge. So I really need you all to rack your brains to think of anything that would give us a clue."

All this remark produced was a long silence. It was finally broken by Miss Edwards.

"I have already said that I am quite certain that Jessica did not stay with the Simpsons. So Mrs. Simpson's appearing at school to collect Jessica's belongings suggests to me that there really was some dirty work, to use your expression, Inspector."

"Yes, Ma'am, that had occurred to me. If you're right it would have been natural for the people she was staying with to do that. And if there had been nothing to hide it would have been natural for them or for Jessica to tell the school where she was living. So, assuming that all this is correct, there was a deception and Jessica was party to it."

Snipe made his first comment.

"Added to which, Miss Thrower and Miss Evans seem to have given a very good description of a young girl in love."

"Thank you, Sergeant", said Miss Thrower. "You've articulated something that none of us wanted to admit, because the implication is that somehow she had found someone and was living with him. There's a fly in the ointment, however. If that had been the case, Mrs. Simpson would have known about it and must have condoned it, which doesn't seem quite in what I remember of her character. You're going to have to find her, Inspector—just another case of *chercher la femme.*"

"But not the usual kind of *femme.*"

154

There was a long pause during which the three teachers seemed to be occupied with their thoughts, and Inspector Phelps wondered whether they were feeling that they had said too much or, perhaps, too little. He rose to his feet and began to thank the two Blenheim Hall teachers for their hospitality, but Miss Edwards interrupted him.

"Forgive me, Inspector, but I should very much like to see the poem that was left with Jessica—for in spite of your reservations I am sure that it was Jessica."

"I don't see why you shouldn't, Ma'am, although I doubt whether you'll gather anything useful from it."

"I really wasn't expecting to—I suppose I'm just being sentimental, but I'd like to see if it gives any impression of this person with whom Jessica was, er, associating."

The inspector produced an envelope from an inner pocket and spread its contents on the tea table while the others gathered round.

"This is a typed copy. The original was written by hand."

"Remarkable", said Miss Edwards.

"Yes", said Miss Thrower, "I think this is the kind of person that Jessica might have liked."

Snipe whispered something in his superior's ear.

"No harm in it that I can see", said the latter, fishing in his pocket again. "I have something else to show you, ladies, and this is not yet public knowledge, so I'll ask you to regard it as confidential. At the funeral on Monday another poem was found, and Sergeant Snipe thinks it would be a good idea to let you see it."

"Someone must have been very devoted to her", said Miss Evans after reading the second poem.

"Or perhaps some two", remarked Miss Edwards, echoing Bill Marjoribanks's comments.

"But . . ." said Miss Thrower. She had turned rather pale and continued with some effort. "It's very odd, but I have a feeling I've seen it before. Unfortunately I haven't the faintest idea where."

The two policemen looked at each other, but this didn't seem to be the time or the place to try to jog Miss Thrower's memory. Phelps did, however, have one more question for Miss Edwards. Realizing that in addition to having red hair and freckles she was short and well, though not heavily, built, he asked,

"Are you by any chance Welsh, Miss Edwards?"

"I was born in Cardiff, but my parents moved to London when I was very young. Why, does it have something to do with the case?"

"Not really. I just wondered."

But he was thinking to himself that Miss Edwards could hardly be described as mercurial or dainty. As he and his sergeant were walking back to the station he articulated the thought that had been bothering him.

"Something odd about that poem, Snipey."

"Yes, Sir. The hair was the wrong color—well, wrong for Jessica."

Meanwhile, Police Constables Chard and Highnam had spent most of the day hunting down all the elderly Simpsons they could find in Gloucester and its suburbs. Chard was waiting at the station when Phelps and Snipe got back from Blenheim Hall.

"No luck, Sir", he said to the inspector. "We've seen nine Mr. and Mrs. Simpsons, three widowed Mrs. Simpsons and a couple of Miss Simpsons, and nobody admits to ever having heard of Jessica Smith. Two of the couples say that they had evacuees during the war, but nobody answering in any way to Jessica's description."

"Did you get the impression that any of them were prevaricating?"

"Not really. Some of the older ones were a bit woolly, but I suppose that's only to be expected."

"So our Mrs. Simpson must be dead, moved or a good liar."

"Or she's just forgotten. Is there anything else you want me to do, Sir?"

"Meaning that you were supposed to go off duty an hour ago?"

"Well, Sir . . ."

"That's all right, son. We don't even know whether this particular haystack has a needle in it."

"And, speaking of needles, or maybe thorns", he went on to Snipe, "I want you to make some unobtrusive enquiries about young Johnson. Find out whether his story about how he spent the war is true, who his friends and relations are and how that business of his is doing. I particularly want to know about family members, brothers, sisters, cousins and so on."

"In other words, who he's covering for."

"Right. Start with the navy—you might not be too late to get something this afternoon"

Phelps returned to his office with the thought that unless Snipe uncovered any juicy items, he was going to be forced to wait for something else to turn up. Quite possibly nothing ever would.

He was busy tidying up the day's paperwork when his phone rang.

"There's a Miss Thrower on the line for you, Sir", said Sergeant Bunn.

"Thanks, Bunny. Put her through", said Inspector Phelps, restraining the loud "Aha" that had almost escaped his lips.

Miss Thrower sounded uncharacteristically agitated.

"There's something I'd like to tell you about. It's quite simple really but somehow I'd rather not do it over the telephone."

"Certainly. Would you like me to come to the school or would you prefer to come to the station?"

"I'll come to the station, Inspector, if I may speak to you in private—not that I expect what I tell you to be regarded as confidential. It would simply make it easier to talk."

"Don't worry, Ma'am. It's very quiet here and we can meet in my office. You can count on me to be as discreet as circumstances allow."

By the time she arrived at the police station, Penny Thrower was quite calm.

"It's about the second poem", she explained, "the one that was found at the funeral. It wasn't about Jessica—it was written *by* Jessica."

Inspector Phelps gazed at his informant with wild surmise.

"Are you sure of this?"

"Absolutely. It was supposed to have been published in the school magazine for 1941, but with all the shortages all we could do was to make a few typewritten copies and stick them on the classroom walls."

Miss Thrower produced a discolored and wrinkled piece of paper.

"I rescued this at the end of the summer term. And I'm sorry I didn't say so this afternoon—I could see what it meant and it was too much of a shock."

"Yes, Ma'am. It means that the remains that were found are almost certainly Jessica's. I'm very sorry."

"Thank you, Inspector. When I realized that this afternoon I was too overcome to talk, but I could have given you this piece of information over the telephone if there had not been other implications."

Phelps already had some inkling of these other implications, but he let Miss Thrower continue.

"This poem was the result of a homework task which was to write a Shakespearean sonnet. Unfortunately, poor Miss Wenlock, Jessica's English teacher, is in a nursing home and unable to recall her own name, but it's possible that I can tell you more about it than she would have been able to."

Miss Thrower paused for a moment.

"You'll have to bear with me, Inspector. This is going to be very difficult. As you know, I was Jessica's form mistress, so it was quite natural for her to show me her poem. The fact that it was about a woman needn't have had any significance since she was writing in the character of Shakespeare, but when I complimented her on how well she had imagined this woman she seemed slightly embarrassed—and this was the only time I ever saw her embarrassed—and confessed that the sonnet was about a real person. As you must have realized, I was much fonder of Jessica than any teacher ever has a right to be of a pupil, and I'm ashamed to admit that my first sensation was jealousy. If I had been on an even keel I should probably have asked her who this wonderful woman was, and it's possible, I suppose, that Jessica might have told me. As it was, all I could do was to repeat that it was an excellent piece of work and suggest that it should be published in the school magazine. That's really all I can tell you."

"Thank you. You spoke of implications and I believe I can see what you mean, but I'd appreciate it if you would explain what you had in mind."

"All right, I'll try. You must have been somewhat surprised at some of the things that were said this afternoon."

"I've been a policeman for a long time, so not much surprises me. It wasn't so much the things themselves as the way the three of you spoke so freely about them."

"I think it was partly that Miss Edwards and I were so deeply involved with Jessica, and we badly need to know the truth. And it's partly Jessica herself, as though she were still with us. Jessica had some quality that aroused very strong feelings in the women around her. I don't think I've ever been the same since I met her."

Conscious of the inspector's gaze Miss Thrower paused.

"All right, I suppose I must say it. I was in love with her, and so, I'm sure, was Miss Edwards. Gwyneth wasn't in love but neither was she impervious. Even Miss Alderley was affected, and all this without the slightest effort on Jessica's part, and, as far as I could see, without the slightest knowledge either. The implication of the poem seems to be that outside the school there was a woman who loved and was loved by Jessica. So when I said that Jessica might have found someone outside the school and might have been living with him, I probably ought to have said 'her' instead of 'him'. And, by the way, I don't think her embarrassment at having to admit that the poem was about a real person was caused by discomfort about its being someone of her own sex. It was just that she was too honest to be able to accept praise for something she hadn't done."

"Thank you for being so frank. Would I be right in saying that it's unusual for girls to have such effects on their teachers?"

"That was very nicely put, Inspector. It probably seems more unusual than it really is. As Miss Edwards said, it's one of the hazards of the profession. When it happens it causes a great deal of pain, most of it to the teacher, who somehow has to maintain a correct relationship no matter what is going on inside her."

"Is that always possible?"

"Well, I managed it somehow; but, no, I have seen it get out of hand, although on very, very few occasions."

"You don't think it happened with Jessica—with someone else in school, I mean."

"I really don't think so. I'm sure that the beloved person in the poem was not one of her teachers. Apart from Gwyneth and me, they were nearly all elderly and rather forbidding. And since I'm being frank, I ought to mention that in spite of any impressions you may have received this afternoon, not all of us are lesbians. I really don't know about Miss Edwards, but my impression is that this happened to her out of the blue and she never got over it. I'm afraid that Gwynny and I did give the game away in the heat of the moment. We were—deeply attached to each other, and when Jessica appeared it was very hard on Gwynny because she couldn't help seeing what was happening. But most of the mistresses are what passes for perfectly normal—middle-aged and elderly spinsters who wanted to teach or got left on the shelf and had no alternative. The younger ones are different. Now it's perfectly possible to be married and have children and teach all at the same time."

"And", Phelps remarked, "the people I met today were those who had been most affected by Jessica. If Miss Edwards had not been in some degree, shall we say, susceptible, we should never have heard of her, and if you hadn't been susceptible you wouldn't have remembered all that you did about Jessica, including the poem. I mean, there must be a hundred or so new girls in the school every year and we're talking about one particular girl from twenty-five years ago."

"So, in other words, Jessica acted like a magnet for women with what you politely call 'susceptibility' and has left us with a sort of posthumous lesbian fan club. No, please don't apologize—it's true, and you never implied that there was anything reprehensible about it. It's not all bad you know. Now that we know more about Jessica and what happened to her it's possible that after all these years Gwyneth and I will get back together, although I don't suppose you would approve of that."

"Now then, Miss Thrower, you mustn't assume that you know what I would approve or disapprove of. As a policeman and a citizen I don't approve of breaking the law and causing death, pain and misery. But some sins, if they *are* sins, are of a generous nature and don't hurt anybody. What concerns me is that someone may have taken advantage of Jessica when she was a fifteen-year-old kid, someone may have killed her, and someone certainly disposed of her body."

"I'm sorry, Inspector. I think perhaps I should go now."

"That's all right, Miss Thrower. I think you're one of the generous ones and I doubt whether you would ever intentionally hurt anyone, except by dishing out extra homework for a kid who deserved it. I just have two more questions, one of which you've already answered, but I'd like to get it absolutely clear. Jessica wrote her poem in the character of Shakespeare, so it was natural for her to make it appear to be about a woman. But couldn't it have really been about a man?"

"A man with 'dainty toes'? It's an interesting theory but I don't think so, although I don't doubt that Jessica was just as attractive to men as she was to women."

"It's important for the investigation because if the poem is about a real person we need to find that person, and it would be handy to know whether we're looking for a man or a woman."

"Apart from the poem itself, I'm pretty sure that the way Jessica spoke made it clear that it was a woman", said Miss Thrower as she rose to leave. "But, of course, that was a long time ago. Oh, I was forgetting—you said you had another question."

"Yes, Miss Thrower. In view of all you've told me about Jessica and the way you felt about her, I'm surprised you didn't think of her immediately when Sergeant Snipe first talked to you."

"The fact is, Inspector, that very few days go by when I don't think of Jessica, and I did think of her immediately. It was simply too hard too say anything, because as soon as the question was asked I knew in my heart what the answer was. You see I had always had the feeling that I should see her again, and it took me some time to face up to reality."

"Thank you. That seems very understandable."

"You've been very kind, Inspector."

"Just doing my job, Ma'am."

There was something about the tone in which this last remark was uttered that made Miss Thrower wonder whether kindness and understanding were the inspector's tools of the trade, to be used, as occasion demanded, to extract as much information as possible from his patients. On the whole she thought not, but she was not at all sure.

"And", Phelps said to himself, after Miss Thrower had left, "what about dear Gwynny? She had a motive for getting rid of Jessica. I'm surprised Miss Thrower didn't see it. Or perhaps she did—she didn't *have* to tell me about her and Miss Evans."

While pondering these goings on it occurred to him that it would do no harm to fill his friends at the Nave in on the latest developments. Woodcock took the call in his office and listened with great attention to the tales of the Penny Thrower, Gwynny Evans and Veronica Edwards.

"That's extremely interesting", he said at the end of the long story.

"You don't sound very surprised. I thought it was a bit more than interesting."

"Well, you know, when you put six hundred people together in a relatively closed community it isn't surprising if a few strong attachments are formed. The really unusual aspect of the story is the character of the girl Jessica, who seems to have gone through the world innocently leaving a trail of emotional wreckage behind her. I'll have to talk to Bill about this."

"Good—and I'd like to talk to both of you."

"All right, how about coming up for a late breakfast tomorrow. We're going to celebrate the end of term tonight, so we're not expecting to get up very early in the morning. Would eleven o'clock do? Ring me just before you leave, and I'll start working on the eggs and bacon"

"Excellent", said the inspector, smiling to himself as he rang off. This was the first time that it had been simply and casually taken it for granted that he knew all about the headmaster's romance with his secretary.

CHAPTER XVII

1940: Sunday, December 22

John Berkeley stood on the bridge of the *Masai* as the early morning light broadened over the grey expanse of the North Atlantic. His convoy was only a day out from Liverpool but it had lost a ship already and he was worried about another merchantman that had been damaged in the attack. It seemed to be listing more heavily and even if it managed to stay afloat it was hardly likely to be able to keep going at the required speed. Abandoning the ship and taking the crew off would be a very hazardous business with U-boats still prowling, but it might have to be done and, if it were, the *Masai* would be involved. Well that was up to the commanding officer. The rules of warfare being what they were, he might decide that the only prudent course was to keep the convoy moving and let the ship try to get back to Liverpool on its own. Meanwhile John's mind kept wandering back to Gloucester.

He had not met the Simpsons but he had seen the house in St. Paul's Road where Jessica would be living, and he imagined her getting ready for school and walking out of the door. He reminded himself that she was just a schoolgirl, doing the things that schoolgirls all over the world do, giggling over the same things, experimenting with the idea of being grown up and developing crushes on people. Unfortunately she hadn't developed a crush on him, although he thought she might have on Susan. What a waste, he thought. Susan was very good at dealing with things like that firmly and kindly, as she had with one of the young nurses at the infirmary. They had laughed about it at the time. John was quite sure that the nurse had been nothing like Jessica, who was physically irresistible, intelligent, humorous and perceptive, and understood things in ways that were beyond the imaginations of most adults. No doubt Susan appreciated all these qualities, but in her business-like way she would by now have put Jessica firmly in her place, packed her off to the Simpsons and got on with whatever came next.

So it was that the captain of the *Masai* was lost in a reverie about a young girl half his age when the stricken merchantman was hit by two more torpedoes in rapid succession. Not that it would have made any difference if his mind had been on his job. He was back in full command instantly, but while everyone's attention was momentarily distracted, his destroyer was struck amidships. There was no confusion or panic. Everyone knew what to do, but the ship soon began to lose way. John knew that the *Masai* was doomed, not because she would be sunk by one torpedo, but because she would now be a sitting target.

Christmas was an austere festival in wartime England but something in the atmosphere stirred Jessica in spite of her agnosticism.

"Let's go to church and sing some carols", she said on the Sunday before Christmas.

Susan's attitude to religion was rather like Jessica's; although Christianity appealed to her emotions she had never found any compelling reason either for believing or for disbelieving. She liked the idea of going to church but there was an element of caution in her response.

"I'd like to very much, but we ought to be careful. I don't want to get stuck in a church porch having a long conversation with one of your teachers."

"I don't think you'd mind if it was Miss Thrower. She's really—well, she reminds me a bit of you."

Susan was surprised by a pang of jealousy. Where her husband was concerned she had never experienced such a thing.

"Susan, have I said something wrong?"

"No, my sweet, it's just me being stupid."

"Darling Susan", said the preternaturally perceptive Jessica, "I wouldn't care if I never saw Miss Thrower or any of them ever again. I love you so much that it hurts."

"I'm sorry", whispered Susan into a mass of black hair, and they held each other so tightly and for such a long time that one might have thought that the whole future of the world depended on their not being torn apart, as, indeed, it seemed to them.

"But we do have to remember that they think you're still living with the Simpsons", said Susan at last.

So they went to the service of carols and lessons at the cathedral, and sat at the side of the nave in the shadow a huge round pillar, where the sound of the invisible choir reached them clearly and sweetly. For a few moments Jessica found herself wishing fervently that she could be a believer, and this reminded her of the conversation she had had with John Berkeley in this same building. "If God wants us to be good", she had said, "why did he make it so difficult?" "Impossible", John had replied. If she were to become a believer she would have to acknowledge that she had been living in sin with Susan, and she would have to repent. Homosexuality was one of the myriad topics that had been discussed during those long evenings and late nights at home before the fatal air raid, and in spite of her words to Susan a few evenings previously she knew what society and the Bible thought about it. She also knew that St. Paul had spoken just as harshly about the accusers as he had about the accused, and she felt that if two people could make each other deliriously happy without hurting anyone else it couldn't possibly be sinful. But she had been reminded of John, and if John knew what was going on he would certainly be hurt. Well, perhaps he would understand and forgive them; would that change matters at all? Thousands of people committed adultery and got divorced and married again. Perhaps it was all right if the original marriage had simply been a mistake. She looked anxiously her lover. Susan seemed lost in the music, but when Jessica's hand sought hers she turned and smiled, drowning all Jessica's thoughts of John, God and society in a flood of warmth, and leaving only a small shadow in an obscure corner of her consciousness.

Two more torpedoes struck the *Masai*, and she soon began to list heavily. The destroyer was no longer able to engage any enemy, seen or unseen and John, hoping to save some of his crew, quickly gave the order to abandon ship. Within a few minutes the list was so severe that it was impossible to launch any more lifeboats, and the well-ordered calm of the ship began to degenerate into chaos, in the midst of which the *Masai* was hit again.

"Using us for target practice", remarked a young officer as he and John clung to the railing of the bridge.

"Time for you to go, Harry", said John.

"I dunno where to. No lifeboats and only a few rafts—I might as well stay here."

At that moment the ship lurched heavily and the two officers slid down to the lower side of the bridge. The water was already over the side and only a few feet below them.

"Maybe you're right", said the officer, seizing his captain by the arm and pulling him over the rail. John offered no resistance. He was a thousand miles away with a young girl. It was a pity that he wouldn't be able to see her again, but this seemed to be a good way out of the mess. Before the waters closed over his head he thought of Susan and hoped with all his heart that she would be all right. None of this was her fault and it would be good that she would never know about his futile infatuation.

As it happened, however, the young officer was a good swimmer with nothing unusual on his conscience, and he thought it would be good idea if he and his captain tried to live a little longer.

Jessica was due back at school on January 7th, which was a Tuesday, and on the previous day Susan received two letters. One was an unusually brief scribble from John to say that he was in Liverpool and would be sailing again on the following day. It was dated December 20th, but the postmark said January 2nd. Evidently John had forgotten to post it and someone had found it and done it for him later. He had also apparently been in too much of a rush to say how much he loved and missed her, and it struck her that if things had been the way they usually were she would have been hurt, whereas in fact she was rather relieved. The other letter was from a government official, telling her that she would be needed for a spell in Portsmouth, starting on Thursday. Portsmouth, the Royal Navy's most important port on the South Coast, was home to thousands of naval personnel and had so far been spared the devastation that the German bombers had inflicted on other south coast cities.

At first Jessica was badly shaken by the news of Susan's imminent departure and tears flowed copiously. Susan knew the things one should say and the reasons one should give for being brave and enduring what had to be, but she was wise enough to keep silent and simply hold Jessica in her arms.

"I'm sorry, Susan", said Jessica at last. "It must be harder for you than it is for me. It's silly really, but I've been pretending that we should be together for ever although we knew something like this would happen."

"We'll soon be together again, darling. It's only supposed to be for three weeks and I'll write as often as I can."

"I'm sorry", said Jessica again, "I really am an awful person. People are being separated for years at a time and being killed and here I am making a fuss about three weeks. And at least it's not London or Southampton—I'd really be terrified if you were going there. It's just that I don't think two people ever loved each other as much as we do."

Susan held Jessica a little more tightly, but again she didn't say anything. She had heard those words before, but on this occasion she thought they might be true in spite of the scepticism of the part of her inner self that kept an eye on her thoughts. There was in both of their minds a fear that neither could articulate or find a way of dealing with—that in spite all their efforts something that would end their love affair lay hidden in the future and that the three weeks of separation would bring them that much closer to it.

That evening when they went to bed Susan said, "Did you know that you've been sleeping with a criminal?"

Jessica thought for a moment.

"You mean because I'm only fifteen? It must be that because I don't believe you've ever done anything wrong."

Susan laughed ruefully.

"I'm not by any means perfect, but yes, I think this is the first time I've ever knowingly done anything against the law. And I think it's illegal anyway, and your being fifteen just makes it worse."

"You don't mean that you want to stop, do you?" asked Jessica, as something seemed to turn over inside her.

"No, I want it always to be like this."

Jessica relaxed a little but her heart was still doing uncomfortable things.

"Please don't ever frighten me like that again."

"I'm sorry, darling. I do understand about being frightened."

"Because of me?"

"Not because of anything that you do. Just that something will happen and I'll lose you."

"But I'll never leave you—unless they put me in prison or something. And if I have to I'll wait for you until I'm eighteen or even twenty-one. Will you wait for me?"

"Of course I will. I've been waiting for you all my life, only I didn't know."

"Susan, what will happen when you see John? I mean, do you think he will understand?"

"I don't know. I don't think there are many people who would. The trouble is that whatever I do he's going to be very hurt, and I truly don't want to hurt him."

"I don't either", said Jessica. "I liked him very much, although he made me feel uncomfortable sometimes."

"How do you mean?"

"I can't really explain it. It was a bit as if he treated me too much like someone of his own age—as if I were a woman he might be interested in."

"But isn't that what I've been doing?"

Jessica paused for a moment.

"This is getting too hard for me. I suppose it's because I love you so much—whatever you do is all right because it's you doing it. Sometimes I feel like a grown-up and sometimes I feel like a schoolgirl and you always seem to love me just the same. I hope this doesn't upset you, but sometimes you're my lover and sometimes you're my mother and I want it always to be like that, even when I'm grown up."

"I think it's often like that with lovers. And it makes me happy, because sometimes I've been a little afraid that when you're grown up you won't want me any more."

"Are you still afraid now?"

"No, my darling, when I'm with you I'm not afraid of anything. And you're very grown up already."

"More than I was a few weeks ago?"

"Much more. Do you like it?"

"Yes—I feel like a woman instead of a kid and it's very exciting. Susan, we're always going to live together and if the rest of the world doesn't like it we can tell it to go to hell."

"And then soon it will be spring", said Susan over breakfast on Wednesday morning, "and we can get on a bus and go out to Newent and gather daffodils and primroses and bluebells in the woods. We used to do that when I was a child, you know. And sometimes when I was older I would bicycle there on my own, early in the morning and have the woods to myself. It was like being in fairyland, and if it wasn't too cold I would take off my shoes and stockings and dabble in the dew and pretend that I had been abducted by the king of the fairies. I was much less grown up than you are, you see."

Jessica's vivid imagination produced an enchanting picture of Susan running through the woods in bare feet and a short flimsy dress very much like the pale green nightgown, and with her golden hair flowing over her shoulders.

"Let's do it, Susan. I'm not too grown up to have feelings like that."

"Neither am I, really."

"Only I don't want the Fairy King. I think that you must be the Fairy Queen, and you've abducted me already and this is the enchanted castle."

"That's funny, really", said Susan.

"I know—let's say 'elves' instead of 'fairies'."

It was their last day together before Susan was due in Portsmouth and they laughed in spite of the deep shadow of parting that was falling over them. Then they both wept a little.

"Can you come home really early tonight?" asked Jessica. "If I have to wait for you for a long time I think I'll die."

"I'll walk out of there at five o'clock no matter what happens."

"And I'll light a really big fire upstairs so it will be nice and warm when you get here."

Chapter XVIII

1965: Thursday, December 23

It was half-past ten on Thursday morning. School was over for two blessed weeks and conversations about the odd events of the past few days were going on in several different places.

Sergeant Snipe had been on the job early.

"What have you got, Snipey?" Inspector Phelps asked as the sergeant walked into his office, looking none too pleased with himself. "Nothing very exciting, by the look of you."

"No, Sir. As far as young Johnson himself is concerned, at least one part of his story is true. His ship was sunk in 1940. He was very ill afterwards and it took him so long to recover that he never returned to active service. They gave him a shore job in Liverpool in 1943 and invalided him out early in 1945. That's all from naval records. From the Parish Register I found out that he was the youngest of three children. He had a brother Thomas, who was the oldest, and a sister Pamela. And from an elderly couple who lived opposite the Johnsons from about 1927 until a few years ago, I learnt that Thomas has a farm somewhere in Shropshire and Pamela died during the war."

"What happened to her?"

"I don't know yet, and possibly the only way to find out would be to ask Johnson directly. According to the old people, she left home when she was about seventeen and they never saw her again. They said that they had asked old Johnson about her once or twice, and as far as they remember he said that she was living in London. Then some time later—they think it was early in the war—they saw him walking along the road and he looked so ill that they went out to see if he needed help. He told them that he had lost his daughter, and that's all he would say. The reason they remembered it was that he seemed so strange. Apparently he never had been very talkative, but on this occasion he just went on walking and wouldn't say any more. The older boy liked to play at being a builder like his father, but Pamela used to run over to the old people—of course they weren't so old then—and they would give her tea and a piece of cake and she would tell them all the things she wanted to do when she grew up. They said that she had a very mischievous look in her eye and was always making them laugh."

"Let's see, how old would she have been in 1940?"

"Well, she was born in 1913, so she would have been twenty-seven."

"And she left home somewhere about 1930. I wonder what she did."

"It looks as if we'll have to ask Henry, and what's the betting he'll say he doesn't know?"

"That's right", growled the inspector. "There must be thousands of Pamela Johnsons in this country—all he has to say is that they were estranged and he didn't hear anything of her until she died. I take it they didn't say anything about young Henry or you would have told me by now. Is there anything else?"

"Yes—the children all had red hair and freckles."

"Like Veronica Edwards."

"Yes, sir. And I've verified everything that we were told about Arthur Williams and Goofy Thomas. Williams's housekeeper exists but rarely goes out, and I don't see how I can talk to her without getting past her boss first. It occurred to me that she might be the lady who was with him and Johnson at the funeral. As far as I've been able to ascertain, Johnson and Sons are doing very well. Plenty of work and no serious friction with their competitors except in the matter of the school."

"Well, scout around a bit more and see if you can find anyone else who knew the Johnsons before the war."

"Yes, Sir. I'll see what I can do. I'll bet you Arthur Williams knows the whole story but I don't suppose it's any use asking him."

"Not yet, at any rate. Just get whatever you can and then we'll make up our minds to pay another visit to young Johnson."

"Mrs. Marjoribanks is becoming quite insufferable", Charles Ferrier remarked petulantly.

"Yes, Mr. Ferrier?" said Mrs. Smail complacently. "What has she been up to now?"

"She hasn't exactly been up to anything—although, now I come to think of it, perhaps she has. But it's her manner that I don't like; a mere secretary and a blacksmith's daughter at that, and she talks to me as though we were social and professional equals. And I'm beginning to think that there's something going on between her and Mr. Woodcock."

"Oh dear", murmured Mrs. Smail, who was also a mere secretary, but a self-effacing and motherly one, "how very unsuitable. Of course, you know her mother was a Gaffney, although by all accounts she was no better than she ought to have been. Like mother, like daughter, I suppose."

"I also have the impression that Inspector Phelps is encouraging the two of them to concern themselves in the investigation of this deplorable business of a young woman's skeleton being found on school property."

He made it sound as if the young woman had been extremely careless in not disposing of her bones in a more appropriate manner.

"In my view", he went on in his most considered and judicial manner, "it is highly inappropriate for the headmaster of a prominent grammar school to be involved in criminal investigations."

Mrs. Smail, who had met Woodcock and been rather taken with him, muttered something noncommittal. Ferrier looked at her sharply.

"Well, don't you agree with me?"

"Oh, yes, of course. Most unsuitable", replied Mrs. Smail, resorting again to her favorite word of deprecation. "But I did hear that they had been very helpful in the investigation of the fire."

This remark increased Ferrier's irritation to the point of causing a mild explosion.

"Nonsense", he snorted. "Phelps is quite capable of conducting any investigation that may be required."

"Of course, Mr. Ferrier, I agree with you entirely", said Mrs. Smail tranquilly. "Perhaps if you said a word to Mr. Woodcock . . ."

"He is quite impervious to anything I say to him—but there may be another way in which I can influence him. Yes, aha . . ."

Ferrier rubbed his hands together and began to look a little more pleased with himself.

"Time for my elevenses I think."

"Yes, Mr. Ferrier."

"Have you got any idea at all about what could have happened to Jessica?" asked Gwyneth Evans. "I mean, did she ever say anything—I mean anything that you wouldn't have wanted to tell the police?"

Penelope Thrower was still working on her exam papers, but the process was mechanical enough to allow her to sustain a conversation at the same time.

"No, Gwynny, we never had any little tête-à-têtes, if that's what you're wondering, so it's a complete mystery to me. I still find it hard to imagine anyone wanting to hurt her."

"I don't know about that—there was a time when I wished that she had never been born."

Penelope looked up and decided that it was time to devote her entire attention to her old friend.

"But you wouldn't have killed her, would you?"

"I don't think so, but I might have wanted to if she had stayed here longer. And perhaps there was somebody somewhere who was in the same position I was or in the opposite position of wanting her and not being able to have her."

"Gwynny! You don't think . . ."

"No, of course not. You would rather have died than let anything happen to her, and I'm pretty sure that even if she had felt about you the way you did about her you still would have stuck to the path of duty."

"I don't know about that", said Penelope with a rueful smile.

"Well you're a much stronger woman than I am, Penny. If that had happened to me I should probably have gone completely off the rails."

"So should I if Jessica had been here a little longer. And now that I'm being forced to think about it I realize that I really have been off the rails for the past twenty-five years. I think if I'd known that she was apt to have that effect on people and I wasn't the only one it might have been different—and if I'd known that she had died. As it was I always had this silly little hope that I would meet her again, perhaps in different circumstances. But it was much worse for you, Gwynny. You were really in the same position as I was except that we had been so happy together, so you were losing something with me that I had never had with Jessica. It does make me realize how someone might really have wanted to kill her."

"But Penny, I really liked her—not the way you and Veronica did—but enough to look forward to seeing her once a week and to enjoy the few minutes' chat that we occasionally had."

"Do you think it's really possible that you could forgive me?"

"I don't know. Sometimes I think about all those wasted years when we could have been together, and I'm afraid it may never stop hurting."

Woodcock had just finished giving Bill the gist of his conversation with Phelps.

"Well!" said Bill. "In a quiet way this Jessica seems to have been an amazing young woman. It certainly changes my opinion of the second poem. For an adult to write something like that would be almost unseemly, but for a child of fifteen it's really quite remarkable."

"It's interesting that you referred to her as a young woman and as a child in the same paragraph."

"Yes. You know I think that's what makes some adolescents so damnably attractive—that is, if they *are* attractive in that way—which is not very often."

"Fortunately. But this one seems to have had something unusually unusual."

"She was physically attractive, athletic, highly intelligent, becomingly modest and quite mysterious. What more could you ask?"

"And women went down before her like ninepins. I wonder what she was like with men."

"I don't know. It's possible that they found her a little frightening."

"Perhaps, but if she was as modest among them as she was with the women, she may have quietly bowled them over too. Childlike vulnerability, hidden depths and youthful idealism still intact—it's a devastating combination."

"I know. That's obviously why you fell for me."

Woodcock looked fondly at his middle-aged lover.

"But of course", he said, and was saved from further comment by the telephone.

"Time to start breakfast."

By the time Inspector Phelps arrived Woodcock had made the air fragrant with the mingled aromas of bacon, eggs, toast and coffee, and Bill had made as cheerful a fire as she could in the typically modest grate of an upstairs room in an English house.

"You know, the fact is that I'm not really quite sure why I'm here", Phelps said rather apologetically as he bent over his plate.

This drew an immediate response from Bill.

"Come off it Jack, the answer's staring you in the face."

"And a jolly good answer it is—it almost compensates for the feeling that we haven't got anywhere with this case yet."

"Well, you've found out who the unfortunate girl was", pointed out Woodcock.

"More by luck than good judgement. Apart from that it looks more like that Sherlock Holmes story than anything else—you know, the red-headed league. We've got a red-headed gym teacher from London, a ginger-haired building contractor with a red-headed sister, only she's dead, and a mysterious red-head who delivered the girl to her school."

"And a red-headed secretary who at this moment is helping the police with their enquiries", observed Bill with a grin.

"Well now, I hadn't thought of that. Let's see, where were you on the night of . . ."

"I never done it", replied Bill with a very realistic whine. "You must be hoping that two of these women turn out to be the same."

"I suppose it would be too much too hope", remarked Woodcock, "that all three of them are the same."

"Well, it did cross my mind and Snipey's, as a matter of fact, that Pamela might have disappeared in London and turned up later as Miss Edwards, and that Miss Edwards might be the red-head who took Jessica to the school. But then you'd think that Miss Thrower would have recognized her, even though she only saw her for a few minutes."

"I don't know", said Bill. "After twenty-five years it's possible that she didn't. What's Snipey doing, by the way? We would have loved to have had him for breakfast."

"I'll tell him. He's trying to find out what happened to Pamela Johnson, so we can be prepared for another go at Henry. All we know about her is what we heard from the old neighbors. We may have to ask him directly—and he's a slippery customer."

"But not a poet?"

"I doubt it, but even if he is he seems to have had a pretty good alibi that lasted for several years. And even if we find the unknown redhead and the mysterious poet, we don't know whether either of them killed Jessica. Apart from finding out about Pamela, all we have to work on is that someone sent Jessica's poem with a wreath and that there's someone at Blenheim Hall had who actually had a plausible motive for putting her out of the way."

"What do you really think of Miss Evans as a suspect?"

"Well, she's the only person we actually know of who associated with Jessica and had a reason for wanting her out of the way. But we haven't found any connection between her and the Nave or Johnson and his pals. She arrived at Blenheim Hall straight from Swansea in 1939.

"Have you considered the possibility that the skeleton was Pamela?" asked Woodcock.

"Yes, but it doesn't seem to work out. If the doctor is right about the victim's age she would have had to have died in about 1929, so she couldn't have had anything to do with Jessica or Jessica's poem."

"What if the doctor is wrong?"

"Well then, supposing that she was the object of Jessica's poem she must have been alive at the beginning of 1941 and she would have been about twenty-seven. I doubt whether the doctor would be so far out, but I suppose we ought to keep it in mind as a possibility."

"In which case Jessica would still be alive and we'd be looking for a mysterious tall, dark woman of about forty who left a wreath and a poem on the coffin."

"And we'd have to explain why she left the school so suddenly in 1941. It just doesn't seem very likely to me."

"Have you got anywhere with the wreath?" asked Woodcock.

"Only that someone posted a large envelope with two fivers, some instructions and an enclosed envelope to Smedley's the florists. 'Please deliver the best funeral wreath you can for the money, and attach the enclosed envelope to it' or words to that effect."

"There's nothing you can trace?"

"They threw everything away after they had filled the order. And the fivers were old and looked as if they hadn't seen the inside of a bank for years."

"You'd better have some more eggs and bacon", said Bill.

"Yes, I think I will. I need something to build up my constitution. I suppose the real reason why I came here is that all we have is dead ends and I thought the two of you might be able to fish an idea out of thin air."

"Well", said Woodcock, "I do have an idea, but it's exceedingly vague and farfetched."

"At this point I don't care how far you have to fetch it."

"All right then—I think that in spite of the evidence of the golden-haired lady, the first poem was written for Jessica by a man, and that he had something to do with the Nave. It's possible that whoever wrote it was present at the burial in 1945 or, at least, knew that it had taken place, and wanted to be near the remains of the beloved. It's that kind of poem, you know. What I suggest is that you trot over to Brunswick House and check up on the past histories of all masters who were appointed to the Nave before about 1947, but especially near the end of the war."

"What will I be looking for?"

"Anything that looks odd or suspicious, or perhaps the absence of something that ought to be there. As I said, this is very thin, but it strikes me that in the normal way, anyone who had somehow been responsible for bringing about the death of a girl, and had got away with it, would probably want to remove himself as far as possible from the scene of the crime. But it's possible that this one had a very elevated romantic reason for remaining on the scene. If that was how it was he may well have taken steps to conceal his identity, and it would have been difficult to supply the usual information about education and previous employment."

"All right, but to be honest, I don't see why there had to be any connection to the Nave at all, apart from the fact that Johnson was putting up the building."

"Well, as I said, it's really just a hunch."

"I believe you have someone definite in mind", said the inspector accusingly.

"Perhaps, but the only real basis for it is a chance remark about Thomas Hardy, and it's so vague that I don't want to mention anyone's name yet."

"I don't blame you; there's too much poetry in this case already. And I think we'd better do this together—I'm not sure that I'd recognize whatever it is or isn't that I'm supposed to look for. The sooner the better, if you don't mind."

"All right—I'll meet you at Brunswick House at two o'clock. Mrs. Smail will be back from lunch but with any luck Ferrier won't."

"Done", said the inspector.

"Now", said Bill, after Phelps had left, "I want to know what you meant about Thomas Hardy."

"All right, if you insist, but it really doesn't amount to very much."

"I've heard you say that before."

"I know, but this time it really is very tenuous."

Woodcock paused and considered. It was hard to put into words something that was not much more than a vague intuition.

"Well, we have a young girl, not yet sixteen, uncannily attractive, immensely talented, unusually modest and, apparently, ill-fated. Now all those things in themselves would not have been enough to put me in mind of Hardy, but it just happened that I quoted him the other day and someone said something that made me think. At that time all we knew was that some unfortunate girl had met her end in a mysterious way, but if I had known then what we know now I should have thought a good deal harder. Although Jessica doesn't exactly correspond to any of Hardy's unlucky heroines, I have the impression that she may have been as ill-fated as any of them—an innocent victim of the universe's indifference to human suffering. That is, of course, if it *was* Jessica."

"Who was the someone?"

"Well, you were standing there at the time."

"Oh, yes", said Bill, "so I was."

CHAPTER XIX

1941: Wednesday, January 8th

By six o'clock Susan and Jessica were sitting in front of the bedroom fire, eating the best tea they could manage. Susan was going over the instructions she had given Jessica for the three weeks in which she was to be alone. It was not so much a matter of buying groceries, dealing with tradesmen and keeping up with the domestic chores—Jessica was perfectly capable of managing those things on her own—as of keeping up the appearance that Susan was still there. The short days and the long blackouts would be a great help. Jessica would occasionally leave the house in the morning, wearing Susan's spare hat and coat, and it would be natural at this time of the year for her be so muffled up that her black hair would be invisible. Her own hat would be in her satchel so that she could change after getting off the bus. She was a couple of inches taller than Susan but in the dim light it was unlikely that anyone would notice the discrepancy.

After tea they looked at each other and Jessica said, "I feel so strange inside."

"So do I. Let's get into bed and just hold each other for a little while."

"Is it getting any better?" Susan asked after a few minutes.

"Yes. Is it for you?"

"Yes."

They were both still wearing their skirts and blouses, and Jessica said, "It's funny to be in bed together with our clothes on."

"Let's try concentrating very hard just on each other", said Susan, "and see if we can stop any of the bad things from getting in."

"I'm all right now", Jessica said a little later.

"So am I"

With great gentleness they undressed each other and helped each other with the nightgowns, Jessica still in red, but Susan now with the pale green one.

"I'm wearing this for you now, Jessica, so that you will know that I'm all new and strong. And while I'm away you can wear it sometimes and pretend that I'm still here."

"I think I'm going to do a lot of pretending."

"So am I. It's a bit more daring than the others so when I think of you wearing it it will make me feel all warm inside."

So red and black mingled with green and gold and made a symphony that lasted well into the night.

"I don't want to go to sleep", Jessica whispered. "It will seem like a split second and then it will be time to go."

"I know, darling. I don't want to go to sleep either. When I was a quite little I hated school, so I used to wait until everyone else was asleep and then turn the light on and read—just to make the night last longer. But the morning always came anyway."

Sleep had its way with them just the same, but in the small hours Jessica woke up. Susan was lying close to her and crying quietly.

"What is it my darling? Oh, my darling, please don't cry. Your Jessica is here. You see?"

Jessica kissed Susan's lips and her wet eyes.

"See if you can tell me what it is."

"It was a dream, only I thought it was real. We went on the bus to King's Square and after we got off I looked round for you and you weren't there. You weren't on the bus or anywhere in the square. And I kept on looking for you everywhere and I couldn't find you."

Susan sobbed inconsolably, and all Jessica could do was to hold her as tightly as she could and whisper, "But I'm here now, darling."

"Are you sure? Are we really here together? Because the dream wouldn't go away—I woke up several times and when I fell asleep again I was still looking for you. And now I'm not sure which is which and I'm so frightened."

"I'm really here, darling. Can you feel my hand?"

She sat up a little, stroked Susan's hair and cheeks and cradled her head between her breasts.

"There", she said. "Those are your little mountains. You really ought to recognize them. You can kiss them if you like, to see if they taste the same."

She went on stroking Susan's hair until the sobbing ceased and Susan said, with a touch of her old humor "I'm sorry, darling. It really is you—you taste exactly right. Can I stay like this for a little while longer?"

"For the rest of the night, if you like."

"Now you're being a mother to me."

In addition to the other little subterfuges that Susan had planned, she had gone out before dawn on the previous day and left her suitcase in her office at the infirmary. Her train was not due to leave until eleven o'clock and she pondered going on the bus with Jessica as far as King's Square so that they could have another half-hour together before parting. But she knew that when the moment came their feelings would be too strong to be expressed in a public place, so they said their goodbyes inside the front door. Jessica was wearing her dark blue school uniform and Susan had put on the long white lace nightgown. They were both struggling with tears and Susan said:

"Isn't it silly—I'm only going to be away for three weeks."

"Three weeks is a very long time", said Jessica, "and I'm scared it won't be the same when you come home."

"Oh my darling, how could you say such a thing?"

Jessica, contrite and for a moment speechless, buried her face in Susan's long golden hair.

"I'm sorry. I'll always love you and I'll never let you down. I think it was because I'm just a kid in a school uniform and you're going away to do something really important. And you're so very, very beautiful in that gown. I feel as if I'm not really good enough for you."

"My dear, sweet idiot", said Susan, "one of the nicest things about you is that you don't know how wonderful you are. You are a much better person than I am."

"Let's promise", said Jessica, her eyes shining.

"Yes, let's."

They stood very upright, facing each other and holding hands, conscious only of each other and quite unaware of the picture that they made; Jessica, if she had but known it, taller and more imposing, her dark blue blazer filling out her slender figure, and Susan, diminutive and vulnerable in her white lace gown, with the morning sun glinting red and green through the little stained glass window over the door.

"I, Jessica, promise that I will always love and cherish you, Susan, and be with you for the rest of my life."

"I, Susan, promise that I will always love and cherish you, Jessica, and be with you for the rest of my life."

"Now I think we're supposed to kiss."

So they did, for a long time.

"What about rings?" asked Jessica.

"I think we're going to have to imagine them. The only rings I have are from John, and I must keep on wearing them until I tell him."

The kitchen clock struck half-past eight.

"You're going to be late, darling."

"I don't mind", said Jessica. They held hands as they went to the front gate before kissing again in full view of the neighbors. Then Jessica was gone. Susan ran back to the house to dress and pack a small handbag. She was very cold now and she had to fight the impulse to lie down on the bed and cry. She and Jessica had been utterly sincere in making their promises, but was there really any hope that they would be allowed to keep them?

CHAPTER XX

1965: Thursday, December 23

Woodcock's strategy for evading Ferrier worked very well up to a point. Mrs. Smail was amused to see the headmaster and the inspector arriving together so soon after she had felt forced to characterize their collaboration as "unsuitable".

"Yes", she said, "of course. Inspector Phelps knows where the files are. Mr. Ferrier won't be back for another hour or so, so you might as well sit in his office and do your looking, as long as you finish before he gets back."

There had been quite an influx of new masters in the years Woodcock had specified, but most of them seemed to be unlikely candidates for consideration as potential poets or murderers. Some had stayed only a short time, some seemed too old to have been involved in a heavily romantic attachment only a few years previously—although, as Phelps remarked, "You never know"—and some seemed impeccably prosaic.

"And you never know about that, either", remarked the headmaster. "However, we seem to have narrowed the field to three candidates, so to speak, and two of them strike me as being unlikely in the extreme."

"And the third?"

"Well look at it. It has everything that you would expect, including the details of his degree, but it doesn't say where he got it. And yet it seems to be common knowledge among his colleagues that he was at Sidney Sussex. And he was a naval officer in the war."

"Like Henry Johnson. But where and what is Sidney Sussex?"

"It's one of the smaller and less fashionable Cambridge colleges."

Woodcock was about to explain further when they heard a disturbance in the outer office.

Ferrier had spent a pleasant hour carefully cultivating the little plan that had begun to germinate in his mind. As it burgeoned and he saw clearly how it might come to fruition he became excited, so he hurriedly paid his bill and strode vigorously back to Brunswick House. When Mrs. Smail saw her superior officer arrive forty minutes ahead of his usual schedule she turned several shades paler and murmured, "Oh dear!"

"What are you muttering about? Is something the matter?" Ferrier asked.

"There are some visitors in your office", said Mrs. Smail bravely.

"Visitors? I wasn't expecting any visitors. Who are they?"

"Well, as a matter of fact it's Mr. Woodcock and Inspector Phelps."

"Woodcock and Phelps? Together?"

Ferrier's voice was getting louder and higher.

"What do they want?"

"They're looking at some old files from the Nave."

"And in spite of knowing my opinion of Woodcock and his efforts at playing the amateur detective you simply let them take over my office?"

Mrs. Smail would have liked to point out that Ferrier had returned much earlier than usual, but since they had never abandoned the polite fiction that his lunch hour ended at two o'clock she could hardly do this. She couldn't think of anything to say, but it didn't make any difference since Ferrier was going straight on anyway. He didn't have a very imposing voice, so when he tried to thunder, "This is intolerable", as he marched over to his office door, it came out as a loud bleat rather than the leonine roar that he had intended. He was about to put his hand on the doorknob when it occurred to him that he had no clear idea of what he was going to say, and that instead of creating a scene in which he might well come off second or even third best, this would be a good time to make a strategic retreat and put his little plan into action; so he turned tail and marched back through the outer office and out to the street. When Woodcock looked out to see what was going on, he caught a glimpse of Ferrier's disappearing coat-tails and a rather better view of Mrs. Smail's highly undignified gape. The lady was equal to the occasion, however.

After closing her mouth with a snap she remarked, "He hardly ever forgets anything, but when he does he finds it extremely annoying."

Inspector Phelps followed his ally out of Ferrier's office.

"We're just going to borrow these three for a day or two. I'll put the rest back exactly as we found them."

"Perhaps I should make a note of them", said Mrs. Smail hopefully.

"That won't be necessary. I'll vouch for their safety."

Phelps had no intention of letting anyone know which masters were under investigation. He and Woodcock had known what they were looking for, but if Mrs. Smail wanted to find out which ones were missing, she would have to sift through the files of hundreds of past and present teachers, and that seemed very unlikely.

The events of the first half of that Thursday had a number of consequences.

A telephone call to Sidney Sussex College elicited the information that there was no one in residence who could find the answer to a question about someone who had graduated in the early 1930's. It was, after all, only a few days before Christmas. Phelps's mild comment to the effect that perhaps the Cambridge police might be willing to help produced the promise to try to locate the College Secretary and find something out in a day or so. With that, Inspector Phelps decided to be content. The corpse had, after all, been awaiting discovery for twenty-five years or so.

Miss Dwight learnt that she would be without a badminton partner for the next couple of weeks as Miss Evans had decided to go on a trip with friend. Miss Evans had forgotten to mention that the trip was only as far as Huntley, a village a few miles outside Gloucester, where she had a small cottage, and that the friend was Miss Thrower.

And the following letter to the editor appeared in the later editions of the *Citizen*.

Dear Sir,

It is with great reluctance that I have decided to air my concerns about the state of education in our city. Gloucester is fortunate in having four grammar schools, some being ancient foundations and all having distinguished records of educational achievement. At three of them traditional standards are, to the best of my knowledge, being maintained, but our Local Education Authority ought to be seriously worried about what is going on at the fourth.

If the recent conflagration at the Nave School had resulted from the malicious activities of nefarious outsiders, we should have far less cause for concern; but the fact is that the public are being kept in the dark about the real nature of what might have been a tragic disaster. It had, in fact, been known for a long time that the building was in a very dangerous condition and yet, to the best of my knowledge, nothing had ever been done to ameliorate the situation. As it happens, however, some of those who are 'in the know' have been willing to let their knowledge percolate into the public domain, and a very disquieting picture has emerged. The whole episode suggests a serious lack of leadership in the school, and there is no reason to suppose that similar events do not lie in wait for us in the near future. It is even more disturbing that at a time when every effort is needed to maintain the school's good name, some of those in positions of public trust and authority continue to set a bad example by openly flouting the conventions of decent behavior.

This parlous state of affairs has been exacerbated by the recent discovery of a skeleton under the ruins of the old science building, so movingly reported in the columns of the Citizen *last Saturday. The circumstances strongly suggest that there is another murky secret hidden behind the smooth façade presented by those in charge, and that there is confusion between the proper domains of the activities of the police and those of the school's internal administration.*

It is to be hoped that our City Fathers will take note of the situation and use whatever influence they can bring to bear to change things for the better.

Yours etc.

Concerned Citizen

(Name and address supplied)

"Well, I'll be damned . . . The bastard, the lousy rotten bastard!"

"Darling, what on earth is it?"

Woodcock generally reserved such endearments for more intimate occasions, but Bill so rarely used any kind of strong language that he knew something unusually awful must have happened.

"I think you'd better look at this', said Bill, handing him the *Citizen*, "and tell me if my diagnosis is correct."

"I don't think there's any doubt about it", said Woodcock, who was a quick reader. "He seems to have taken some trouble to sound anonymous but he can't control his tendency to be pompous and sententious."

"He doesn't know he's pompous and sententious. Why aren't you gibbering with rage?"

"Actually I am, but I'm trying to look on the bright side and gibber intelligently."

"Do you think it's actionable?"

"I don't know; I'm sure he thought of that and decided that we wouldn't want to wash our dirty linen in public. But I do think that he got very angry this afternoon and acted hastily without weighing the consequences quite carefully enough. This will certainly have repercussions in the L. E. A. and the City Council, and if it comes out that Ferrier wrote it he's going to find himself in hot water."

"That may be difficult. It's obvious to us, but some of our city fathers are not so quick on the uptake."

"True, but I have another idea brewing. Five days ago Ferrier was responsible for a report in the *Citizen*, and the immediate consequence was a letter from Veronica Edwards. I think it's quite possible that this letter may stir someone up. If Jack is right about the goings on on

Friday night, Henry Johnson and his friends must already feel that the ice is pretty thin beneath them—and if I'm right there's someone in the school who's in the same condition. That's the 'murky secret' that the writer says we're hiding under our 'smooth façade', and I think that Jack would have every reason to find out who he is and question him—the writer, I mean. If that were to happen I doubt whether he would be able to remain anonymous."

Rather a lot of sleep was lost on Thursday night. Bill's fury had abated somewhat but she was still steaming inwardly when she and Woodcock went to bed, taking a bottle of Burgundy with them.

"Why are you so calm?" she asked her partner. "It's not natural and it's probably not good for you."

"Well it's partly that I have a vision of Ferrier stewing in his own juice, and partly that I can't help feeling sorry for him."

"Sorry for him!"

"Well, he doesn't like his wife and he doesn't like his children. His one great comfort in life, apart from the sense of his own importance, is Mrs. Smail, and yesterday *she* let him down. If he lost his job he'd have nothing left—in fact he'd have a negative balance."

"Whereas if we got the sack, I could get a job as a secretary and you could stay at home and look after the house—and write a nice juicy memoir about the doings at the Nave. Is there anything left in that bottle?"

"Absolutely, and there are two more in the cupboard."

"That should just about see us through. What, if anything, do you think is going through the minds of the city fathers?"

"I suspect that the dominant feeling is one of curiosity. The patriarchal pennies tend to drop rather slowly, so it's highly probable that some of them are still wondering what on earth the letter is about. When you try as hard as Ferrier did to say something without quite saying it, you are dependent on the sharpness of your audience. They'll all get it eventually, but some of the more dim-witted ones will have to have it explained to them. Unfortunately there's a certain amount of truth behind some of the insinuations. I mean, in spite of our efforts to be discreet, some people must have tumbled to the fact that we have been flouting the conventions of whatever it was."

"'Decent behavior.' And I don't think it's unfortunate. I've been enjoying the floutation."

"So have I, and I intend to continue floutating—unless you feel the urge to make an honest man of me."

"Well as a matter of fact . . . But I don't want to do it just because Ferrier has been shooting off his mouth. It would be too much like a shotgun wedding. On the other hand I don't want to *not* do it just because etc."

"All right. May I propose to you sitting up in bed or would you like me to get out of bed and kneel?"

"I have a better idea."

"Yes?"

"You could propose lying down."

Woodcock emptied his glass and complied with Bill's suggestion.

"Will you marry me, Bill?"

Bill followed suit and asked, "Now?"

"Absolutely."

Meanwhile the righteous indignation that had sustained Ferrier throughout the day was subsiding, and he realized that he had no desire to explain to his wife, who had far more common sense than he had, how he had spent the latter part of the afternoon. All he would say was that he had had a very trying day and that he thought it would be good for him to go to bed early.

"I suppose it hasn't occurred to you that I've had a very trying day too", said his wife. "Perhaps it has escaped your attention that today is the first day of the Christmas holidays and I've spent most of it running after three children, trying to do some shopping and getting meals ready. All you have to do is sit on your bottom and dictate letters to a fat fool of a woman whose main duty seems to be to make tea for you whenever you feel a little jaded."

Ferrier had often had to defend Mrs. Smail against such attacks, but it could hardly be denied that she was a bit overweight, and on this particular day he was not feeling very pleased with her.

"Yes, dear, but I've had to deal with all the awkwardness arising from that confounded skeleton and today my office was invaded by Woodcock and Phelps."

"How awful of them to disturb your tranquillity! And next I suppose you're going to complain about this idiotic letter in the *Citizen*. How anyone could think that a letter like that would help the situation I can't imagine—or why the *Citizen* would print it. It must have been someone with a pull at the editor's office. But I'm surprised they didn't ask you about it—you've always been pretty thick with them, haven't you."

"I don't know, my dear. I thought it made some rather good points."

The hint of smugness in Ferrier's voice caught his wife's attention. She looked at him with growing suspicion.

"It was you, wasn't it? It's exactly your style. You don't like those people at The Nave and you took your chance to get back at them. Don't you realize that if this gets out you'll have to resign? How did I come to marry such a blithering idiot?"

But Ferrier was already halfway up the stairs, muttering something about a headache, so the question was never answered.

The next morning Phelps made up his mind.

"Time to take another shot at Henry Johnson", he told his sergeant. "I want to try the name of Jessica Smith on him and ask him about his sister. He'll probably still stonewall us but we might just get an indication that we're on the right track."

There was more than a hint of world-weariness in Johnson's posture as he received the two policemen, but he still wasn't giving anything away.

"Well, I have to hand it to you for persistence, but since I haven't got anything else to tell you I'm afraid it's still going to be a waste of time."

"Perhaps that's so, Mr. Johnson", said Inspector Phelps, "but we do have a few new questions for you."

"I can't imagine what they are, but fire away."

"All right. First we'd like you to tell us what happened to your sister Pamela."

For the first time Johnson lost his composure.

"Why are you bringing Pamela into this? What could it possibly have to do with her?"

"We're simply acting on information received, Mr. Johnson. Is there any reason why you shouldn't tell us?"

"No, and as far as I can see there's no particular reason why I should."

"Well, perhaps you could tell us if it is correct that she died during the war."

"Yes. If you must know she was killed by a V2 in 1945."

"I'm very sorry, Mr. Johnson, but I do have to ask these questions. Do you have any record of her death?"

"No, damn you, the whole building she was in was blown to bits and no one was ever identified."

"What did she do during the war?"

"She was a WAAF, and that's all I can tell you."

"Very well. I have just one more question. Does the name Jessica Smith means anything to you?"

"No, Inspector, not a thing", Johnson answered quite firmly, but as he spoke he sat down heavily and, for the first time, looked shaken.

"You're sure of that?"

"Yes, I'm sure"

"And I'm sure he was lying", Snipe remarked as he and Phelps walked back to the car.

"Yes. We may not have cracked him, but at least we've confirmed that he's involved. And he may be lying about his sister being killed by a V2. They didn't start until 1945, but old Johnson's neighbors said that it was near the beginning of the war when he told them that he had lost his daughter."

"Right", Snipe said, but they were both thinking that there are more ways than one of losing a daughter.

A few seconds after they had pulled out, an old Ford Prefect passed them in the opposite direction. Looking in his driving mirror Snipe saw it turning in to Johnson's yard.

"I've seen that car before", he said, "but I can't think where."

CHAPTER XXI

1941: Thursday, January 9

When Susan arrived at the infirmary to pick up her suitcase the first person she saw was Jill Simpson.

"Oh, Mrs. Berkeley, I'm so glad I bumped into you. Something really awful has happened. Look at this. It's from Jessica's Uncle James's solicitor."

Susan took the letter from Mrs. Simpson's agitated hand and read:

Dear Mr. Simpson,

I regret to inform you that Major James Phillips has been killed in action. Following his instructions we shall continue to make monthly payments to you from his estate for board and lodging for Jessica Smith, until a period of three years has elapsed or until the cessation of hostilities, whichever event occurs sooner, or until Jessica is no longer residing in your household. Please inform us immediately if there is any change in Jessica's situation.

I trust that you will find a suitable way of conveying this sad news to the young lady, of whom Major Phillips appears to have had an extraordinarily high opinion.

Yours truly,
Edwin Mortimore

The letter added considerably to Susan's inner agitation, but she managed to retain her outward poise.

"What an awful thing", she said. It sounded like a purely conventional remark, but what it meant to Susan was that she was the only responsible adult left in Jessica's world—only she had forfeited the right to be considered responsible. "I'd better keep this and write to the solicitor explaining the situation."

"But what is the situation, Mrs. Berkeley? I don't want to get into any trouble over this."

"I'll tell him that Jessica has only just moved to our house, so there won't be any trouble for you. Now I really must go."

"All right, Mrs. Berkeley, if you say so. Well, I'll see you when you get back."

Susan thought that there was a note of suspicion in Mrs. Simpson voice, but there was nothing she could do about it. She had just enough time to catch her train.

Jessica would have enjoyed living on her own if she hadn't missed Susan so terribly. She made up for this to some extent by writing long letters to her lover, although she didn't yet know her address. The weekend, having been the most treasured of times, was now the most dreaded—the days seemed so long and empty. When Jessica turned on the radio its impersonal voice only emphasized her loneliness, so she spent most of the time in bed, doing her homework and writing more letters. She was therefore spared the knowledge that on Friday, the day after Susan's arrival, Portsmouth had suffered one of the worst air raids of the war, in which schools, churches, hospitals and houses had been destroyed and many hundreds of people killed.

One of Jessica's tasks gave her the chance to do something else for Susan. It was to write a Shakespearean sonnet, and Jessica, her imagination filled by the picture of Susan dancing barefoot among the woodland flowers, knew exactly what she wanted to do. She finished the poem on Sunday evening, and thought to herself that perhaps when she got home from school the next day there would be a letter from Susan.

At Blenheim Hall there was a certain amount of discussion about Jessica.

"I've never seen her like this", said Miss Wenlock to Miss Thrower on Thursday, the day of Susan's departure. "I thought she seemed very preoccupied yesterday, but today she could hardly stay awake."

"I know. I actually thought that she had dozed off in algebra, but when I spoke to her she was awake and seemed to know what was going on. She just seemed very, very far away."

"She's probably in love", said Miss Wenlock, unwittingly thrusting a dagger into her colleague's heart.

Jessica seemed a little brighter on Friday, however, and on Monday she amazed Miss Wenlock by producing her sonnet, three days before it was due.

"I think Jessica must be all right", reported Miss Wenlock to Miss Thrower. "Look at this."

Miss Thrower read the poem and felt the dagger twisting slowly.

"It's wonderful", she said, trying to give a good imitation of her normal voice.

Jessica had made a copy of the poem for Susan, with grass and flowers adorning the borders, and at lunch time she showed it to Miss Thrower, who managed to sustain a conversation for a few minutes before excusing herself on the ground that she had to speak to another pupil. What she actually did was to walk round the corner into the park, and reason with herself for a while before returning to school and teaching for the rest of the day as though nothing untoward had happened. As soon as the girls had left for the day she sat down in her classroom and composed a letter offering her resignation as of the end of the week. It didn't seem possible to her that she could survive the emotional torture of being in such close proximity to Jessica for more than a few days. The next morning, however, when she looked at herself in the mirror, she said, "You're a fool, Penny Thrower", and tore the letter into little pieces. Ostensibly this was because she didn't want to let a young girl make such an idiot of her, but being an honest woman she had to acknowledge the real reason, which was that as long as Jessica was at Blenheim Hall she couldn't bear the idea of not being there.

When Jessica got home from school on Monday afternoon there was a letter from Susan. It was very short but it seemed to Jessica that it said everything that really mattered.

> *My darling,*
>
> *I'm here in the hospital in Portsmouth and I'm writing straightaway so that you will have something from me on Monday—that is, if the post office is still working. I didn't get here till nearly five o'clock and then the head of the hospital wanted to talk to me for a long time. Then I taught until nine o'clock. It looks as if I'll be working at least twelve hours a day, but I don't believe a minute will pass when I don't think about you. I never dreamt that anyone would make me so happy. If I were a proper kind of person I should be reminding you of all the things you are supposed to do, but all I want to do is to keep telling you how much I love you.*
>
> *I have a little room in a house almost next door to the hospital. It's very bare and chilly but I'll keep warm by imagining you sitting in bed with the green nightie. I'll write some more to you tomorrow, my darling love, but I want to make sure that this leaves as early in the morning as possible so I'm writing before leaving the hospital and I'll post it on the way to my room.*
>
> *If you try very hard you can feel me kissing you.*
>
> *I love you now and always,*
> *Susan*

Susan had written her address at the top of the page, so Jessica went straight upstairs and without waiting to take off her coat or light the fire started writing.

An hour and several pages later she wrote:

> *I am still sitting on the bed with all my clothes on. Being in love with you keeps me very warm, but I think I'd better stop for a few minutes and light the fire and have something to eat. Then I'm going to put on your green nightgown, get into bed*

properly and write some more. Since you went away I haven't worn anything in bed because that's how we slept together in the beginning, but now I think the nightgown will help me to feel that you're still with me.

Jessica lit the fire, undressed and put on the nightgown. She looked at herself in the mirror. Her shoulders were a little narrower than Susan's, so the straps had a tendency to slide down her arms and the whole nightgown, which had fitted Susan quite loosely, was in danger of ending up on the floor.

"Susan is much more beautiful than you are", she said to her reflection. "I wish she were wearing it now."

One idea led to another. Remembering what Susan had said about the nightgown, Jessica couldn't help picturing her in bed with John. This resulted in a painful spasm of jealousy. What were Susan's feelings? Had she actually enjoyed it? Jessica couldn't bear to think about it. She got slowly back into bed and forced herself to remember what she had been thinking in the cathedral a few days earlier, that John had done nothing wrong, and that he was somewhere at sea, longing for Susan and having no idea of what was going on in his own bedroom. On that occasion Susan had held her hand, smiled and chased away the thoughts that she didn't want to think, but Susan wasn't here now. It seemed to Jessica that if she were a really good person, she would go back to her old bedroom and restore the house to its proper order. When John eventually came home, it would be as if nothing had ever happened. Perhaps by then she would be able to go back to London, and Uncle James would help her.

All that these good thoughts did was to increase her misery.

"I can't", she said, addressing the God she had never quite been able to believe in. "I'm sorry, but I can't. It's too hard for me. And what about Susan? She wouldn't be able to live with him the way she did before. And I promised to love her and always be with her, and I do and I will. She didn't make this happen. Why did you send me here? Just because you liked what you did to Adam and Eve and you wanted to do it again? What did you expect them to do? You gave them Paradise and then you made it too hard for them to stay."

She got back into bed and pulled the blankets up to her chin. Against her will the picture of Susan in bed, in this flimsy nightgown, in John's arms came back to her. Trying to stop her thoughts from going further into the unbearable, she picked up Susan's letter. Beneath it was the sonnet. She read the poem and the letter and then the poem again. What could Susan, dancing among the bluebells with her golden hair and her pale green nightgown, have to do with this man, with any man? John had had his chance and instead of staying with Susan he had gone off and joined the navy. If he had loved her as much as Jessica loved her he couldn't possibly have done such a thing. In any case, the marriage was a mistake from the very beginning (but a little voice reminded her that that wasn't John's fault) and no matter what Jessica did, Susan would never sleep with him again. Susan was right about telling John, but Jessica didn't want to leave her to do it on her own. They must tell John, as kindly as possible, that they meant to spend the rest of their lives together and that he would have to . . . What would he have to do? Live somewhere else and find another woman? How would he react? Susan had said that he wouldn't understand but they would have to try. It had not occurred to Jessica before to be frightened of John, but now she was afraid. She wished that she and Susan could just go away together. It didn't really seem possible, but she would ask Susan anyway. She picked up her writing pad and her pen and tried to gather her thoughts. It was no use blaming God. If he was there at all he was probably doing his best, and perhaps it was just as hard for him as it was for Jessica and everyone else. After writing for half an hour she noticed that it was nine o'clock, so, not having heard the news for several days and feeling that she ought to find out what had been happening in the war, she turned on the radio. Having missed the first sentence or two the first thing she heard was that the death toll from Friday's air raid on Portsmouth was now in the thousands, and that many more were leaving the city because they were homeless or feared further destruction. The fragile calm that Jessica had achieved while writing the last part of her letter disappeared into a dark pit of fear and desolation. With no more news and no way of finding anything out, her imagination began to conjure terrible pictures. The enemy must surely know about the naval hospital and would aim at it deliberately. If Susan had survived the raid she would at this moment be working to save the badly injured, as she had been trained to do, and would therefore be in the target area for more bombs. If not, was she, like Jessica's parents, lying dead under a heap of rubble?

Jessica felt a sense of acute claustrophobia, enclosed in her room where there was warmth and light, while outside darkness stretched in all directions and was penetrated only where the fires of war were burning. It was as if the darkness were really in her room, in her heart, while she had a vision of people all over England, Europe, North Africa, wherever the war was being fought; people with smoke-blackened faces stained red by the glow of fires, coping with fear, pain, death, bereavement and the necessity to continue with their tasks until they could no longer stand. This was what war meant, and this was how Jessica thought of Susan. Susan would never give up as long as there was one person left in need of help. It might have been a great relief to let go, to cry helplessly and to wallow in self-pity, but Jessica knew that in so doing she would not be meeting the required standard, and would be less than a fit companion for her beloved Susan. Instead she took up pen and paper again. It was much harder to think clearly now, but the effort helped her, and she began to feel just a little more hopeful that she and Susan might have some kind of future together. By ten o'clock she was asleep.

Susan arrived at Portsmouth Naval Hospital late on Thursday afternoon and was immediately summoned to a conference with the Director, after which she was set to work with a group of nurses. Most of them seemed completely unprepared to deal with the kind of injuries that occur in wartime, the living and breathing souls with crushed limbs and mutilated bodies. When the session ended at nine o'clock she was extremely tired, but she managed to write a brief note to Jessica before leaving the hospital, so that she could post it on the way to the house on the nearby side street where she would spend the night. In the past Susan had scarcely thought about her lodging while on one of these trips. All she had needed was a room and a bed and a little respite between sessions, but now the little room with its single bed seemed strange, as if it belonged to another world. Although Jessica was never far from her thoughts, Susan had been fully engaged with her work during the day; now at night the real world was wherever Jessica was. The seven weeks in which they had lived together, culminating in the ceremony that they had improvised in the morning, had built something between them that went so far beyond promises that the separation was physically painful. The room was very cold and Susan was thankful that she had brought a long flannel nightgown with her. She undressed as quickly as she could, got under the covers, closed her eyes and set her imagination to work. Jessica was with her in bed—was she wearing the green nightie or nothing? Susan decided on green and swiftly transformed her own flannel into black gauze. Soon they were in each other's arms . . .

Susan's imagination was fighting a losing battle against her exhaustion. Within a few minutes she was asleep.

The next day was divided between giving classes and helping the often bewildered young nurses in the big wards of wounded servicemen. Once again Susan returned exhausted to her room and prepared herself for sleep. This time, however, her thoughts of Jessica were interrupted by the sounds of air raid sirens going off all over the city. Within a few minutes she heard the heavy, throbbing drone of the incoming bombers and the fierce cacophony of the anti-aircraft batteries. Then came the more terrible sounds of the first bombs, deep, earth-shaking explosions that made the house tremble and everything in Susan's body feel as if it were falling apart. She quickly got dressed and tried to decide what to do. Ordinary citizens were fleeing to air-raid shelters or finding some flimsy refuge under the stairs or the living room table, but just round the corner was the hospital and for Susan there would be work to do. She had just set foot in the dark street and was groping her way to the hospital when a huge explosion seemed to take place all around her. The earth swayed and she was thrown from her feet. Then, although everything was brilliantly lit by flames shooting into the sky above the nearby houses, there was dead silence. Susan lay still for a moment before trying to sit up. Apparently she was not seriously injured. She stood up and tried to walk. There seemed to be something wrong with her sense of balance, so she leaned for a while against a lamp post. The ground still shook under her feet and gradually the popping of the Bofors guns and the roar of the heavier explosions became audible. She tried to walk again, and slowly made her way to the corner of the main road. The flames were coming from the hospital, and as she got closer she saw that the whole front of the building had been destroyed. Rescue parties and ambulances were arriving, a few survivors were standing in the street, and bodies were being pulled from the wreckage. Susan had a great deal of experience of working with badly, sometimes hideously, injured people, but she had never been present at a raid before. She found the scene horrifying. As she approached, one of the first-aid workers took her arm.

"Nothing you can do here, Miss. You ought to be in a shelter—you never know when the next one's going to land."

"I'm a nurse with special training for work like this", said Susan, "and there's a lot I can do. Where are they taking the injured people?"

"To the general hospital, Miss. It's only half a mile from here and I'll bet they'd be glad to see you."

Within a few minutes Susan was sitting in the back of an ambulance with two patients on the way to the general hospital. The raid went on for several hours and Susan worked at the hospital for the rest of the night and most of the next day, in the course of which she learned that scores of people had died in the Naval Hospital. It was getting dark when she made her way back past the wreckage to the house on the side street. It seemed surprising that it was still there, and there was something almost welcoming about the little room, as if Susan had somehow invested it with a tincture of Jessica's spirit. She did not plan to stay there, however, only to collect her belongings and go back to the hospital, where she would get a few hours of sleep before returning to the wards.

Survivors were still being brought in on Sunday, a day that was very much like the previous one except that everyone was even more exhausted. That evening Susan lay on a couch in the nurses' room, realizing that she had been wearing the same clothes for three days and that all she could do was to wash her face and put on some clean underwear. She pictured Jessica as she had last seen her, looking brave, beautiful and composed in her school uniform. She would do very well under fire, Susan thought, and as she was thinking this, it struck her with the force of a bomb that Jessica must have heard about the raid on Portsmouth, and might even know that the hospital had been destroyed. Knowing what Jessica must be going through, Susan was deeply distressed, but with no telephone and no possibility of sending a telegram at that late hour, there was nothing that she could do. The next morning she talked to the matron with whom she had been working and learned that telephone and telegraph services had been disrupted and no one knew when they would be back in operation. It was while this conversation was going on that Susan saw the headline on the front page of a newspaper that someone had left on a chair.

"HMS MASAI SUNK: DESTROYER LOST WITH FEW SURVIVORS."

The paper was several days old and appeared to be reporting events that had taken place a week before publication. The article gave few details beyond the fact that the *Masai* had been torpedoed off the coast of Northern Ireland and that the presence of an unknown number of enemy submarines had made rescue attempts very difficult. There were very few survivors, it said. Next of kin were being informed.

Susan sat down, closed her eyes and tried to get a grip on the thoughts that were racing through her mind. Although her experiences with Jessica had given her an entirely new perspective on what it meant to be in love, she had genuinely loved John and she didn't want him to be dead. She wanted him to be alive and happy, and it was with this thought that she realized that if he was still alive he might at this moment be on his way to Gloucester; he might, in fact, be there already. Sailors were usually given a short leave after a disaster like this. She knew that of the whole crew the captain was one of the least likely to survive. If he was dead there would be a letter of condolence from the Admiralty. She had asked Jessica to read any official looking letters, in case there was something that needed to be attended to. In either case, but especially if there was a chance of John appearing at the house, Susan needed to be with Jessica.

"That's my husband's ship", she said, showing the article to the matron. "I'm sorry, but I must go and try to find out what has happened. They may have written to me in Gloucester. I'll come back as soon as I possibly can."

"But, Mrs. Berkeley, we really need you here. I'm sure we can find out from the Admiralty as soon as the telephones are working."

"That may be true", Susan thought, "but there's another reason why I have to go to Gloucester and I can't possibly explain it."

Torn between the impulse to wait and see if it was possible to find out from the Admiralty and the need to be with Jessica as soon as possible in case John appeared, all she could say to the matron was,

"All right, I'll think about it." It seemed that her body knew the answer, however, for while she was still trying to make up her mind her legs carried her out of the main entrance and into the railway station, which was only a few minutes' walk away.

At half-past three on Monday afternoon, John Berkeley walked out of the L. M. S. railway station in Gloucester and made his way to the bus stop in King's Square. His first thought had been to go straight home, but it struck him that school would soon be ending for the day at Blenheim Hall, and that if he walked though the park to St. Paul's Road he might see Jessica. Her most likely route would be through the park, over the railway by means of the footbridge, round the corner of Weston Road and past New Street, but there were other possibilities so he decided to wait at the corner of New Street and St. Paul's Road, where he could keep an eye on No. 32 without attracting the attention of its occupants. His state of mind was such that every time he saw a girl in the distance he thought it was Jessica and hurried towards her, only to find that there was no resemblance at all. At the same time he was becoming more and more dismayed by his lack of self-control and more and more determined to find Jessica, even though he had no idea what he was going to say when he did. He waited in St. Paul's Road until nearly five o'clock before coming to the conclusion that for some reason Jessica wasn't coming home or that she hadn't gone to school that day. Perhaps she was ill. By that time it was quite dark and he had no idea what he was going to do next. He couldn't bring himself to knock on the door of No. 32 and ask for Jessica, and he felt in no condition to go home and talk to Susan. She would soon realize that something was wrong. So he wandered back to the station, bought a platform ticket and went into the waiting room, where they served ersatz coffee and stale buns. The coffee was undrinkable and the buns inedible, but at least there was a little light and somewhere to sit. He took out a small pad and a pencil and began to write slowly, a few words at a time.

The waiting room closed at eight o'clock, but John remembered that there was a small pub next to the station where there might be some watery beer. The pub was empty and when he tasted the beer he realized why.

"No wonder you haven't got any customers", he said to the landlord.

"I can't help it, Sir, it's all we can get."

"Perhaps", said John, "or perhaps not. What have you got under the counter?"

"Nothing, Sir", replied the landlord, eyeing John's naval uniform and scenting a potential customer rather than a government snooper, "but if you were to come with me into the back I might be able to find something for you."

They went into a grubby parlor with a microscopic fire in an ugly little grate. The landlord produced a half-bottle of Scotch of dubious origin, and named an outrageous price.

"We have to pay through the nose to get this stuff and then there's the risk, so I can't let you have it for less."

"Does it have any alcohol in it?" asked John suspiciously.

"Now you're pulling my leg, Sir. Look at the label."

John was too tired to argue so he paid up and took the bottle and a glass to a dilapidated armchair by the fire. The whisky was coarse but effective. John got out his notebook and wrote a little more, but an hour or so later, when the landlord looked in, he was asleep.

"Sorry to disturb you, Sir, but I was wondering whether you would be requiring anything else."

John looked at his watch. It was nearly a quarter to ten.

"Good God", he said. "How late do the buses run from King's Square?"

"Till about ten o'clock, Sir."

John ran groggily to the square and caught a Cheltenham Road bus just as it was leaving.

"Is this the last bus?" he asked the conductor.

"Yes, Sir. This is it for the night."

Susan had to wait until nearly midday for a train from Portsmouth. When it did come it took her only as far as Bristol, stopping at every station on the way and frequently between stations. There was no room to sit down so she traveled in the corridor, wedged between two morose soldiers with large kit bags that made it impossible for her to stand up straight. Between her inner turmoil and the sheer physical discomfort she found that any kind of thinking was out of the question, and her mind was filled with images of John getting home and finding Jessica in his bed. She was quite sure that Jessica would be unable to lie her way out of the situation and doubted whether she would even try. Having no idea of John's actual state of mind, Susan anticipated several different kinds of outcome, but it seemed unlikely to her that he would become violent. Unlikely, however, is not impossible, and the physical discomfort of the crowded train was nothing compared to Susan's mental anguish as she imagined Jessica's stumbling attempts to explain, John's incredulity, and his reactions when the truth dawned. At best it would leave Jessica horribly scarred and might well mean the end of their love affair. By now Susan was quite convinced that against all the odds John had survived and was on his way to Gloucester. The only possible salvation was for her to get there first, so that Jessica was not left to deal with this impossible situation on her own.

The train stood for an hour almost within sight of Temple Meads station in Bristol, and when it finally arrived it took Susan half an hour to find anyone who could tell her when the next train would leave for Gloucester. It wasn't until a quarter past seven that she found herself packed into a smoke-filled compartment in a non-corridor train that crawled for two-and-a half hours through small towns and dark villages on the thirty-five mile trip to Gloucester. Now Susan had the added anxiety that she would miss the last bus and have to walk out to the house on Cheltenham Road. It was a quarter to ten when the train pulled into the Great Western station, but it took her several minutes to disentangle herself from her compartment and get out of the station into Railway Street. She might be able to get to King's Square in time if she ran all the way, but running was difficult in the heavy darkness. The area around the bus stop was dimly lit with a few carefully shaded lamps, and as Susan entered the Square she thought she saw a tall figure step onto a bus just as it pulled away.

The Square was now deserted. Susan had no doubt that she had just seen the last bus depart. She began to run again, as fast as she could. It was the longest mile she had ever traveled.

When John entered the house he was immediately aware that something was different, although at first he couldn't tell what. He went to the living room and switched on the light. It was cold and there was no sign of a fire. He noted that the wireless was missing. It was odd that the hall had seemed slightly warmer than the living room. He looked into the kitchen. Everything was neat and tidy and looked the same as usual. Susan must have taken the wireless upstairs. He went up into the bedroom and saw the glowing remains of the fire.

Jessica had been in a deep sleep but by this time she was vaguely aware that someone was moving about in the house. As John entered the room she sat up and said, "Susan?"

She reached out and switched on the bedside lamp. John took in the scene—the fire, the wireless, Jessica's papers on the tray by the bed and Jessica sitting up in Susan's nightgown. After a day spent obsessing about her, searching for her and trying to drown his pain in whisky, John felt his legs turn to water and he sat down abruptly on the edge of the bed. When he spoke his voice was weak and shaky.

"Jessica, why are you here? Where's Susan?"

Torn between fear, guilt and her love of Susan, Jessica was speechless. John repeated his last question.

"She's working at a hospital in Portsmouth."

"And you're staying here on your own?"

"Yes."

"Why aren't you at the Simpsons'?"

This would have required a long explanation and Jessica couldn't bring herself just to say, "I didn't like it there", or "They were horrible people." Although Jessica was quite capable of telling a small fib, she had never acquired the art of serious lying, even as a last resort. Thinking that John must have realized what had been going on she began haltingly to explain.

"I'm sorry John. It's just that we love each other so much. And we were going to tell you as soon as we could."

"Who?" John asked, but the light began to dawn. There wasn't anyone else so it must be Susan. "You and Susan?"

"Yes."

It was the merest whisper. John stood up. His heart was still pounding, but the blood which had seemed to drain from his limbs was coursing through his whole body now, and he had suddenly begun to perspire freely.

"You and Susan?" he repeated loudly and with a note of incredulity. "You and Susan? That's very funny." He walked around the room, shaken with hysterical laughter. Jessica cowered terrified in the bed with the sheet pulled up around her shoulders. John returned to the bed and sat down again.

"What a wonderful twist on the old story. 'Sailor comes home to find wife in bed with best friend.' 'Sailor comes home to find best girl in bed with wife.' Only wife isn't here and girl is wearing wife's nightie. So girl will have to make do with sailor."

He tore the sheet from her grasp and threw off the bedclothes.

"John, please . . ."

"Does that mean 'Yes, please' or 'Please, no'?

"John, we didn't mean to hurt you."

John kicked off his shoes and started undressing before he replied.

"Ah, but you don't understand, do you? You see, I fell in love with you too and for the last two months, whenever we weren't actually under fire, all I've thought about is you, sleeping with you and making love with you. Yes, making love. So you needn't worry your lovely little head about me and Susan. She could have had a love affair with anyone she liked and I wouldn't have cared. But it had to be you of all people. All this time I've been wanting you and she's been having you. But now she isn't here and I am, and I can have you if I want to. You look very pretty in that nightie, but it doesn't really belong to you."

The thin straps had fallen from Jessica's shoulders and John pulled them down so that her breasts were exposed.

"There, now I can really see you, and the only question is, am I going to do this with your consent or without it? After all, it's only fair, you know. You did it with Susan and now you have to give me my turn. So be a good girl and let's get rid of this silly nightie."

As John pulled at the nightgown, Jessica made one more effort.

"I don't believe you love me or you wouldn't hurt me like this. How much do you really love me?"

"Don't you understand? I can't stop now—it's impossible. And I'm not going to hurt you—just make love to you. Then you'll know."

There was a hint of pleading in John's voice and it flashed though Jessica's terrified mind that if she submitted and let him have his way it might count as an act of atonement; and with that, but more powerfully, came the thought that she would at last know and understand what Susan had experienced as John's wife. With a great effort of will she let her body relax.

But John was not a natural rapist or even a natural philanderer; now that what he had desired and vividly imagined for the past two months was his for the taking, he hesitated, and it was at that moment that Jessica heard the front door key turn in the lock.

"Susan, Susan", she screamed.

John let her go and backed away as he heard Susan crossing the hall. Jessica leapt from the bed and ran from the room. As she reached the landing, the nightgown slipped down and entangled her feet, so that she plunged headlong down the stairs, carrying Susan with her as she went. The collision caused Jessica to spin round and there was a horrifying crack as the back of her head hit the hardwood floor. John stumbled to the landing, and in the dim light from the bedroom door he saw her lying on her back, with Susan kneeling beside her. Drops of blood from a gash on Susan's temple fell on Jessica's white cheek and flowed into the pool that was collecting around her head. Susan wiped the blood from Jessica's face with her hand and called to her, her voice rising in agony and falling finally to a whisper.

"Jessica, Oh my darling, my darling Jessica, please don't leave me, please don't leave me."

Jessica's eyes opened and she spoke in a high, childlike voice.

"Darling Susan, when can we go and gather daffodils and bluebells in the woods?"

Her eyes closed again. Susan, skilled in the experience of death, covered Jessica's body with her own and kissed her lips. And John Berkeley, quite sober, captain of the lost destroyer *Masai*, standing naked at the top of the stairs, heard the sound of grief such as he had never heard before; unassuageable, inconsolable, unendurable.

209

Chapter XXII

1965: Friday, December 24

When Inspector Phelps and Sergeant Snipe returned from their visit to Henry Johnson, Sergeant Bunn greeted them with the news that there was a message from Cambridge.

"Here it is, Sir", said Bunn, handing Phelps a piece of paper, "but I can tell you the news in one sentence: no one by the name of John Hume ever matriculated at Sidney Sussex College."

"Well I'll be damned! Now how the hell did he know?"

Without specifying who "he" was, Phelps marched into his office and telephoned Woodcock. But the headmaster was neither at home nor in his office. He and Bill were, in fact, sitting in the parlor of Bob Roberts's cottage enjoying a nice hot cup of tea. Bill, who had met Bob only briefly before, when her children were pupils at The Nave, found the man and his cottage charming. Funnily enough, at that moment the subject of the discussion was Inspector Phelps.

"A splendid person", Bob was saying, "although it took him some time to explain who he was. I thought he had come about the drains, and the remarkable thing is that the very next day Mr. Pettigrew actually called here after I had been trying to get him to come for several weeks, and I'm sure that the inspector had a hand in getting him here. Pettigrew was extremely annoyed and told me that he really didn't consider that a smelly drain was a police matter. But he did something to the drain and I let him go away under the impression that I had complained to the police. Inspector Phelps was also very polite about my bicycle and did not appear to think that it was a sign of eccentricity."

Bill was sitting back and enjoying the conversation, but Woodcock was rather anxious to get to the point.

"I have been somewhat concerned about John Hume and I'd like you to try to recall the circumstances under which you appointed him in 1946."

"How very extraordinary!" exclaimed Bob. "I hadn't seen Hume since my retirement, but yesterday he came to see me, and now here you are enquiring about the subject of his visit—and all this immediately after a policeman comes to see me about a skeleton."

"I'm afraid it isn't all coincidental", said Woodcock. "I don't believe Hume killed anyone, but I do think he probably knew the victim. In some ways it would probably be better to leave whatever old griefs lie behind this mystery in peace, but it's not good for the school to have it hanging over our heads, especially in view of the letter in yesterday's *Citizen*"

"Yes. Of course I wouldn't say this in public, but Ferrier has always been a fool."

As Bob continued his visitors tried to avoid showing their astonishment at his acuity.

"I hadn't thought about this for years, but Hume's visit brought it back to me. When he applied for the post early in 1946 he had had no teaching experience, but in other ways he was by far the best applicant. He had read natural science at Cambridge, had specialized in chemistry and had a good honors degree. He had a record of distinguished service during the war and was in the process of obtaining an honorable discharge."

"Can you tell us which college he was at?"

"Yes. In fact, he had to remind me—it was Sidney Sussex."

"According to the people at Sidney no one of that name ever matriculated."

"Ah well, you see, thereby hangs a tale—*the* tale, one might say. He told me that he had changed his name because of a family entanglement that he wanted to place as firmly as possible in the past. But he gave me his old name so that I could verify his story—which I did."

"And what was his old name?" asked Bill.

"Well now, I'm sure it was something that I ought to remember. There was some little oddity about it but I'm sorry to say that I can't recall it."

"And it isn't written down anywhere?"

"No. You see I was very careful to make sure that it didn't appear on any papers that other people might see."

"Why did he come to see you?"

"Well that seemed very odd to me. As I said, when I appointed him he was very anxious that his old name should remain unknown, which was easy enough since everything connected with the appointment had been done in terms of his new one. But yesterday his intention seemed to be to let me know that there was no longer any need for secrecy. It was almost as if he wanted the facts to come out."

"And his old name wasn't mentioned in your conversation?" asked Woodcock.

"No. He seemed to think that I knew it, and I didn't bother to ask him since I had no idea that I should ever be called upon to discuss the matter."

"Well, this has been very enlightening. If you should happen to remember Hume's original name please let me know. And thank you for the excellent tea."

"Not at all. And if you see Inspector Phelps would you thank him for sending the man about the drains—and perhaps you would mention that I have been waiting for the geyser person for over a month. Oh, and wish him a Merry Christmas and, of course the same to you and Mrs. Marjoribanks. And congratulations!"

"A Merry Christmas to you too" replied Bill, "but what are you congratulating us for."

"Well, you are getting married, aren't you?"

"How did you know that?" asked a startled Woodcock.

"Now that you ask, I'm not quite sure. I suppose it seemed obvious."

"Well", said Bill, "we only made up our minds yesterday and it hasn't been announced yet."

"Don't worry", said Bob. "I seem to be quite good at forgetting things."

"Do you think that was genuine", asked Bill as she and her fiancé drove off, "or is he a crafty old so-and-so?"

"I'd say the answer to that is definitely 'Yes or no'. And if he's crafty I must admit it was very neatly done and I fell for it hook, line and sinker. *And* if he's as crafty as that I wouldn't be prepared to guarantee that he's telling the truth about forgetting Hume's real name."

"Meaning that he would prefer to let sleeping dogs lie?"

"Perhaps. But on the whole I think the simple explanation is the likeliest. He just can't remember."

When Bill and Woodcock got back to the Dower House they found a note from John Hume pinned to the door. It was addressed to Bill, and while she was reading it the telephone rang.

"Hello, Jack, what's up?" asked Woodcock.

"News from Cambridge—I've been trying to get you all afternoon."

"We've just spent the afternoon with Bob Roberts, probably with the same result."

"So you know that no one called John Hume ever went to Sidney Sussex. In fact you knew already—that's why we raided Brunswick House."

"No, Jack, I really didn't know—I only thought there might be something unusual in his past. Actually he did go to Sidney Sussex, but under a different name, which Bob either can't or won't remember. And I don't really see where this gets us. There's nothing criminal about changing your name, so I'm still left merely with the suspicion that he knows something about this business, in fact that he may actually have known Jessica. Can you hold on for a moment—Bill's waving something at me."

Woodcock read the note from Hume.

"Hello, Jack. I'd like to talk something over with Bill and then ring you back. It will only take a few minutes."

"All right, I'll be here."

"So Hume wants you to go and see him", said Woodcock after replacing the telephone.

"Yes, and it sounds urgent. He couldn't get me on the phone, so he drove up here and left the note."

"You know him quite well, don't you? I remember your telling me that he used to ask you to go to concerts with him because going on his own made him too melancholic. Have you any idea why he wants to see you?"

"I have a feeling it's something to do with Jessica, but further than that I can't say. I think I should go."

"Yes, I believe you should. It's possible that he feels that he can tell you things that he can't bring himself to tell the police. And I really don't believe there's any danger."

"Danger?"

"Well, you know, this may be a murder investigation, so you should keep an eye on him. Now I have a suggestion. He lives only five minutes' walk from Nave House, so if you get the impression that he knows something that would be useful to the police, see if you can persuade him to come to my office. I'll have Jack waiting there with me."

"Do you think Jack will agree to that?"

"I think so—anyway, we can soon find out."

Phelps gave his approval to the plan and added another piece of information.

"We think Hume went to see Henry Johnson today. We're not sure because we only caught a glimpse of the car as it turned into the yard, and it didn't dawn on us that it might be Hume's until we were back at the station. Of course, there are still scores of old Ford Prefects about, but we've checked and it was the right color."

"So we have a possible connection between two people who may know something about Jessica."

"Doesn't sound very exciting, does it? But I think we should go ahead with your plan."

"All right. I'll take Bill to Hume's place and see you in my office in twenty minutes."

Bill was looking pale but composed when she knocked on the door of Hume's flat. She liked John Hume. If he had been involved in anything criminal or morally reprehensible she would have preferred not to know

214

about it; but the poems written for and by Jessica, and the descriptions given by her teachers, even though heard only at second or third hand, had given Bill the feeling that she knew Jessica almost as a real, living person. She wanted to find out what had happened to her.

Hume opened the door and took Bill's coat without a word. He pointed to an armchair and placed a thick folder in her hands.

"Thank you for coming", he said at last. "This is an odd way of spending Christmas Eve, but I think you'll understand if you read the first few pages."

There was no title on the outside of the folder and no title page inside. On the first page under a Roman numeral I Bill read:

Sometimes I want you so much
That I wander through the streets
Or in the park,
And often see you
At a street corner
Or through the trees:
Only then it isn't you
Or anyone I've ever seen before.
But my heart won't stop pounding
So I walk a little more,
Trying to be calm and remember
That Gloucester is a big place
And I should really go home:
But I keep on wandering,
And there you are again:

Only then it isn't you.

Bill turned the page and was not surprised to find that she had seen the second poem before.

You asked how much I loved you
And I said:
Let the Queen require . . .

Bill looked up.

215

"Do you want to talk about it, John? Is that why you asked me here?"

"I wasn't really sure what I wanted, but I've realized that I can't keep it to myself any longer. You have always been very kind to me, but to have to listen to me unburdening myself would be a much greater imposition than just holding my hand at a concert."

"It was never an imposition, John. I always enjoyed myself. And if this is what you want I'm ready to listen. But I must tell you before you start that I don't want to be put in the position of having to keep secrets for you."

"I don't want you to. The truth is that I've been living with this for twenty-five years. Now that the reason for my being in this place has gone, I can't bear it any longer. But it's very hard to start. Everyone here seems to think of me as a nice, slightly eccentric old fellow and quite a good chemistry master, and it's not easy to have to explain that I was responsible for a girl's death in shameful circumstances. I thought that telling you about it would be easier than telling the police."

"All right, John, but remember that this may not be any easier for me than it is for you."

Hume had still not decided exactly how he was going to start, how much he wanted to say and how much he was going to leave out, so there was quite a long pause before he began.

"I was a naval officer during the war and my wife was a nurse. We lived in Gloucester for a few months in 1940 and Jessica came to stay with us in November. She was fifteen, which was rather old for an evacuee, but her parents had been killed in the blitz and she seemed to have no remaining relatives except for the divorced husband of her mother's sister, who, I suppose, was technically not a relative at all."

"What about the aunt?"

"She was with Jessica's parents when the house was hit. Jessica's uncle—she still thought of him as Uncle James—was an old friend of mine. He was very fond of Jessica and wanted to adopt her, but he was off to the North African front. He wanted to find a safe place for her for the time being, and he thought of us in Gloucester. I was there on a short leave and my wife was often away for several weeks at a time, training nurses in hospitals all over the country, so it really seemed impossible for us to take her. My wife found her a decent home to live in, with one of the older nurses at the Royal Infirmary, but unfortunately her husband was taken ill and Jessica had to stay with us for a few days until he recovered. Now I'm coming to the difficult part. Jessica arrived on a Thursday and I left early on Sunday morning. I was thirty-one and she was fifteen and I fell violently in love with her. This isn't something that I expect anyone to understand, let alone to condone, but the fact is that it was something over which I had no control."

"Did she have any feeling for you?"

"I think she liked me, but I had the impression that she was slightly uncomfortable with me, as if she had sensed that there was something in the air that wasn't quite right. I hope you can understand that being in love with her was very painful and I wanted it to go away. I went through all kinds of mental contortions to make it stop, but nothing worked and even when I was back on my ship I couldn't stop thinking about her. I was hoping that time and absence would have some effect, and I wished to God that I had never seen her and I was back in the old days with my wife."

"Were you happily married?"

"Yes, we were. It wasn't exactly ecstatic, but we loved each other. We were comfortable together and I always thought that in its way it was better than ecstasy. And having had a sort of whiff of ecstasy with Jessica I believe I was right. I think if Jessica had fallen for me I might have died of it. Well, I went back to sea hoping that it would wear off, but I crossed the Atlantic twice and it had no effect at all. Then on the second day out from Liverpool on the next trip my ship was torpedoed and went down off the coast of Ireland. Most of the crew were lost and I would have been quite glad to be lost too, but my radio officer happened to be a good swimmer and he pulled me up onto a raft. It took another miracle to get us picked up, and then we were back in Liverpool in another two days. We were both quite ill but for some reason I recovered a lot faster than Harry, so they sent me home for a short leave before assigning me to another ship. It was the worst thing that could possibly have happened—all I could think about was Jessica. I knew where she was supposed to be living, so as soon as I got back to Gloucester I went looking for her. I thought I might see her on the way home from school, and I every time I saw a girl in school uniform I thought it was Jessica. But I didn't see her and I didn't have the nerve to go and knock on the door of her house, so I went and found a pub and got drunk. I've always been apt to write poetry in times of stress and while I was still relatively sober I wrote the one at the beginning of that folder. I fell asleep and when the proprietor woke me up I realized that if I wanted to get home at a reasonable hour I'd have to run for the last bus. I just managed to catch it and when I got home the house was dark. I thought my wife must have gone to bed, but when I got upstairs I found that she wasn't there. I had just sat down on the bed to try to think things out when I heard Jessica's voice coming from the bedroom where she had slept when she stayed with us. She thought I was Susan . . . Oh, God!"

"John, why didn't you want me to know your wife's name?"

"I wanted to keep her out of it. None of this was her fault."

"Where is she now?"

"She died twenty years ago."

"Then surely nothing that happens now can hurt her."

"I can't explain it—I'd just prefer to keep her completely out of it. I went to Jessica's room. She had switched on the light and was sitting up in bed. She was wearing one of Susan's nightgowns and it had slipped off her shoulders. I asked her why she was there, and she said that the Simpsons had been very unpleasant. Susan was trying to find somewhere else for her to live, only Susan had been sent to Portsmouth and Jessica was going to stay until she got back. I was still pretty drunk and the sight of her bare shoulders nearly drove me out of my mind. I told her that I was in love with her and I wanted to sleep with her. She begged me to leave her alone but I put my arms round her and tried to take off her nightgown. She was still pleading with me when we heard the front door open. I let her go and she tried to run downstairs, but she tripped and fell. Susan had come home from Portsmouth because she had heard about my ship and wanted to know if there was any news. Jessica landed on the back of her head and died a few minutes later. The last thing she said to me before I let her go was, 'How much do you really love me?', and I've never been able to get the question out of my mind."

There was a long pause before Hume continued. Bill looked around the room. She had examined Hume's bookshelves before. Philosophy, psychology, religion, music, art, chemistry, astronomy—all dedicated to understanding the world and its strange population of unpredictable human beings, and all powerless to help a man catastrophically in love with a young girl.

"I wanted to get a doctor but the telephone still hadn't been connected and Susan knew that Jessica was dead. While Susan had been away she had heard the news that Jessica's uncle had been killed in action, so there were no relations left at all. We both knew that we ought to call the police and it would have been easy enough to say that Jessica had simply fallen down the stairs. That's another thing that I can't really explain—I think it was the idea of the elaborate pretence and all the lies that would have been necessary. Susan had lived in Gloucester when she was younger and had an old friend who she thought would help us. It meant a long walk in the dark for Susan while I stayed with Jessica. I brought a basin of water and washed as much of the blood out of her hair as I could. Then I wrapped her in a sheet and a blanket and carried her upstairs. It seems absurd now, for I knew that I would soon have to carry her down again, but we thought that she shouldn't be left lying on the bare floor even for an hour. I was, and still am, agnostic to the point of atheism, but as a ship's captain I had done burials at sea. We gave Jessica a Christian burial service at the bottom of Susan's friend's garden. I really can't tell you any more about that since it involves this other person—or about how Jessica's body came to be found in St. Mary's Square. But at the end of the war I applied for my discharge and when it was granted I came here. It was completely illogical, but I felt that someone who knew and loved Jessica ought to be here for her."

"Wasn't that a bit risky? I mean there must have been people in Gloucester who might have recognized you and asked questions."

"I don't think so. I never saw Mrs. Simpson, and the only people who knew me by name were the neighbors on Cheltenham Road. I thought the chances of anyone remembering me from five years previously were pretty remote."

"Are you still in love with her?"

"No, not in the usual sense of the phrase. It ended even more suddenly than it had begun, when Susan opened the front door and Jessica ran away from me. Susan was the closest approach to a purely good human being I have ever met—as kind, clean and sane as fresh air—and it seemed as if the demon that had taken possession of me saw that there was no point in staying any longer—it had done its work."

"Do you believe in demons?"

"Not really—it's just how it seemed at the time."

"But you must believe that somehow Jessica is still here or you wouldn't have felt that it was so important to be with her."

"That's another question I can't answer. I don't believe in God any more than I ever did, but until the last few days I have always felt Jessica's presence very strongly. Now I have the feeling that she's going away."

This appeared to be the end of the story, and Bill found it highly unsatisfactory. The beginning rang true but not the end. Susan would surely have sensed what was going on, and yet she cooperated in concealing the crime, which, in any case, could easily have been disguised as an accident. Expressions of sympathy and understanding seemed unwanted and out of place and she had only one question.

"Now that you've told this to me, are you prepared to tell it to anyone else?"

"I ought to tell Mr. Woodcock. I'll be resigning, of course."

"How about Inspector Phelps?"

"I don't know. What do you think?"

"I can't tell you, John. All I can say is that I doubt whether he can charge you with anything unless you positively want him to. You're the only witness."

"I think I'd better do the job properly. Yes, I'll tell him."

"Then if I may use your telephone I'll let them know. They're waiting for you in Mr. Woodcock's office."

Hume smiled wanly.

"So you had it all planned."

"I thought we should be ready. May I telephone?"

"Yes. Let's get it over."

Chapter XXIII

1965: Friday, December 24th

When Woodcock arrived at Nave House two visitors were waiting on the doorstep. One, as expected, was Jack Phelps; the other was Bob Roberts.

"Mr. Roberts bicycled all the way in from Brookethorpe", said the inspector. "He came to see me at the police station with a very useful piece of information. I told him that we would be meeting here shortly, and he said he would like to explain it to you personally."

Bob wanted to launch into his explanation immediately, but Woodcock managed to get him indoors and seated in the office.

"I've already told Inspector Phelps that I was less than straightforward with you this afternoon. Now I ought to apologize for holding something back a year-and-a-half ago when we talked about the staff. At the time it seemed inconsequential and I was influenced by an undertaking that I had given twenty years previously. As you know, Hume changed his name before applying for the position. But for the fact that I needed his original name in order to verify his qualifications I don't think he would have mentioned it. The undertaking that I gave was that I would keep this knowledge to myself unless some compelling reason emerged for revealing it. When he came to see me yesterday he seemed to have been deeply shaken by something, and I thought perhaps that after sleeping on it he might change his mind again. After all, if he wanted you to know his old name all he had to do was to tell you. But after thinking about it I concluded that it might have saved you and Inspector Phelps a great deal of trouble if I had told you this when you first came here, and that I had better tell you the truth as soon as I could. So now I'll leave you to continue your investigation."

"But what was the name?" asked Woodcock.

"Oh, yes, of course. It was Berkeley."

"I might almost have guessed", said Woodcock. "Not George, by any chance?"

"No, he kept the same Christian name. I have been told that it's harder to change the Christian name than the surname, although I have never understood why. But it did lead to an interesting little philosophical discussion in which I suggested that he had moved to a more advanced form of scepticism. He said that that was probably true and had had something to do with the choice of name."

"Well, Sir, we're very much obliged to you for coming in and I don't think you need worry about holding up the investigation. It's only in the last day or so that we've had any indication that Hume's past would be worth looking into. And if I may say so, I'd feel a lot happier if you would let Constable Chard drive you back out to Brookethorpe. It's a long way in the dark, and we can tie your bicycle onto the back of the car. All the neighbors will be watching the telly so no one will see you."

"Do you know", said Bob, "I really think I will. I have never had a ride in a police car."

While they were waiting for Chard to arrive, Woodcock made a little conversation.

"What would an existentialist say about Berkeley and Hume?" he asked.

"You must be referring to my sonnets", Bob said with a chuckle. "I'm interested in existentialism but I'm not really an existentialist. I simply write them for fun. When people ask me about them I give an explanation that is even more baffling than the poem. I find that it's an interesting test of character, and I enjoy watching them struggle to give the impression that they understand what I'm talking about. There are not many who admit their bafflement, and even fewer who charge me with talking nonsense."

"Berkeley", said Phelps after Bob had left. "Wasn't he the bloke who said that the tree wasn't there unless someone was looking at it?"

"Yes, and someone pointed out that the tree was always there because God was always looking at it."

"And where does Hume come into it?"

"Well, assuming you mean the philosopher and not the chemistry master, Berkeley was sceptical about matter, but Hume seems to have been sceptical about almost everything."

"Including God?"

"Yes."

"So what did he think about the tree?"

"You know, that's an excellent question. I've never heard it asked before."

The telephone rang. Woodcock took the call and listened silently for a few minutes.

"All right Bill. We'll see you shortly", he said, and continued to Phelps, "Hume has confessed to being involved in Jessica's death. Bill didn't say so explicitly, but she gave me the impression that he didn't tell the whole story."

"In that case", said Inspector Phelps, "I have a call to make."

He dialed a number and spoke.

"Yes, Mr. Johnson, this is Inspector Phelps. I'm calling from Mr. Woodcock's office in Nave House and I think you should know that John Berkeley has admitted to being responsible for the death of Jessica Smith and is on his way here to make a formal confession . . . No, Sir, that's all I can tell you . . . Because I thought it might be helpful if you knew . . . No, Sir, that's all. Goodbye."

"Bill said 'involved', not 'responsible'", remarked Woodcock. "I gather you're trying to stir something up."

"Yes, I want to get the whole story. I'm convinced that Henry Johnson had something to do with it, and I don't think it's Hume that he's been trying to protect. With your permission I'd also like to have Snipey here. It's always a good idea to have a second policeman handy."

"I have no objection, but Hume isn't expecting anyone else to be here, so I don't know how he'll react."

"All I can say to that is that there may be others turning up too, and I want to be prepared. That's probably him now."

Phelps went to answer the door and came back with Sergeant Snipe. Before they were seated Bill appeared with Hume. Woodcock sat at his desk with Phelps on his right and Hume, with his back to the open door, at the corner of the desk on the headmaster's left. Bill and Snipe made themselves as unobtrusive as they could, further off to the inspector's right.

Phelps began the proceedings.

"Good evening, Mr. Hume. I gather that you have something to tell us."

Hume looked round at Bill and Snipe, hesitated for a moment and began his story. It was expressed more stiffly and with less color, but in essence it was exactly as Bill had heard it. During the pause when he got to the end he looked round and saw that Snipe was no longer there.

"What's happening?" he asked.

"Don't worry about it, Mr. Hume. Sergeant Snipe is just obeying orders. Now I have one or two questions for you. First, what would have happened if your wife had not arrived at that moment? You said that you couldn't stop, but Jessica was still pleading with you. Would you have raped her?"

"I don't know. I wanted her to love me and to consent, and at the last moment I thought that she did. I'm still not sure whether I would have been able to go through with it, but in any case it doesn't really make any difference. It was my behavior that caused her death."

Hume was unaware that when he began this last statement Sergeant Snipe was standing just inside the door with Henry Johnson and the woman who had been with him at Jessica's funeral. She was wearing the same overcoat but her head was uncovered and little flashes of pale gold showed in her white hair.

"You told us that you had help in disposing of Jessica's body, but you have refused to give us any information about how it was done."

"I have told you that I can't answer any questions about that."

"And you have said that you wished to keep your wife's name out of this although she had been dead for twenty years. Why is that?"

"My wife was a wonderful woman and I don't want her even posthumously to be dragged through this muck that I created."

"John, you mustn't do this." It was the white-haired lady who spoke. "We must tell the whole story, so that the inspector knows that it was just as much my fault as yours."

Hume turned and saw the newcomers.

"Susan, my dear, Jessica loved you and that made all the difference. You shouldn't have come."

"No John, we must tell the whole story so that they can understand what it was that made you so unlike yourself that night."

Susan Berkeley turned to Phelps and Woodcock.

"It's a very long story and I don't know how far back to go."

"Perhaps I can help you", said Woodcock. "Are you the golden-haired lady of Jessica's poem?"

"Yes, although Jessica made me sound much more wonderful than I really was."

"And Jessica came to your house and you fell in love with her."

It was a statement, not a question.

"Yes. How did you know?"

"Inspector Phelps has talked to two other ladies who fell in love with her, one of whom, I think, bore a considerable resemblance to you. It seems that Jessica became quite fond of them, but in your case there was something different. Her teachers at Blenheim Hall have described the way she was in school—quiet on the outside and bubbling with secret happiness on the inside. And, of course, there is the evidence of the poem. She fell in love with you."

"Yes. It's hard to say this in front of my husband, even though he knows it already, but for nearly two months Jessica and I were ecstatically happy. We slept together and used the bedroom as living room, dining room and study too."

"Before we go on", interjected Inspector Phelps, "we'd better have some introductions. Sergeant, please find chairs for Mrs. Berkeley and Mr. Johnson. Now, may I take it, Mrs. Berkeley, that at one time you were Pamela Johnson and that Mr. Johnson is your younger brother?"

"Yes, I'm Harry's sister, Pamela Susan Johnson. They used to call me P. S. as though I were an afterthought, so I decided just to be Susan."

After performing the remaining introductions the inspector continued.

"And may I also ask if your brother was the officer who saved your husband's life after his ship went down?"

Johnson stirred.

"Yes, Inspector", he said. "So it would be just as logical for you to blame me for Jessica's death as to blame my sister and brother-in-law."

While Inspector Phelps groped for words, Woodcock turned to Johnson with a smile.

"It seems to me, Mr. Johnson, that from beginning to end you have acted out of the most unselfish motives. You must be extremely fond of your sister."

This shot seemed to penetrate Johnson's armor.

"Yes", he replied uncomfortably, "my sister is the salt of the earth—and so is the Captain. I did whatever was needed to protect them."

"Including making up that story about Mrs. Berkeley having been killed by a German rocket in 1945", remarked the inspector.

"You must understand, Mrs. Berkeley", Phelps went on, "that although I am not at the moment taking this as a formal statement, I shall at some point have to consider whether to institute criminal proceedings. Mr. Woodcock and Mrs. Marjoribanks are here at your husband's request and Sergeant Snipe is here to assist me. I have to ask some questions, but you are not under any compulsion to answer them. In view of one of your statements I have to ask whether you and Jessica had sexual relations."

"Yes, we did. I have spent twenty-five years thinking about this and I bitterly regret having treated John as I did. I know that whatever guilt he feels really lies on me, and that I am responsible for Jessica's death, which was a grief beyond imagination. But I find it impossible to feel remorse for the way Jessica and I lived together. It wasn't perfect, you know. We had doubts and fears about the future, particularly about how it would be for John, and yet there was something at the center that really was perfect. We used to talk about Adam and Eve quite often and it seemed to me afterwards that for those few weeks we had lived together as Adam and Eve might have done if they had been allowed to stay in Paradise after the fall, waiting for God to decide what to do with them."

Phelps grunted unintelligibly. Religious analogies were all very well but he wanted a few more facts.

"Now I'd like to go back a bit. One thing we found out was that the people Jessica was supposed to have stayed with were called Simpson and that it was Mrs. Simpson who collected Jessica's things from her school after she died. And yet she seems to have spent the whole time with you."

"I took Jessica to the Simpsons' house a few hours after John had gone back to his ship. I think we were already in love, although I hadn't quite realized it at the time, and I was very worried about how she would get on there. I spent the rest of the day trying to get back to normal. I couldn't sleep that night and I was up very early the next morning. I opened the blackout and stared into the darkness for a long time, and then, when it began to get light, I saw Jessica coming along with her suitcases. I can't possibly explain to you how brave and beautiful she looked. I ran downstairs and opened the door for her, and we fell into each other's arms."

Inspector Phelps sighed inwardly. He had been hoping for something a little more succinct, but by now he had realized that a great deal of patience would be required. It was clear that Susan Berkeley was still deeply preoccupied with Jessica, that she saw everything in terms of their relationship, and that she could not be hurried. Phelps guessed that everyone else in the room had come to the same conclusion; Henry Johnson sat upright and expressionless, but Hume was slumped forward with his head in his hands. Sergeant Snipe had gone back to his seat next to Bill and the two sat there rather like a Greek chorus waiting to comment on the action. In spite of being almost at the center of things, Woodcock had somehow managed to efface himself so thoroughly that the others were hardly aware of his presence.

Susan continued:

"Jessica told me what had happened at the Simpsons', and Mrs. Simpson confirmed it in different words. Mr. Simpson was a very nasty old man and Jessica decided that she simply couldn't stay there. She might have gone back to London, where she had friends who would have taken her in, but we both wanted each other so much that London never came into the picture. We went to bed in different rooms that night, but Jessica had a nightmare and we ended up together. It might help you to understand Jessica's frame of mind a little better if I mention that three soldiers tried to rape her on the train from London, and would have succeeded if a sergeant hadn't realized what was going on."

"So on top of losing her parents all this must have left her in a very vulnerable state."

"Yes, Inspector, and I know that the implication is that I took advantage of her. Yet she was amazingly resilient, and when we gave ourselves to each other it was a relationship of equals. I think, after all, I ought to tell you how she dealt with the Simpsons."

Susan told the story just as she had heard it from Jessica, and amid all the tensions of the situation, even the case-hardened policemen, the headmaster with a thirty-year backlog of dealing with juveniles, and his worldly-wise secretary couldn't help smiling at the recital of the young girl's exploits. But Hume did not look up and Henry Johnson remained outwardly unmoved.

"Thank you, Mrs. Berkeley. That certainly helps us to understand Jessica's frame of mind a little better. Just for the record, what was the address of these Simpsons?"

"They lived at 32, St. Paul's Road."

Phelps fished for a paper in his briefcase and ran his finger down a list of names and addresses.

"Well I'll be darned. There's still a Mrs. Simpson there now. Widow, and claims never to have heard of Jessica Smith. Something to do with the money, I shouldn't wonder."

"I'm afraid I'm responsible for that, too. I encouraged her to keep the money as a way of restraining her curiosity."

"Well that's immaterial I suppose. Now, Mrs. Berkeley, I'd like you to tell us about Jessica's death and what followed.

"Yes, Inspector. First I'll tell you what my husband didn't mention. When he got home that night he found Jessica in bed in our room. He saw the wireless from downstairs and the remains of the fire in the grate. You must remember that he wasn't expecting her to be there at all. He had no idea what had been going on, so it would never have occurred to him that Jessica and I had been having a love affair if she hadn't started talking about it. You see she thought that John must have realized as soon as he saw the way we had arranged the room. I only know this because John told me about it after we had . . . Well, I'll come to that in a minute. Jessica had been very worried about John and she told him . . ."

Hume interrupted.

"She said, 'We didn't want to hurt you, it's just that we were so very much in love.' I'm sorry, my dear. I still don't think any of this was your fault."

"And I have never blamed you, John. Shall I go on, Inspector."

"Yes, please, Mrs. Berkeley."

"When John realized that Jessica and I had been having a love affair it drove him out of his mind. You know what happened after that. He did things that he would never have done and in the end I don't believe he would have hurt her."

"Yes, Ma'am, but she didn't know that, did she? However, what you have told us certainly puts a different complexion on things. Now I want you to tell us what happened to Jessica's body."

"John's first thought was to get a doctor and call the police, but I knew that Jessica was dead, and I could see that in the mood that John was in he was going to tell the police what had happened and take all the blame for it. If that had happened I should certainly have told them my half of the story and shared the blame with him. But then I thought about Jessica and imagined how the story would be told in the newspapers, and my soul rebelled at the thought of her being made the object of sensation and notoriety, which she had done nothing to deserve. We knew that Jessica had no relatives, so there was no one left to wonder what had become of her. I persuaded John that it would be better to let her go in quiet anonymity. I decided that although my father and I had been estranged for some years I would go and ask him to help. As a builder he was allowed to have a certain amount of petrol for his lorry, and I thought we could give Jessica a decent burial in his grounds. I walked up the Cheltenham Road and all the way along Longbridge Lane. It was well after one o'clock when I knocked on the door . . ."

Chapter XXIV

1941: Monday night, January 13

It was midnight when Susan left the house on Cheltenham Road, and she didn't notice that it was raining until she had been walking for several minutes. Still wearing the clothes she had worn on the trip from Portsmouth, she had nothing to protect her head, but she was so filled with the experience of Jessica's life and death that the water that soaked her hair, ran down her neck and gradually penetrated her overcoat was of no consequence. It was as if all these physical discomforts were being suffered by someone else. Even the task of finding her way through the darkness to her father's house barely reached the surface of her consciousness. It was fortunate that she had grown up in this part of the world, so that while her mind was elsewhere her body could carry her in the right direction, out into the rural area beyond the suburbs. She could see only the very dim outlines of trees, hedges and gates and found it best to walk in the middle of the road, hoping that she would be able to see the white signpost that would show her where to turn into Longbridge Lane. As her awareness of the actual moment and the journey she had undertaken gradually increased, she realized that she had no idea how long she had been walking, and began to be terrified that she had missed the signpost and would go on walking all night, while Jessica waited for her to return. It was impossible to grasp the reality that Jessica, now wrapped in a warm blanket and lying on the bed in the room where she and Susan had had their greatest happiness, was dead and without thought or feeling.

The rain decreased to a heavy mist and a little dim moonlight penetrated the clouds. Susan saw the signpost with its long finger pointing to the left. The night was still too dark for reading but Susan knew what it said: 'To Tewkesbury Road 1¼ miles.' The lane was narrow and rutted, with a deep ditch on the right and a steep bank on the left. Susan struggled along as quickly as she could, but it was getting harder and harder to keep moving. She felt sick and dizzy, and there was something wrong with her breathing. It did not occur to her that she had had nothing to eat since early that morning, had made an exhausting train journey, and had run most of the way from the station to the house on the Cheltenham Road—and all this on top of three hellish days in Portsmouth. She stopped and stood for a moment while the mud crept over the tops of her shoes. "Jessica is dead", she would have thought, if she had been capable of crystallizing a thought. "I didn't really know it before, but now I know it." It wasn't a thought, but something that tangibly penetrated her whole body and her whole consciousness, like the approach of her own death, robbing her of her remaining strength and willpower. She sank to her knees and the moonlight flickered and went out.

It lasted for a few seconds. When Susan struggled to her feet she felt like a very old woman, or someone who had undergone a serious operation and was trying to emerge from anesthesia. She took a step forward, tripped and fell into the mud. She raised herself again and found that at last she was able to focus her mind on what she was attempting to do. Jessica was dead. It was John who was waiting and Susan who must get help. Slowly she began again to put one foot in front of the other.

William Johnsons's house, like everything else, was in total darkness. When Susan knocked on the door she realized that she had no idea what she was going to say, and it came over her that it had been a stupid mistake to try to get her father to help. She waited for a long time before knocking again. Perhaps it would be better if no one answered. When the door at last opened and she summoned her failing courage to explain why she was there at that time of night, soaked, covered in mud, exhausted and incoherent, she found to her inexpressible relief that she was looking into the face of her brother.

"Susan, what on earth . . . Come in and let me help you—there's still a little bit of a fire in the living room. Then you can tell me what's up."

Harry helped her off with her coat, took her arm and gently guided her to a chair in front of the remains of the living room fire. He picked up the poker so that he could stir it up and add some more coal, but Susan stopped him.

"Don't bother with the fire, Harry. Something dreadful has happened."

Struggling to overcome her exhaustion and accept her shame and humiliation, Susan told her brother about Jessica and her love affair, about her husband's infatuation and the final catastrophe. She tried to explain why they had not called the police.

"There's no need to explain, Sue. You and the Skipper decided what to do and that's that. The big problem is how to deal with Dad."

"Oh, so that's what I am—your big problem. First my daughter's queer, then she's a murderess, my son is going to be an accessory and I'm a big problem."

William Johnson was standing in the doorway. Apparently he had heard the whole story.

"Susan isn't a murderess, Dad. If you've been listening you know that. I'm going to get the lorry out and bring the Skipper and the dead girl here and we'll bury her under the trees at the back of the garden. It's invisible there from the road and the neighbors and no one will ever know."

"Don't you think it would be a good idea to get my permission first? I might call the police myself."

"Isn't it about time you remembered that Susan is your daughter? She's never hurt you or anyone else, and you've been treating her like dirt all these years."

"Pamela was my daughter. This Susan—I don't know her. And now I don't think I know you any more. Do whatever you want, but don't expect any help from me."

William Johnson stumped back up the stairs and Harry said:

"It won't be light for another five hours, so there's time for you to go up to your old room and find something to wear. Everything's still there. I'll make you something hot to drink, otherwise you'll catch pneumonia."

Susan, wearing old overalls and a Mackintosh, and sipping hot Bovril while Harry went to start the lorry, was amazed to see her father reappear, now fully dressed.

"I told you that you and your girlfriends would come to no good in the end. But Harry and the Captain need help. You can't bury her without a coffin. How tall is she?"

Startled and confused, Susan tried to answer in feet and inches and found that she couldn't.

"I don't know, Dad."

"Pull yourself together, girl. Is she taller than you?"

"Yes—an inch or two."

"All right, that's near enough. It won't be a proper coffin but it will be better than nothing. There's the lorry. You'd better go. And tell Harry that when you get back he can drive the lorry down the lane and use the headlights to dig by. It'll be pointing away from the road and no one will see."

Old Johnson put on his hat and went out to his workshop. The blackout had some advantages after all. Nobody would ever know that inside the workshop there was a man making a coffin.

"All right, Susan?"

It was Harry at the front door. He helped his sister up the long step into the cab of the lorry. Its headlights were fitted with metal covers that allowed only thin shafts of light to emerge into the foggy darkness, making the journey along Longbridge Lane almost as precarious in the lorry as it had been on foot. Under normal circumstances Harry would have gone the long way round, following the main road into Gloucester and back up the Cheltenham Road to the Berkeleys' house, but policemen were apt to be curious about the doings of solitary lorries in the small hours of the night in a country at war, so Susan soon found herself back in the lane, leaning out of the window and trying to help her brother avoid the ditch as they edged along at not much more than walking pace. When they finally reached the main road the cessation of this activity brought a return to blank misery and it was only when they drew up in front of the house that she began to picture the return journey.

"Harry, we can't just put her in the back of the lorry."

"But I don't see how . . ."

"I'll stay here and you and John must put her on my lap, in my arms."

To Harry there was something abhorrent about the idea of his sister thus carrying the dead girl to her grave, but he could see that the matter was beyond argument.

"All right, Susan, if that's what you want."

Susan waited in the truck, but she no longer knew that she was waiting. She had moved out of time into a region where events do not happen consecutively but are present as coexistent states: Susan and Jessica asleep in each other's arms, the frenzied journeying from Portsmouth, Jessica lying at the foot of the stairs in a pool of blood amid the lamentations that still sounded in Susan's ears, the appalling passage of Longbridge Lane, the confrontation with her father, and that which in ordinary time was still to happen—the burial . . .

Several minutes elapsed before John carried Jessica out of the house. Harry followed him and stood on the running board of the lorry while John lifted Jessica into his arms and thence to Susan's. There was very little room. Susan sat with one arm holding Jessica to her body and the other supporting the dead girl's head on her shoulder. The sense of time had not returned. Jessica was both alive and dead. John had done his best to wash the blood out of Jessica's hair, and the feel of the damp hair against Susan's cheek added more pictures to the tableau—the bathroom, clouds of steam and Susan helping Jessica with her hair. *Oh my darling, my dearest love . . .*

John climbed into the back of the lorry and the return journey began.

Susan sat in her father's living room with Jessica, who lay in a long rectangular box of plain elm boards. The damp, freshly cut boards filled the room with their soft woody fragrance. It was raining heavily again and the sounds of digging came faintly through the heavily shaded windows. Time and present reality were gradually returning to Susan. The clock on the mantelpiece said half-past four. They had been digging for two hours. Susan looked at Jessica's face. While she could see it, it made a tenuous barrier between her and her grief, but now she wanted this part to be over and Jessica to be at peace.

Harry, soaked to the skin, came into the room. He looked at Susan and at the lid, which lay beside Jessica's coffin.

"Yes, Harry", said Susan. She stood up and touched Jessica's cheek.

"Dad has got out his prayer book and the Skipper's going to read the service. And the Skipper asked me to put this in the coffin."

It was a little oilskin pouch bound with copper wire. Harry carefully placed it on Jessica's breast before he put the lid on the coffin and fastened it with brass screws.

John came in and looked at the coffin, tried to speak and couldn't. Old Johnson followed him in a few seconds later and handed him the prayer book. Hesitantly at first, but with growing force and resonance, John read words that are apt to stir the souls even of unbelievers.

> *I am the resurrection and the life, saith the Lord: he that believeth in me, though he were dead, yet shall he live: and whosoever liveth and believeth in me shall never die . . .*
>
> *Lord, thou hast been our refuge: from one generation to another. Before the mountains were brought forth, or ever the earth and the world were made: thou art God from everlasting, and world without end . . .*
>
> *For as in Adam all die, even so in Christ shall all be made alive . . .*

Old Johnson, torch in hand, led the way to the back door, followed by Harry and John carrying Jessica's coffin, and, last of all, Susan, walking as if to her own grave. Johnson opened the door, and the air was filled with the sound of water, drumming on the roof, sibilant in the trees and chattering down the sloping garden in newly formed runnels. All except the old man were hatless, and the rain seemed soft, clean and almost refreshing. The last part of the journey was uphill, passing the lorry, which was now dark and silent, and ending at the graveside on a little knoll set among oak trees, whose heavy wet leaves lay thick on the ground. The earth had been piled at each end so that thick ropes could be stretched across the grave and staked firmly. Harry and John laid the coffin across the ropes and stood back. Old Johnson passed the prayer book back to John, removed his hat and used it to shade the book from the rain.

John read by the light of the old man's torch:

> *Man that is born of a woman hath but a short time to live, and is full of misery. He cometh up, and is cut down like a flower . . .*
>
> *In the midst of life we are in death: of whom may we seek for succour, but of thee, O Lord, who for our sins art justly displeased . . .*

Old Johnson put the book into his pocket. John and Susan stood on one side and Harry and his father on the other. John detached one of the ropes from its stake.

"Can you do this, Susan?"

"I think so."

She braced herself as well as she could and took the rope. It was as much as she could do to hold it against the weight of the coffin.

"Please don't let it be long now", she whispered.

The three men took up their ropes and the coffin was slowly lowered. The ropes were only just long enough and by the time it came to rest all four bearers had been pulled to the very edge of the grave.

Harry and his father picked up the shovels and John, now holding the torch and the prayer book, read the final sentences.

> *We therefore commit her body to the ground; earth to earth, ashes to ashes, dust to dust; in sure and certain hope of the resurrection to eternal life . . .*

Susan heard the words and her thoughts flew far away. Jessica wasn't earth, dust and ashes; she was pure fire, swept on a wild breeze. The wet earth thudded down, imprisoning her body in its coffin, but where was her spirit? Surely not meekly enduring all the purifications and humilities described by the church. Yet Jessica had not been proud. She had merely done what occasions demanded. Perhaps that was what she was doing now. Susan ached to be with her and know, for it was impossible to think of her as utterly dead. By mutual consent Old Johnson and Harry paused and leaned on their shovels. They spoke a few words but their voices receded into the infinite distance. The rain had become very quiet, too. Susan swayed and fell.

When Susan woke up she was lying on the floor in front of the living room fire, and Harry, the dead whiteness of his face emphasized by the shiny wetness of his red hair, was kneeling beside her. He had washed the mud from her face and hands, removed her shoes and wrapped her hair in a towel, but she was still wearing the bedraggled mackintosh.

For a moment she had no idea where she was. All she knew was that every bone, joint and muscle in her body hurt intolerably. Memories, equally intolerable, flooded back.

"Jessica's gone, isn't she?" she asked.

"Yes, she's gone, and I was afraid you were gone too."

"What happened?"

"You fainted and fell into the grave. Dad and the Skipper are finishing up and covering it with leaves. Then they're going to bring the lorry and I'm to take you both home—the Skipper said there are things you have to do there. Can you stand up?"

"I'll try."

Susan rolled carefully onto her side and struggled to her knees. With an effort Harry stood up, helped her to her feet and guided her to a chair. Her body might be in the last stages of exhaustion, but her mind was clear. She and John must go back to the house on Cheltenham Road, restore it to the state in which they had found it, and leave as soon as possible. She must return to Portsmouth, and John would have to find somewhere to wait for his new posting. She heard the front door open and close, and the mumble of voices. John came into the room and looked anxiously at Susan.

"I'm all right", she said. "Where is my father?"

"He went up to his room. I tried to thank him but he wouldn't listen to me."

"I ought to go up and see him."

"No, Sue", said Harry. "It won't do any good and you've been through enough already. We'd better go—it's going to start getting light soon."

John helped Susan into the passenger's seat and climbed into the back again. Harry seemed to have some difficulty getting into the driver's seat, and after he had started the engine nothing happened.

"Harry, what is it?"

"I don't know"

Harry's voice was faint. "I don't seem to have any feeling in my arms. I don't think I can drive."

Susan touched Harry's forehead. It was burning hot in spite of the chilly night. She opened the door and called to John.

"Harry's ill and he can't drive. What shall we do?"

It was not an easy question to answer, but one thing was obvious—Harry was too sick to take any further part in the proceedings.

CHAPTER XXV

1965: Friday, December 24

Phelps looked at his watch. Nine o'clock: people would be celebrating Christmas all over the city, and Mrs. Snipe must be wondering when her husband would get home. Bill and Woodcock had their own ways of doing things and would undoubtedly be happy to do their celebrating at whatever time and place it became possible. Henry Johnson's wife had remained hidden and anonymous, and once again the inspector pondered the advantages of being single. Realizing that Susan was still talking and that his mind had wandered a little he pulled himself together

"By the time we got Harry into the house he was almost too weak to stand. We had no thermometer, but he was coughing and he obviously had a high fever, so we decided to take him to the Infirmary. We got him into pyjamas and an overcoat and then we found that he was too far gone to sit up on his own, so he had to travel on my lap just as Jessica had done. Nobody in the Infirmary seemed surprised in the slightest—it was just another wartime emergency. I stayed there with Harry, while John drove the lorry back to my father's house and told him what had happened."

"He wanted to drive straight to the hospital", Hume said, "but when I told him Susan was there he changed his mind. I walked home and cleaned the house and put it back together as best I could. Later that morning I caught a bus into Gloucester and went to see Harry. It was pneumonia and it was touch and go at first. Susan nursed him continuously for about seventy-two hours. After what she had been through I can't imagine how she did it."

"I love my brother, Inspector. I loved Jessica and, although you may find it hard to believe, I have always loved my husband; but Harry has been my best friend for as long as I can remember. He protected me from my father and in the space of about ten days he risked his life twice, first to save John and then to protect us from the consequences of Jessica's death. For all these years, and especially in the last few days, he has gone on protecting us."

"I appreciate that, Mrs. Berkeley. If it's any consolation to Mr. Johnson I should mention that we realized very early that he was covering for someone, and it wasn't himself. Now I have a few questions. First of all, how did it happen that Mrs. Simpson went to Blenheim Hall to tell them that Jessica had gone back to London?"

"I saw her at the Infirmary—in fact she actually helped me with Harry. So as soon as I felt capable of dealing with her I told her that Jessica had gone back to London and that since Jessica was supposed to have been staying with her it would be good if she would speak to the headmistress herself. I'm ashamed to say that I hinted that this would be the best way of avoiding any awkwardness about the money she had been receiving for having Jessica with her."

"And why did you move the body to St. Mary's Square?"

Henry Johnson explained.

"It's fairly simple, Inspector. Since I wasn't allowed to go back to sea, I was able to get home and see my father fairly often. Susan was away all the time, and in any case he didn't want to see her. My older brother was in the army, so Dad was alone, and having the grave at the bottom of his garden began to prey on his mind. I'm not sure to this day how religious he really was, but he couldn't stand the thought of the grave being out there completely unmarked. He wanted to put a cross over it, but knew that he couldn't because someone might go down there and start asking questions. One time when I came home on leave I found that he had started building a summerhouse over it. It's fortunate that it wasn't visible from the road, since using materials for such a purpose would certainly have been frowned upon. He said that once it was built he would be able to mark the grave properly, so I helped him finish it, and he made a wooden cross and hung it on the wall over the head of the grave. But it didn't really satisfy him. Eventually he became so preoccupied with it that he could hardly think of anything else. He was becoming so disturbed that I thought that he might start talking about it to people or even tell the police. I was invalided out in 1945 and when he got the job of putting up the building for The Nave I was well enough to do some of the work for him. We started on the Monday after school closed for the summer holidays. By the Thursday of that week we had cleared the site and dug the hole for the boiler room. That evening I told him what I was going to do. He didn't like it but I didn't give him any option . . .

CHAPTER XXVI

1945: Thursday, July 31

"The Skipper's in port until Monday. He'll get here tomorrow, so on Saturday you can go to bed the usual way and when you wake up in the morning she'll be gone. We'll bury her under the boiler room and no one will ever be any the wiser."

"You'll need another coffin."

"I can attend to that, Dad."

"No. It's got to be done properly. The poor young thing ought to be given a decent burial in the churchyard, and now you want to put her under a boiler room. I'll make her a coffin and you can put her next to the boiler room so she's not so deep down."

"It'll only be her bones, Dad. It isn't as if she's really there."

"You don't know where she is, do you? She died in sin, poor girl, and not of her own making."

"All right, Dad, we'll do as you say."

The next morning, when Harry and his father arrived at the building site, they found Siggy Harescombe staring into the hole that they had dug for the boiler room. It was about a third full of water.

"What the hell are we going to do?" muttered Harry.

"You'll have to pump it out and put in a waterproof floor and walls", said Harescombe.

"I doubt whether it can be done", said old Johnson. "There's a lot of water there, and this is August. There'll be more in the spring."

"So what do you propose to do with the boiler?"

242

"We'll have to accommodate everything above ground, Mr. Harescombe. It could be done quite easily if you weren't so finicky about everything."

"Finicky? What the devil do you mean by that? Putting the boiler on the ground floor will ruin the whole design."

"And putting the boiler where it might be flooded will wreck a lot more than that. If you want a basement you'll have to build somewhere else. You may know a lot about science, Mr. Harescombe, but you don't know the first thing about building."

"I know that people have been putting basements and cellars in damp places for thousands of years . . ."

"And usually it leads to nothing but trouble."

"Only if the builder is too lazy to do the job properly."

"Oh, so now I'm lazy! What about you, spending most of your time sitting on your hindquarters talking to little boys and being on holiday nearly half the year?"

Siggy bit his lip. Obviously this conversation wasn't going anywhere.

"Before you do anything else I want to know what the architect thinks."

"He's going to think exactly the same as I'm thinking."

"If so I'll apologize. But he's in Scotland at the moment, so we can't find out until Monday."

"All right", interposed Harry, "that's what we'll do. Come on, Dad, we can't do anything here now."

Old Johnson glared at his son and at Siggy.

"All right, Mr. Know-all, we'll do as you say. But I'm right, you mark my words, I'm right."

The Johnsons got back into their lorry and drove off in silence.

"First thing tomorrow", Harry said when they got home, "we'll fill in the hole up to about two feet above the water level and get the rest of the site ready. After that we'll come back and dig up the girl's remains. Then early Sunday morning we'll put the coffin in, fill in the rest and pour the concrete over it. The square will be deserted—the church has no service until eleven o'clock. And then it won't matter what the architect says. And, Dad, Susan is coming here tomorrow, and I want you to remember that she's your daughter and treat her decently."

"I have no daughter. Do whatever you like, but keep her out of my way."

Saturday was cool and bright, but the summerhouse stood in the shadow of a large oak, and it was quite dark inside. By early evening there was only just room for the piles of earth that John and Harry had raised around three sides of the grave. Susan knelt in the space that had been left between the fourth side and the new coffin, terrified of what she might see but unable to look away for an instant. All her training and experience of death had done nothing to prepare her for the sight of the bones that had been encased in the living flesh and blood of Jessica's body.

The lid of the old coffin had collapsed along one edge, leaving only a triangular space inside, but in spite of the conditions under which the burial had taken place the interior was fairly dry. Another hour of careful work revealed that the bedclothes in which Jessica had been buried had largely decayed, but that the pouch containing John's poem was still intact. Harry removed the side of the old coffin and slid a new elm board beneath the remains of Jessica's body. Together they raised the board and placed it next to the new coffin. Jessica's skull was visible and Susan forced herself to look at it.

"How strange", she murmured to herself. "It looks just like any other skull."

Harry, who was usually the most matter-of-fact of people, said, "Can you feel anything? I told Dad that it was only bones and Jessica wasn't really here, but I think I was wrong. Or is it just imagination?"

"I don't think so", said Susan. "I can feel her too. But perhaps she isn't always here—maybe it's because of us."

"I think she's been here all the time", said John, "and that's why your father got so obsessed about her grave."

Susan looked at her husband in surprise but said nothing. She had intended to cover Jessica's remains with a new sheet, but at that moment they heard someone approaching the summerhouse.

"It's Dad", Harry said. "I don't know what will happen if he sees this."

John went outside to talk to old Johnson, while Harry quickly lifted the skeleton into the new coffin and fastened the lid. By the time the old man entered the summerhouse there was nothing to see but a deep hole, piles of earth and a closed coffin.

"It won't do you any good", he said. "It will all come out in the end."

Turning to Susan, he added, "This is all because of you and your queer ways. Why couldn't I have had an ordinary daughter, like everyone else?"

At five o'clock on Sunday morning the people who lived around St. Mary's Square were astonished to be awakened by the sounds of earth being moved and cement being mixed. No one had the energy to go and investigate, however. The hole had to be filled in within two feet of ground level to make a dry base for the coffin but the grave would be protected by several inches of concrete and a whole building would rest on top of it. Within four hours the job had been finished, and Harry had roped off the area and put up several signs warning passers-by about wet concrete.

They listened to the church bell striking nine o'clock, and Susan said "I'd like to go to the service at St. Mary's."

Rather surprisingly, John agreed.

"So would I. I don't believe in God any more than I did before, but somehow I think that Jessica is still here and it might help her. Completely illogical, I know."

"All right", said Harry. "In that case I'd better come too. We just about have time to drive home and put some clean clothes on."

It was less than two months since the Allies had declared victory in Europe, and the war was still going on the Pacific. The themes of the service were thanksgiving for deliverance—the Vicar was careful not to say "Victory"—prayers for peace, and the necessity of forgiving one's enemies. Harry's conscience was relatively clear. Admittedly he had assisted in the illegal disposal of a body and might be considered an accessory after the fact, but he had done so to help others and had no particular qualms about his actions. It was different for Susan, who was still shaken by her father's last remarks and found the general confession very disturbing.

"*We have erred and strayed from thy ways like lost sheep. We have followed too much the devices and desires of our own hearts . . . We have done those things which we ought not to have done; and we have left undone those things which we ought to have done; and there is no health in us . . . Spare thou them, O God, which confess their faults. Restore thou them that are penitent . . .*"

In her state of tenuous unbelief she didn't know whether any of this mattered. She was really in the church for Jessica, not for God. But if it did matter, did confession just mean to God or did it include the police as well? And although there were things about which she really was penitent, there were others at which she could only look back with joy.

John did not require the General Confession to make him regret his actions, which seemed to him to be the consequences of primal stupidity. It was absurd that something commonly known as love could lead to such a terrible end. This love or lust, or biological exigency, which for two months had controlled his thoughts and actions, had been a palpable, almost a personal, presence in his mind and body, an unwelcome visitant who had stayed just long enough to end Jessica's life and ruin his own and Susan's, and had then left, as if with a mocking grin. Now that the time for action was over he felt limp, helpless and hopeless. But he still experienced Jessica's presence, and although he could not ask for God's forgiveness he hoped fervently for hers.

CHAPTER XXVII

Christmas Eve, 1965   10 pm

"One rather trivial question, Mr. Johnson", said Inspector Phelps. "May we take it that the water got into the hole without your assistance?"

"Yes, you may. I can see what you're driving at, but we would have been quite happy to bury Jessica next to the basement, as my father wanted. Then she might never have been found. She would have been several feet down and the boys would never have found her. I suppose somebody might have noticed something when the excavator went in but . . . I'm sorry, Susan."

"It's all right, Harry", said Susan, who had gasped. "I couldn't help picturing it."

Everyone in the room imagined a load of debris, with a bone, perhaps even a skull, falling from those huge jaws into the lorry.

"Did you know that your father went to see Mr. Roberts about it?" the inspector asked.

"Yes. He was very angry with Mr. Harescombe and he wanted to set the record straight. But he said he might just as well not have gone—Mr. Roberts seemed to have no idea what he was talking about."

"I can well believe it. Let's get on to the subject of poetry. Mr. Hume, I gather that you were responsible for the poem found in Jessica's grave?"

"Yes, Inspector. A foolish thing to do, I suppose. I wrote it while I was waiting with Jessica's body. I have always found that focusing my mind on something like that helps me to get through desperate times when there is nothing to do but wait. The oilskin pouch was what I kept my identity papers in, and I picked up the piece of wire somewhere in Harry's house—the sort of thing that a radio operator is apt to have lying about. I wanted there to be something there that in some way gave Jessica's body an identity and said that she was loved."

"And Mrs. Berkeley, I presume that it was you who sent the wreath and the other poem to Jessica's funeral."

"Yes. Again it probably seems foolish, but it was a way of telling her that I was close at hand and still loving her. And I think that with the discovery of Jessica's skeleton, John and I both began to feel that we wanted to tell the truth to someone."

"Yes", said Hume, "my reason for being at the school had gone and Jessica had been properly buried. What finally pushed me into talking to Mrs. Marjoribanks was the letter to the *Citizen* that complained about goings on at the school. It seemed to me that the least I could do would be to get one mystery out of the way."

This produced a murmur from Woodcock.

"I had an idea that that letter might have an effect that its author didn't anticipate."

"And", said Inspector Phelps, "that was why you went to see Mr. Johnson this morning. We saw your car when we were leaving."

"Yes", Hume replied. "I wanted to tell him that it was time for me to confess and that I intended to do it without involving Susan or him. I think he would have tried to persuade me not to, but you had just started making enquiries about Susan, and it seemed to us that the best way of protecting her was for me to go through with my plan."

"But . . ." the inspector began, and several other people in the room were thinking the same thing.

"You want to know why I didn't just say it was accident, just as we might have at the very beginning. Obviously after all the evasions and lies I can't claim that I simply wanted the truth to come out."

"As far as I can see, Mr. Hume, the only time you told any lies was today when you gave your statement, and those were intended to shield your wife."

"That may be so, but I have depended on Harry to tell lies on my behalf, and that now seems to me to be more blameworthy than telling them myself. The fact is that I have been living with this situation and seeing it from a certain angle for a very long time. The night before last, in mulling it over for the hundredth or the thousandth time, I saw it from a different angle—almost from Jessica's angle. A picture came into my mind of her up there somewhere. She was looking down at us and thinking how absurd it was that Susan and I had remained so utterly preoccupied with her for such a very long time. If Susan had died Jessica would have been just as grief-stricken as Susan was and she would have remembered her lovingly for the rest of her days. But I'm sure that she would have got on with her life, even if there had been some personal guilt to deal with."

"That's true", said Susan, "and I wish I had seen it long ago. Jessica was a very truthful person, but if we had decided to lie our way out of the situation at the very beginning I don't think she would have minded. But John, although I would not claim to have loved Jessica any more strongly than you did, I was much more deeply involved."

"Yes, Susan." John made the observation without rancor. "You had had what I wanted, so it was much harder for you. Well, be all that as it may, I decided that it was time for me, as schoolmasters are apt to say, to make a fresh start. But I could decide that only for myself, not for Susan and Harry. I gave you an edited version of the story and left certain things out, in the hope that Jessica's remains would finally be at rest under her own name and I could take the responsibility for what I had done."

Inspector Phelps coughed. "I hope you understand what you are saying about taking the responsibility, Mr. Hume. If this had happened in peacetime and you had made this confession, it might well have ended up as a hanging matter, and if all the other facts had come out the least you would have got away with would have been manslaughter—and Mrs. Berkeley would certainly have gone to prison. As it is, with the circumstances of the war, the experience of losing your ship and almost your life, your subsequent service and twenty-five years having elapsed—and, furthermore, with no witnesses other than yourselves—I can't say for certain what will happen. I'll have to put it before the Chief Constable. Now, in order to fill in the picture, I'd like to go back a bit and hear how the two of you spent the rest of the war. I know that you stayed in the navy until 1946, Mr. Hume, but perhaps you would be a little more specific."

"I was given another destroyer and sent back to the same beat as I had been on before. It was a good thing for me personally to have a job like that where I was responsible for a great many other people—otherwise I might have done something silly. I managed to avoid getting torpedoed for a year or two and then we were sent to the Mediterranean. We saw some action and got strafed a few times."

"Since he won't tell you this himself", said Harry, "I'll just mention that his ship was bombed almost out of existence off the Italian coast and they gave him the D. S. O."

"It's kind of you, Harry, but I can't see that it makes any difference."

"In the Chief Constable's mind it might make a great deal of difference, Mr. Hume. And you, Mrs. Berkeley, what did you do when you had finished nursing Mr. Johnson?"

"I stayed here at the Infirmary until Harry was well enough to go home. He wasn't well enough to look after himself, but John still had a few days of leave, so after cleaning up the house where we had lived he stayed with Harry as long as he could. After that my father had to take over. I had been away from Portsmouth for nearly a week and I decided that I had better go back there. There had been no more raids but the naval hospital had been demolished and the director and most of his staff were dead. I found out that I was officially dead too, and it struck me that that might not be such a bad thing—but I wanted to keep on working, so I got in touch with the higher ups and they sent me to London. I spent the rest of the war there, training and nursing."

"And being blitzed", added Harry.

"And you weren't killed by a V2?"

"No", said Harry, with the slightest of smiles, "I made that up on the spur of the moment."

"And had the presence of mind to tell Mr. Hume!"

Susan continued:

"For a long time I didn't know where Harry was, and he didn't know where I was, but I wrote to him at home and eventually he got the letter and wrote and told me about the difficulties with our father. After the war was over in Europe, I went back to see Harry, and we agreed that if we could find some way of moving Jessica's remains we should do so. Well, you know the rest. But Harry, I suppose we ought to explain about Arthur."

"I suppose so. Arthur Williams used to live with his widowed mother almost next door to us on the Tewkesbury road. He's only a few years older than I am and he wanted to join the navy too, but they discovered that he had something wrong with his heart, so they wouldn't take him and they found him something useful to do in Gloucester. He got married during the war and they lived in his mother's house, thinking that they didn't want to leave the old lady all by herself. Well, the night we moved Jessica to St. Mary's Square, Arthur's wife was taken ill. It turned out to be appendicitis and she was in a bad way. He hadn't got a telephone so he came to our house very early in the morning to call for the doctor. We were just getting into the lorry and he saw the coffin in the back. He was too upset about his wife to think anything about it at the time. He just telephoned the doctor and went home. They took her to the hospital but she died the next night of peritonitis. I spent a lot of time with him after that, and it seemed to help him when we talked about other people and their troubles. Somehow or other I let something slip about Jessica and he remembered seeing the coffin, so I had to tell him part of the story—just that John and Susan had been very fond of this girl and that the circumstances had made it impossible to call the police. A few months later his mother was taken ill and he needed a nurse for her, so I asked Susan if she was interested. Her war work was over and she could have got a job in any hospital she liked, but she had told me that she just wanted to fade into the background somewhere. So she moved into a room in Arthur's house and nursed his mother until she died about a year later, leaving him quite a lot of money. He told me that he didn't expect to marry again but wanted to find new place where he could live quietly on his own. So he bought one of the new houses that they were building on Longbridge Lane and asked Susan if she would keep house for him."

"Arthur and I are about the same age", said Susan, "so I'm sure the tongues were wagging pretty freely, but in the year I spent nursing his mother we had a lot of long talks and I knew that he had been completely devastated by his wife's death. He was just as deeply preoccupied with her as I was with Jessica. I didn't tell him explicitly what had happened, but he realized that there was a dark secret. It was also clear to him that John and I would not be getting back together and that I was not interested in any more romance or marriage. After his mother died I went away for a few weeks while he moved into the new house, and then returned as unobtrusively as possible. After that I was practically invisible for the next nineteen years."

"So that's why he didn't want me in the house", Sergeant Snipe murmured. Susan smiled at him and continued.

"Arthur didn't need to work, so he was at home most of the time. He did all the shopping and took the deliveries. I did all his cooking, cleaning and washing. After a while he began to feel better and more like his old self, but he decided that he liked the arrangement. He said that matrimony was a wonderful institution but that the chance of finding anyone you could be really happy and comfortable with was very small, and that since he had already done it once it was very unlikely to happen again. Harry comes to see me quite often and, as you must have realized, he and Arthur are great friends."

"Tell me, Mrs. Berkeley", asked Woodcock, "how did you occupy yourself for those nineteen years? There must have been a great deal of time when you weren't actually housekeeping."

"I have done a lot of reading and a certain amount of writing—and, of course, a lot of thinking, most of it, I'm afraid, about Jessica. With Arthur's help I venture out occasionally to a cinema or a concert. I thought that as time went by I might begin to understand things better, but I must admit that I don't and after all this time I doubt whether I ever shall."

"Forgive me for asking, but what exactly is it that you don't understand?"

Phelps stirred and caught Snipe's eye. He thought it was clearly time for the two of them to wind things up. What Mrs. Berkeley didn't understood about life was scarcely a police matter, but he found that he wanted to know whether she had come to any conclusion beyond the hopelessness of the attempt, so he allowed the conversation to continue.

"Well, I suppose what happened in our house after Jessica arrived is not too much of a mystery—just an unusual version of the old eternal triangle. But what was it about Jessica that made such a thing possible?"

"And about you and your husband?"

"Yes, I suppose so—but it was Jessica who was extraordinary. I'm not so very unusual in having a lesbian orientation and John is not unusual in suffering a grand passion for a young girl. But we were both well on the way before she had been with us for thirty-six hours, and from what you have told me we weren't the only ones. So part of it is that I don't understand Jessica. The other part is that I don't understand the whole scheme of things any better than I did when I was a child."

"Not many of us do, Mrs. Berkeley."

"But perhaps you don't need to. I imagine that you have led a fairly blameless life and will eventually die with a reasonably clear conscience. But people like me who have committed grave sins—although I still don't believe that our love affair was in itself sinful—we have more to worry about. How can we ask God to forgive us when we're not sure that he's really there?"

"I think the church's answer would be to try it. 'Oh taste and see.' But I expect that you know that and have tried."

"Yes, I have, as well as I could. And nothing ever seems to come back. It's like sending an urgent telegram and getting no response, or crying into the void where there isn't even an echo."

Susan's remarks were not comfortable hearing, even for a confident Christian, and there was a long silence. To Inspector Phelps the atmosphere suddenly seemed intolerably claustrophobic, so he rose abruptly and opened a window. The air that came in was cold and clean, and bore with it the sound of the clock of St. Mary's church ringing the quarters. No one spoke as the deep bell chimed eleven o'clock. Finally Sergeant Snipe stood up.

"Time for me to go home and wish the Missus a Merry Christmas."

Chapter XXVIII

1965: December 27th

By the third day of Christmas a persistent drizzle had washed away the remains of the snow. For most of the citizens of Gloucester, fantasies about partridges, turtle doves and French hens had been replaced by the reality of work on a Monday morning. At nine o'clock, Bill Marjoribanks and Colin Woodcock were dawdling over their breakfast and, once again, contemplating matrimony.

"I think we're very lucky", Woodcock said. "I have no parents and yours are simply rejoicing to see you happy and optimistic. Of course, they don't know me well enough to realize that your optimism is completely misplaced."

"I know. They won't discover their mistake until they see the bruises all over my body and I start asking them for money."

"But for the present they don't seem to care how or whether we get married as long as we're enjoying ourselves."

"Each other."

"Each other? Oh yes, of course—silly of me. And you're sure your family won't mind our getting married at the Registry Office."

"Not a bit, and for our more distant relatives I have a plan."

"Aha!"

"Well, the Registry Office is only a few steps from the cathedral, so after we're married we can have our photographs taken in front of the cathedral entrance. It's quite imposing."

"That's a very good idea. That just leaves us with the task of deciding how we're going to explain this to Mr. Kingston."

The Reverend Charles Kingston was Vicar of St. Bernard's, the church at the foot of Robinswood Hill which the couple attended regularly on Sunday mornings.

"Are you sure we can explain it to ourselves?" asked Bill.

"Not really, but I suppose we should start by admitting that it isn't altogether a matter of principle. I mean a big part of it is that we want to avoid all the fuss and pother of a church wedding."

"True, but we can't say that to His Reverence. How about telling him that we've both been married in church once and we'd like to try a different method?"

"Don't forget he has a weak heart—I don't want to have the death of an elderly clergyman on my conscience. I suppose the biggest problem really is that we've been living in sin long enough for it to become fairly common knowledge, and a fancy wedding will give such wonderful opportunities for remarks ranging from the merely catty to the positively ugly. With a Registry Office wedding there'll just be a brief announcement in the *Citizen* and most of what is said in response will not be in our hearing."

"True again, but you still haven't said anything about matters of principle."

"All right. I'm sure the Rev. would be very happy to marry us, but he's probably one of the few people in the parish who don't know that we've been living together for the past two months. I think I should feel compelled to tell him about our 'manifold sins and wickedness' before letting him do the deed."

"I don't think it would come as such a shock to him. He must be aware that most people no longer regard chastity as a virtue."

Woodcock gazed at his fiancée with mild surprise.

"Bill", he said, "I believe you want us to marry in church after all."

"Well", Bill began, but her reply was interrupted by the doorbell. "That'll be Jack and Snipey."

Having arrived at the station at seven o'clock, Inspector Phelps and Sergeant Snipe had covered enough ground to enable them to take an hour off for a quiet cup of coffee and a post mortem on the case of Jessica Smith.

"This is about the most unsatisfactory case I've ever had", the inspector remarked as he watched his cup being filled. "We know who the girl was, how she died and who was responsible. I think the Chief Constable did the best thing in deciding not to prosecute—and yet I feel completely dissatisfied."

"Well, it really *is* unsatisfactory", said Bill. "Two unusually good people go off the rails, behave in a highly reprehensible manner and cause the death of a talented and beautiful girl. We've met these people and it's almost as if we've met Jessica. Perhaps the Berkeleys couldn't help falling in love with her, but they were both experienced, responsible people and they knew perfectly well that what they were doing was wrong. As you said the other day, if this had happened in peacetime they'd both be spending the next umpteen years in prison."

"Perhaps it wouldn't have happened in peacetime", Woodcock pointed out.

"That's what the C. C. said", remarked the inspector. "Not because the circumstances wouldn't have arisen, although that's true, but because—so he says—people tend to lose their moral bearings in wartime. He feels that Berkeley or Hume or whatever we call him now was unhinged by the loss of his ship and most of his crew and his own near drowning. And he had no intention of killing the girl. But I can't help seeing it from the other side—no matter how good and likeable they are they ought to be in jail. And then the C. C. said something else that I really couldn't stomach. I had given him a pretty detailed account of Jessica, the kinds of things she did and how some of those other women had reacted to her, and . . ."

"Let me guess", said Bill. "He said it was her fault for being so talented, beautiful and attractive."

"Well, not quite in those words, but more or less. And he said that in all the circumstances he might have gone off the rails himself. I think the old boy has a fairly vivid imagination—I could almost see him mentally twirling his moustache as he said it."

"Well, Sir", said Snipe, "he's been a widower for thirty years and old gentlemen are entitled to their little fancies as long as they don't try to put them into practice. I think it would have been only right for Mr. and Mrs. Berkeley to have gone to prison, but it's too late now for that with Mrs. Berkeley, and it would be very difficult with Mr. Hume if he decided to plead 'not guilty'."

"So", asked Woodcock, "are we to take it that the Chief Constable's decision was really based on purely practical considerations and that the rest was just moral fantasizing?"

"If I were a proper policeman", Phelps replied, "I'd say, 'yes', and leave it at that. That's what I do ninety-nine times out of a hundred. Unfortunately this case has got under my skin a bit and I'm a little too involved with the characters, and that includes Jessica, even though she's been dead for twenty-five years. I think the C. C. was wrong in the way he put things, but you can't deny that the whole case revolves around her and her character."

Woodcock was not quite so sure.

"That may be an illusion brought about by the circumstances. I don't deny that she was unusual but don't forget that the whole sequence of events was brought about by the death of her parents. If she had not gone to live with Miss Edwards it's very doubtful whether that lady would have become so overwhelmingly involved. To Miss Thrower she was a swan among geese. And although the two of them were important in the investigation they weren't actually involved in Jessica's death. You could just as easily argue that the whole case revolves around the Berkeleys and their peculiar situation. They had been separated for most of the previous five years and although they were undoubtedly fond of each other, their marriage had not become quite what they had expected. It's quite possible that any attractive and intelligent girl thrown into the middle of that situation might have stirred something in them."

"Maybe", said Bill, "but I doubt it. Anyway, Colin, you're being inconsistent. Yesterday you said that Jessica was unusually unusual and now you're saying she was just unusual. You probably would have fallen in love with her yourself."

"Probably—old men can be quite silly about young girls. And how about you?"

"How about me what?"

"Would you have fallen in love with her?"

Bill was very broadminded about other people's activities as long as they excluded such things as cruelty and dishonesty, but she wrinkled her nose at the thought of a love affair with someone of her own sex.

"Not my idea of fun", she said, "but *chacun à son gout,* I suppose."

But it flashed through her mind that perhaps she could not be quite sure what would have happened if her marriage had been unsatisfactory and she had met someone with Jessica's armor-piercing personality. It would have been interesting to find out, but Jessica was dead, gone and unlikely to recur. Perhaps that was a good thing, or perhaps not. Bill became conscious that her fiancé was looking at her.

"A penny for 'em", he said with a smile.

"Never mind. But I think you're wrong, Colin. Or half wrong—I don't know . . ."

"Well", said the inspector, "no doubt we're all a little bit right and a little bit wrong."

"Yes, Sir", Snipe said, "Jessica and the Berkeleys were like the Titanic and the iceberg—all fine and good as long as they stayed apart, but put them together and you get a disaster."

"But it's hard to say which was which, isn't it. And Jessica was more like a magnetic mine than an iceberg."

"Jack!" said Bill, outraged.

"I'm sorry. Sometimes it's hard to remember that they were adults and she was a child. And the Berkeleys were unusually talented and attractive, too."

"Oh, come off it, Jack. Look at the four of us sitting in this room. We're all unusually talented and attractive, but people are not throwing themselves at our feet all the time."

"Well", said the inspector, "I thought coming here might help me to get things a bit clearer in my head, but it doesn't seem to have helped very much. As far as I can see there's only one satisfactory thing about the whole case, and even that's a mixed blessing. I looked in on the building site yesterday and the darned hole is half full of water. Come on, Snipey, we'd better get back to the station and see what the locals have been up to. A bit of ordinary run-of-the-mill crime might help us get our feet back on the ground. Thanks for the coffee, and let's hope you're spared any further adventures—you've got enough trouble already with this new building going up."

"Not to mention suddenly having to find a new chemistry master."

"Oh Lord, I hadn't thought of that."

"Does he know about the Chief Constable's decision?"

"Yes, I talked to him as soon as I had the chance."

"How did he take it—I mean, did he seem relieved?"

"Not so as you'd notice. He just seemed neutral—ready to take whatever happened."

The doorbell rang.

"I'll bet you that's him now", the Inspector added.

"If it is just tell him to come up."

CHAPTER XXIX

1965: December 27

Woodcock waited at the door while the policemen rumbled down the stairs.

"I'll only stay for a few minutes", said Hume as he came in. "I just wanted to tell you personally something that you have probably realized already. I know it will make things very awkward for you and the school, and I'm very sorry, but I'm sure you understand."

"Yes, I'm very sorry too, but in your position I'd do the same thing. May I ask what you intend to do next?"

"I'm not sure. All I can say for certain is that I need to get away from Gloucester. Susan has decided that she needs to get away too, at least for a while, and we're thinking about going together—we're still married, you know—although we wouldn't go as husband and wife, perhaps as something more like brother and sister. We have no idea how it will turn out but we think the most likely thing is that we'll spend a few days sorting things out and then set about arranging a friendly divorce. We have enough money to last for a few months and then Susan thinks she can get back into nursing and I'll look for another teaching position for September."

Hume was still standing just inside the door. As he turned to leave he appeared to remember something.

"Oh, Bill, there's something I wanted to give you, but I forgot to bring it up. It's downstairs in the car."

Bill interpreted the look on Hume's face.

"I'll come down with you."

Hume shook hands with Woodcock and Bill followed him down the stairs. The old Ford Prefect was standing in the rain, a dripping collage of green paint, mud, rust patches and holes where the metal had given way altogether.

"There's something for the poet in me", said Hume with a wry smile. "'The embodiment of patience, awaiting its master.' Only I won't be writing any more poetry, so I thought I'd give you this."

He gave Bill the folder from which she had read on Christmas Eve.

"Why not?" asked Bill.

"Well, for one thing I don't think I'm very good at it. And for another, I've come to feel that there's something self-indulgent about it, as if I'm wallowing in my distress and saying, 'Look, folks, can't you see how much I'm suffering.'"

"But the folks never got the chance to see. And, in any case, isn't that what poets are supposed to do?"

"Perhaps, but not all the time. I mean, even Hardy wrote a cheerful poem occasionally. I can only write poetry when I'm depressed, and then it always seems to come out sounding like somebody else or several other people. And now that I come to think of it, giving you a collection of bad poetry isn't much of a compliment."

"I don't think it's bad", protested Bill, "at least, not the ones I've seen."

"Well, you see, the only even half-decent ones are about Jessica. I've already thrown away most of the other rubbish, and Jessica is gone now, so I have to find something else to think about. While I was waiting for the police to decide what to do I was almost looking forward to being put in prison—at least I should have felt that I was paying for what I had done."

"John, you've been paying for the last twenty-five years. I think it's enough. For goodness sake go out and start living again. And don't forget there are other things in the world besides teaching. The real problem is that you let Jessica knock all the stuffing out of you—and you the captain of a destroyer by the time you were thirty! I know it's pointless to tell you to forget her, but she had something that you haven't shown much of recently—fighting spirit. Remember what you and Susan said the other day about what Jessica would be thinking?

Well, I'm different from you. I really believe it. And, by the way, am I right in thinking that you lured me down here because you wanted to talk? Because if so let's go into the porch and out of the rain."

"All right—but only for a moment. I really wanted to thank you for seeing me through on one or two occasions when I thought I wasn't going to be able to cope, especially this last time. I'll do my best to fight back, but when you've been cursing yourself every day for twenty-five years it's hard to get out of the habit. I'm not sure that I want to be a schoolmaster any more, but I can't think of anything else that I'd be any good for."

"How about going back to sea?"

"I can't go back to the navy after all these years. I suppose I might be able to get a job on a merchant ship, although at the age of fifty-six . . ."

"Well, for goodness sake try something. Oh, I'm sorry—I know it's easy enough for me to talk. Do you know whether Susan has anything in mind?"

"You've only seen Susan in her housekeeping guise, but she's still a very attractive woman and I think she would like to find somebody. I'll go now and I'll try to take your advice. Goodbye, Bill"

"Goodbye, John. Take care of yourself—and I'll take care of your poems. You never know, you may want them back one day."

"Oh", said Hume as they shook hands. "At the end of the folder you'll find a copy of a letter that Jessica wrote that night. I think it might help you to understand her a little better. And there's one other thing. I think she ought to have a proper headstone, and since I can't very well do anything about it I was wondering if you and Mr. Woodcock might be willing to put your heads together with the Vicar of St. Mary's. I don't know how much such things cost, so I've left an open check in the folder. Anything within reason. Goodbye and good luck."

Bill left the porch door open and sat down on the bench just inside. She liked the sound and smell of the rain, and she wanted a quiet look at Jessica's letter. The folder was much thinner than it had been the last time she looked at it, and she realized that Hume must have done quite a bit of pruning.

There were, in fact, only half-a-dozen pages of poetry before she came to Jessica's letter, which John had painstakingly copied in his small, precise handwriting.

Darling Susan,

After I wrote the last bit I listened to the news and heard about the air raid in Portsmouth. For a long time I was too terrified even to think, but now I realize that I must try to be as brave as you are. And I think that if something had happened to you I should know. So I'm going to try to write what I was thinking before I heard the news.

It's about us and how hard it is to decide what is right and what we ought to do, and I'm feeling happier because I think I understand things a little better. Also I've thought of a way that we could live together and no one could do anything about it.

You know how we talked about Adam and Eve and temptation. It was as if God had two children, and when they did something he had told them not to, he threw them out of the house. It made me think of you and your father. I know he didn't exactly throw you out, but he didn't understand you and he made it too hard for you to stay. My parents were the best that anyone has ever had, but still there were things in me that they couldn't understand and I couldn't explain. And there were things in them that I couldn't understand. Well, I think God had these two children and when they started to grow up he didn't understand them either. You know how some parents want their children always to be children, and when they start growing up and asking questions and being disobedient the parents can't stand it? Well, I think that's how it was with God. He wanted his children to be free to decide things for themselves, but when they didn't decide them the right way it made him so angry that he threw them out, and one thing he didn't realize was that after they had been outside for a very long time their children and grandchildren and so on might forget who had created them in the first place. Of course, in the Old Testament he kept on reminding them, but that doesn't seem to happen any more. And I think that eventually he realized that there were all these millions of people who were really his children, only most of them didn't know, and he had no idea what it was like to be a child. So he sent Jesus into the world to find out and help him to understand them better, and also to remind them where they had come from and who their father really was. But

I'm not sure that it really worked because in some ways Jesus turned out to be too much like his father. He healed the sick and forgave people's sins, but only on his terms, and if you didn't believe properly all you got was weeping and gnashing of teeth. And he never admitted that God had ever made a mistake. And I think he must have, because even the angels rebelled. My mother used to say that when people have children they have no idea what they're letting themselves in for, and I think it must have been the same with God. I am really beginning to feel sorry for him. You know I've never been sure that he even exists, but I'm beginning to think that if he does he's up there like an anxious parent who really loves his children and feels very upset about the way things have turned out. And he can't decide what to do next. If that's true it must be very hard for him to help us decide what we should do. Well, you and I did decide and I think we got it right. And I still don't understand, and I don't think I ever shall, how you can make yourself believe something just because someone tells you to. It must have been different if you were actually there with Jesus, but even then a lot of people didn't believe.

And I've been thinking about what being in love is. At first I thought it meant that I had these enormously strong feelings in me and you had them in you, and perhaps that was true at the very beginning, but now it feels as if whatever it was that was inside each of us has come out and got all mixed up together and that we live in it and breathe it and splash about in it, sort of like taking our bath together except that we're splashing about in love instead of water. Even when you aren't here I can still feel it in the air. I have an idea that I can't explain at all that it has something to do with God and that he likes it when we love each other, which is even more confusing since I'm still not sure that he's there. And I think that somehow our bodies have got mixed up with each other, because I feel as if half of me has been cut off and taken away.

We've been reading some of Shakespeare's sonnets and I'm sending a surprise for you in this letter. We read one on Thursday that made me think of you and miss you so much that I almost cried in class and Miss Wenlock asked me if I was all right. This is the bit that did it.

"So you are to my thoughts as food to life
Or as sweet-season'd showers are to the ground."

But the rest of the sonnet was a bit disappointing, as if he'd said everything he really needed to say in the first two lines and had to work very hard to fill in the rest.

I think I've had a wonderful idea only I'm not sure. Since Uncle James is not really my uncle any more I don't think I have a parent or guardian of any kind. So I think you should adopt me. I'm sure they wouldn't allow it if they knew what we had been doing, but nobody does. Could you find out about it? If you could we could live together for the rest of our lives and nobody could say anything. I know that we still have to talk to John and try to make things right with him, and it will be very, very hard for him, but tonight I am beginning to have the feeling that in the end everything will be all right.

When I put the light out at night and look at the reflection of the fire on the ceiling I always cry for you. I just can't help it. And I'm afraid I'm going to cry again tonight because I love you so very much. I'll write a few more words in the morning and post the letter on the way to school.

After the letter there was a copy of Jessica's sonnet. Bill read it again and wondered whether Jessica had written it naively and unselfconsciously, or whether she had been aware of its derivativeness.

"I think she was", Bill said to herself, "and perhaps it didn't matter. It doesn't make it any less sincere. And what the hell would Mr. Kingston say about the letter?"

She was beginning to feel cold, so she closed the door and went back up to the flat.

"Well", she said, "it's an odd world."

"Very odd. Are you referring to the fact that there are two agnostics, who are actually married to each other, preparing for a period of celibacy, while here we have a couple of practicing Christians fornicating to their hearts' content?"

"That's part of it, though there seems to be some doubt as to how long the celibacy will last, at least in Susan's case. But look at this."

Woodcock read Jessica's letter in silence. When he had finished he looked at Bill and gently shook his head.

"What I don't understand", she said, "is why he speaks to some and not to others—even when they desperately need him to."

"I know. Sometimes nothing seems to make any sense at all. I can't think of any way in which you and I are better people than Jessica and the Berkeleys, but for us he's there and for them he apparently isn't. And although it's true to say that we poor human beings can't hope to understand the ways of God, it doesn't seem to make the whole thing less unfair."

"No, it doesn't. It would have been different if they had been the usual kind of boring atheists with the usual kind of specious objections based on the usual kind of ignorance of what Christianity actually is. But . . ."

Bill trailed off and there was a long silence.

Finally she asked, "Is she right about God? I mean, is he actually suffering?"

"Not according to standard theology, but I'm not sure that that's anything to go by. I think Jessica's version might be a little closer to the truth in that respect. If she had lived she might have wanted to reconsider some of her other conclusions, but she was still child enough to say things that an adult might have shied away from—and much closer to God than she imagined."

"And she *was* unusually unusual, wasn't she?"

"Yes. Extraordinarily so."

"It makes me feel that it's time for us to stand up and be counted."

"I agree. I'll telephone Mr. Kingston right away."

On the following Wednesday four formal announcements appeared on different pages of the *Citizen*.

A small paragraph on page one reported that the remains found in St. Mary's Square were those of Jessica Smith, a wartime evacuee from London with no known relations. The paper commended the police on their quick work and added that further explanations were expected later.

"And as far as I'm concerned they can go on expecting", Inspector Phelps remarked to Sergeant Snipe.

On page two, which was reserved for important local news, it was announced that Mr. Charles Ferrier had offered his resignation as Director of Education for Gloucester, and that the Local Education Authority had accepted it without comment.

"I see you've got your name in the paper this time", said Mrs. Ferrier sarcastically. "What a pity you couldn't have resigned anonymously."

Evidently the editors felt that people who actually teach are far less important than those who merely administrate; John Hume's resignation "for personal reasons, after twenty years of devoted service" appeared unobtrusively at the foot of page four, drawing an acid comment from Woodcock.

"How the devil I'm going to find a new chemistry master by the week after next I can't imagine. And if I do he'll have to wait another month before there's a lab for him to work in."

"Don't worry, darling, there's always Gibbet and Thong", said Bill, mischievously referring to the notoriously dilatory educational agency reputed to be the last hope of junior masters sacked by their previous employers.

And on page six, among the births, marriages and deaths it was proclaimed that the engagement of Mr. Colin Woodcock, Headmaster of the Nave School, and Mrs. Wilhelmina Marjoribanks, daughter of Mr. and Mrs. John Jones of Brookethorpe had been announced and that the wedding would take place at the Church of St. Bernard at the end of January.

Mrs. Smail was highly intrigued. "In other words, as soon as the banns have been read three times—I wonder if she could possibly be pregnant"

Bill found two other things tucked away in a pocket at the end of Hume's folder. One was a program from the concert that Bill had attended with him in April. At first it seemed to her that it must have been left there by accident, but then the last item caught her eye.

Quartet No. 14 in D minor ("Death and the Maiden") Schubert

"Well, I'll be damned", she muttered. "Why didn't I remember that? No wonder he was upset."

Then there was another poem, evidently his last one.

Life was fine, the grass was green,
The house was relatively clean,
The dishes washed, the table cleared;
The sky was blue when Love appeared.

Oh Love, we weren't expecting you,
But as a host is bound to do,
We put you in our finest bed
And saw you entertained and fed.

But now your welcome here is gone.
The wrinkled sheets you feasted on
Give no more promise of good cheer,
So why, Love, do you linger here?

Love, the unexpected guest,
Will serve his needs and take your best,
And then he'll linger for a space,
To gloat upon your fall from grace.

But when your house in ruins stands,
Why then he'll wave his wanton hands,
Traverse the cracked and gaping floor
And saunter through the broken door.

When Bill and Colin had their pre-nuptial chat with the Vicar, the reverend gentleman expressed no curiosity about the way in which they had been conducting themselves, but he did enquire about the poor young lady whose remains had been found in St. Mary's Square.

Bill told him as much as she could, which wasn't very much, and absent-mindedly mentioned that she had been left with the task of choosing an inscription for Jessica's headstone. While she was trying to decide what to say if the Vicar asked her who had given her this assignment, Woodcock hurriedly remarked that he thought it ought to be short, simple and scriptural. The Vicar immediately made a suggestion ("Quite a favorite thought in this parish") which Bill promptly accepted before making another change of subject.

Thinking about it on the way home she said, "I don't know about that inscription. It's fine for anyone who doesn't know the story but . . ."

"I know", said Woodcock. "To Susan Berkeley, for instance, it might convey an unintended meaning. Would you like to choose something different?"

"No", said Bill. "I know it's naughty, but I rather like the idea. I think Jessica would have appreciated it."

So the headstone was erected and Jessica was finally left in peace.

Jessica Smith

1926-1941

"Today shalt thou be with me in Paradise."